The Ballad of JJ McHale

Seamus Moran

First published in 2017 by
Seamus Moran
Dublin
Ireland

Paperback   ISBN: 978-1546713-623

Also available as an eBook

Typesetting by Dinky Typesetting
Cover design by Leanne Willers

"*The mimic warfare of the evening became at last as wearisome to me as the routine of school in the morning because I wanted real adventures to happen to myself. But real adventures, I reflected, do not happen to people who remain at home: they must be sought abroad.*"

– James Joyce "The Encounter" (*Dubliners*)

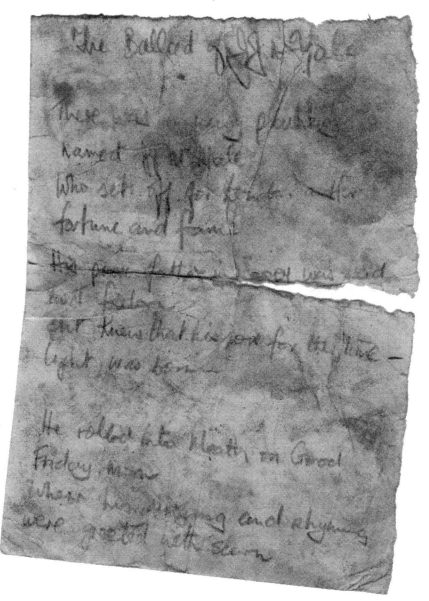

SKETCH OF THE AREA IN WHICH THE BATTLE OF ASHBOURNE WAS FOUGHT

1

JJ's Last Ride

IF JJ MCHALE HAD BEEN able to hear the squeaking front wheel of the tall, black Rover safety bicycle as it crunched its way homeward, over the rough stone roads that meandered through the boggy, undulating landscape of east Sligo, he would have noted that its pitch and rhythm matched, almost perfectly, the pitch and rhythm of the squeaking springs of the bed he was kneeling on. Apart from the fact that the bicycle was some distance away and well out of earshot, JJ was far too engrossed in his own activity to be aware of anything outside the delightful little cosmos he had created for himself here, in this farmhouse bedroom, on this fresh April morning.

Beneath and before him on the bed was the plain-looking but shapely Mrs Bartley Comer. She was kneeling too; not in supplication, for he was no king; not in adoration, for he was no god; but definitely in anticipation. Her hands clasped the ornate metal headboard. Her long hair, unfurled now, was sprawled over her naked back, shoulders and arms, as she raised her head to heaven, her back arching spontaneously. She was like a feral animal. If JJ had been able to hear the squeaky front wheel of the bicycle now, as the middle-aged rider, his lined face set in grim determination, pushed it up the final steep hill before home, he would have remarked that the rhythm was much slower and more irregular than the squeaking springs of Mary-Ann Comer's bed as she purred, moaned and cried out in paroxysms of ecstasy.

JJ McHale would also have observed that the squeaky bicycle wheel almost came to a stop just short of the brow of the steep hill, as Bartley Comer, sweat beading on his furrowed brow, contemplated dismounting and pushing the bicycle the final fifty yards to the top, a yard for every year he'd lived here. But something innate, deep inside, a stubbornness that forbade surrender, forced Bartley Comer to grit his teeth against the searing pain in his calves and pedal those final yards. He was further spurred on by the fact that his beautiful, thirty-year-old wife waited at home, preparing a dinner of boiled, home-cured bacon with savoy cabbage, curly kale and floury new potatoes from their own garden. He rose out of the saddle like a jockey astride a thoroughbred and pushed with every fibre until finally he edged over the crest of the hill and almost instantly picked up speed, the squeak in the front wheel rising to a squeal as he freewheeled the final few hundred yards home. In fact, in a rare moment of euphoria, he sat back into the saddle, spread his legs wide and whooped loudly to the empty landscape.

Not much more loudly than Mary-Ann Comer cried out from beneath the firm grip of JJ McHale's soft hands, but with none of her intensity, as lightning bolts of pleasure exploded from every nerve ending. Just before his own moment of release, JJ noticed a thin film of perspiration on the smooth, arched lower back of the woman pressed against his loins. Then, looking out the bedroom window, he thought the piercing cobalt sky, between the few puffy cumuli that tried hopelessly to block it out, had never looked so blue. The colour seemed to flood in through the glass, engulf the room and stream in through his eyes, filling his entire body, which shuddered and jerked as he drifted into a sensual haze. As he threw his head back, the colour became a musical note, as it always did at moments like this, the purest note he had ever heard, a note that only an angel, if you believed in them things, or a rare song-bird might be capable of singing.

If any of JJ's senses had been alert, as he collapsed onto the bed beside Mary-Ann, he might have heard the dull squeak of the big black Rover, as it trundled to a stop in the farmyard outside. He probably wouldn't have heard Bartley Comer dismount and lay the bicycle carefully against the low front wall of the flower garden of his house, though. Had Bartley not paused for a few moments to enjoy his front garden, which his wife had transformed from a muddy, barren piece of ground into a pleasant display of colour and diversity, he would have doubtless discovered that same young wife lying naked in the arms of that useless wastrel JJ McHale and smiling in a way that she had never smiled for him. Indeed, as Bartley inhaled the sweet fragrances that filled the air, he may have been thinking that Mary-Ann was not the most beautiful woman in the district. Her features were just a little too sharp. Her lips were too thin. Her grey eyes were small and just a bit too close together. But she was industrious, an excellent cook and shapely. She went in and out in all the right places, as they say. Being honest with himself, he had to admit that her plainness was possibly why no one else had claimed her and why the large-nosed, middle-aged bachelor farmer was able to convince her to marry him. That and the fact that she knew she would be comfortable for the rest of her life.

By the time Bartley Comer entered his house, the kitchen was empty, the water all but boiled out of the bacon pot. The cabbage and spuds had been washed but not yet put on to cook. Admittedly he was early but not by much. He'd sold his couple of heifers quicker than expected and for a good price too. He'd had one bottle of stout to celebrate but declined vociferous invitations to stay for more. Why would he, when he had a lovely young wife waiting at home with a fine feed ready to put in front of him. He called out his wife's name as he made his way towards the stairs.

"Mary-Ann? Mary-Ann!"

JJ, who was just emerging from his sonic afterglow, heard the call, even if the shapely Mary-Ann had not, and instantly guessed what was about to unfold. By the time Bartley Comer had started to climb the steep, wooden stairs that led to the bedrooms, JJ was pulling on his trousers, stomping into his boots and grabbing as he went any other items of clothing he could find in the mess of sheets, blankets, corsets and bloomers. He was also trying to shush Mary-Ann who, still oblivious to her husband's approaching footsteps, was moaning far too loudly.

"What are you doin', a graween?"

"Shsh."

"What's your hurry away?"

She grabbed him by the wrist and pulled him towards her.

"Shshsh." He pulled his hand free and pointed frantically at the bedroom door, his eyes searching the room for a hiding place or, better still, an escape route.

"Is that all I am to you? Is it?"

"Shshshsh!"

JJ heard Bartley Comer's footsteps stop for an instant, imagined his head craning, his furrows deepening, as he wondered if that was his young wife's voice he was hearing.

"Just a plaything, is it? To be cast aside the instant you've had your pleasure?" she shouted.

By the time Bartley Comer had leapt up the final few steps of the stairs, certain now that something untoward was afoot, JJ McHale was battling the catch on the sash window, cursing it, cursing Mary-Ann's stupidity.

"What the bloody hell are you doing, woman?"

As Bartley Comer flung the bedroom door wide, certain that some marauder, or maybe a bastard of a British trooper, was attacking his wife, or worse, seeking to rob him blind, the catch of the window finally snapped loose. Before Bartley had revised his notion and concluded what had in fact occurred, JJ was out the window, jumping onto a water tank and from there onto the ground below, just as Bartley Comer's bulbous nose and bald head appeared at the bedroom window.

By the time Bartley had grabbed his shotgun and made it back downstairs, leaving his wife to clothe her shapely body and concoct a tale that would cast McHale in the role of blackguard and herself in that of the defiled maiden, JJ had hobbled – he'd wrenched his ankle in the second jump – around to the front of the house and mounted the big, black Rover safety bicycle. As he pedalled furiously away from the house, he burst into song, a song in the old language that seemed to fit the moment: "Alliliu, buillailiu, ailliliu, tá an puc ar buile/ Alliliu, buillailiu/ Ailliliuuuuu, tá an puc ar buile!"

The frantic squeaking of the bicycle's front wheel was drowned for only an instant by the reports of the double-barrelled shotgun. Even if Comer had been a good shot, JJ was too far away by now for the pellets to do any real damage. When JJ reached the hill that Bartley Comer had freewheeled down only minutes earlier, so uncommonly euphoric that he should have known something bad was about to happen, the squeaking wheel slowed, filling Bartley with new hope that he could still catch this odious villain. The farmer fumbled two new cartridges into the shotgun and lumbered after his young prey. But JJ McHale was a much younger, fitter man than Bartley Comer so, despite the exertions of the previous hour and his throbbing ankle, he rose out of the saddle and climbed that hill much quicker than his pursuer could run. By the time the echoes of the next two gunshots had died, the sound of the squeaky bicycle wheel was fading quickly, down the far side of the hill and away from Bartley Comer, his shapely young wife and, although he didn't know it right in that instant, away from everything JJ McHale had known up to then.

This wasn't the first time the notion of flight had crossed JJ's mind but this time was different. This time he knew in his body before it had registered in his brain that he wouldn't stop, couldn't stop. He knew that Comer would already be cycling to his father's small farm. Oh, no, he couldn't cycle now, could he? Well, no matter to Bartley Comer. When that man got a notion into his head there was no stopping him. When that man came home to find you in bed with his shapely young wife, there was definitely no stopping him and no telling what lengths he would go to to exact revenge. JJ could picture him marching the five miles across fields and over ditches to JJ's father's house. Alternatively, and better still, he could have yoked his auld mare to the turf cart, but JJ doubted Comer would have the presence of mind to think of that. Once there, he would demand that Pat McHale deliver his renegade son to him, right there and then, so he could inflict the punishment he deserved or else shame his father into punishing the lad himself, like a real man would do. And, of course, Pat McHale would be only too willing to serve his wastrel of a son up on a platter to the demented farmer, lathered in sweat and carrying a loaded shotgun.

"You made your bed, now lie in it," he would say as he cast his feckless son to the raging lion.

So there was no going back now, not this time.

2

Foiled Escape

—⁓—

THE FIRST TIME JJ BOLTED, he was only fourteen years old. He'd long grown sick of his father's moods and the unrelenting pressure on him to work the farm, go to school, study, dig, build, fetch and carry. Most of all, though, he'd tired of his father's inability to understand what it was that brought pleasure and fulfilment to his youngest son's life. Not like his mother. His father failed abysmally to recognise that his son was a natural performer, a boy with a gift who was not destined to be a common grafter, a small farmer, shackled to a miserable patch of barely arable land. He seemed to have no idea that his young son was, in fact, destined for adventure, travel and ultimately fame and fortune. Mind you, it took a little time for the realisation to dawn on JJ himself. Aside from a vague feeling of satisfaction that he got from watching the enraptured faces of his audiences whenever he sang at parties, funerals or wakes, the first time JJ got a real sense of what his future might be was when the fit-ups came to town.

He had just turned fourteen and had been waiting for that day for weeks, bubbling with excitement and expectation. Looking back on it, he often felt that he must have had some inkling of the profound effect the events of that day and night would have on him. Of course, at the time, he hadn't a clue. It was simply a great opportunity to mitch school and avoid farm work, for one day at least. The caravan or convoy or whatever you call it rolled, or rather lolled, into the village around ten o'clock. First there was breakfast in Lynch's bar, with creamy pints and golden whiskeys lining the counter. From the gait and carry on of some of the cast of colourful characters, it looked like they would just be topping up. For the upstanding citizens of the district, the players, as they called them with a somewhat disparaging curl of the upper lip, were an uncouth bunch of reprobates, and the whole rigmarole was an unseemly display of ignorance. Still they would turn out in numbers for the show that night.

JJ had never seen anything like it before, though: the colour, the ribaldry, the devilment, the pure fun. He loved it all, couldn't wait to be right in the middle of it. But beyond any of that, he had what a more educated man than JJ might have called an overpowering sense of fraternity, a feeling of belonging, even before he had met or as much as spoken to any of the players. It was like he understood it all instantly, intuitively. He would need little or no explanation. Anything they asked him to do he would do willingly, unquestioningly, without a single moan or bellyache, in marked contrast to his behaviour in school or on the farm. Anything he didn't understand he would quickly figure out for himself or would ask a member of the troupe and drink up any instruction or advice, no matter how gruffly delivered. Yes, this was his world, his destiny. He just knew it.

After the liquid breakfast, the cavalcade processed flamboyantly down to Murphy's field, the Sraith, as it was known locally. There, after some liberal pissing, accompanied by manly banter and wisecracking, horses were untethered, fed, watered, and the tent for the evening's performance was erected. Not everyone was required to engage in this busy but uncomplicated operation. For the women it was optional, many of them preferring to arrange and repair costumes, prepare bedding for those who would sleep under the stars and arrange digs for those who liked and could afford more comfort. One or two of the older male actors, too, were excused, either due to frailty or because they were busy pacing around the perimeter of the field reciting speeches, great tracts of complex poetry, pure music to the young boy's ears. This provided JJ his opportunity to get involved.

If his father had done nothing else for him, and he hadn't, he had taught him to be a good carrier, an efficient runner and fetcher, and the long hours of physical work had made him strong for his age. So without being asked or asking, he was immediately in the midst of the action, tugging on tent ropes, fetching hammer and pegs, carrying and placing benches. No one complained. Why would they? They were getting a pair of strong hands and broad young shoulders at no cost. If anyone passing by didn't recognise JJ as Pat McHale's son, they'd have been certain sure he was one of the actors they would see on stage later that night. Indeed, they'd doubtless not recognise him then, either, befrocked and made up to look like a young woman or scarred and bloodied like a pirate or scrubbed and besuited to look like the son of the lord of the manor.

A little later, the work done, the stage set, so to speak, the whole crew sat around in a haphazard formation. Bread and cheese, buttermilk supplied by one of the friendlier local farmers, and home-cured ham, bought earlier in Lynch's bar, were passed around. Most of the men were happy to slug buttermilk or spring water now, in preparation for the evening's performance, although two men and one older woman huddled together under a tree sharing a bottle of cider and a slim, aromatic, rolled cigarette. JJ was quite happy sitting among the troupe, sharing their food and jollity, listening wide-eyed to their amazing tales, until one of them addressed him directly.

"So, who are you, lad?" He was a tall, muscular, stubble-faced man, the sort, JJ imagined, who played the roles of the thief, the highwayman or the brigand. "What stone did you crawl out from under?"

JJ was shocked at first, thrown by the man's directness, his gruff, abrasive accent. He was suddenly shy in this new company.

"Leave the lad be," said a milder, thinner, more soft-spoken man, the sort who probably played the gents or the romantic, poetic lovers, who fell for the girl but never won her because she was more attracted to the highwayman, the brigand or the drunkard, even though she knew he would make her life a living hell, before casting her off for a younger, prettier maiden.

"I'm JJ McHale, sir, and I'm from Ballysumaghan, just up the road."

"Are you, now?" continued Stubble Face. "So why aren't you at school, then, or helping your father at home?"

"Coz ... I'd ... I'd rather be here with ye," stuttered JJ, disappointed at his own timidity.

"Yeah? Sittin' on your arse, eatin' our food and guzzlin' our milk and water?"

JJ wasn't sure now if the man was still a little drunk and serious or just practising for his role in that night's play. Encouraged by the latter notion, JJ was about to respond with some clownish buffoonery, mimicking the man's drunken demeanour and gruff speech, when a booming voice interjected from behind and above him.

"Leave him be, Quigley, you great lumbering oaf. You know he's been here all day, labouring as conscientiously as anyone." The voice came from a tall, imposing man who was glaring self-assuredly at Quigley. He was accompanied by a statuesque, slightly aloof beauty, an actress JJ assumed, the one who always played the leading lady, the depressed heroine, the femme fatale. She smiled gently but thinly at JJ, then looked away distractedly.

Quigley was silent for an instant, glowering back at the older man, but then he leapt to his feet, and both men towered above JJ.

"Fuck off, O'Donnell. This has nothing to do with you!"

"Oh please, Jarleth," chimed the statuesque actress.

O'Donnell put a gentle hand on her wrist. "Oh but it does, Jarleth," he replied, quietly this time, measured and controlled. "As long as I run this company, anything that affects the welfare of its members is my concern, and this young man, by dint of his efforts this day is, at least for now, a member of this company."

"For fuck's sake," said Stubble Face, "do you ever get tired of the sound of your own voice, Marcus? I was only tryin' to rise the young fella, isn't that right, JJ?"

"Ehm . . ."

Well, how was JJ supposed to answer that? Initially, he had certainly been convinced that the Quigley fella meant every word he said, but he had put that down to him being a damn good actor. But even though he hadn't understood most of what O'Donnell had said, he sensed that the man was standing up for him. He really liked the older man too, but he was more than a little scared of Quigley. Oh, life could be so confusing sometimes.

"Ehm . . . I suppose so," he said.

Quigley ruffled JJ's hair, almost knocking him to the ground. "Go on with you!" he said and then turned to the older man. "See you later, Marcus. Sarah." And he strode off like the hero in a history play.

Sarah smiled. O'Donnell threw his eyes to heaven.

And that was the exact moment that JJ had decided that he would run away. This motley gang of players would be his escape from his father's rule-bound world and his passport into a wide-open world of limitless possibilities. A world where you were free to be what you were, where you could follow your dreams, celebrate your achievements and share your disappointments without fear of mockery or disdain.

Back at his father's house, he tried to behave as normally as possible and stick to the evening routine that had been established over time – there was no question of asking if he could go to the performance in the village. His father wouldn't be seen dead at such a frivolous, amoral event and neither, by extension, would any of his three sons. But that was a good thing too, though, if JJ could manage to slip out, unnoticed. And this he felt he could do if he could get to go to bed early, climb out his bedroom window, clamber along the back wall then into and away through the back field. So once he had finished their plain evening meal of boiled potatoes and buttermilk, he feigned a sick stomach and dizziness. This alone was never going to fool his father, and he didn't expect it to. He knew he would have to be on death's door to get out of his evening chores: driving the milk cows over to the Lios field, sweeping out the milking parlour and feeding the calves in the Garraí. This was but phase one of his plan.

He staggered off to do the first job, under the suspicious eye of his father, and skipped the second job, which would have left him too late and too smelly to go to a show in a tent. Instead he began filling the bucket of feed for the calves in the Garraí, groaning and making as much noise as possible.

"Are you feeding the wanelings already?"

"What?" he replied weakly, as if in a daze.

"Did you sweep out the milking parlour yet?"

"The milking parlour?" he echoed, as if he had never heard of such a place before.

This was enough to draw his father away from his own evening task of sharpening his slean for a hard day's turf-cutting the next day.

"What divil's got into you tonight?"

"Hah?"

His father glared.

"I dunno. What?"

"You're acting like a right cluasánach, that's what!"

His father's colour was rising fast. JJ rolled his eyes obligingly and made sure to step out of the shadows so that his father could witness the full effect of the white marl he had rubbed into his cheeks to drain them of their colour. He wobbled a bit then, almost stumbled and replied, barely above a whisper, "What? I'm all right. Is it morning yet? Need to feed the calves before the morning."

JJ turned and staggered out the door, straining exaggeratedly under the weight of the bucket of feed, sensing his father's astonished eyes burning into his back. When he sensed the time was just right, he dropped the bucket; collapsed onto his knees, threw his head back, emitted something between a sigh and a whimper, then fell forward onto his face, careful to use his hands to break his fall. As he lay there, virtually inert, his mouth half full of shit-stained grass, it seemed to take his father an age to react, whether out of genuine shock or an innate suspicion. Eventually he did edge his way over to his prostrate son, grab him by the shoulder and yank his head around so that they could see each other, eyeball to eyeball.

"You've spilled the whole bucket of feed, you feckin' loodramawn!"

"What?"

JJ wasn't acting. He really couldn't believe the insensitivity of the man, though there was more than sufficient precedent.

"I . . . I'm sorry." He tried to get up but slumped back down so that his father had to haul him up by the arms.

"Go on, get in to bed. You're useless to me in that state!"

Yes! JJ had to fight to restrain a smile as he hauled himself up. He was about to skip back into the house but remembered in time to stagger a little and sigh, leaving his disgruntled father to refill the bucket and go down to the Garraí to feed the baying calves and sweep out the milking parlour. This gave JJ enough time to root under the stairs for an old dressmaker's dummy his mother used to prop on the kitchen table when she was sizing dresses for her few customers, in the good old days. It was worn, moth-eaten, but just the right size to fit in his bed, under his blanket, giving the impression that he was in fact there in person. An old mummer's straw-mask of his brother's, laid on the pillow and tucked well under the blanket, would give an adequate impression of his blonde locks. All the elements of his plan were now neatly in place. Finally he wrapped and knotted some bread, potatoes, a shirt and a pair of trousers in an old sheet. Then he just had to wait for his father to return and resume his slean-sharpening, before slipping out and away into the village to the show in the tent, to freedom and the beginning of his new life.

With no money to pay the entrance price, JJ slipped in under a tent flap, which he had ensured earlier was left unsecured, and wedged himself in beside a large farmer and his petite wife. She smiled when she recognised him and slid over to make more space on the bench. He had missed the first couple of items on the programme but got the final minutes of an entertaining comedy sketch that had the entire audience doubled with laughter. Then Sarah, the elegant actress from earlier, sang a spellbinding version of "I Dreamt I Dwelt in Marble Halls" while the stage was being set for the main entertainment of the evening, a comic play, *The Shaughraun,* by the famous Dublin playwright Dion Boucicault.

The shaughraun of the title was a witty, lazy, alcoholic and ne'er-do-well whose intuitive cleverness saves the day. The play was fast-moving, the dialogue sharp and funny. JJ and the audience were enthralled by the action and the performances. Jarleth Quigley was playing Robert Ffolliott, a young Irish gentleman under sentence as a Fenian; that's what they called rebels in those days. JJ had heard there were still some Fenians around but he had never met one. Ffolliott was in love with the beautiful Arte O'Neil, played by Sarah, naturally. JJ thought that Quigley didn't look the perfect Irish gentleman, particularly since he clearly hadn't shaved in several days, but then, Ffolliott was a man on the run and Quigley carried off the aristocratic accent and bearing very well. He also stumbled a number of times and slurred his words occasionally, leaving JJ unsure whether that was how Quigley chose to portray the character or if the actor was in fact drunk.

Then, about half way through the second act, the play took a sudden and alarming turn. Robert Ffolliott is in jail, where the distasteful local magistrate Kinchela surprisingly gives him a chisel and offers to help him escape because he is fond of Robert's pretty younger sister, Claire. His plan is to have Robert moved to the Old Gate Tower, where the wall is only one course thick and the mortar still fresh from a recent repair. Once there, he can easily chisel his way to freedom.

Enter then the beautiful Arte O'Neil and local priest Father Dolan, played by Marcus O'Donnell, to visit Robert. They are dismayed that Robert is talking to Kinchela, a man of questionable motives for whom they have no regard. When Kinchela had exited, Father Dolan remarked, in an accent much easier to understand than O'Donnell's own: "When Saint Patrick made a clean sweep of all the venomous reptiles in Ireland, some of the vermin must have found refuge in the bodies of such men as that."

"And maybe in your own body too, O'Donnell," said Ffolliott, or Quigley, JJ was unsure. Had he not called the other actor by his real name?

"What ails you, *Robert*? Do you not see that it's *Father Dolan* you address?" said Arte/Sarah.

"Yes, and . . . ehm . . . ehm . . ." The priest/O'Donnell searched for an ad-lib.

Quigley was sneering now and swayed slightly as he stepped towards Arte.

"Hope!" shouted the priest, suddenly inspired. "Where do you find it?"

"In her eyes," says Quigley, smirking and taking Arte first by the hand, then by the waist. "I was in prison when I stood liberated on American soil. But now I am in prison, this narrow cell is Ireland." He pulled Arte/Sarah close and tight. "I breathe my native air and am free."

Then he kissed her hard and deep. She struggled. The priest was visibly shocked.

"Quigley! Egads!" roared the priest/O'Donnell as he tried to come between the kissing couple. "What effrontery. Before a man of the cloth!"

Arte broke free of Quigley's grasp.

"Spare us your sanctimonious clap-trap, Father Dolan!" Quigley roared.

Surely this was not the script as written by the playwright, thought JJ.

"Robert," squeaked Arte, "you forget yourself." Then, as an aside to the priest, "What's going on, Marcus?"

"I have no idea," said O'Donnell. Then: "Sergeant! Sergeant!"

The sergeant instantly stumbled on, fumbling to get his cap on properly, as Ffolliott/Quigley swigged from a hip flask.

"Ehm . . . Ehm . . . sorry, I was . . ." mumbled the sergeant, clearly surprised to be on stage.

O'Donnell glared and gestured to him to proceed.

"Ehm . . . We are ordered to shift you to the Old Gate Tower!" said the sergeant, glancing at O'Donnell for reassurance.

"No!" roared Quigley.

"The guard is waiting, sir, when you are ready."

"I am ready but I refuse to accompany you, sir."

"Robert?" Arte pleaded.

"Damn you, Quigley," spat the priest, though there was more of O'Donnell than Father Dolan in it.

"And damn you too, O'Donnell. What's the point? Why not just cut straight to the chase? Stop this arsing about and let everyone get to the pub earlier, which is where we'd all rather be anyway!"

"Jarleth! Stoppit, please," said Sarah/Arte.

Quigley ignored her, faced the audience and addressed them directly: "Kinchela has set a trap to kill myself and the shaughraun as we attempt to flee because he loves you, Arte, and sure why wouldn't he, and he knows that I have been pardoned and am free now to be with you, except I'm not, am I, Marcus? But the shaughraun will eventually save the day. We will escape, Kinchela and his crew will be exposed, Claire will marry Molineaux and I will have you, Arte, as I have you now."

He grabbed Arte/Sarah again. "Come away with me, Sarah. You know I love you."

He kissed her again. She relented, kissed him back, but then broke free just as O'Donnell grabbed Quigley by the shoulder and wheeled him around, snarling, "You bloody bowsie! You drunkard. Go and be damned!"

"Be damned yourself, O'Donnell!" and he punched Marcus and sent him flying off the stage and into the startled audience, causing a chorus of moans, groans, shrieks and cheers.

Sarah rushed off, while the other actors on stage tried to restrain Quigley, who was now ranting like a crazed lunatic and flailing at anyone who approached him. Actors rushed on from the wings, some to restrain Quigley, others to support him, and soon a maul formed around the raging actor. The more timid members of the audience tried to escape, while others, fired up and smelling blood, pressed forward, removing jackets and rolling up shirt sleeves in anticipation of a good riot. The maul teetered on the edge of the stage for several moments, arms flailing and fists lashing out, before plunging headlong into the baying crowd. JJ stayed well back, taking up a safe position from which to observe the fracas.

Egged on by the locals who were pushing, shoving, jostling, even throwing the odd speculative punch, the scrap quickly escalated in energy and scale until it outgrew the cramped tent. One of the central poles snapped under the weight of the maul and the other fell over, causing the tent to come billowing down, smothering the combatants for several minutes, though some nonetheless managed to land an extra blow or two.

JJ's brother Michael, on his way home from the village, heard the ructions in the Sraith and was drawn in by a mixture of curiosity and a good nose for a fight. JJ emerged from under the tent just in time to see and be seen by Michael.

"What the hell are you doing here? I thought you were sick in bed."

"What are you doing here?" JJ blurted, genuinely taken aback.

"I had business in the village for Da. Don't be so cheeky, you little óinseach."

By then the brawl had spilled out through several gaps and tears in the canvas. JJ's brother smiled with relish at the imminent fisticuffs.

"Here, hold that," said Michael, as he took his hand off his bicycle and began to roll up his shirt sleeves.

JJ leapt forward to catch the bike before it hit the ground.

"And don't be thinking of scooting off on it in either," his brother warned, pointing a thick index finger. "Your father'll have a thing or two to say about you being in this place tonight, so he will." Then he dove into the midst of the scramble, swinging left and right. His flailing fists had no real impact on proceedings until they met the chin of Marcus O'Donnell. Time seemed to freeze for an eternity as the stunned actor/manager appeared to hover on his heels, his eyes rolling back in his head, before he fell backwards onto the heaped canvas like a massive sack of potatoes.

JJ almost applauded but the instant, perceptible change in the atmosphere stopped him. Up to that point, the dispute had been more or less between Quigley and O'Donnell, with a few ancillary onlookers and cast members, extras you might say, taking the opportunity to let off some steam in the generalised dust-up. With Michael's punch, however, the company of actors immediately closed ranks, and Quigley took on the role of O'Donnell's heroic avenger. It was players versus locals now, fit-up versus village, a proper faction fight.

Quigley it was who confirmed the change in tenor by landing a thundering, reciprocal haymaker on Michael's chin, lifting the lad clean off the ground and landing him unconscious in the middle of a thorn bush. Looking on the bright side, and JJ always did, that punch had instantly revived his chances of making good his escape. Within seconds, however, weapons had been found or quickly fashioned from boughs, tent poles, horse harnesses, anything solid that was to hand and could cause injury, and the two bands of men – and women, because some of those actresses were fiery individuals too – were at each other's throats.

After close to an hour of fierce hand-to-hand combat, both sides had suffered some fairly serious-looking injuries and it was difficult to say who had won, if indeed there had been a victor. The fighting had abated though. The company had hurriedly packed up its belongings and was limping out of the village, weapons still in hand and escorted by a similarly equipped band of villagers. A still dazed O'Donnell attempted to throw oil on troubled waters but his pleas for a reasonable resolution fell on deaf ears, on both sides. He, after all, had "slept through" the worst of the fighting. As had JJ's brother.

Michael! JJ had forgotten completely about him, so engrossed had he been in the affray. But now, as he contemplated stowing away in one of the fit-up wagons, sure that he could negotiate a peace later with O'Donnell, Quigley and the others, he was forcefully reminded of his brother's presence when he heard him call out – no, shout out . . . no, roar his name – from the other side of the Sraith, where he had been given some poteen to revive him.

"JJ? JJ McHale!"

JJ knew in an instant. That was it. Game up. Prisoner recaptured. Sentencing would be handed down on the morrow.

And a harsh sentence it turned out to be. What he had thought of heretofore as a tough, cold existence became tougher and colder than anything he could ever have imagined. What had previously been disdain and a bemused lack of understanding of his father's view of the world, grew to utter disgust and hatred of the man and everything he represented.

So now, four years on, as the front wheel of Bartley Comer's black Rover safety bicycle continued to squeak loudly beneath him, he knew that this time was different. This time there would be no recapture. This time there could be no return to that world. Opportunity had presented itself a second time, fully formed and in one fell swoop, his future, his destiny encapsulated in one defining moment, and JJ McHale was not afraid to seize it with both hands. This time his escape had been unplanned and utterly impulsive but, like many impulsive actions, it had been lying dormant for a long time, a seed waiting to be germinated by the right set of circumstances; a tinderbox awaiting the spark that would ignite it.

3

Racquet Court Cinema

———•———

IF BARTLEY COMER HAD TAKEN a little longer to sell his few meagre
beasts at the fair, or had stayed for a couple of extra bottles of porter
with his fellow farmers, things might have been different. JJ would have
left a gratified Mary-Ann, smiling over her pot of steaming cabbage,
and watered the cattle in his father's field that bordered Comer's farm.
He would doubtless have grinned wryly at a tipsy Comer, freewheeling
down the boreen, as he himself walked home across the fields. He
would have swung by Lynch's bar and shop to buy a couple of bags of
slag, with the ten shillings his father had given him for the purpose. He
would have humped the bags of fertilizer on his shoulders, arriving at
the house tired and sweaty and just in time for the customary dinner of
spuds and buttermilk. After doing his chores in silence, he would have
spent twenty minutes before bed going through his growing pile of
pictures and articles, cut from the *Freeman's Journal*, *Evening Telegraph*
and any other newspaper he could get his hands on. Every article and
picture had to do with performers, actors, singers, theatres and the latest
phenomenon to have hit the country, motion pictures; most articles on
the latter featured the biggest star of that medium, Charlie Chaplin.

His experience with Marcus O'Donnell's fit-up company, the bitter
disappointment of his thwarted escape, did not dampen his interest
in the life of the actor but rather intensified it. He used all the charm
and natural appeal he'd been gifted, especially with the fairer sex, to
acquire as much knowledge as was possible in such a backwater. He
read and reread newspaper reports about plays, touring companies and

the latest films making their way to Ireland from the United States of America. He had only been to the cinema once, and had seen just three films, but it had proved a life-altering experience for JJ McHale.

Just over a year ago, his father's brother had died in Galway and, in an uncharacteristic display of fraternal devotion, he brought JJ and his brothers to their uncle's funeral. His father and his uncle had never been close, and JJ was convinced the only reason he went was because he hoped his dead brother might have left him a few quid in his will. Ever a pleasant and convivial man, his uncle had married well, into a Galway merchant family, and had managed one of their big shops in the city.

"At the very least, they'll have to throw the young fella something for singing so well in the church and at the graveside," he overheard his father mutter.

Indeed all of his cousins and many of the mourners were moved to tears by his plaintive rendition of "Amhrán Mháinse": "Dá mbéadh mo chlann sa mbaile agam/ An oíche a bfhaighinnse bás."

His father received no remuneration, however, and thankfully didn't notice JJ's aunt slip a folded ten-shilling note into his palm as she shook hands to thank him, begging him to sing another later, back at the house. When called upon to do so, he chose the beautiful "Cailín Deas Crúite na mBó", a favourite of his mother's that tells of a man's infatuation with a comely milkmaid.

He chose the song for his sad but comely fifteen-year-old cousin, Hannah, who was not a milkmaid. She was sitting on the arm of her father's chair by the fireside in the cosy parlour, holding the framed photograph of him that had adorned the coffin. She gripped it like she believed she could somehow keep him longer among them if only she didn't let go. How like a painting of some tragic heroine she looked as JJ sang in the old language about the sunlight of the milkmaid's eyes, her lips sweet as berries, her skin whiter than milk. But it was the musicality of the words, the deep broad vowels, the guttural *ch*, the long alveolar *l*, the sensually sibilant *s* that JJ enjoyed most and that carried him through the song as if he were floating in a luscious dream.

> Tá a súile mar lonradh na gréine,
>   . . . Ar lasadh measc craobha na gcnó,

Tá a béilín níos dílse ná sméara,
's is gile ná leamhnacht a snó,
Níl ógbhean níos deise san saol seo
Ná cailín deas crúite na mbó.

He knew the English translation but didn't think it came anywhere near the beauty of the Irish, and judging from the rapturous applause and congratulations from the assembled mourners, he was not alone in that. Before he could wallow too much in the affirmation of the crowd though, his father was roaring for him to do one of his own favourites.

"Never mind that yoke. Do Robert Emmet, 'Bold Robert Emmet'. Go on, son!"

JJ must have hesitated for an instant, probably not wanting to sing such a rousing ballad at his uncle's funeral, sensing too that few if any of the mourners shared his father's bombastic, froth-and-no-beer republicanism. Either way, his father was shouting again, his brothers forming a chorus of approval.

"It was a favourite of your uncle's."

Everyone knew it wasn't.

"Sing the 'Bold Robert Emmet'. Sing it!"

JJ had little choice, so he began, as quietly and apologetically as he could. "The struggle is over, the boys are defeated/ Old Ireland's surrounded with sadness and gloom."

"Good man, son. Sing out!"

"We were defeated and shamefully treated—"

"Don't ever be ashamed of what you came from!"

"And I, Robert Emmet, awaiting my doom."

He thought about ending it there but his father and his filial choir had already leapt into the chorus, singing at the top of their lungs. He continued to sing along with bridled passion.

Bold Robert Emmet, the darling of Erin.
Bold Robert Emmet will die with a smile.
Farewell companions both loyal and daring,
I'll lay down my life for the Emerald Isle.

JJ couldn't think of anything more ridiculous than laying down your life for anything, let alone the Emerald Isle. Life was for living, not for laying down. He was about to drift into the next verse, when he realised that the overwrought passion of his father and siblings had been self-defeating. By climaxing at the end of the chorus, they provided the perfect opportunity for the mourners to cry out, "Well done! Fair play!" and clap politely, before drifting back into conversation and drinking.

"Woohoo!" That was his father. "One of the greatest Irish rebels!"

"There'll soon be plenty more like him," chimed JJ's brother Tomás to mostly deaf ears and several disapproving glances.

In the heel of the hunt, there was to be no inheritance for his father, but while he spent the rest of the evening drowning his sorrows in a barrel of porter, JJ skipped away to a film show at the Racquet Court Cinema Theatre, where he got all the riches he desired, for the time being at any rate. He cannot claim credit for making that decision though. It was his cousin Hannah who took the initiative. She was a couple of years younger than JJ and just beginning to bloom. She was approaching the peak of her beauty. Genetics, visible in her mother and aunts, and the struggles of life, would soon begin to ravage her pretty features and distort her slender body. Right at this moment though, her skin was perfectly smooth, her breasts ample but contained, her hips shapely, her lips delectably moist and full. But her eyes were her crowning glory, a dark Spanish brown and pool deep.

As they picked their way along Buttermilk Walk, through a throng of traders and beggars, Hannah laughed and talked with the innocence and giddy excitement of youth, but JJ knew she was no skittish ingénue – that's what they called the vulnerable young actresses in the newspaper reports he'd read. She was bright, intelligent, witty and his first cousin. She loved her father deeply, a milder more amenable parent than his own, but she had cried her fill – her eyes were still red from the tears, which made them even more captivating – and she needed a break, to be a young girl again for an hour.

When they turned into Middle Street, they were met by a queue that stretched from the corner to the cinema doors. This gave them time to get to know each other better. He was happy for her to do most of the talking; she had more to tell; a more interesting city life to recount than the boring, repetitive, chore-laden days of farm boy JJ McHale. She had interesting and adventurous friends. In the family shop she got to meet all sorts of colourful characters. When they finally reached the Racquet Court Cinema, the façade was nothing special but, once inside, JJ felt like he had stepped into a fairy tale. The colour, the music, the fuss, he loved it all. Almost full to its five-hundred capacity, the noise of chatter and the unwrapping of sweet papers was almost deafening to his ears, used only to the chirping of birds and the plaintive calls of sheep and cattle. Overhead he noticed six lavish private boxes, complete with curtains, only two of which were occupied. The red-velvet-covered, tip-up seats at the back of the theatre, the "dear seats", were like something you would only see in a bishop's palace or the like. Even the basic cloth-covered seats they sat in were softer and more comfortable than anything he had set his arse on before.

The first film was a dreary enough seventeen-minute romantic drama, *The Lad from Old Ireland,* about a young Irishman who flees from poverty to America, where in ten years he makes himself rich through hard work and clever investments, finally rising to become mayor of New York itself. It was made by three American fellas and the audience seemed delighted when the hero came back to save his half-forgotten sweetheart from eviction and then married her. JJ thought it was mushy and sentimental because it went for the corny happy ending but he was impressed by the young hero's ambition and the fact that he'd realised his dreams in America.

The second film, *Caught in a Cabaret,* starred Charlie Chaplin and was the funniest, most entertaining thing he'd ever seen. He'd read about the film in one of his paper cuttings. It had been shown in Dublin earlier in the year: " . . . one of the best comedy pieces in cinematography yet shown in Dublin . . . In all its details it proved a most laughable piece and drew forth loud applause." He couldn't believe that he had got to see it for himself and all thanks to his poor uncle's untimely death coupled with his father's greed, followed by his cousin's need to escape the morbid funeral house. To receive this unexpected pleasure was wonderful; that the film starred Charlie Chaplin was a bonus. He'd read so much about this actor from London, England, who had come from a background as poor and dismal as his own. JJ stared wide-eyed at the screen. Seeing his hero like that, in such times, was as good as meeting him in person. Not that JJ didn't dream of doing that too someday.

JJ's amusement and awe was quickly replaced by boredom when the third film got underway. *The Huns of the North Sea* was a dull factual film about laying mines in the North Sea, which was somewhere between Scotland and Norway. Or was it Sweden? God knows why the Huns would be bothered with that cold, dismal part of the world anyway. JJ was stirred out of his boredom, though, by the sudden, tingling warmth of Hannah's hand on his knee. When he looked into her dark pools of eyes, he noticed a flicker of hesitation, just enough to allow him to politely demur, if he chose, without causing her undue embarrassment, but not enough to admit that she was sorry or felt guilty for broaching the subject, as it were. He smiled, which she interpreted as a signal to proceed. So, by the time he kissed her, her hand had moved up to his crotch. This prompted him to rest his own hand on her left breast. It was then that he wished they had been able to afford the dear seats at the back, not just for their comfort but also their relative seclusion. It was not long before a chorus of hushing and tutting began. Smirking, JJ took her by the hand and within minutes they had slipped up the stairs, where they willingly surrendered to the sum of their combined passions, behind the curtains of one of the empty private boxes.

Maybe it's wrong to have relations with your first cousin. Maybe it's especially wrong to do so on the day of her father's funeral, taking advantage of her grief. Certainly few people would approve of doing it in a private box in a packed cinema, during a screening. But JJ McHale saw nothing wrong with what happened between Hannah and him that day. He, after all, had not initiated anything. He saw what he did as an act of kindness towards a girl for whom he cared, in the way you do for your first cousin, and who, he was certain, was in need of comforting, on such a dark day.

After that day, as he saw it, he had two ways of escaping his father's claustrophobic world, from the existence that was mapped out for him, and realising his dream to become rich and famous. Option one was to do like the fella in the first film and hightail it to America, work hard, invest well and become mayor of New York. There were certain obvious drawbacks to this option. Firstly, he was not enamoured of hard work, at least not the heavy-lifting, back-breaking, long-hours kind. Secondly, he had no idea how he would ever manage to get the fare together. He did broach the subject with Hannah, after the picture show, but she confessed to having meagre savings and, now that her father was deceased, would have to work full-time in the business. She also talked about maybe, in time, saving enough money for both of them to go away together, which was moving far too quickly for JJ. Finally, that option would simply take too long and, while it worked in a film, was unlikely to succeed in real life. No, JJ had a much better idea.

Option two was to make his way to Dublin, something that could be done at relatively little cost. Once there, he would earn money by singing on the streets and at fairs and festivals. Having gained some recognition, he would become a performer at the Theatre Royal, the Olympia, the Coliseum, the Tivoli or the Queen's. He might even try the Abbey Theatre, although he'd heard they only did dull plays about the past and how wonderful it was to be Irish, as long as you were a famous warrior, a mythological god or a fairy. Anyway, with all the work he would get, with all the rich gentlemen and, more especially, rich ladies who he would charm out of their gold, he would quickly save the fare to London. Once there, he would find and join the Karno Troupe as a singer-actor and, in no time at all, he would be on a steamer to America with them. He would then make his way out west, to California, and into the films with Charlie Chaplin and his gang. That would bring him the fame and riches he craved. If a poor waif from the backstreets of London could do it, why couldn't he? He just needed to be in the right place at the right time. And Ballysumaghan was definitely not the right place.

4

The Beast of Riverstown

—•—

THAT HAD BEEN JJ'S PLAN for the past year, but he had not expected
to be putting it into action so soon and so impulsively. Here he was
though, cycling east, away from his father, his brothers, Bartley Comer,
the countless girls whose hearts he'd broken and the many women
whose honour he'd impugned, much to their enjoyment and their
husbands' displeasure. He was cycling east and towards his future and
the endless possibilities that lay ahead. He was cycling east on Bartley
Comer's bike with the squeaky front wheel, the squeak that now, he
was becoming aware, was almost deafening and the front wheel that he
noticed was wobbling far more than it should be, unless it was warped,
or worse, loose. That final thought had barely crossed his mind when
the wheel squeaked for the last time, parted company with the fork of
the bike and shot into the ditch. The unsupported fork seemed to hover
in the air for an instant before it nosedived and dug into the surface of
the road, flinging its passenger headlong over the handle bars. He tried
to use his hands to break his fall but his momentum carried him, head
over heels into the wet, peaty ditch. Bike and rider protruded from the
marshy landscape of Riverstown, like two sore thumbs.

The next thing JJ McHale knew, he was staring through watery,
unfocused eyes at some class of a mythological, horned beast with the
body of a man, towering over him, ready to strike him dead with the
long spear it was brandishing in its gnarled claw. Naturally JJ screamed
and jolted up and back, in a pathetic attempt to elicit help or at least
dodge death a little longer.

"In ainm fuckin' Dé, cén diabhal atá ionat, a mhacín?"

JJ recognised the old language but had no idea what it meant. Some dreadful incantation as a prelude to slitting his throat, gouging out his innards and eating them raw? This second fright gave him enough energy to leap out of whatever he had been lying in. But as soon as he hit solid ground again, his legs buckled under him and he crumpled in a heap on what felt like a cold stone floor. So maybe he wasn't in hell after all.

"Ná bíodh faitíos ort. Tá tú i mBaile Idir Dhá Abhainn. Cathaigh tú fanacht sa leaba go dtí go bhfuil tú réití!" This was barked like a threat, as the beast caught him under the arm and hurled him back into whatever he'd been lying in and loomed over him again.

"Fan ansin go bfaighfidh mé tae dhuit!"

JJ's vision was beginning to clear now, and thanks to the light streaming in through the small window to his right, he could see that the beast had a human face, a huge hooked nose, lined leathery skin, half a mouthful of teeth. The implement in his hand appeared to be a shepherd's crook and not a primitive spear. Then, when the beast turned and walked abruptly away, his horns remained. JJ saw now that they were ram's horns, attached to a skeletal head that was nailed above the door of what, he realised, was actually a small bedroom and not a cell in the Underworld. He was lying on a hard, rough-hewn, settle bed.

"Ow."

He was suddenly aware of how sore his head was and felt the large lump and moist scar that he had obviously received during his fall from the bike. That bike, Bartley Comer's bike. His recent history replayed itself in short, jumpy flashbacks, like a Keystone film, only he wasn't laughing.

"Seo dhuit!"

The beast-now-a-man was before him again, shoving a large mug of tea into his face.

"Chuir mé braoinín uisce beatha istigh ann."

"Thanks."

He took the mug and drank. Whoa, it had a kick like a donkey. He remembered now, ishka baha, whiskey, or in this case, more likely poteen.

"Tá sé láidir," said beast-man, with a laugh like a bucket of pebbles, as he sat on the settle bed.

"Níl Gaeilge agam," JJ replied apologetically, because he still didn't know if this fella was friend or foe. It was the only bit of Irish he could remember, other than song words, but it proved useful.

"Is mór an trua. Shame on you, lad. But no matter. Still would've been wrong to leave you on the side of the road."

"Thanks."

"You're from Sooey, aren't you?

"What?"

How the hell did this stranger know where he was from? Had he been ranting during his unconsciousness? What had he said?

"You're Tom McHale's lad. I've seen you at the fairs with him sometimes. He's a bastard to drive a bargain!"

He could have stopped at bastard, but JJ just said, "Yes, that's me, Ballysumaghan."

"You'll be grand, so," said the stranger. "I sent word with the egg man. He'll be over that way in a couple of hours. Doubtless your father'll come and fetch you home."

"Doubtless," mumbled JJ, the grim thought hitting him like a fist in the solar plexus. "The doctor from Ballymote is on a sick call in Drumfin as it happens, poor auld Miley Burke, I doubt the craythur will see the end of the week. I sent word in with the postman, so he should be here in a whileen."

"Great," said JJ with a smile that was somewhere between grim and wry. Wasn't he a great man for sending the messages all the same? JJ was being well looked after but his gallop was going to be well and truly halted if he didn't do something quickly. He tried standing again but wobbled and almost spilled his tea. The man grabbed him roughly with his huge right hand.

"Céard sa diabhal atá ort? Lie down, would ya. Get some rest."

This last order brooked no argument and, with the combined effect of the poteen and a mild concussion, JJ found himself unable to fight off the tiredness.

When he awoke, he was aware of voices coming from the other room. The dim light and his inability to hear clearly made him feel like he was in some sort of a motion picture, a spy thriller or a war story this time that had him trapped behind enemy lines, awaiting torture then execution. The two men were prattling away in the old language, but he quickly recognised the gruff tones of his rescuer-jailor and recalled where he was. He sat up and found that the dizziness wasn't as bad as before. His head still hurt but he was able to stand now. He shuffled over to the doorway, where a blanket hung from a couple of homemade nails. He peered out the gap between blanket and wall to see who owned the second voice. It was an older man too, in his fifties maybe, in a worn, tight-fitting suit with a bag that looked like it was made of leather in his left hand. This must be the doctor. He was feeling cornered now and knew he needed to act immediately. A reflex drew his vision to the small window, little more than a hole in the whitewashed wall. As he shuffled over to it, he smiled when he heard the soft nicker of a horse outside.

Once at the window he saw that the horse was yoked to a trap, the doctor's trap and a viable means of escape.

"Tá sé thíos sa seomra anseo," he heard the farmer say, his voice getting louder and closer, as he led the doctor down to the room. JJ instantly thrust himself hands first through the window opening and began to tug and wriggle. The horse took a couple of steps backwards, whinnying loudly. The window, however, had not been designed with such an activity in mind and so was a little too narrow for his girth. But JJ McHale was not going to be so easily defeated. Ignoring the questioning look and dismissive snort from the horse, he continued to twist and flail.

"In ainm fuckin' Dé!" he heard from behind him.

He thrashed, tugged and flailed even harder, until he had got himself as far out the window as he was ever going to get. He was stuck, wedged, jammed in and going nowhere. He looked up to see the doctor's bemused face looking back at him, as he reined in his startled horse. JJ smiled sheepishly and his mouth made an attempt to form some words of explanation, perhaps, or exhortation. But before anything comprehensible could emerge, he shot backwards through the opening and found himself lodged in the arms of the beast-man, like an errant sheep or an unruly calf after a difficult birth.

"Bíonn driopás ar na h-amadáin nuair a bhíonn drugal ar na h-aingil."

The metal stethoscope was cold on his bare back as the doctor bade him inhale and exhale at regular intervals.

"Well everything is fine in that department."

"More than can be said for upstairs," rasped the farmer, tapping his own head. "What in the name of God were you playing at? Sure aren't we only trying to help you. Óinseach!"

"I know."

"Maybe he wanted a different help than we were offering," suggested the doctor.

"Sure he needs that head patched up, doesn't he? Wasn't he lucky you were around, God damn it!"

"He doesn't look like he counts himself lucky. What were you over here for, anyway?"

"Nothin'."

"Were you coming or going?" pressed the doctor.

"I was coming, but I was going too, sort of," said JJ, trying not to sound like a smart aleck.

"You little fecker," growled the beast-man, raising the back of his hand to strike.

JJ raised his arms to defend himself. The doctor raised his hand to calm the beast-man, then addressed JJ directly, eye to eye.

"Look, if it's going you were, east instead of west, away from home and not back to it, then who are we to stop you?"

"What?"

"You're a man now. Eighteen?"

"Yes."

"So you're well capable of knowing your own mind and making your own decisions."

"I ... suppose."

No one had ever credited him for knowing his own mind before and certainly had never recognised his right to act independently.

"Don't tell me you're off to join them daft rebels in Dublin," scoffed the beast-man.

"That's a fine way to talk about brave men who are willing to risk their lives for the rest of us," responded the doctor in a dignified tone.

"Stupid men, more like, and I never asked anyone to risk his life for me!"

"Well, let's hope it won't come to that," said the doctor with finality as he packed the implements of his profession into his bag.

"Well, are you?" the beast-man barked at JJ.

"What?"

"A stupid, deluded fool on his way to Dublin to become a hero?"

"No," said JJ defensively. "I'm headed much further afield," he added with an irrepressible grin, "but you might still read of my exploits in the newspapers, one day."

The beast-man was too perplexed to add anything further and now seemed to lose interest, having nothing to scold JJ for.

"In any event," said the doctor, "you still got a nasty knock to the head and your bike is in no longer roadworthy, so . . ."

There was a pregnant pause as the beast-man looked quizzically at the doctor, at a loss to know what conclusion he had reached.

"So?" asked JJ.

"I'm going back into Ballymote after this. I'll take you with me. I have spare beds. You can rest up for the night, and if you're still intent on venturing east in the cold light of tomorrow, there's a train will take you all the way to Dublin."

JJ smiled broadly then stopped to look to his rescuer-jailor. The old farmer raised his hands wide with an expression that indicated it was no skin off his large nose what this daft young fella or any other daft young fella did. He had done all he could.

Half an hour later JJ was sitting alongside the doctor in his trap. They had to make one other house call along the way to another small farmhouse on meagre acreage. They chatted a little as they trotted, the doctor telling of his time at university in Dublin, JJ of his love for singing and acting. The doctor had been a frequent theatre goer during his time in the city, mostly "serious theatre" as he described it. It was something he missed, but he expressed no particular interest in this new cinema fad, convinced it would never replace the thrill of the live performance. As they drew close to the farmhouse, the doctor spoke in a lowered tone, with an expression of concern mixed with intent.

"I don't need to know any more than you've already told me. But if it is the case that you are heading to Dublin for noble reasons, the man of this house will give you any help you require. He does not share the views of our previous client."

He closed this short speech with a wink, as they slowed to a stop in front of the thatched farmhouse then waited for a response. JJ hesitated for an instant but the doctor's unflinching gaze demanded he say something, besides which, he didn't want to look a gift horse in the mouth.

"All I need, Doctor, is some food and somewhere dry to lay my head for the night," JJ answered with an enigmatic grin.

The doctor smiled knowingly. "The latter you will have with me and welcome, the former will be provided presently."

Within minutes, JJ was munching potatoes and boiled mutton, washed down with a can of fresh milk mixed with cold, refreshing spring water. The farmer who had so kindly fed him was a strong, lean, red-faced man. His deep eye sockets and heavy brows gave the impression of a naturally secretive person. He smoked his clay pipe and chatted about nothing in particular, but JJ couldn't help feeling that he was trying to figure out his motives, trying to get him to open up. JJ was too busy enjoying the food, though, and imagining the lovely accommodation that awaited him in Ballymote, to engage with this man beyond the demands of polite conversation. As they were leaving, the farmer shook JJ's hand so hard he thought he would break bones. He stared JJ in the face, a tear forming in his eye. "Go dtugfaidh Dia misneach dhuit, a mhac!" he said earnestly.

JJ hadn't a clue what it meant but knew how to say thanks for the food and hospitality. "Go raibh maith agat, a chara."

The tear rolled down the man's cheek as he released his vice-like grip, and the doctor stirred the horse into motion with a swash of the leather reins.

5

The Dublin Train

————*————

JJ McHale was awoken on the morning of Thursday, 20 April by the sun streaming through lace curtains that fluttered in the breeze brushing in through the partly open sash window. He was rested, refreshed and smiling. Although it took him a few moments to register where he was and recall how he had got there, his spirit knew instantly that he had taken his first significant step towards a future bright with expectation.

A note on the kitchen table told him the doctor was gone out on an urgent call and that he should help himself to the home-baked bread and fresh eggs on the table, the former made by his housekeeper the previous day, the latter provided by a patient as payment for his services. Both were flavoursome and satisfying.

As he made his way through the small town in a topcoat, a gift from the doctor along with a clean shirt and a flat cap, he thought it must be Sunday, such were the numbers of people making their way towards the church. Had he been unconscious for days rather than hours? A polite enquiry provoked an irate response from a grey-haired woman with a head scarf, knotted tightly under her chin.

"Do you not know that it's Holy Thursday, you heathen, the day before the Lord died on the cross to save us from our sins?"

More talk of people dying to save the rest of us. What was the country coming to? She was gone by the time he'd mumbled, "Thanks."

The mention of Holy Thursday, and the sudden doleful chiming of the church bell, brought words and notes flooding back. Back home in Ballysumaghan, he would have been heading to a similar ceremony in Sooey church: the blessing of the baptismal water, the re-enactment of the symbolic washing of the apostles' feet, the last supper later, to celebrate the Passover and the flight from Egypt to freedom and the Promised Land. "Live as children of the light, performing actions good, just and true." Before he knew it, the Latin words and notes were flowing from his lips like the waters of an immaculate fountain.

> Ave, ave verum corpus
> Natum De Maria virgine
> Vere passum,
> immolatum in cruce pro homine
> Cuius latus perforatum
> Unda fluxit et sanguine
> Esto nobis praegustatum
> In mortis examine.
> In mortis examine.

By the time he'd finished singing, the woman with the knotted scarf was back before him, to berate him further. He hunched his shoulders against the onslaught.

"Go mbeannaí Dia thú," she said, her eyes misted, "maybe you're closer to him than the rest of us," she concluded as she blessed herself, hugged him with a gentleness he didn't think she possessed, and kissed him lightly on the cheek.

"Thank you, mam," he answered, taking the flat cap from his head instinctively. Misinterpreting the gesture, she smiled and tipped a penny into JJ's cap. The assembled congregation followed her lead, tossing pennies and halfpennies into it. Despite his surprise, JJ's natural inclination to entertain took over and he launched into a couple of verses of a traditional hymn, "A Íosa, Glan Mo Chroíse" and finished off with a verse of "Panis Angelicus". Not knowing the meaning of the Latin words, he was oblivious to the gentle irony, but smiled beatifically as the jingle of coins rang in his ears like the sweet song of angels.

> Bread of the Angels is made bread for mankind;
> Gifted bread of Heaven of all imaginings the end;

Oh, thing miraculous! This body of God will nourish.

The train station was quiet for the same reason the town was busy. There was a lone man, in his late twenties, JJ guessed, wearing a felt hat and a long Mackintosh, the collar pulled up around his ears. He smoked two cigarettes while they waited for the train and exhibited no desire to have any interaction with anyone else. JJ waited beside a youngish woman with three young children in tow. She was on her way to spend the Easter weekend with her sister in Tullamore and spoke to JJ like he was her brother or a close friend of the family. She revealed that her husband had stayed at home because he didn't get on with her sister, though she thought the real reason was that her husband had always wanted to marry her sister and that he only settled for her after her sister rejected him and married a Tullamore man who worked for the railway, instead. Her husband, she confessed, couldn't bear to be reminded of that fact and avoided being around whenever the two sisters were together.

Thankfully the train arrived before she could get too far into a long list of her children's ailments and the various remedies that had been provided by that doctor, in the town, who was only an auld charlatan.

"I mean who's to say he even studied medicine at all and didn't just forge his degree or whatever it is they get from those universities."

JJ didn't bother telling her about how helpful and considerate he had found the same doctor.

The fare was twelve shillings and sixpence, his father's ten-shilling note plus half of what he had just collected outside the church, but it was worth every penny. He was well and truly on his way now. As they trundled out of Ballymote towards Boyle, through Kilnaharry, Killined and Tawnaghmore, spectacular Lough Arrow just visible in the distance, the beautiful landscape floated by his carriage window like it was a cinema screen. Once through the jagged Curlew Mountains, they descended into Boyle, the lush green fields a marked contrast to the flat, heathery bogland around Sooey. Next they passed Lough Key, the huge forest, and on into the lush valley of the River Shannon towards the busy market town of Carrick. JJ was soon lulled into reverie by the rhythmic chugging of the train, like the drumming of a bodhrán, tapping out a reel or a hornpipe. Melodies swirled around in his head, an accompaniment to the fabulous technicolour moving picture he was watching through the window of his carriage.

JJ McHale couldn't remember when he started singing but anyone who knew him growing up said he was singing before he could talk. That's probably an exaggeration, but who was he to contradict his elders? He was definitely very young when he first began to take the floor at parties to entertain his neighbours, at Meitheals and Seisiúns in their houses. He had no memory of the songs sung back then, but his parents' friends, especially the women, adored him: women as big as heifers, women as delicate as wrens, women from eighteen to eighty. They would wrap their arms around him like a big blanket and snuggle him into their chests, crowing giddily.

"Ooh, come here, a graween."

"Couldn't ya just eat him up?"

"He's like a cup of fresh cream."

"Wouldn't you slip him under your shawl and take him home with you? Wouldn't you?"

He remembered well the warmth and softness of their bosoms as they squeezed his face tightly into the tender, fleshy mass. He remembered feeling safe and cherished for those moments. The memory was warm, whiskey coloured. Life doesn't stay like that though.

He remembered clearly the day his mother died. He would have liked to recall that it was a frosty day in February or a dreary, rain-sodden late afternoon in November, after a day picking cold, wet potatoes out of the hard, broken earth, but he couldn't. He knew it was a day in mid-May, the month of Mary, the blessed virgin, whatever that meant.

It was a gorgeous, gorgeous day and he sped home from school, hoping that his mother might be well enough, on such a perfect day, for him to lift her out of her bed for an hour, so she could maybe take him back the boreen to pick wild flowers for the May altar in school. But instead he was met by his father. He was dressed in his best black Sunday going-to-Mass suit. His face was fixed in an angry glare. It was like he had lassoed a dark cloud and was carrying it around on his shoulder, like Jesus carrying the cross to Calvary.

His father ordered him inside. "Get cleaned up. The priest is coming."

When JJ got inside and called to his mother, she didn't answer. Probably asleep. So he climbed the stairs quietly and tip-toed into her darkened room. The floral curtains were shut, the window too. The air was stale, sickly, a vomity, sweaty sort of smell that the single lighted candle couldn't mask.

"Did you not see the candle? You fuckin' loodremawn!"

Why the hell hadn't it dawned on him what was after happening, with the closed curtains, the smell and the stupid fucking candle? His father was right, he was a fucking eejit. Thinking she was asleep, he had edged forward and planted a delicate kiss, like a petal, on her cheek. Her cold cheek. Although his lips barely brushed it, he sensed the intense iciness, the intractable hardness of her skin. Her face was as still as the far lake in summer. Was there even breath coming out of her? He placed his shaking fingers on her face. This was not a natural coldness. Her skin was hard and stretched tight. It was already becoming difficult for him to imagine that adamantine face smiling or laughing or singing along with him in the chorus of a favourite song, their very breaths in perfect harmony.

"She's gone from us, son. Now get cleaned up."

But how could she be gone? His mother would never leave him. Surely she must have been taken. Some diabhal, a pooka or some fairy maybe, something unnatural or supernatural, like in the stories she told him, must have slipped in unnoticed after he left for that damn school this morning. It must have stolen her, right from under his fucking-gobshite-of-a-father's nose. God damn and blast it! Why didn't he stay home from school altogether? If he'd stayed here with her, he could have saved her. He'd never have let anyone, man nor beast, ghost nor goblin take his beautiful mother from him. He'd have minded her. Not like *him*. He glared angrily at his father.

JJ was eight years and one month old.

It rained the day of her funeral.

"The angels are crying for your mammy, JJ."

At her funeral mass, he sang "Amhrán Mháinse". He could sing it, feel the music of it, but he didn't understand it. As he sang in the cold, darkened church, the auld wans all bawled their eyes out.

He didn't sing for a whole year after that. When he did, it was different than before. The listeners still loved it, were even more effusive in their praise, the women even more generous with their hugs and cuddles. But when he had sung before, he had been aware of only notes, melody and words. He had simply hopped, skipped and skimmed from crotchet to quaver, like a harvesting bee, or a fresh breeze playing with autumn leaves. But now he felt like he was being swallowed by the song and was floating around inside it, being tossed and turned by the melody, chilled and warmed by the sounds of words he often didn't even know the meaning of but now felt the full weight of. It was like he was the flower; he was being played by the breeze.

The first time he sang again, it was in the house of the prettiest of his neighbours' wives, Fionnuala. At least to his young eyes she was. Her hair was long, soft and wavy, like golden clouds shrouding her plump face. Her bosom always seemed too big for her frock and her smile made him feel like the sunshine used to. It was Fionnuala's birthday and she asked him, begged him, to sing her favourite song. She held his face in her soft-as-a-buttercup hands, planted a motherly kiss on his forehead, promised him an extra slice of apple tart then hugged him close, his cheek squeezed against the exposed flesh of her breast. He agreed to break his musical silence, not for the slice of apple tart but in return for the delicious thrill her hug had sent shuddering through his young body. The skin of his cheek was still tingling when he reclaimed it from the embrace of his pretty admirer.

> If I was a blackbird, I'd whistle and sing
> And I'd follow the ship that my true love sails in
> And on top of the riggings I'd there build my nest
> And I'd pillow my head on his lily-white breast.

If he had known that day that he would spend the next ten years in a sullen glowering contest with his father, he would have run away right there and then. But he didn't, because you don't think like that when you're still only a child. No. When you're a child you search only for the next possibility; you ferret out the positive; you treat your life like a great, endless adventure. And that's what JJ tried to do, but his father was having none of it. If he had taken off his black suit in itself after the funeral was over, there might have been some hope for him. Instead he chose to keep it, or the shadow of it, always about him. JJ never again saw the man smile. His touch, which up till then had been manly and strong, became rough and ungenerous. His language was spiteful. His words were sharp. His emotions were tight. And JJ seemed to get the worst of them all. He was the youngest, the baby, as his father constantly reminded him in a snide, cutting drawl. He was useless, a waste of space and "sure if he was good in school in itself?" The raised inflection implied that it was a question that begged no answer.

It wasn't like JJ didn't try his best to fit his father's restrictive mould. He'd help out with the milking, in the bog, at the hay in the summer, keep the house clean and tidy, though he would never do that as well as his mother had. But he was only a boy, and a boy whose head was full of dreams and imaginings, quicker to spot an opportunity for adventure in the woods or down by the river than to spot a cow stuck in a drain or a job needed doing. Between his father and his two older brothers, there was hardly anywhere on his body that wasn't black and blue from digs and belts and horseplay. In a house of grieving men, he became a punch bag. By the time he was big enough to hit back, he had lost interest in them and their pettiness.

Indeed, if he had been good at school in itself? School had always been a prison for him too. He could never understand why supposedly intelligent adults believed that locking children in a schoolroom for hours on end was good for them. What of use would they ever learn caged in like that? They'd all have been much better off being released into that great, big, wonderful world outside the window that was just sitting there, waiting to be explored, discovered, tasted and relished. He could never concentrate, either, on what the Master had to say, could never take in any of the knowledge he was imparting. Maybe if he'd sung it or made a story of it, there might have been some hope. Why, he used to wonder, did they seem to pick the men with the dullest, most monotonous voices to be teachers? Surely a good ballad singer or a seanachaí would be much better? Sure JJ had only to hear a song once, twice at the most, and he had it, the rise and fall of it, the skittery flit and flittery jit of it, every word, syllable and sentiment of it. And if he heard a seanachaí tell a story about the ancient Celts, the Tuatha Dé Danann, the Fir Bolg, Fionn MacCumhaill and the Red Branch Knights, he had it for the whole class the next day. Maybe not word for word, but he'd have the gist of it, certainly, and sure anything he couldn't remember, he would make up. He was good at making things up like that, filling in the gaps, inventing, whenever the narrative flagged, then embellishing once he had his audience in thrall.

"If you knew your arithmetic as well as you know them stories, McHale, you mightn't be such a dunce as you are!"

That too got even worse after his mother died. When she was alive, at least he had the joy of her to look forward to in the evenings. He loved their chats, she going on about wild flowers that he hadn't a clue about nor any interest in, other than they interested her. He loved the musicality in her voice, and there was nothing she didn't know about those flowers. Names, smells, curative properties, and there was a story going with each one. Strolling back the boreen, holding her hand and singing with her seemed the most natural thing in the world. It needed no learning, no practising, no homeworking, and it was always flawless, perfect. Sometimes he'd even finish his schoolwork in double-quick time in the hope that he would be released early and get to spend longer with her.

After she died, though, the days dragged and the evenings seemed interminable. He found himself staring out the classroom window even more than before, not in the hope of escape, but lost in wondering. Wondering where she was. Wondering if he would see her again. Wondering if she would, could come back to him. Wondering would he ever be happy and carefree again.

"McHale, I asked you a question!"

"Sorry, sir."

"Answer me!"

Red hands again that evening.

There was one young teacher who did make an impression on JJ. He was a trainee or substitute or something, with a great love of plays, especially Shakespeare. Not the literature of them, not the technical why and wherefore of the theme, the rhyme or the structure, but the blood and guts of them. He talked about the characters as if they were real: Hamlet, King Richard, Juliet, Romeo. What did they want? What drove them on? What stood in their way? What was their fatal flaw?

"We all have a fatal flaw," he would say.

"Not one that will necessarily kill us, but one that will constantly have us work against ourselves and prevent us reaching our full potential or at least delay us. These plays are lessons for life," he declared.

"Life is a series of obstacles that we must overcome and learn from so we can grow and flourish!"

Then he would read a speech from Shakespeare: "Soft, what light through yonder window breaks?/ It is the east and Juliet is the sun." "A horse! A horse! My kingdom for a horse!" Or he might get a couple of the pupils to read a scene from some other classic by Ibsen, Chekhov, Shaw or Wilde. JJ lived for these happy interludes in their otherwise dull, didactic, algebraic days. He particularly liked the speeches, responding to the music of the words and the melody of the rhyme. He soaked them up as he did the songs and stories of the local seanachaí. Unfortunately that teacher spent only six months at the school but his influence on JJ was lasting.

When JJ did get out of school for good, it was the best day of his life. Well the best day since . . . Anyway, he was fifteen when he was finally released. His father got him a job in the village shop, which he thought would suit JJ, since he seemed to be allergic to hard work. It was a grocery shop in the village and he loved it. Why the hell couldn't the gobshite have done this long ago, instead of forcing him to keep on in school? Was it trying to torture him he'd been? But that was all spilt milk under the bridge by then, so no point looking back. That was what was happening right then and there and it was good. No. It was very good. For one thing, it got him away from that den of bitter men. For another, it was mostly women did the shopping, so he was in his element. Between keeping a smile on their faces in the shop by day and a twinkle in their eyes at the night-time sing-songs, life had really started to look up for young JJ McHale. And when the women hugged him then, there was more than a tingle running through his pubescent body. When they brushed a free hand carelessly along the inside of his leg, it caused activity where once there had been none. Oh yes, JJ had started to smile again and it was hard to "wipe that stupid sthreel off his face," no matter how often his father roared at him or how hard he hit him. JJ McHale was finding his feet, beginning his steady march towards his destiny.

6

Bullocks on the Line

———•———

JJ's REVERIE WAS SHATTERED ABRUPTLY when the train pulled in to Carrick. Carrick on the River Shannon, the heart of Leitrim, the gateway to Connaught. The doors shot open and hordes of people piled on, chattering, lugging, pushing and bumping. His own carriage was invaded by a large extended family. Each member of the troupe carried a bag and several had musical instruments: bodhrán, fiddle, tin whistles. They were led by the parents, hefty, red-cheeked country people who smelt of butter, cow shite and rose oil. They laughed and nattered, one topping the other, as they herded their charges aboard. There were five children between the ages of about nine and fifteen, an older girl around nineteen or twenty and a couple in their sixties, apparently the grandparents. JJ got tired just watching them as they hustled and bustled into the seats beside and across from him. The youngest two, a boy and a girl, sat opposite him, the boy struggling to stem the flow of snot from his reddened nose with the sleeve of his threadbare hand-me-down jacket. The oldest, a brawny lump of a lad, sat in beside JJ. The father, the older girl and the other boy and girl sat across the aisle, while the mother took the two grandparents to the next seats along.

The upshot of this little set dance was that JJ had a perfect view of the attractive older girl, sitting at the window seat diagonally across from him on the far side of the aisle beside her smiling curly-haired sister. She used the window to avoid having to look at JJ, preferring instead to stare out at the ever-changing scenery.

Once settled, the farmer stretched a meaty, calloused hand across the aisle to JJ.

"Duignan. Máirtín," he said, smiling broadly. "Kilclare."

JJ took his hand, mirrored his smile. "JJ McHale. Ballysumaghan, Sligo."

The oldest lad scowled from beneath a head of hair like an upturned bowl.

"Good man. That's Eibhlín and Colmeen," Duignan said, waving in the direction of the two children opposite JJ. "Pádraic, Seán, Orlagh and that's the eldest, Peggy," he added, nodding at the attractive young girl who was still gazing out the window.

"That's the wife and her parents behind."

The wife saluted JJ and he responded with a smile and a flick of the head, before turning his attention back to Peggy. Hardly missing a beat, Duignan struck up a virtually one-sided conversation with JJ about everything from the price of cattle to the war in Europe.

"I'm glad to see you haven't been duped by all that English recruitment bullshit. We need our young men at home here, not flittin' off to France to fight someone else's battles!"

Eventually he moved on to talk about his passion – music – and JJ became interested. Duignan insisted that the Leitrim style was the purest in the country, no matter what the Sligo shower claimed. JJ would have been quite happy to concede but a strong objection might make him more attractive to the dark-haired, brown-eyed beauty, still staring out the far window. At the very least, a lively debate might draw her out of her self-imposed shell. So he objected strenuously to the father's claim and made up an elaborate tale of how a number of the finest Sligo songs, all in the old tongue, had been passed down from a famous blind fiddler from his own place, Ballysumaghan.

"Gifted to him by the gods."

"Go 'way out o' that."

"I'm serious," JJ said. "The fiddler swore they had seeped up through the bog, perfectly formed, the music of dead generations that lay preserved deep within the peaty earth."

Duignan threw his head back and laughed loudly but seemed half convinced, nonetheless, so sincere was JJ's account. The dark beauty in the corner hardly moved a muscle, but when JJ went on to sing a few lines from one of those old songs, mar dhea, he was certain her eyes flickered in his direction.

> Shiubhalfainn féin an drúcht leat is fásaigh ghuirt,
> Mar shúil go bhfaighinn rún uait nó páirt dem thoil.
> A chraoibhín chumhra, gheallais domhsa go raibh grá agat
>   dom
> 'S gurab í fíor-scoth Sligeach í, mo Róisín Dubh.

Yes. He had her now. He knew it. He had played this game before, was well used to it. She was pretending not to notice him so that others wouldn't notice that she was attracted to him. He pounced, confidently.

"So what about you, mo Róisín Dubh? You must have a nice Leitrim song to match my Sligo air?"

"Hot air is all I'm hearing," said she, "and it's of no interest to me, sir."

She never took her eyes from the window. Her father laughed his outrageous laugh again. JJ smiled widely, covering his disappointment and amazement that his ploy hadn't worked. She truly seemed uninterested. How could that be?

"Well damn it to hell," he said. "If Róisín Dubh doesn't move you, you must have a heart of stone."

She didn't flinch.

"Now, now," said Duignan, "easy, let ye."

JJ laughed a hollow laugh to restore his composure. "What about yourself, sir? You must have a song?"

"I don't but I have an air or two. Givvus the fiddle there, Colmeen."

The snotty-nosed kid opposite JJ reached under the seat to retrieve the man's fiddle. He played a haunting slow air, "Port na bPúcaí", about a woman stolen and kept hostage in the kingdom of the fairy women. It almost brought a tear to JJ's eye but drew only a sneer from his dark Róisín in the corner. Without pausing, the man followed on with an uplifting reel, "Farewell to Leitrim", then a jaunty jig, "The Connaughtman's Rambles".

Delightful and all as the music had been, dazzling and all as Duignan's fiddle playing, JJ was glad to escape to the toilet for a few minutes. As he unlocked the door and stepped back out of the cubicle, he was grabbed by an unseen hand. Caught unawares and literally off balance, he was whipped back against the exit door. The rushing wind whipped in through the half-open window. The mechanical grinding of the bogie filled his ears. Sharp nails dug into his neck and a bony knee pressed into his crotch.

"You're some boyo, so you are."

It was a woman's voice, a young woman, smelling of rose oil. When she whipped her thick mane of jet-black hair back off her face, he saw the brown eyes of his dark Róisín.

"The way you sang that song, you blackguard."

Her face was close to his now, her eyes softening, her breath warm, slightly milky.

"I wanted to jump out of my seat and swallow you whole, right there and then."

Before he could think of something clever to say in response, she had attached her mouth to his, and her tongue was plunging deep into his throat.

Within minutes they were back inside the locked toilet cubicle, loosening and tearing off only the garments that stood in the way of their mutual pleasure. It was not lovemaking, it was pure animalistic lust with an urgency to it that's normally only found in life-threatening situations. He was barely able to keep up with her, so voracious was she, as she did indeed swallow him whole and take him as deep inside her as he had ever been inside anyone. Although it lasted no more than five minutes, he was left breathless, exhausted, spent, while she looked like she could go again, several times more. She grasped his face between her hands.

"Don't think I wouldn't like some more of that, mister."

"JJ."

She held his gaze for an instant. Her eyes smiled slightly. "If I don't go back, they'll be wondering."

"Right. Peggy."

"I can't be talking to you in there, either, like I have a thing for you or anything."

"Of course not." He couldn't restrain a grin.

"Not that I have a thing for you! Mister JJ."

"Sure why would you?" His grin widened to a smile.

"Jesus, you're some boyo all right." She smiled now too. It lit up her face for an instant. Then darkness again and she was gone.

Once back in their seats, they managed to be civil to each other without appearing too interested. Duignan played some more and JJ sang. He and Peggy conversed through her father or the youngsters, using them as conduits to pass coded messages. They took two more toilet breaks.

About two hours later, and just after they had pulled out of Maynooth Station, the train screeched to an unscheduled halt in the middle of the countryside. It quickly became clear that something was amiss. There was a proliferation of voices outside, urgent and panicked. Some people were sure they could see soldiers and police milling around the front of the train. The man in the Mackintosh and felt hat who JJ had spotted on the platform in Ballymote walked urgently through the carriage towards the rear of the train. Finally, the train groaned its way back into Maynooth and the reason for the hold-up was explained. There was a pair of bullocks lying across the tracks, not an insurmountable obstacle in itself. Closer inspection, however, had revealed that the bullocks had been shot through the head and stuffed with dynamite, primed to be detonated by an intricate booby-trap device. The word was that it had been set by rebels, Irish Volunteers, determined to disrupt the instruments of British rule. Clearly, the only disruption was to the unfortunate passengers aboard the train, poor auld Irish peasants and farmers trying to make their way to Dublin for a bit of a holiday or some other equally innocent reason. The train would be delayed indefinitely, maybe even overnight, until the device was made safe by the military and the obstruction removed. The train hadn't even stopped at the platform when JJ saw Mackintosh-man jump off and scurry out of the station.

Once the train had stopped, Duignan made a quick decision. Since he and his family had planned to travel on to the races in Fairyhouse anyway, to play music and have a few days' holiday, they would take to the road. It was only about twelve miles across country. They could walk or maybe get lifts from farmers, heading home to Meath having emptied their carts in Maynooth. The only reason they had been going to Dublin first was because Peggy was due to start work in the General Post Office the following Tuesday. Sure she could easily make her way to the city on Easter Monday, after the races. When JJ heard about the crowds that would be in Fairyhouse for the Grand National, about the drink that would be consumed and the money that would be spent, he was in no doubt that it was the place for him too.

"Sure Dublin empties itself anyway for the weekend," Duignan told him. "A singer as good as yourself could make a right killing in Fairyhouse, fill your pockets with copper and silver, maybe even a pound note or two."

Then there was the added attraction of Peggy, mo Róisín Dubh, as JJ liked to think of her. He smiled. "Why not."

He noticed Peggy fumble with her bag to conceal a self-satisfied grin.

Being Holy Thursday, there was little traffic on the roads, so they split into three smaller groups. Duignan took the grandparents, his eldest boy Pádraic and most of the bags and instruments. His wife took two of the younger children. JJ and Peggy paired up and took the final two youngsters, Eibhlín and snot-nosed Colmeen. The father's group got a lift before long, in a farmer's cart headed for Dunboyne. Who could leave two aged grandparents on the roadside? The children slowed everyone else down, so it took them the rest of the day to walk the six or so miles to Dunboyne.

The younger children saw it as a big adventure at first, helped by a few of JJ's songs and made-up stories. The diversions into fields for a quick wee or an impromptu game of hide-and-seek were amusing at first but quickly became tiresome. Then, after only two miles, feet began to hurt, throats began to dry, tummies began to rumble and the children began to grumble and whine. Peggy was able to put a little smacht on them, but ultimately they were just children and six miles was a long walk for small feet. JJ carried Eibhlín on his back the last three miles. The family managed to get reasonable lodgings in the town. They couldn't afford to pay for JJ, though, and he insisted anyway on finding his own. Truth be told, he had had more than his fill of playing happy families.

With only some loose change in his pocket, he was content to sleep in an empty outhouse and have a few pints of porter instead. He found adequate accommodation in a farmyard on the edge of town. Later he enjoyed a few pints and swapped stories with a gang of stable lads from up the country, who would be continuing on to Fairyhouse the next morning. He struck up an instant rapport with one of them, Ollie. With a crooked grin and a sideways cap, Ollie was a good man to tell a story himself and he loved JJ's singing. He offered JJ a lift in their transporter, as long as he didn't mind sharing with a couple of feisty thoroughbreds. JJ was delighted to accept. In fairness, he did think of trying to get a lift for everyone, the grandparents and Peggy at least, but the mode of transport on offer was far from suitable and he was unwilling to face another day of moaning youngsters. He was sure they would have no trouble getting there. Ollie told him to be ready to leave at dawn. Anaesthetised by the alcohol, JJ spent a relatively comfortable night in the outhouse on a bed of loose straw.

Before departing next morning, he scribbled a brief note to Peggy's father, including a veiled apology to the dark one herself, which he slipped under the door of their lodgings. Then he scrunched into the back of a motorised horsebox, between two spirited thoroughbreds, a dark gelding and a bay colt. He would definitely need a good wash and a change of clothes after this trip.

Unfortunately, after his mother's death, the welcome mat that sat inside their front door, for visitors and residents to wipe the dust and grime of the day off their boots or shoes, had long since worn thin and been thrown out. So how could JJ know that there might be a similar mat inside the door of the lodging house and that his note would slip under it, where it would remain unfound for the next several days.

7

Fairyhouse

———✦———

THE FIRST SENSE JJ HAD that they had reached their destination was when the horse transporter slowed and turned off the main road onto what felt like little more than a dirt track. The vehicle jerked and bounded fiercely. The horses snorted and whinnied, as they shifted restlessly in their confined quarters. The colt fired a couple of kicks at the wooden sides of the box, narrowly missing JJ's head. Then, just when it seemed the journey couldn't get any more uncomfortable, they left the dirt track and roller-coasted across a humpy, rutted field, before skidding to a halt, throwing JJ face first against the flank of the dark gelding. He felt twelve years old again as he looked up sheepishly into the flaming eyes of the disgruntled steed who was clearly unimpressed with this gauche young farmer's son.

The doors of the transporter's front cab opened and banged shut again. The horses began to skitter and jig about excitedly. The two stable lads flung open the back doors. The horses recoiled, startled by the sunlight that flooded in. JJ, dazzled too, regained his balance and composure, fixed his clothes as best he could and presented a brave, smiling face to the world. The two stable lads laughed loudly at their young passenger who was not nearly as composed as he thought, shirt tails dangling, straw in his hair, jacket buttoned askew.

"Pleasant trip?" said Ollie with a smirk.

"Not exactly a first-class carriage," said JJ.

The two equine aristocrats whinnied loudly in a tone that JJ took as indignation but which was, in fact, joy at being untethered and led out by their minders. They leapt, gambolled and kicked, the arms of the grooms straining on the ropes. The dark gelding reared, towering over JJ as he stepped gingerly out of the transporter and onto the lush green grass. JJ was struck instantly by the freshness of the air, the sweetness of the grassy odour, the cool of the breeze and then the warmth of the sun. He smiled widely and inhaled deeply as the lads led the horses off for water and meal.

It was only then that he became aware of the noise surrounding him. Theirs wasn't the only transporter in the field or the only horses. There was a row of various-sized motorised and horse-drawn transporters parked in a higgledy-piggledy line behind him and to his right and left. In front of him stretched a long, wide grassy field, uneven and rutted, the one they'd just driven across. It was bordered by a high stone wall. The fertile plains of Meath stretched beyond, towards the low-lying hills of Dublin to the south and the sea to the east. The Irish Sea. The sea that soon would take him to England and his destiny. He watched as several large groups of stable lads, grooms and other young fellas with the gimp and gait of jockeys grouped around an array of shining, statuesque horses. The animals were being patted, walked, fed and watered, delighted to be able to stretch their legs properly again. Others were in the care of a single man or boy and on much longer leads. These were being trotted or cantered, in circles or up and down the field. Still others were back at their boxes, being carefully rubbed down, brushed or having their manes braided. JJ marvelled at the care the stable lads and grooms took, at their attention to detail. When it came to their own appearance and personal habits, he had noted a marked absence of either care or attention.

He plucked a tráithnín and slid it between his teeth as he wheeled left and walked to the end of the line of transporters. His eyes widened at the sight that greeted him. It was a racecourse. Just a racecourse. He'd been at the races before, a few times, in Sligo. But there, the track was small with tight bends and nestled in a boggy valley that became sodden in the winter or whenever there was a heavy fall of rain. There the outer boundary was an irregular stone wall and four rudimentary, curved wooden railings demarcated the bends, while the spectators stood on a natural hill to view the racing. But this here, this was a real racetrack.

It was expansive, a huge elliptical arena, bordered outside and in by gleaming white railings that traced perfectly the pleasing undulations of the track, like an artist's line drawing. On the far side of the track there were two monoliths set against the backdrop of a blue sky, the two tall, purpose-built viewing stands; one of metal, for the gentry and those with money; the other of wood, for the Seáns and Síles, the hoi polloi, the ordinary punters who possessed little more than the desire to escape reality for an afternoon and immerse themselves in the endeavours and excitement of others. He had to admit, they really knew how to do things up this end of the country.

JJ spun round, startled by two sudden explosions of sound. A barrage of bangs, cracks, roars and thuds followed before he identified the source of the rumpus. About half way down the higgledy line of transporters, a beautiful chestnut gelding, coat glistening in the midday sun, was rearing and kicking for all he was worth. Despite the best efforts of four strong men to hold him, he had smashed both guide rails on his transporter and was now kicking and jerking his way free of his holders. One smaller lad went flying head over heels against the back wheel of the transporter; a second man, forced to release his grip on the rope to avoid a similar fate, danced away from the gelding, arms flailing, before finally losing his balance and sliding across the grass on his belly, like a stone skimming across the surface of a lake. The two remaining men let go of their ropes, no longer able to restrain the recalcitrant horse. The gelding jumped, twisted and reared in a demonic circle, then flung his head skywards and, with an arrogant flick of his mane, galloped towards the boundary wall, heading for the sea. Perhaps his destiny too lay somewhere further east and not here, on this lush, green racetrack. Straightening his sideways cap and fixing his crooked grin, Ollie sidled up to a wide-mouthed JJ and filled him in, squirting the facts through the side of his mouth.

"All Sorts. Temperamental gelding out of Avidity by Piersfield. Owned by James Kiernan and trained by Mr Richard Cleary in Bishopstown, Cork. Not really expected to win the National on Monday but you can never write off the Bishopstown lot. I certainly wouldn't fancy his chances after that display though."

"Why not?"

"Just not up for it, I'd say. Strange beasts, you know. Minds of their own."

"Strange is right."

JJ looked after the fleeing chestnut gelding, All Sorts. As he reached the boundary wall he thought better of attempting to leap the eight-foot-high obstacle. He chose instead, wisely, to slow on the turn, skidding slightly, and run along its length, in search of a gap or a lower section. By now his way south and north had been blocked by several helpful lads from other stables. That's how it seemed to work in this world. They watched out for each other, had each other's back. There was intense rivalry yes, bordering on hatred at times, but the animals were prime. They were their livelihood and no one wanted to see a fellow horseman done out of his livelihood. Finding himself semi-corralled, All Sorts seemed to calm somewhat and a tacit compromise quickly established itself; the humans kept their distance and the horse stayed put, settled and began to chomp on the sweet grass. Peace was restored and everyone returned to their tasks as if nothing had happened.

"Come on if you're coming with us!" Ollie said, slapping JJ across the shoulder as he headed in the direction of his transporter.

As JJ turned to follow, spitting out his well-chewed tráithnín, his eye was drawn towards the west again, as he noticed broad, colourful canvas sheets fluttering in the wind in the area around the viewing stands and also in the centre of the white, wooden ellipse. The chatter of voices and the chirrup of laughter drifted on the wind, competing with the rattle of tin cans and buckets.

"Hucksters!" roared Ollie. "You'll see plenty of them over the next few days."

"Come on!" demanded the driver as he slammed the bonnet of the engine shut. JJ hopped, skipped then sprinted over, not with the grace of a thoroughbred but with the determination of a jockey, careening down the home straight towards the finishing line.

"They'd sell you anything, those hucksters," Ollie said, as he closed the back doors of the transporter.

"You need to watch them!" he shouted through the small air vent between cab and box, as they bumped and jerked back onto the main road again, bound for the nearby village of Ratoath.

"They'd sell you your own breath," said the driver as he strained to straighten the steering wheel.

"Keep your hands in your pockets!"

"Oh we're good at that, all right, the Irish," blurted Ollie's fellow groom, "keepin' our hands in our pockets and doin' nothing!"

Ollie and the driver were dumbstruck at his sudden outburst.

JJ was too busy avoiding the hooves of the frisky bay colt to respond.

When they disembarked in Ratoath, JJ's spirits soared yet again. Although a mere village, it was much bigger than Sooey, and today it seemed to contain the population of a city. Traps, sidecars and horse-drawn wagons of various sizes criss-crossed haphazardly, while the few cars, vans and trucks on the streets honked and squealed impatiently, teasing a way through the pandemonium. It was like the village had been invaded, taken over by a colourful army of hawkers, hucksters, traders, chancers and clowns. And this was only the vanguard, he was reliably informed by his new companions. These were the ones who had farthest to come and so arrived earliest, to find their feet before the big day, or to have a couple of days' holiday, or those who simply wanted to extract the maximum fun, devilment and money from the event. Their number would most likely double over the next twenty-four hours. This, after all, was the highlight of the year in this part of the country, the weekend of the Grand National. It was one of the most important race meetings on the calendar, featuring the most prestigious and valuable horse race of the season.

JJ parted company with his transporters at their boarding house. They invited him to join them but he was unsure whether the invite was to stay for free and, anxious to remain unencumbered so he could glean his fill from the cornucopia of pleasures that surrounded him, he declined politely and skipped off into the throng, whistling as he went. He had never seen so many people gathered in one place. He had been to the big fairs in Sligo town with his father. But they were cities of animals, with only a fraction of the number of people that now buzzed and scutted past and around him. In a world that was generally monochromatic, the array of colour on display was extraordinary, dazzling. Most of the men were in their customary greys and blacks, with white shirts, but many hucksters, peddlers, tinkers and musicians strutted about like peacocks, displaying flashes of green, red, vermillion, blue and serge, sporting elaborate, flowing scarves, harlequin waistcoats and chequered jackets. Top hats, bowlers, boaters and panamas bobbed on a sea of well-dressed men, while the ladies swished and swirled, creating a dazzling scene for the young, wide-eyed farmer's son from Sligo.

A slim young man, head down and walking fast, bumped against JJ's shoulder, knocking him slightly off balance. A sensation of pressure in his jacket and trouser pockets caused him to spin clumsily, clutching his pockets as he did. They were still empty. He had to grab a fellow pedestrian by the shoulder to stop from falling on his arse on the footpath.

"Hey, get off, you bloody brigand!" shouted the athletic young gentleman whose shoulder he had just grabbed. He was glowering at JJ, shaking his black cane. JJ spread his arms, hands skywards, but before he could declare his innocence, the gentleman had moved on. A red-faced RIC sergeant, with a bulbous nose, stopped on the other side of the street, his attention drawn by the shouting. He glanced over, frowned and appeared to make a mental note before continuing on his way. JJ shrugged, confused, unsure what had just occurred but certain that he was going to have to keep his wits well and truly about him in this place.

As he shuffled and sidestepped onwards, unable to properly gauge the pace and rhythm of the throng, his attention was drawn by two shawlies, tinker women with long unruly ringlets falling onto colourful, quilted shawls that were pulled around their shoulders. Singing loudly in unison, they staggered drunkenly across the busy road, causing several vehicles to halt abruptly. Unperturbed, they squealed gleefully and continued to sing raucously. It was a tune very similar to one that JJ was sure he had sung before or maybe had heard his mother sing, but he didn't recognise their words. He thought maybe they were singing in Irish but then realised it was their own shelta dialect.

Their singing was suddenly cut through by the faint but shrill whine of uilleann pipes from further down the street. As he looked beyond the shawlies and tuned his ear, he also discerned the sweet lilt of a fiddle, maybe two, then the twang of a banjo. He was unable to make out the tune being played and was having difficulty locating the source of the music, until an exuberant bodhrán joined the mix, giving the tune a definite rhythm, the unmistakable 6/8 of a jig, "The Mug of Brown Ale"!

Then the sea of people and vehicles seemed to part so that he could see the group of musicians clearly, sitting on a selection of orange boxes, beer crates and a three-legged stool. There were indeed two delicious fiddles, a rather squeaky set of uilleann pipes, a banjo, button accordion and the ubiquitous bodhrán. As he drew closer, JJ could see that there were dancers too, not organised, informal, several couples, stirred by the music to break into a series of impromptu set-dancing figures, all arm-hooks and energetic twirls. One man swung his partner so hard her legs left the ground and for an instant it looked as if she might take flight until her screams caused the man to rein in his enthusiasm and his flying partner. Oh boy! This was like heaven on earth.

He stayed for an age, clapping and lilting along with abandon, savouring the stirring music, marvelling at the energy and spontaneity of the dancing.

He might have stayed even longer had he not been distracted by an incident on the opposite side of the street. His attention was drawn by the loud, rather pompous voice of a rotund gentleman in pin-striped tweed who was imparting directions to a thinner, less well-attired man. The rotund gent was elaborately waving about his decorative walking cane as he glared condescendingly at the thinner man who'd somehow managed to lose his way in this small village. Indeed, the stray didn't seem to be terribly bright either, as he had to ask the gent to repeat several of the directions and indicate them more precisely by pointing his cane.

But this was not what kept JJ enthralled. He was watching instead what was happening behind the Arbucklesque gent's back. A young man of around his own age had slipped from a doorway and in behind the gesticulating gent. Then, in the blink of an eye, he slipped his hand into the gent's hip pocket and relieved him of his wallet, which was almost as plump and over-packed as its owner. Instinctively, JJ shouted and dashed across the street to try to intercept the thief. A brief shemozzle followed, almost a dance between felon and Good Samaritan, the two men interlocking arms and hands, as JJ attempted to retrieve the wallet, shouting to draw attention to the larceny in progress.

"Stop! Thief! He's got your wallet, sir! Stop!"

But in a twinkling the thief had twirled JJ, spun around and was gone, leaving JJ disoriented and clutching the now-empty wallet. The lost man had vanished in the opposite direction and the red-faced RIC sergeant with the bulbous nose was back on the scene. He grabbed JJ by the rear of his jacket collar just as the rotund gent confirmed that his wallet had indeed been purloined and was now in the hands of this rather scruffy young country boy.

"What the hell are you up to, sonny?"

"Ehm . . . this wallet. They took it." JJ stammered in response. "From him." He pointed the wallet at its owner.

"I see," said the sergeant as he snatched the wallet from JJ's grasp and checked its contents. "Empty!" he announced as he handed it back to the irate gent.

"What? There was more than one hundred pounds in there! What have you done with it, you bloody rapscallion?" he roared, beating JJ on the back with his cane.

"What? Stop!" JJ cowered.

"No point wasting your energy on this one, sir," said the sergeant. "He'll have passed the cash on to one of his accomplices!"

"Good Lord!" He beat him twice more, harder still.

"Come on, sonny, time to take a little walk."

"What?" said JJ, who had no compulsion to exercise at this point in time.

"What will you do?" asked the portly gent of the sergeant.

"I'm taking him into custody, sir."

"Custody?" cried JJ in confusion. "You're arresting me?"

"See if we can't get him to give us a few names before we send him down for daylight bloody robbery," said the sergeant with a wry grin.

"No," pleaded JJ. "I was trying to help!"

"You'll need to come too, sir, to make a statement."

"No. You're making a mistake!" said JJ. "It wasn't me!"

"As if I haven't heard that one before!" The sergeant jerked JJ forward.

"This is damned awkward," snarled the ungrateful victim, "a bloody disgrace that a gentleman can't go about his business without being assaulted in such a manner. You should be ashamed of yourself, young man!" His cane slapped across JJ's shoulders once more.

"No! Please! I was trying to stop them. I swear!"

But he was wasting his breath.

The sergeant had clammed up and was frog-marching JJ away from the scene. They passed a smiling man of about forty, in a lurid red shirt and black leather waistcoat. He was twirling the handle of a small, decorative barrel organ that was strapped around his left shoulder and under his right arm. He grinned widely as the rude instrument churned out a slightly atonal, pitch bent version of the popular "Hold Your Hand Out, Naughty Boy", which rendered the whole scene more surreal still for poor JJ. A plump red squirrel in an emerald-green waistcoat sat tethered atop the organ, holding a tin can between its tiny paws. As they passed, the animal chirruped maniacally, a loud, trilling rattle, as he shoved the can into JJ's face. How the hell was he going to get out of this jar of pickles?

8

The Hole in the Wall

———•———

WHAT JJ DIDN'T KNOW UNTIL they reached their destination was that there was no barracks in Ratoath. The closest were in Primatestown and Ashbourne, about four miles north and west respectively. A wagon transported prisoners hourly to one or other of these barracks, the sergeant had explained to the panting gent who was struggling to match the policeman's brisk pace. In the meantime, recalcitrants were detained in a temporary holding cell, instituted for the duration of the festive weekend. So when the sergeant marched JJ down a laneway, guarded by a single RIC constable armed with a rifle, and shoved him into a small, dusty public house, he was astonished. A sign above the array of bottles of stout and spirits on a rough wooden shelf read HOLE IN THE WALL – THE OLDEST PUB IN IRELAND. Another wall displayed a painting of an English gentleman in a red officer's uniform – the man reputed to have established the drinking den in the previous century for his off-duty troops.

"Ah, Sergeant O'Connor. Another fish for the barrel?" A thin, bespectacled man of around fifty stood behind the counter, pouring whiskey for two well-built customers, farmers by their dress and bearing, who seemed to view the world out of the corners of their eyes.

"The place is awash with them, Timothy," O'Connor replied.

The farmers leaned an elbow each on the counter and conversed in hushed tones out of the sides of their mouths. Neither greeted the policeman nor he them. The counter was so scratched and coated in dirt and detritus that it was difficult to age it. The room itself was dimly lit and shadowy.

"Get yourself a drink there, sir," Sergeant O'Connor told the rotund gent. "I'll be with you in a jiffy."

He gave JJ a second shove, which threw him face first against the whitewashed back wall and the sergeant's weathered right boot separated JJ's legs, almost causing him to fall. His arms were grabbed and spread apart so that he stood like a misshapen star against the wall. O'Connor's big, rough hands checked JJ's clothes, pockets, socks and boots for concealed weapons. Next, apparently satisfied that his pickpocket was unarmed, he led JJ to a second door made of old planks. As he unlocked the door, he called over his shoulder to the man behind the bar.

"Put up a quick bottle of stout there, Timothy."

Then he lifted the latch.

The plank door opened onto a small muddy yard with high walls, quite a bit taller than the height of two men, with rows of jagged broken glass embedded along the top. JJ saw that there were three other sorry-looking souls already in the yard. The door slammed shut behind him and the lock was re-engaged. One man was curled up and asleep in the corner, comatose from drink no doubt. A second was lolling against the back wall of the pub smoking a cigarette. The third was sitting, but not slouching, against the back wall, propping his handcuffed wrists on his raised knees. The weaselly smoker was the first to speak.

"Welcome to the Hole in The Wall gang. What you in for?"

"Ehm. They think I stole a wallet."

"But you didn't do it, right?"

"Yes. I mean, no. I was trying to stop it being stolen."

The man smirked as he flicked the butt of his cigarette into the mud, which sizzled for an instant before quenching.

"That's original. Do you have any smokes?"

"No."

The taut, wiry man seemed almost angry at him for this omission. He began pacing the length of the yard, playing a small stone through his fingers as he did. JJ smiled thinly and nodded to the handcuffed man who was staring back at him like a crazed killer. The man didn't flinch or avert his gaze. He wore a strange, wide-eyed expression that could have been determination or insanity. JJ preferred to think it was the former. He certainly must be in for something serious since he was the only one in handcuffs.

"What's your name?" It was the weaselly smoker again.

"McHale. JJ."

"From?"

"Ehm. Bally . . . Sooey."

"Are you trying to be funny?"

"No. It's in Sligo."

"Soooeee?"

It was a strange, mocking sort of pronunciation of his home place but JJ decided it was best to nod agreement. He was after all among criminals with questionable morals, if any at all.

"What about yourself?" he ventured tentatively, hoping to humour the temperamental inmate.

"What about me?"

Boy, this was going to be tough. He should probably just shut up, but that wasn't in JJ's nature. "Where you from?"

"Here and there."

"Hmm. And what's your name?"

"Depends on who I'm talking to."

"Right."

"In ainm fuckin' Dé. Can you not tell him your fucking name!" snarled the handcuffed man, barely moving a muscle.

"Fuck you too!" retorted the smoker with a sneer and he spat on the mud by the other man's feet. The other man sprung up athletically and squared up to the smoker, who stepped back, blinking, throwing his arms forward instinctively. Then he remembered that his assailant was handcuffed and become a little bolder again.

"Yeah? Go on then. You going to show us what you're made of?"

The other man calmed again, instantly, with the reserve of someone who was above such backstreet brawling or who felt he had some higher purpose in life.

"Fucking óinseach!" He turned instead to face JJ and proffered a cuffed hand to shake. "Is mise O'Cofaigh. Cathal. Deas castáil leat."

JJ was glad to accept. It was a curt business-like shake. He smiled. O'Cofaigh didn't. Without another word, he sat back down and reassumed his meditative pose. He could definitely be a psychopath. Clearly he was not a common thief. JJ wondered what he had been arrested for.

Time seemed to drag, and nothing more was said by anyone, apart from a couple of incoherent outbursts from the drunkard in the corner. All that could be heard from within were the muffled mumblings of the customers and the occasional creak of the outer door as someone came or went. The silence was as thick as the mud underfoot. JJ was feeling cold and hungry. He was glad it wasn't raining at least. Then he became aware of some activity on the other side of the back wall. It was barely audible at first, but to his keen ear, it sounded like grass rustling, like feet scurrying along the wall. A twig snapped. The handcuffed man was alert now. A voice called out.

"Hey!"

The shout was cut dramatically short, overpowered by a dull thud.

"Oogh!"

Even the weaselly one noticed that.

Next there was a crack, like a plank of wood splitting, followed by a heavy thud, like a sack of spuds being dropped onto the ground. O'Cofaigh sprang to his feet again. The smoker was no longer slouching against the wall but standing, ready for action, fists clenched as if he expected trouble. There followed an eerie silence that lasted only seconds but seemed to go on for an eternity. Then the sound of metal on stone and mortar reverberated through the wall. O'Cofaigh stood facing the wall now, his eyes focused on that section from where the tapping, chipping sounds were emanating, staring as if he might burn through the cut stone. Within minutes, one of the stones, about three feet from ground level, seemed to move, become loose, and O'Cofaigh bounded into action again, peering, searching in the mud for something, a stone, an implement. He found a sliver of old bone, a chip off a larger radius, ulna or rib, discoloured by the elements. JJ hoped it had been from an animal and not some other poor unfortunate human who, like himself, had been unjustly arrested and incarcerated here alone, forgotten about until he died of starvation. Had he rotted to become one with the soil or been buried in a shallow grave? Either way, JJ felt slightly sick to think that flimsy shard of bone was all that remained of him.

JJ snapped himself out of this most un-useful flight of imagination and watched wide-eyed as O'Cofaigh used the piece of bone to scrape frantically at the powdery mortar surrounding the disturbed stone block. Within seconds it had been loosened, dislodged and shoved through into the yard.

"Bhfuil tú istigh, a Chathail?" The voice was male and urgent but not shouting, slightly conspiratorial.

"Tá mé, Liamy. Chuinnigh oraibh!"

The tapping and chipping continued, faster now, and as each stone was dislodged, it became easier to remove the next one. Within about fifteen minutes a wide enough hole had been created to allow a skinny teenager to slide through, and the mood in the dismal yard had been transformed. O'Cofaigh stopped scraping, frozen.

"Hishsh. Éistigí!"

His hearing was even sharper than JJ's. There was some commotion inside in the bar. Bellowing. Shouting. Glass shattered; something heavy crashed against the plank door. O'Connor, it sounded like, was roaring angrily, his words indecipherable. The door was unlocked, unlatched, and a huge bull of a man came hurtling through, crashing into O'Cofaigh, and sending them both careening against the back wall. O'Connor came charging in on the heels of the giant prisoner, followed by a constable who slammed the door shut behind them. As the two policemen laid their weight against the door, O'Connor's face displayed a slowly dawning amazement. He was looking at the huge backside of the new prisoner who was lodged in the back wall, his head seeming to have crashed right through it, like a human battering ram. Surely this wasn't possible? Before O'Connor could work out what was unfolding, the huge new prisoner had extricated himself from the hole in the wall and was charging him like a bull. O'Connor took him full in the stomach. The constable drew his truncheon and felled the sergeant's attacker, with two heavy blows to his hairless head. The wall-breakers, eschewing all subtlety now, were widening the hole with alacrity.

Just as the new prisoner dropped, trapping O'Connor momentarily, a revived O'Cofaigh got to his feet and slipped his handcuffed arms over the constable's head and around his throat before he could land a third blow on the big man's head. As he grappled with the lawman, he seemed also to be exhorting JJ to action.

"Cabhraigh liom. Cabhraigh liom. In ainm fucking Dé! Tabhair buille dhó!"

JJ had no idea what he was saying but the intent seemed clear. O'Cofaigh wheeled the constable around to face JJ, who hesitated for an instant before landing a well-aimed kick right between the policeman's legs, causing him to crumple into a more manageable heap in O'Cofaigh's arms. By now O'Connor had hauled himself out from under the stunned mass of the new prisoner and was drawing his truncheon. JJ was too far away to respond, but all was not lost. The smoker was clearly not without guile, so it shouldn't have been surprising that he was able to contribute.

"Hey, peeler man, watch your back!"

O'Connor spun round, truncheon raised, to be met by two fists full of gloopy muck that splattered over his face, blinding him just long enough for the new prisoner to regain sufficient composure to grab O'Connor by the shoulder, turn him and floor him with a haymaker that struck his lower jaw like a sledgehammer. The sergeant crashed in a heap in the mucky yard several seconds after his constable had collapsed from the force of a blow of his own truncheon delivered by O'Cofaigh.

The actual hole in the wall was now big enough for even the massive new member of the 'gang' to get through. The rescuers were shouting at the captives to get out as quickly as possible, before all hell broke loose. Not that a fair bit of hell hadn't already broken loose.

"Go. Gabh amach!" O'Cofaigh was shouting, whooshing JJ and the new prisoner ahead of him through the wall.

"Fair play, O'Cofaigh. I'd never have thought you had it in you," said the smoker with a wry grin.

"Ní dhearna mé é seo dhuitse, Óinseach!" replied O'Cofaigh with an enigmatic smile. Then he swung the truncheon up and across the smoker's face, sending him hurtling backwards and crashing against the plank door, unconscious.

"Is everything all right out there?" whimpered a timid voice from inside the bar, doubtless Timothy, the bespectacled barman.

"Yeah. All under control now," retorted O'Cofaigh, as he and the giant prisoner hauled the two policemen against the plank door to delay any pursuit.

Once outside, and despite the fact that they spoke mainly in the old tongue, JJ ascertained that O'Cofaigh was one of these crazy rebels that he'd heard about; Fenians or Sinn Féiners he'd heard them called. They referred to him as captain, saluted and chanted, "beir bua agus beannacht!" JJ almost tripped over another RIC constable, a sentry, who lay crumpled in an unconscious heap on the ground. A butty sort of a fella in a long grey overcoat and black flat cap grabbed his elbow.

"Are you alright?"

"What?"

"I'm Liamy. It's good to have you onboard." He was shaking JJ's hand now.

"Bhfuil tú linn?" O'Cofaigh asked JJ urgently, as his colleagues set to splitting his handcuffs with a rock and a chisel.

"I don't speak the Gaelic. Sorry."

"Are you with us?" Liamy repeated.

"Me? No. I'm just here for the races. I'm a singer. I'm going to be an actor."

This statement and JJ's impish smile were greeted with a blank look from O'Cofaigh and a titter from the rest of his crew.

"You'll need to be careful round here now," Liamy said. "They'll be looking for you."

The handcuffs snapped apart and within seconds the rebel, his rescuers and the giant new prisoner were gone and JJ was left alone, stunned and briefly inert. A loud, dull groan from the other side of the wall soon spurred him into action, though, and he fled in the opposite direction from the rebels, back to safety and civilisation.

9

The Battle of the Ratoath Inn

———·———

JJ SPENT THE REST OF the day on high alert, every fibre of his being focused on self-preservation. Once he felt safely lost among the throng again, his next priority was to eat. To eat he needed money. The only way he knew to make money was by singing. So despite his recent trauma and the fact that he was still a wanted man, within half an hour JJ McHale was boldly standing at the crossroads in Ratoath, singing a selection of popular ballads, with one eye out for the dark-green uniform of the RIC and a strange new tremolo in his voice, more nerves than artifice. He started with "Brian O'Linn", about a resourceful young farmer with a creative approach to clothing. Next "The Ballad of Master McGrath", not about a horse but an Irish greyhound who won a big race in England in 1868. The racegoers loved that one. Then, as an ironic nod to his own recent misadventures, he sang "The Peeler and the Goat", an elegy to an unfortunate goat arrested under false pretences. His lips curled in a soft smile again, as he watched the flat cap in his hand fill with copper. He moved to three other stands, dodging down laneways or mingling with groups of drinkers whenever he spotted a flash of dark green, before he earned enough money to keep him in food and drink for the rest of the evening and into the night.

The singing left him thirsty so he wet his whistle with a couple of bottles of stout before feasting on fried pork, boiled cabbage, soda bread and jellied eels, bought from a street vendor. Crowded and all as the town had been at the start of the day, the numbers seemed to have doubled by evening. The bars were packed and noisy, the streets humming. There was music on every corner, dancing in the streets and drunkenness appeared the natural state. The couple of drinks brought the redness back to his cheeks and a broad smile to his face. He sat on a low stone wall to eat, the spot not casually selected; there were two men performing directly across the street.

One was slim and fit, in a three-quarter-length fawn-coloured coat, decorated with old war medals and brooches. A pheasant feather brightened up his battered top hat and he played the fiddle with a deft ferocity. His companion was older and sported a full, white beard. A collarless shirt, under a dark waistcoat, was tucked into bright red trousers that surely had a story going with them. They had thrown an old wooden half-door on the ground and the bearded man was dancing on it, his hobnail shoes tapping out the rhythm of a hornpipe, while his knuckles beat a complementary rhythm on the bodhrán in his left hand. Their energy was infectious, their dexterity and musicianship impressive. JJ sat, listened and munched as if he were in paradise.

Suddenly something grabbed the back of JJ's collar, forced him forward and up onto his feet. Damn! Had he allowed his guard to drop and a policeman to catch him unawares? Bam! A heavy, unidentified missile came hurtling in from the side, to catch him squarely on his ear, knocking all cogency clear out of his head. The blow sent him reeling and what remained of his food flew out of his hands. A number of bystanders broke his fall but as they hoisted him upright again, two hands of meaty fingers grabbed his jacket and heaved him up until his face was only inches from the face of the owner of those hands.

"What did you do to my sister?" growled a thick Leitrim accent.

"Sorry?" was all JJ could manage in response.

"You heard me, you bloody tinker!"

JJ's ear stung, his head was buzzing.

"Pádraic?"

He blinked and squinted at his assailant through watery eyes but there was no mistaking that head of hair like an upturned bowl. Then Peggy's face appeared behind her brother's shoulder.

"Peggy? What's going on?"

"That's what I'd like to know Mister Sligo."

"Thought you could just leave her in the lurch you shleeveen, without a word!"

"I never did."

"Are you calling me a liar?" Pádraic shouted and swung another hammer-like fist, but JJ saw this one coming and was able to duck so that it caught the side of his head instead of his jaw. Although the blow caused his head to buzz loudly again, the solidity of his skull had also stung the lad's knuckles.

"You bastard!" he roared as he shook the pain from his hand.

"I thought you liked me?" Peggy asked.

"I did. I do."

"I'm not bothered, one way or the other, but why didn't you just say something instead of skulkin' off like some sort of slítheán?"

"I left a note!" said JJ.

"What note?" Pádraic grabbed him by the lapels, tightening the collar around his throat.

"I gosh a lift in a horsh transhborter." JJ was barely able to breathe. "Shoved a noshe undger the dchoor. Shaid I'dge meet you at the rayshes."

"There was no note. Did you see a note Pádraic?"

"No." Her brawny brother tightened his grip on JJ's throat.

"Jeeshis Pawick! I lecht ung!"

"What?"

"I lecht ung!" JJ repeated, his face reddening, his eyes pleading.

Peggy laid a hand on Pádraic's shoulder. He released his grip and JJ collapsed backwards. Several bystanders broke his fall and kept him on his feet, not out of compassion but because they were keen to see this fracas escalate. He regained his balance and sat down on the low wall.

"We saw no note."

"I left one. I swear. I would never have done that to you Peggy. I . . . I like you."

"I told you, I'm not bothered. I just thought you'd . . . "

But before she could finish the imposing form of Sergeant O'Connor materialised. He had doubtless been drawn by the noise of the dispute, which must have travelled on the cool evening air. Instinctively, JJ leapt up, grabbed Pádraic around the waist, buried his head in his oxter and began to stagger as if his legs had no bones.

"What the hell are you doin' ya loodramawn?!"

He tried to pull away but JJ clung even tighter and, to complete the picture, he began to sing a drunken version of "The Real Old Mountain Dew" – well, it was the first song to come into his head – going straight into the chorus:

> Hi the ditheryal the dal, dal the dal the dithery al,
> Al the dal dal dithery al dee,-
> Hi the ditheryal the dal, dal the dal the dithery al,
> Dal the dal dal dithery al the dee.

"Shut up, would you!" Pádraic was shouting.

Peggy began to sing along, taking JJ's free arm and draping it across her shoulders. JJ squinted out from his hiding place, like a naughty child who has covered his face with his hands and, thinking that he is hidden, peeks out between his fingers to see if he's been spotted. Peggy smiled and winked. Pádraic seemed to follow his sister's lead.

O'Connor had placed himself in the path of the ribald trio and was frowning at Peggy and her brother. JJ buried his face deeper in Pádraic's oxter.

"Is he going to be all right?" O'Connor asked.

"Don't worry, Sergeant, I'll take care of him," said Peggy without breaking stride and deftly steering her drunken companion around and past the sergeant.

"Grand so," said the peeler with a nod, glad to have one problem fewer on his hands on this day from hell. Pádraic jerked his chin up in response, clearly happy to avoid the unnecessary intrusion of the law, and they proceeded on their way, JJ launching into the second half of verse one of his song. He sang with renewed verve as he was hauled off to relative freedom.

> Oh the gaugers all from Donegal, Sligo and Leitrim too,
> We'll give them the slip and we'll take a sip
> Of the real old mountain dew.

"Good Christ, Peggy! What the hell possessed you to hitch up with this omadawn?!"

*

The misunderstanding with Peggy had by no means been smoothed over though and several strings of harsh words were unleashed on the journey back through the village, but JJ was on a roll. His confidence had returned, his spirits raised by having eluded the ubiquitous Sergeant O'Connor. Plus he had, after all, truth on his side. So despite the lack of hard evidence to the contrary, and Pádraic's open scepticism, Peggy believed JJ had left her a note that had somehow gone astray, and sure wasn't he here now and repentant and charming and as gorgeous looking as ever and, with the effects of the stout, nice and frisky too. Whatever residue of hurt or anger that remained was quickly suppressed by their inability to keep their hands off each other. They left Pádraic perplexed, as they strutted off in each other's arms, almost dancing along to the music that wafted up from the streets on the night air, crisis resolved, wounds healed, life to be lived.

An hour later, the lovebirds were in a crowded public house drinking, laughing and singing. They had met up with JJ's cheeky new friend, Ollie, and a group of other stable hands. Once things had settled, introductions made, compliments and jibes exchanged, the lads opened up and shared stories aplenty about great horse races, close finishes and underhand tactics. Ollie himself was close to tears when he told a story about a horse called Genesius that he had looked after when he first started at the Galway stables of Mr Harry Ussher. The horse was a terrific jumper and had won several quality races on the way to being entered for the prestigious Conyngham Cup at Punchestown, with a first prize of £150, a significant purse. The horse was expected to win, although his closest challenger, Majestic Star, was expected to run him close. Genesius would need to be on his best form, in tip-top shape and, right up to the day of the race, Mr Ussher was happy that he was, and even though Ollie was only six months at the stables, he had got to know the horse well enough to agree.

On the morning of the race, though, Ollie noticed something awry.

"Genesius just wasn't himself. 'What do you mean?' Mr Ussher asked me. But I couldn't put words on it, you know? The horse just seemed off, like someone who'd got out the wrong side of the bed or was suffering from a bastard of a hangover. Well that's not exactly the language of horse racing is it? So how could you expect Mr Ussher, a trainer with years of experience, to take me seriously? He asked me how the horse had been behaving and I told him he was jumpy and jittery, nothing like his normal, relaxed self.

"'They're almost human you know, Ollie,' says Mr Ussher. 'Maybe he realises this is a big one, a step up for him.'

"'So you think he's just nervous like?'

"'Could be Ollie, could be. But we'll know for sure by this evening.'

"So that was it. Nothing more was said or done, even though the horse got even more restless, almost angry. It was like a friend I'd known for six months suddenly went from bein' a jolly, good-natured companion to an angry, disagreeable blackguard.

"The jockey felt it too, once he got to saddle and mount him. Said he was a lot friskier than normal and was pulling hard, even in the enclosure. And this from a horse that never pulled. Then, Mr Ussher himself started to get worried when the jockey dismounted down at the start. He didn't remount until the starter's flag was raised and had barely got himself back in the saddle and the horse turned when the field took off with Genesius at the rear.

"Once the race settled, Genesius seemed to find his rhythm, you know, and he sat in nicely behind the leading pack. The race was being run at a good lick, led out by Royal Maiden, a fairly decent mare. So, as they rounded the bend farthest from home, the placings had changed very little and Majestic Star was sitting right on Genesius' heels, as expected. But then, everything changed in a flash. Our fella started pullin' hard again and throwin' his head like mad, so the jockey was forced to switch to the outside, for safety, and surrender poll position on the rails to Majestic Star.

"Next of all, they rounded the third bend and were jumping the fourth from home when Genesius threw his head way back, almost reared, and all but unseated his rider. I was straining to get a better view, hoping Genesius was just trying to make his move too early and the jockey was having to battle with him."

Such an extreme reaction from a strong stallion like Genesius would leave the jockey with only two choices, Ollie explained: continue to rein him in, making a fall almost inevitable, or give him his head and take a chance that he would have the stamina to claim victory. The jockey chose the latter, and in a twinkling, the horse's head dropped and strained forward, he pinned back his ears and took off like he had been shot from a gun.

"I'd never seen Genesius run so fast, even when he was pushed, back home on the gallops. He was sprinting like there was only a couple of hundred yards to go, but there was two and a half furlongs left. There was no way he could keep that up. He left Majestic Star well and truly stranded as he flew up the outside of the field and, after jumping the second last, he was six lengths clear of the field. Then, phittt! Like a candle being blown out. His four legs collapsed from under him, his head hit the ground, the jockey tumbled off, and the poor auld Genesius slid along the grass for almost fifty yards before he came to a halt, close to the outside rails, and rolled onto his side. I was already sprinting down, but before I even got there, I knew by the gimp of the jockey that it was even worse than I feared. Genesius was lyin' dead on the damp grass. Poor fucker. His face was all contorted, frozen in a look of . . . shock. I'll never forget it. I've never seen anything like it."

After sniffling back a tear, Ollie told how Majestic Star won comfortably by three lengths and went on to make a lot of money for his owner. No one knew or could say for sure what had happened that day but the suspicion was that Genesius had been poisoned, some fatal concoction injected, or slipped into his feed, in return for thirty pieces of silver, a guinea or two at least.

Vigilance around the stables increased from that day on, feeding was closely monitored and no one was ever trusted implicitly again. It made for a difficult atmosphere sometimes, but Mr Ussher was determined that nothing like this would happen again. Apart from the financial loss, there was the loss of reputation, which in turn affected everyone who depended on the stables for their livelihood. It also affected them personally.

"It was like a death in the family," Ollie concluded.

He was a terrific storyteller. He had everyone in the tight group hanging on his every word. JJ was impressed by Ollie's ability and noticed how he skilfully manipulated the reactions of the audience at each of the dramatic turning points in the story. JJ would never have believed he'd have had such a good acting lesson from a simple stable lad. There was applause for the story, despite the mood being muted somewhat by the sad ending. Ollie immediately called for another round of drinks and JJ broke instinctively into song to lift the mood. "Master McGrath" was a perfect antidote followed by the doleful but beautiful "Flower of Magherally".

"For the ladies and the lovers among you!" he said, bringing a blush to Peggy's cheeks.

After the song the group disbanded naturally, breaking into couples and threesomes and mingling with the crowd in the pub. JJ was intrigued to see Ollie's fellow stable lad, who had withdrawn sulkily from the group during the story, deep in discussion with a wild-looking young fella with a mop of red curls and an honest face, taller but of similar age. Then Peggy grabbed JJ's arm and took him out onto the floor for a few reels. After half an hour of hopping, swinging and twirling they found themselves breathless, sweaty and thirsty on the far side of the large, barn-like public house. JJ went to get fresh drinks to slake their thirst. When he returned, weaving deftly through the crowd so as not to spill the creamy contents of the glasses, he accidentally bumped into the shoulder of a young man who, along with his companion, had occupied JJ's space and was chatting to Peggy who was smirking and flirting back.

"Oops, sorry!"

The man turned his head and gave JJ a withering look. It was only then that he noticed the men's uniforms. Thankfully, they were not the dark green of the RIC but the pale green of the Dublin Fusiliers, complete with Sam Browne belts. Presumably they were home on leave from the war in Europe or enjoying a few days' rest and recreation before heading out for the first time.

"Thanks for the drinks," said the one JJ had bumped into.

He was as young as JJ, skinny, with a gaunt face. His uniform seemed a little too big for him. He wrapped his fingers around the two glasses and tugged. Surprised, JJ tightened his grip and smiled.

"Ehm, no, sorry, they're our drinks."

"Are you trying to mock us?"

"No."

"You think we're not worth buying a drink for?"

"No."

The skinny soldier bristled, tightened his grip on the glasses, set his face in a sneer. "Why the fuck not, you measly fucking gouger?" he snarled.

"Sure it's okay, JJ. I have enough anyways," said Peggy, sliding her arm around JJ's lower back.

JJ gave her a reassuring nod, then looked the skinny soldier in the eye. "That's not what I meant."

"What then?" He was clearly spoiling for an argument.

"I'm just saying, these are our drinks."

"Do you have any idea what we've been through, what we've done for the likes of you and all these other ungrateful fuckers here?"

The last words were shouted for the benefit of the revellers.

"Easy, Mickser," said his fellow trooper, laying a conciliatory hand on his friend's shoulder.

"I don't have the money to be—"

"You're a fucking waster!"

Mickser shook his friend's hand off his shoulder, which, combined with the competing grips on the glasses of stout, caused quite a spill, some of which splashed onto Mickser's uniform. His face tightened, his eyes narrowed.

"Is that the respect you have for this uniform?"

"That wasn't my fault!" said JJ.

"Leave them have the drinks, JJ. It's not worth it," said Peggy.

"What did you say? We're not worth it?"

"Come on, Mickser."

"No, Billy. Did you not hear this fucking tart?"

"Ah here now." JJ was getting a bit fed up of this man's carry on.

"She says we're worthless too! This fucking whore and her fucking tinker boyfriend think we're worthless fuckers, Billy!"

Billy's hands were gripping Mickser's arms.

"Don't you dare speak about Peggy like that!" said JJ.

"Let it go, sunshine. Don't push it," Billy advised JJ.

"We're over there in hell, dying like fucking flies to keep fuckers like this safe from the Huns and they think we're fucking worthless," shouted Mickser.

"Come on, JJ, please," said Peggy.

"No! You heard what this phocaide called you!"

"What did you say?" Mickser's grip on the drinks tightened further.

"Right," said JJ firmly, "please take your hands off our drinks and leave us alone."

"You fucking bastard!"

Mickser changed from grabber to tosser and flung the contents of the two glasses into JJ's face and onto the heads and shoulders of several other customers behind him. It took JJ a few seconds to clear his eyes and respond. By then, Peggy had been brushed aside and knocked onto her arse by two men who, also hit by the flying stout, had lunged forward to attack Mickser. He fought as he looked, like a terrier, hitting, kicking, biting. Billy backed him, adopting a more orthodox approach, addressing his assailants like a trained boxer.

Shouts of "Fucking troublemakers!", "Fucking traitors!", "Go back to England, you fucking Brits!" came from the crowd, as blows were traded, bottles smashed over heads and chairs hurled across the room.

JJ was astonished by the outpouring of emotion from those who were assaulting the soldiers and the few patrons who backed them. He knew a lot of people didn't agree with Irishmen fighting for England but he had clearly underestimated the extent of the animosity. No one from Sooey had joined up, despite several recruiting campaigns. But that was because the young men were needed to work the farms and felt no compulsion to sacrifice their lives for someone else's cause. JJ himself had no interest in any cause but he was not going to be treated and spoken to like that by anyone.

Mickser's face was before him again, blood streaming from a cut above his left eye. "You bastard!" he snarled, as he drew his arm back to strike.

But before he could land the blow, JJ slammed his boot into his adversary's crotch and floored the Fusilier with a sharp, downward right cross to the face. As JJ shook the pain of the blow from his fist, Billy caught him with a haymaker from behind and he toppled onto the floor. His head was pounding, his vision blurred.

By now, several more Fusiliers and a couple of lads from the Irish Rifles had provided reinforcements, but the antagonistic locals still outnumbered the troopers and their few civilian supporters. Peggy had regained her composure and was slapping JJ's face. His vision began to clear and the sound of RIC whistles filtered through the ruckus.

"Jesus, what the hell was that?" he asked, rubbing his cheek with his hand.

"Can you stand?"

"Of course I can."

He got to his feet but his legs wobbled. Peggy caught him and he managed to get an arm around her shoulder.

"The police are here so it'll soon be sorted out."

"Police?"

Now he could clearly hear the peelers' whistles. "We have to get out."

"You can hardly stand."

"I can now."

He couldn't really, but with Peggy taking some of his weight, they were able to stagger and stumble to a rear door and get out before the pub was overrun by RIC, who were swinging their truncheons left and right, obviously deciding it was more expedient to quench the vigour of the feuding factions than to try piling them all into the tiny yard at the rear of the Hole in the Wall. Especially now that there actually was a hole in the wall.

Back in the peace and seclusion of the small hayshed behind Peggy's lodgings, they lay together on the small spread of hay left over from winter feeding. They talked about the future. She was looking forward to starting work in the post office the day after the races. There was nothing for a young girl in remote Leitrim, other than to marry an old farmer and become a baby machine, or go to England to work in a munitions factory. She was delighted to have landed a job in the expanding post office service and looked forward to her independence, making new friends and meeting people who lived real lives, exciting lives. JJ, of course, recounted his dream of becoming an actor and singer.

"I suppose you'll have little need of a simple girl from Leitrim so, when you're rich and famous," she said.

"And I suppose you'll meet lots of handsome mickey dazzlers in Dublin that'll sweep you off your feet. So you'll soon forget about your poor actor boy from Sooey."

"Ugh," she snorted. "Why does life have to get so complicated?"

"It doesn't, a stór. It's only us who complicate it by living too much in the past or thinking too much about the future."

"You're a fine one to talk."

"I know."

With that, he pulled her close, fondled her breast and kissed her full on the lips. As they continued to disrobe and their limbs entangled eagerly, hungrily, the air seemed to fill with the music of the distant whinnies of tightly tuned thoroughbreds and the rush of the gusting wind through the leaves of the strong oaks and chestnuts that surrounded the barn.

10

Anima Christi

———◆———

THE TREES EXPLODED INTO LIFE when a murmuration of starlings burst and swirled upwards towards the clouds that floated across the crisp ice-blue sky. Church bells pealed joyously in the distance like an accompaniment to the melodious birdsong. Then the volatile bird-cloud swooped downwards, as if it might smash headlong into the leafy arms of the tall trees. It didn't crash, though, but instead furled sheet-like, the skilled aviators using the warm air to slow them to a virtual hover, a spectacular, unified black wave, moving in slow motion and teetering for an instant on the brink of breaking apart, before alighting like a host of dark cotton balls on the welcoming branches.

The morning was beautiful and alive with promise as JJ woke and lifted his drowsy head from his bed of hay. He was alone. Peggy had slipped away sometime during the night, needing to return before her father discovered she was missing. Even for such a bohemian family, being seen to have spent the night with a young man out of wedlock would be severely frowned upon. But he felt reinvigorated, the slate wiped clean and ready to be filled again with a whole new set of adventures.

Down below, on the streets of Ratoath, a much less raucous but equally joyous flock of worshippers was making its way to the local church. It was Easter Sunday, the anniversary of the resurrection of Jesus, the son of God made man, our Saviour, who died for our sins but was reborn into eternal life on the third day. What a fittingly glorious morning to celebrate such an event, the happy gaggle must have been thinking, as it made its way through the sunlit streets. Their clothes, too, reflected the universal jubilation that needed no alcohol to fuel it. Women wore brightly coloured scarves; ladies sported bonnets or extravagant picture hats trimmed with frills, lace and flowers. The dresses were flouncy, party-like and colourful, swishing and flicking as the women sashayed along with steps as light and flippity as dancers. After the bleakness of the long Lenten period of fast and abstinence, this was like the true beginning of spring. You were allowed to smile along with the sun again, sing along with the birds, float along with the butterflies.

Not surprisingly, JJ had lost all sense of time and his place in it so had no idea what day it was. When he did eventually make his way down to the village, he wondered why the streets were so quiet. When he finally discovered it was Sunday and that the main activity was in the church, he made a beeline there. Not because he was a devout Catholic but because he just loved singing, any singing, in any company. The songs of Easter Sunday morning and the gusto with which they were sung were irresistible to him. He was late, though, and not for the first time in his life. The priest was finishing his sermon and waffling on about the immorality of violence and how the taking of life was the sole realm of God himself. JJ noticed many of the congregation turn their heads to cast admonishing looks at a small group of worshippers over to his left, who in turn straightened their backs and stared defiantly back at their chastisers. Curious. But then JJ was well used to small-town politics, though he never got involved himself. Meanwhile, the priest was urging his congregation to use the celebration of the Resurrection to re-evaluate their lives, examine the mistakes they had made, the sins they had committed, and to make amends for past transgressions, to be reborn themselves in Christ, and to go forth and not sin again.

The sermon finished and the offertory began with the singing of the simple but beautiful "Anima Christi". Maybe it was tiredness from the night's exertions, maybe a latent hunger or maybe he was just hungover, but the voices of the choir seemed to soar up through the roof, the vowels and consonants dispersing in the warm, midday air like flower petals. When JJ joined in the singing, he felt light-headed, almost transported. He definitely needed to eat soon. Whenever he sang this hymn in the church at Sooey, he was always asked to sing the mid-section as a solo.

Ne permittas me separari a te.
Ab hoste maligno defende me.
In hora mortis meae voca me.

So maybe that was why he sang it with a bit more power and passion than the rest of the congregation. He had not reached the end of the first line, when one member of the small group the priest had seemed to admonish in his sermon turned to look at him.

He thought at first it was a man; the long dark coat: the lack of frills or affectation, the tight, plain-knit woollen hat concealing any hair. But as he looked closer at the stern, frowning face, he noticed that the nose was thin and fine, the eye lashes long and feminine, and a tiny auburn ringlet had escaped from under the hat and was playing delicately with her ear. She stared at him with an intensity he had not witnessed since . . . well, for longer than he could remember. But her feelings were unclear. At first he was sure she was looking at him with disdain, disgusted by his boldness, a stranger singing so boastfully in her church. Or could it be that she simply didn't like his voice? Unlikely. He noticed, too, that her skin was pale but clear, her cheek bones high and her eyes green. Before he had reached the end of the second line, her full lips parted slightly and curled in a barely perceptible smile. Her eyes seemed to become glazed and assumed a vaguely mystical quality in the sanctified atmosphere. As he began the final line, smiling slightly too beatifically back at her, her companion, definitely male, turned to see what was distracting her. He was tall, tanned, with a full head of thick, wavy hair and a carefully manicured moustache. There was admiration in his gaze too, though, but his intrusion had shattered any spell JJ imagined had been cast. She turned back to face the altar without even an acknowledgment. Her companion did likewise, while the choir seemed to swell and take over again, leading the congregation through the final three lines and onto the elongated, climactic "saecula saeculorum, amen."

Back out on the streets, the mood was very different from the previous day. There was still an air of celebration, still music and singing, but there was less drinking, less boisterousness, less hustle and bustle. There seemed a sort of tacit agreement to permit joyous celebration without going overboard, allowing families with young children to enjoy the stalls and entertainers that abounded. While JJ personally welcomed this contrast to the much-too-hectic Saturday, it was not good for business. He was not a children's entertainer and knew few suitable songs, as Peggy's sister, Eibhlín, would no doubt testify. His speciality was the romantic, the comic, the drinking song or, when necessary, the fiery rebel song. He didn't starve though. Peggy made sure he got whatever her family could spare. It also afforded him an opportunity to wander around as a spectator and enjoy some of the activity for himself.

JJ was particularly taken with one performer, a tall man, at least six foot, sporting a black top-hat with a huge paisley scarf tied around it as a decorative band. Before he began his magic trick, he removed his ostentatious hat, revealing a head as bald as a duck-egg, and set it down as a coin collector. The flared sleeves of a mustard-yellow shirt with a jabot bloomed from beneath an old, dark-green morning coat, with large, deep side pockets. Next he lined up three small tin cups in a row on his makeshift table – an upturned tea chest – and placed an unripe plum under each one. He lifted each cup in turn, several times, to show that the mini plums were still underneath. Then he took a plum from under one of the cups, replaced the cup upside down on his little box-table and asked his audience how many plums were left.

"Two!"

He reiterated the word before lifting two of the cups to reveal a plum under each one. As he replaced the second of these cups he took away the plum that had been under it and was shouting again, asking how many were left now and which cup was it under. Well, any fool could have told him that there was only one plum left and that it was under the middle cup. JJ shouted out the answer at the same time as several others, getting caught up in the fun and suspense. The audience then dutifully went through the motions with the magician, waiting expectantly for when the trick would occur, when they would witness the magic.

"Are you sure?" he called out, building the tension.

"Would you bet your life on that?" He was raising the stakes, goading the audience into investing further in his magic and in him. He lifted the cup to reveal that there was in fact one plum left and it was indeed under the middle cup. But then, in a flourish that caught everyone by surprise, he lifted the first cup again to reveal a plum under it too.

"How come this one is back, then?"

He smiled broadly, took the plum back from under the cup and appeared to slip it into the pocket of his dark-green morning coat. He was moving swiftly now, with slick, deft hands. He lifted the first cup again – empty – the third cup, and there was a plum under it. How? He appeared to take back that plum, then casually raised the middle cup to reveal not one but two plums under it. The audience gasped. JJ was incredulous. How was he doing this?

"So how many here now?" the magician asked with an impish grin as he lifted and replaced the middle cup again.

"Two!" the audience chorused, trusting their own eyes implicitly.

"Three!" he retorted as he lifted the middle cup yet again to reveal not two but three mini plums beneath. The audience gasped, cheered and applauded.

The magician went on to do several variations of the trick and the audience rewarded him with a trickle of copper – farthings, halfpennies, an occasional penny.

JJ was mesmerised. The man certainly had the gift of the gab and, no matter how closely he watched, followed the man's hands, the movement of the cups, he could not see how he managed to get the plums to disappear and reappear at will, wherever and whenever he wanted. It truly was magic. But, impressive and all as that was, JJ didn't see how he could make more than the price of a few drinks or a good meal.

Then a stranger stepped boldly forward from the crowd and challenged the magician, betting half a crown that he could follow the plums and tell their final destination. The magician claimed he was not a betting man, but the stranger, black hair combed in a cow lick, plain jacket and collarless shirt, insisted that he take the bet, calling him a charlatan if he didn't. The stranger had the crowd on his side now. They were people who loved a bet and admired a courageous gambler. They cheered him and jeered the magician, goading him into accepting the bet. The magician began his banter and set about his routine. He placed the plums under the cups, lifted the cups to reveal the plums still underneath. He performed the trick as before but his movements were nervy, his shtick less confident. Finally, he finished and spread his arms, inviting the gambler to indicate the whereabouts of the plums. Beads of sweat had gathered on the magician's upper lip. The punter squinted at the three upturned cups. He touched the first cup and simply said, "Plum." The magician lifted it and indeed there was a plum beneath. There were oohs and ahs from the crowd. The punter's hand now hovered over the middle cup as he seemed to try to divine what was underneath it, before passing over and onto the third cup.

"Plum," he said again, even more emphatically than before.

The magician lifted the cup to reveal another plum. The crowd cheered loudly, relishing the magician's discomfort. Finally the stranger returned to the middle cup, tapped it confidently and said, "Empty!"

The magician lifted the cup slowly and sure enough, there was nothing beneath it. The crowd went wild. The punter snatched his own half-crown and the magician's two and six with a self-satisfied grin. The magician raised his hands and had to shout to be heard above the clamour.

"You have to give me a chance to win back my money," he pleaded.

"No, thanks. Quit while you're ahead," retorted the punter, pocketing his winnings. "Perhaps one of these good people might like to relieve you of some more silver, my friend," he said and swaggered off, laughing. The magician looked suitably glum.

Another punter stepped quickly forward, waving a shilling under the nose of the magician.

"If he can do it, I reckon I can too." And he slapped the shilling on the table.

"I'm not a betting man, I said!"

But the chorus of boos and cries of "charlatan" left the magician with little option but to accept or move on. He repeated the trick, seeming to move even more slowly now, his dexterity clearly affected by his loss. JJ watched closely, certain this time that even he could see that the conjuror had slipped one plum under the first cup, one under the middle cup and the third into his jacket pocket. And sure enough, those were the selections of the punter and the correct locations of the plums. JJ smiled for the punter but felt some sympathy for the poor magician, a fellow street performer, forced to hand over another hard-earned shilling. Whatever about quitting while you're ahead, this illusionist should think seriously about quitting before he got any further behind.

"Doubles or quits!" cried the most recent punter as he left his shilling on the magician's table.

"Are you trying to put me in the workhouse, a mhac?" cried the magician.

"Come on. Are you a man or a mouse, magic man?"

The conjuror set about the trick again with undisguised impatience, a hint of anger audible in his truncated banter. JJ had barely time to concentrate before it was over, the magician moving slickly again, without any hesitancy. This time the punter, much less certain, selected the middle cup, last cup and pocket. Wrong. There was one plum in the first cup, two in the middle and the last cup was empty.

"At last!"

The fickle crowd cheered the magician now and laughed at the greedy punter's red-faced disappointment. The magician slipped the coins into his trouser pocket and started to run through his routine with the cups again.

"That was just a bit of luck!"

"It was indeed, and good to have some finally."

"I'll go again."

The punter threw another shilling on the table, hoping to at least win back his original stake. The trick was repeated, the magician beginning to play with his audience now, throwing looks, the occasional wink, taking them into his confidence, into his world, much as JJ would do while singing a song. The punter guessed wrongly again. He did this twice more before deciding he had lost enough money to this conniving magician. But there was another man ready and more than willing to take his place and then another, each one betting either a shilling or a tanner. Sure isn't that what the races were all about – laying a bet, taking a chance, having a punt. JJ watched the magician pocket fifteen shillings and only lose three in the space of barely half an hour, before he picked up his upturned tea chest, tin cups and plums and moved on to wherever his next pitch might be. Well, well, well, not such a bad way to make a few quid after all. It would take JJ a week of singing to earn as much.

JJ passed the next hour wandering the streets taking in the sights and the diversity of people enjoying the Easter festivities: punters, paupers, gents and spivs, farmers and hawkers and ladies, oh ladies galore. He bought a rose from a flower seller to bring to Peggy. On his way back to her lodgings, he took a shortcut through a narrow lane behind O'Callaghan's public house. He was astonished to see the magician in close conversation with the stranger, the gambler who had almost cleaned him out. As JJ approached, he was even more surprised to see the magician hand over a share of his takings to said stranger, as they shared a laugh. JJ was practically upon them before they spotted him. The stranger quickly pocketed his cash and regarded JJ with a quizzical expression. The magician was more open.

"Good afternoon, my friend. Isn't the weather fabulous for the festive weekend?"

"I suppose. Good for the magic tricks too," said JJ with a frown.

"Ah, did you get a chance to see my performance earlier?"

"I did."

"And?" said the so-called gambler, his black cowlick falling down over his eye.

"And it was quite the trick," said JJ.

The gambler clenched his fist and looked to the magician for a lead. The older man waved a calming hand.

"Frankie was just going."

The other man looked surprised, even a little disappointed.

"I'll see you tomorrow, as arranged."

Frankie grunted and left, his fist still clenched.

"Now, why don't you let me buy you a drink, my young friend?" said the magician to JJ with a broad smile, glowing with reassurance. JJ gladly accepted the intriguing invitation.

In the pub, over two bottles of stout, the conjuror introduced himself as Stephen McNamara, a Dublin man, illusionist and raconteur. JJ didn't know what the last word meant but he liked the man, felt warm in his company. By the time they started on their second stout, it was like they were long-time friends, soulmates even. And then, just as he was about to quiz him about what had passed between himself and Frankie, his new friend came clean, unprompted. He explained that Frankie was in fact his assistant, as it were.

"An associate, if you will."

He assured JJ that everything he himself had done was legitimate sleight of hand and that without the magic, there would be no act, no show. Frankie's role was to, he seemed to search for the right words, demonstrate to the assembled punters that it was indeed possible to win money by betting against Stephen's dexterity. JJ queried if that was not in fact stealing, or at least cheating?

"Oh, no, no, no, no, no!" He was nothing if not emphatic. "It's definitely not stealing. On the contrary; it's simply instilling confidence in people, so that they have the courage and self-belief to place the bet. I still have to outwit them with my skill."

"But you let Frankie win. They can't possibly win."

"Of course they can win. You saw later, three more people were successful."

"You let them win too," said JJ with a grin.

Stephen couldn't prevent a self-satisfied smirk. "Perhaps I lost concentration for a moment. Perhaps I was too slow to properly create the illusion. Perhaps they just concentrated a little harder for that moment. Or maybe they just got lucky. It's all just an illusion anyway, JJ."

"What is?"

"Everything. Life. You flit from moment to moment, from event to event, thinking you are shaping your life, that you have some control over it. Am I right?"

"Well, I don't know . . ."

"We all do it, JJ. I do it myself! But you don't have control. It's all in your imagination, my life in mine, Frankie's in his and we're all colliding and interrupting and altering each other's stories all the time."

"Ah now, you can't think everything is total chance!"

"No, not entirely. But we can only control moments here and there, get the crowd with us for a short time, for example, but only for the briefest instant."

"Like with your magic trick?"

"Exactly! Then it becomes real and for that tiny moment, we are real too. So are they."

"I see." JJ didn't really understand but didn't want to appear stupid or ungrateful.

"We performers do that best of all, JJ. We are the gifted ones."

The conjuror drained his glass.

"So you see my young friend, you need a story, a context, if you want to make it pay."

JJ couldn't help but admire Stephen's restrained bravura. He was a born actor. JJ recalled how convincingly upset and ham-fisted he had appeared when acting out his little scenario with Frankie the Punter. JJ smiled, said, "Sláinte mhaith!" and drank too.

"I have a proposition for you, my friend," said Stephen, as he wiped the yellow froth from his upper lip and leaned closer to JJ, resting an arm on his shoulder.

He explained that the next day was one of the biggest days of his year, but it had its difficulties. It was relatively easy to instil confidence on a busy street. There's a constant turnover, a steady flow, people move on, move about and he too can move his pitch to the opposite end of the town at regular, judicious intervals. The race track, though, was a more confined space and the people stayed around for the entire day, found a nice spot and set up camp. Therefore, he liked to have at least two assistants, so that there was less chance of people spotting the collusion. His second associate had vanished, left without any explanation.

"An unfocused young fella with a mop of red hair but a great face for winning over the crowd," he told JJ.

JJ thought of the lad he had seen talking to Ollie's fellow groom in the pub the previous night.

"So I need someone to take his place," Stephen went on, "someone with the necessary attributes, who possesses the right qualities."

"What qualities?"

"You need to have a natural honesty and be capable of playing the part of an inexperienced gambler who strikes it lucky. You have to appear shy, diffident, almost unwilling to bet and then astonished when you do win. A natural actor like yourself could carry that off, I believe."

JJ, feeling like his coaching had already begun, was flattered to be considered and a little dismayed at this stroke of good fortune. After all, as Stephen had said, it wasn't like stealing, it was just, how had he put it again, instilling confidence in the punters.

"You would get a 25 per cent share of the net takings," said Stephen.

JJ wished now that he'd paid more attention during maths. He had no idea what 25 per cent might translate into in hard cash, but it sounded well worthwhile, and he couldn't care less if it came in a net or not.

"I'll do it," he said, grinning widely and shaking Stephen's hand vigorously.

JJ felt compelled then to buy his new friend and employer another drink, to seal the deal and cement the friendship. Stephen threw his arm around JJ's shoulder again and pulled him close, in a sort of sideways bear hug.

When JJ skipped up to the lodging house several hours later, the rose still tucked in his inside jacket pocket, he couldn't believe that Peggy was refusing to come down to him. She did eventually concede to talk to him from the window of the first-floor landing, if talk be the word. She harangued him for his tardiness and presumed drunkenness. When he tried to explain why he had been delayed and deliver what he saw as his good news, he stuttered and stammered, at a loss to put it in terms that didn't make it appear an illegal or at least disreputable scam. When he eventually took the flaccid, slightly withered rose from his inside pocket, and presented it as a peace offering, she scowled, harrumphed and slammed the window so hard, JJ was surprised the glass didn't shatter. It was going to be a quiet night alone in the hayshed then. Ah well, at least the weather was seasonably pleasant, and he had much to look forward to.

11

A Horse! A Horse!

—◆—

The crowing cock that woke JJ next morning sounded like it was perched right next to his ear. The fright made him raise his head so suddenly it set off a seismic throbbing. He groaned loudly and collapsed back onto his jacket-for-a-pillow. He would have liked to have gone back to sleep for several hours but he had to get to the racecourse where a big payday, by his modest standards, awaited him. The most expedient way to do that was to make contact with Ollie. They would be heading out at first light to begin preparations. JJ revived himself by washing quickly with cold rainwater from an old barrel in the yard. He grabbed a fistful of wild water mint on his way out the back gate and chewed on a few leaves to freshen his breath. The remainder he rubbed vigorously between his hands then massaged the fragrant salve onto his face and neck. By the time he reached Ollie's lodging house, the horse transporter was already pulling out. He galloped after it shouting and waving until Ollie spotted him, swung open his door and hauled his young friend into the cab beside him and the driver.

The journey back out to the track at Fairyhouse was much more comfortable than his previous trip. If JJ hadn't been jabbering so excitedly about the great day ahead it might have occurred to him that he was in the cab because they were a man down. He did eventually notice that Ollie and the driver were silent and sombre.

"Is everything all right, Ollie?" JJ asked casually.

"Of course it is," Ollie snapped. "Why wouldn't it be?"

"Right. Where's wee whatshisname?" he asked brightly, trying to change the subject.

Ollie glared. "The little bugger skedaddled during the night!"

"Fucked off without a word to anyone!" added the surly driver.

"Probably up to Dublin for that fuckin' parade he was goin' on about," spat Ollie.

Apparently the lad had joined a local group of Fenians back home in Galway, just over a year previously, and used to train and drill with them a couple of times a week. Neither Ollie nor anyone else in the stables took it at all seriously, but one thing was sure, this little adventure into Dublin city, today of all days, Grand National day, would cost this particular stable lad his job.

"Bloody fool!"

When they arrived at the racetrack, the two other men were already in work mode. JJ scanned the course to get his bearings while they opened the back doors of the transporter. It was a fabulous late-spring morning with the faintest whisper of summer in the air. There was a light dusting of frost on the grass, a thin film of fog veiled the rising sun and the horses' breath shot plumes of steam from their flaring nostrils. This was going to be a very good day. As Ollie led Ballyneety out, JJ noted that the brown gelding was a little subdued, not at all as lively as he had been on the journey down from Dunboyne. Cherry Branch, on the other hand, was as excitable as a young kitten.

"Give us a hand here, JJ, would you?" snapped Ollie as he struggled to get the skitter-jittery colt out of the box without injury. JJ jumped to it and led the calmer Ballyneety out of their way. Cherry Branch almost clipped him with a flailing hoof, as he leapt out of his confinement. Ollie roared at the frisky colt and whipped him across the neck with the leading rein.

"Is there anything else I can do to help, Ollie?"

He shrugged and scowled. JJ waited for a better answer.

"You could be our second lad, I suppose. If you really want to help."

"Me? Ah Ollie. I wouldn't have a clue what to do."

"Just follow my lead. You'll be grand."

"But I have my own work on today."

"You'll still fit that in, and there'll be a few bob in this for you, too."

As they began to walk the horses on long reins, Ollie outlined what JJ's duties would be. Once they had stretched the stiffness out of their joints, the horses would be given a quick trot or a short canter to check that they were okay. JJ had been on a horse's back before. Every farm had a workhorse and often, as a young lad, he would have raced their piebald mare against his friends, around one of the bigger fields or across the bog in summer. But this was different. He had never even sat on something with the aristocratic power and temperament of these thoroughbreds.

"It's only a stretch out. He'll do it for you. You just have to hang on."

"Right."

"And stay calm. They're clever. If he senses you're unsure, he'll throw you."

"Very reassuring, thanks."

"After that you just make sure that he settles into his stable for the day, and get the correct owner's colours to the jockey."

Ollie could manage the pre-race plaiting and grooming himself but he would then need to concentrate on getting Ballyneety ready for the big race. The gelding needed socks – a thick piece of wool wrapped around the horse's front legs, between the knee and the hoof, and bound with cotton bandages. Ollie explained that he hadn't been jumping as well as usual and the trainer felt this would help him to be braver over the rigid fences on the testing Grand National course. So while Ollie did that, he needed JJ to lead Cherry Branch to the saddling enclosure about twenty minutes before the race and hand him over to the trainer, Mr Ussher, and the owner, Mr Malcolmson.

"The owner?"

"Don't worry, he'll hardly even notice you. He'll only want to talk to the jockey, give him instructions, trying to sound like he knows what he's talking about. I'll let Mr Ussher know that you'll be helping us out."

JJ sighed heavily. He would still be able to work with McNamara and even fit in some busking, but this was a distraction he could have done without. He couldn't not help his new friend, though, who had been so good to him when he was in need.

"I might have some valuable information for you, too," added Ollie.

JJ managed to canter a frisky Cherry Branch the few hundred yards up and down the gallops, without coming a cropper. There were a few hairy moments, when the horse twisted and reared and it looked like he and his mount might part company. But a few stern shouts from Ollie and some feigned confidence from JJ averted disaster and the horse ran out well. He reminded JJ of some of the better athletes in his village on annual sports day, twitchy, keen and eager to get out onto the track, just get on with it, and more than a little sweaty.

"Too sweaty. He's overheating." Ollie said after the brief workout. "We need to get a few buckets of cold water over him."

They doused the horse with several buckets of cold water, which the colt didn't seem to relish, but it did the trick and calmed him down. Ballyneety, in contrast, seemed sluggish and uninterested.

"Has he got a hangover or something?" JJ asked lightly.

"What do you mean?" said Ollie with a frown.

"He just seems a bit out of sorts."

"Hmm . . . temperament. Let's get them to their stables," Ollie said and he peeled Ballyneety away.

His morning chores complete, JJ made his way to the main concourse. The whole place was beginning to come to life, slowly, like a huge old dinosaur waking and stretching its large, cumbersome limbs. The area around the grandstands was being swept and made ready by official-looking men in white coats accompanied by several gentlemen in jodhpurs and well-cut jackets. Posh food stalls were being set up in a corner of the main concourse. But it was the inner centre of the track that interested JJ, the area enclosed within the railings. This huge corral would be home to the thousands of ordinary folk – families, women and children, those with only a passing interest in the racing. They were on their holidays for the day and determined to enjoy themselves, spending what little money they had been able to put by for the occasion. Later, this would be the setting for dramatic scenes of great activity and vibrant colour, the score provided by musicians, singers and excited chatterers. For now, there were only ripples of what was to come: the flapping of canvas tarpaulins, the rap-a-tapping of hammers on wood, the clinking of metal on metal. He walked into the middle of this hive of preparation like a child allowed into a sweet shop before it opened to the public. He was goggle-eyed and grinning stupidly, when he heard McNamara call his name.

"McHale! I thought you'd got cold feet, a mhac."

"Stephen. No. Here I am."

"Here you are."

That was Frankie Ronan, whose scowl was far from welcoming.

"Frankie, howya."

"Hmph." He stubbed out his cigarette. "I'll see you after the first race, then."

"Sound," said McNamara, and his accomplice was gone.

Alone with his new sidekick, McNamara rehearsed what would be required of JJ. They went through it several times until JJ was absolutely clear about his role. McNamara played to an imaginary audience and skipped through his patter like the old pro he was, even doing the voices of punters, detractors and sceptics, as he mesmerised JJ again with the magic of his hands. Then, on one of several prearranged cues, JJ had to interject as the callow gambler, still wet behind the ears. Unlike Frankie who played the experienced, challenging punter, JJ had to stammer, stutter and lay his money falteringly on the makeshift table, unsure if he was even permitted to place a bet. McNamara, in this scenario, would welcome the bet, invite him to wager more if he so wished, gushing with confidence that he would easily relieve this naive youngster of his money. When it played out for real, the audience would be delighted to see the inexperienced punter strike it lucky and get one over on the smug magician. And sure if a green-horn like that could do it, surely they could too? Once JJ was secure in what he had to do and say, McNamara threw in a few ad-libs, which distracted JJ at first.

"You changed the lines!"

"There are no fixed lines in this business, kid," said McNamara. "You have to improvise, get a feel for the audience and respond to whatever is thrown at you, as if you really are that innocent, untutored gambler you're pretending to be. Just an ordinary country lad who happens to hit the jackpot!"

JJ pursed his lips, nodded then smiled. Yes, he understood. He was going to be good at this and he was going to enjoy it. This was real acting.

Several hours later JJ had been back to the stables and discharged his duties there, bar taking Cherry Branch to the saddling enclosure, and was returning to perform in McNamara's little sideshow. As he strode back through the centre section of the track, it too was thronged. The stand and concourse, as well, on the other side of the railings, were beginning to fill with owners and their families, trainers, jockeys, bookmakers, racing stewards and wealthy punters. The finery on display was something to behold. There was taffeta and lace, fur and fleece, ruffles and bustles of all shapes and sizes. There were lavish gowns from the haute couture stores of Paris, set off by extravagant picture hats and bonnets with coloured ribbon and veritable gardens of flowers atop; one was even adorned with oranges, apples and grapes. These were outfits bought to make the ladies look their best and as unabashed displays of wealth and status. Likewise the men, though their costumes were less flamboyant. A not too close inspection of the fabrics and cuts would reveal their expense. Because it was the races, with its sense of carnival and an acceptable opportunity for ostentatious public display, there were stripes, contrasting lapel and pocket trims and bright coloured waistcoats only seen on special occasions. People had travelled by railway, coach, gig, wagon, on horseback and, particularly those in the centre of the track, on foot. The jockeys, already in their silks for the first race, added to the colour and spectacle.

The central corral was filled with people, noise, music, and the colour and flap of a huge variety of stalls. There were several bars selling alcoholic refreshment, which were already well patronised. Bookmakers had also set up stands; while the gambling would not be as fierce, or the wagers as large as in the main concourse, there was still money to be made. Some were dressed in scarlet, others wore peculiar hats, something to set them apart from the throng, and each man bawled the odds for the first race in his own inimitable style and accent. There were also roulette wheels and card tables. A huge wheel of fortune was spun by a fat lady with red cheeks and a deep, gravelly laugh. There were jugglers, acrobats and clowns, some employed as a distraction to facilitate the many pickpockets in their particular sleight of hand. A group of four young girls danced reels and jigs, accompanied by another girl on a small melodeon. Several gypsy fortune tellers' tents were doing a roaring trade. JJ thought about paying one of them a visit, to find out what the future held in store for him, confirm that he was on the right track. But that would take all the fun out of it and spoil the surprise. Also, if he were to believe Stephen McNamara, it would be a total waste of money. They were all at the same game, conjuring illusions of control to assuage and hearten the floundering masses.

JJ stopped as a loud, insistent drumming split the air and the crowd in front of him parted to reveal a large pair of shoes and two trouser legs that were longer than any he'd ever seen. His eyes followed the trouser legs up to the waist and further again to the body and finally to the head of the tallest man JJ had ever met. He must have been nine or ten feet tall, in a striped suit beneath an exotic-looking, sleeveless, sheepskin coat, with a red, green and blue tam o' shanter on his head. He had three wooden clubs, which he juggled intermittently as he strode through the crowd. His dwarfed companion beat a military snare drum and had a leather shoulder bag to collect coins from the amused, wide-eyed spectators.

Here too, there were some fashionable displays, although none of the costumes had come from Paris. It was also a day for the less well-off to take down their finest gown or suit. The vehicles that had transported them here had drawn up in the vicinity too, many with bumpers full of food and drink. JJ was impressed at the unstinting hospitality on display; a livelier, gayer or a happier sight he was certain sure could not be seen anywhere.

By the time he reached McNamara's table, it was already surrounded by a sizeable crowd of curious onlookers. JJ was astonished but he was prompted into immediate action by a surreptitious glare from his paymaster. This was it. The audience waited, expectant but unsuspecting, and the conductor stood in the midst of all, weaving spellbinding circles and arcs with his charmed hands. JJ took a deep breath. It was show time. He slipped into character like a seasoned pro and delivered the performance of his life. The audience was enthralled by the drama that unfolded between the magician and the guileless young lad from the country, who seemed to have been born under a lucky bush. They were completely taken in and, as JJ left with a self-deprecating shuffle, shyly pocketing his winnings without even counting them, there was a surge of people keen to bet against McNamara, certain that they too could increase their meagre coinage two-, three- or even fourfold. Once out of sight, JJ smiled, threw back his shoulders, cocked his head and sang at the top of his voice as he roamed through the swelling crowds, his confidence at an all-time high.

As I roved out thro' Galway town to seek for recreation,

On the seventeenth of August, my mind was elevated.
There were multitudes assembled with their tickets at the
      station,
My eyes began to dazzle and they goin' to the races.
Agus fáim arís an crúiscín is bíodh sé lán.
It's there you'll see the gamblers, the thimbles and the garters
And sporting Wheel of Fortune with the four and twenty
      quarters
There was others without scruple pelting wattles at poor Mag-
      gy
And her father well contented and he looking at his daughter.
Oh, it's there you'll see the pipers and the fiddlers competing
And the nimble-footed dancers and they tripping on the
      daisies.
There was others crying cigars and lights, and bills of all the
      races
With the colours of the jockeys and the prize and horses' ages.

By the end of the song, small groups of people had formed an irregular circle around him, most of them children, surprisingly, and were following him as if he were the Pied Piper himself. A few of the adults had joined in the choruses and the final applause was generous; a few cheered and some even called for more. The mood, tone and humour of the song had been perfect for the occasion, and the spot JJ found himself in was perfect for busking, close enough to the other stalls and spectacles to draw a crowd but far enough removed from bawling bookmakers, rowdy punters and mellifluous melodeons. He sang throughout the first race – the majority of people in this central area were more interested in the carnival than in the horses – and continued for a further fifteen minutes after the winner had passed the post. By then, he had earned two shillings and three pence for his singing, which, together with what he would get from Magic McNamara, would see him going away with pockets much heavier than he had coming, not always the case after a day at the races.

Ollie was giving Cherry Branch a final brush down when JJ got back to the stables. As he checked the horse's hooves and shoes, he exhorted JJ to get the animal down to the saddling enclosure as quickly as possible.

"I will, I will. Not a bother."

Ollie handed him the long rein and the horse whinnied loudly then rose onto his hind legs, like a giant warrior setting himself to charge into battle.

"Christ, he's well ready for this, isn't he?"

"He is. Bit young yet, though, but might have a chance, with Anthony on his back."

"Anthony?"

"Jack Anthony! From Wales. Champion jockey two years ago, won the English national when he was only seventeen."

"Really? Jaysus. And he's riding for Mr Ussher?"

"Came over to ride Alice Rockthorne in the big race, but once the boss heard, he booked him post haste."

"Should we put some money on him then?"

"Well, she's coming off a good run against Punch at Downpatrick and the weights are in her favour, but she's a bit out of her depth today."

"Right. And how about Ballyneety?" JJ asked, looking into the gelding's stable.

"You have him looking lovely."

He was indeed beautifully turned out, his mane neatly plaited, his coat brushed to gleaming. Ollie glanced at the horse, pursed his lips and gazed thoughtfully at JJ, his eyes narrow slits. He shot a sharp glance left and right before summoning JJ to one side, with a quick jerk of the head. "This is just between you and me, right? You must tell nobody."

JJ hoped that this was as important and urgent as he was making it seem.

"Ballyneety has no hope of winning today's race."

JJ had no idea how shocking or otherwise this news was. "Oh. And he was expected to?"

"Well, he was in with a great chance, you know. You can never be one hundred per cent when there are fences involved, but," admitted Ollie.

"But you seem certain that he won't win."

"Someone's got to him."

"Got to him?"

"Slipped something into his feed during the night."

"Poison, you mean? Like the horse in your story?"

Cherry Branch threw his head back and raised his front legs impatiently. JJ pulled the rein, ordered him to calm and then gave him a bit more rein.

"Yes, but not enough to kill him by the looks of things, just to leave him sluggish and out of sorts."

"But how? When?"

"Chrisht!" exclaimed Ollie, irritated. "If we knew all that sure we could stop it happening."

"Of course. Sorry."

"Look, there's always someone willing to do shite like that for a few extra bob. None of us is rich, like."

"Too true," said JJ, though the corners of his mouth might have betrayed a slight smirk as he contemplated the earnings likely to come his way later that day.

"So ye have no clue at all?"

"Oh indeed we have clues. It's proof we lack and without that you're wasting your time. But these kinds of things come back to bite you on the arse, don't you worry, someday, down the road a piece." Ollie nodded and looked wistfully across the racetrack, like a wise old sage.

After a brief, weighty pause, JJ said, "So, who do you think, then? And why?"

"Well, Punch has been got to as well, we're told, and being last year's winner, the ground perfect for him, Harrison on his back and coming off a good win up north, he'll probably be the favourite. He was the one we all felt we needed to beat."

"Right. So with two of the best horses out of the race . . ."

"That leaves the way clear for Civil War. Mr Laurence King's horse. He's a Sligo man. You might know him?" Ollie was looking at JJ with just a hint of suspicion.

"Laurence King? No. Never heard of him."

JJ was too distracted to notice the suspicion in his friend's gaze, the doubt in his tone.

"Mmm, sure why would you?"

"So you think he's the one behind it?"

"Chrisht Almighty! Well, he's the one with the most to gain from it."

"Right." JJ had no idea why that was.

Ollie tutted impatiently. "He won it two years ago with the same horse, Civil War. He's a good gelding but not good enough to beat Punch or Ballyneety at their best."

"But with them at less than their best . . ."

"He's got a good weight and the owner is riding, so he'll know how to keep him out of trouble on the way around."

"Out of trouble?"

Cherry Branch whinnied again, dropped his head and skipped from his hind onto his front legs a couple of times.

"Keep him from getting bunched in, so he gets a clear run, space at the fences. So, barring a freak fall, you'd have to put your money on him."

"Really?" said JJ.

"Be daft not to. As near to a dead cert as you'll get in this game. Probably get him at a good price too, six- or seven-to-one, maybe."

"And there's nothing ye can do?"

"Oh yeah, there'll be objections lodged after the race, all horses will be examined by the vet, but, like I said, without definite proof . . ."

"I'm really sorry, Ollie."

"All part of the game. Nothing can be done now, except maybe make a few bob out of the whole thing." Ollie smiled wryly. "Now, get this fella down to the saddling enclosure!"

"Right. Yes."

"And JJ? Not a word of this to anyone or the finger of blame will come right back to us. Do you understand?"

"Yes, of course. Right, I'm off."

Cherry Branch gave a final quick rear and a shake of the head, as if to say "About time!"

Mr Harry Ussher was a well-known owner and trainer from Loughrea in County Galway and carried himself as such, at least out here on the racecourse. If you met him at home or on the street, you would likely think from his dress and gait that he was a simple farmer. But today, his tailor-made brown plaid morning suit and neat black bowler, sitting nonchalantly on his head, gave him the appearance of a country gentleman. As JJ led the giddy colt across the saddling enclosure, Ussher was in close discussion with his jockey, Mr Jack Anthony, pointing his light, hooked walking cane at several points on the racetrack, and projecting all the confidence and powerful presence that went with being successful in the racing game. He glared at JJ, whose confidence evaporated instantly, and he lost control of Cherry Branch for a moment. The gelding reared and threw back his head so violently that he almost wrenched the lead rope from JJ's grasp. Mr Ussher stiffened and Jack Anthony sprang forward instinctively, ready to take the necessary remedial action. JJ tightened his grip and managed to at least keep the horse from bolting and the adrenalin coursing through his veins gave him the strength and determination to get the animal under control again. Indeed, he thought maybe he had gone too far, shouting angrily at the frisky thoroughbred, as his father had often tongue-lashed JJ whenever he hadn't carried out his instructions properly or had messed up some task or other. At any rate, it worked. The horse steadied and calmed again, Ussher relaxed, nodding approvingly at the young lad's alacrity, and his jockey stepped back by his side.

As JJ got the colt alongside, he noticed that Jack Anthony was quite tall for a jockey, having several inches on the other riders in the ring, but as thin as a whippet. Anthony said very little, and the trainer continued to give instructions that were incomprehensible to JJ.

"Break cleanly . . . sit tight . . . not too much rein . . . he lugs in . . . don't let him get a big heart for the race . . . likes one good run."

What little Anthony said in response was in a thick accent that JJ presumed was Welsh. The wiry jockey grabbed Cherry Branch, unhooked the lead rope, threw it to JJ by way of thanks and mounted, with a leg up from Mr Ussher, who then disappeared behind the horse to chat to the owner.

His presence no longer required, JJ made his way out of the ring and through the elegant crowd in front of the grand stand, back in the direction of the centre of the track. He was quickly stopped in his tracks, though, when he spotted a group of four young Dublin Fusiliers. He instantly recognised the skinny, gaunt Mickser from the pub the previous Saturday night and, just as he averted his gaze, Mickser spotted him too. Shit! JJ immediately swung to his left and quickened his step, but the young soldier, used to dealing with much more elusive and highly trained antagonists, instantly changed direction. His comrades, adjusting automatically, skirted a group of partying punters. JJ diverted slightly. Then, with quicker, lighter, dance-like steps and longer strides, the infantryman was suddenly standing right in front of JJ, his arms spread wide, palms open and his feet square, like an animal ready to pounce. JJ stopped and turned to retreat, only to find that Mickser's colleagues, reacting like the tightly knit, battle-hardened unit they were, had taken up strategic positions to his rear and flanks. JJ was surrounded, and his nemesis, free from the calming influence of his friend Billy, was relishing the moment.

"Well, well, well," he drawled in his working-class Dublin accent, a little hoarse after a heavy night's drinking, "if it isn't the slimy little bogman from the other night."

JJ's mind was racing.

"Do yiz notice the smell, lads? The smell of cow shite?" sneered Mickser.

"Look, I don't want any trouble, lads." JJ tried to take them all in with a look, to appeal to their better judgement and lack of personal involvement. He even held his arms up in front of him, almost in a gesture of surrender. But they remained unflinching, fused by a loyalty and brotherhood that comes from shared adversity.

"You seemed to want plenty of it the last night?"

"You were upsetting my girl. What was I supposed to—"

"Your girl?" scoffed Mickser. "She was a tart, fair game I'd say. What do yiz think, lads?"

They laughed lightly, a scoffing laugh and tightened the circle, anticipating a reaction from JJ. Instead, he mustered what restraint he could and put on his best poker face. "You know what, my friend, you're right. She was a tart and I should have let you have your time with her. I apologise for the misunderstanding."

JJ held out a hand that he hoped wasn't trembling noticeably, and Mickser was momentarily taken aback. He laughed, then ignored JJ's hand and pressed ahead again.

"Well, smart aleck, it's a shame you didn't think of that before. It's a bit late for apologies now, bog man. Time for you to prove you're a real man and give me the satisfaction I'm entitled to."

They were almost nose to nose and JJ got the sickly-sweet whiff of stale whiskey off Mickser's breath.

"Ah now lads, this isn't the place to go fighting, is it?" he asked and glanced around at the blur of passing faces, hoping that one might notice his dilemma and come to his aid. Then he eyed each soldier individually again, pleadingly, as they tightened the circle further.

"Oh no, bogger, not here, that'd be stupid, wouldn't it lads?"

He winked, nodded slightly, and before JJ knew it, two of Mickser's colleagues had grabbed him by the elbows, lifted him off the ground and were carrying him through the crowd to some quieter spot, he supposed, where Mickser could get his pound of flesh.

Damn it! What could he do now, he wondered, as he was whisked across the crowded concourse like a naughty child, his legs swinging, as if pedalling an invisible bicycle. Some lines came into his head, from a recitation he'd learned in his final year at school. "If you can keep your head when all about you/ Are losing theirs and blaming it on you," he began, quietly, for himself. "If you can trust yourself when all men doubt you," he continued, louder now, bolder. "But make allowance for their doubting too . . ."

The crowd was beginning to pay him some attention. People were slower to clear a path for the strange ensemble, thinking they were being treated to some unusual performance. Some even stopped what they had been doing and followed. The Fusilliers had to change direction several times, weave a path through the spectators as best they could.

"Shut up, would you," snarled one of his bearers.

There was no quieting JJ, now he had an audience. "If you can wait and not be tired by waiting," he declaimed. "Or being lied about, don't deal in lies," he shouted as he began to swing his legs forward and back, as violently as possible. The soldiers were suddenly uncertain. This was something they had not been trained for.

"Stoppit you little bollocks!"

"Shut that fucker up lads, would yiz!" Mickser snarled.

"Or being hated, don't give way to hating," JJ recited. "And yet don't look too good, nor talk too wise," he concluded, as, with one final swing, he threw his legs high in the air and, using his bearers' arms as leverage, catapulted himself upwards and back.

"If you can dream – and not make dreams your master . . ."

He executed an almost perfect backflip and landed on his feet, with only a slight stumble, while his two bearers, discombobulated by the sudden acrobatic stunt and pulled backwards by JJ's counter movement, lost their footing and fell on their arses.

"Yours is the Earth and everything that's in it,/ And – which is more – you'll be a Man, my son!" And he spread his arms wide, cocked his chin haughtily.

The passing punters and those who had followed the progress of the comical ensemble clapped, some cheered, a few laughed. It was only this that drew Mickser's attention to what had just occured. As he turned to see what had caused the reaction, JJ ducked, in anticipation of the fourth Fusilier, who had been running behind as a sort of rearguard. The trooper, his arms outstretched to grab JJ by the shoulders, went flying over JJ's crouched body and clattered onto his two supine comrades.

JJ stood again and bowed quickly. "Thank you, ladies and gentlemen. Thank you!"

Then he smirked and gave Mickser a cursory salute, before turning on his heels and fleeing, spectators clapping him on the back as he passed and forming a defensive wall between him and his pursuers.

As he wove his way through the crowd he glanced back to see that Mickser, having burst through the human barricade, was in hot pursuit and gaining fast. JJ almost collided with a wall of punters queuing to place a bet. He changed direction deftly but tripped or slipped onto his hands and knees. As he picked himself up, he could see Mickser grin manically as he came charging towards him.

"This way a mhac." A butty young fella, in a long grey overcoat and black flat cap, was beckoning him.

Where had he seen him before? No matter. JJ ran towards his apparent ally just before Mickser could lunge and grab his hated enemy.

"Go! Go!" shouted the butty lad.

JJ nodded and ran ahead, then glanced back, to see his ally shoulder-charge Mickser in the chest, as he sprinted past. The lad then scuttled away in the opposite direction, leaving Mickser stunned and flummoxed on the ground and JJ racing to freedom.

Fuelled by his exhilaration and the adrenalin coursing through his veins, JJ skipped and scurried away, weaving a circuitous route through the crowd to be sure he had shaken off all pursuers. Then he galloped behind and around the grand stand. As he skidded around the far corner, he ran into what felt like a solid brick wall, ending up on his backside looking back up at an RIC sergeant. Not just any RIC sergeant but his old friend Sergeant O'Connor.

"You'd want to watch where you're going, sonny."

"Hmm. Yeah, sorry, sir."

He stared at the ground as if he'd lost something.

O'Connor stretched out one of his huge hands and hauled JJ to his feet. "Why in such a hurry? What are you running from?"

"Me? Huh? Nothing."

"Nothing?"

"I mean, not running from, running to."

"To what?"

"To . . . put on a bet."

"A bet?"

God, he was a tough bugger this sergeant. "I have a hot tip for the next race. Ehm . . . Cherry Branch, ridden by Jack Anthony."

"Jack Anthony? The champion jockey?"

Great. He was a racing man. "Yes. I'd throw a few bob on if you have it to spare, Sergeant."

"Would you, now?"

"I would," said JJ, smiling wanly, tipping his forelock and stepping to his right, eager to be on his way.

The burly sergeant halted him with a shovel-like hand. "Do I know you?"

Shit. He stopped but didn't turn to face O'Connor. "No. Don't think so."

"Oh, I think I do. In fact, I'm sure I do." O'Connor stepped around to look JJ in the face again. JJ kept his head bowed.

"Ehm . . . maybe . . . it's my older brother you know?"

"Your brother?"

"Ehm, yes. McNamara? Stephen?"

"Is he from these parts?"

"Ehm . . . no. He's a magician. We come here for the races every year. Maybe you . . .?" JJ couldn't think of anything else to add and was suddenly aware that several figures in military uniform had appeared at the front of the stand, behind the sergeant's back. When they turned the corner, JJ recognised Mickser.

"McNamara, a magician?" The sergeant, scratched his cheek. "Hmm, yes, I do know him."

"There he is, lads," cried Mickser. "Hey, you! Bogger!"

Mickser charged, flanked by his red-faced comrades.

"I didn't know he had a brother, though," said the sergeant, glaring at JJ.

"Well, he does!" replied JJ indignantly. "But if I were you, Sergeant, I'd be more worried about those fellas than about me."

JJ pointed at the fast approaching soldiers. Sergeant O'Connor turned to look and saw the strange band of brothers charging towards them.

"What the bloody hell are you lot so fired up about?"

Mickser's comrades slowed but he continued undaunted.

"Come back here, you fucking bogman!" shouted Mickser.

By the time the sergeant turned around again, JJ had disappeared.

Once clear of his predators, he slipped back over to the much safer and friendlier enclosure in the central corral, sans soldiers, sans stress, sans Sergeant O'Connor.

12

Irish Molly

———*———

NESTLED IN THE DUSTY WARMTH and relative safety of the whiskey tent, JJ downed a large one to steady his nerves. It didn't quite but it made him feel a lot better and a little more relaxed.

"You all right, my young friend?"

Stephen McNamara was munching on a cheese sandwich. The second race had started and he was taking a quick break.

"Yeah, fine. Just . . . trying to do too much."

"Life's too short for that, JJ. Here, get some food inside you. Plenty of punters out there waiting to be relieved of their money."

"Aw, thanks, Stephen."

"No problem. You all right, Frankie?"

Frankie Ronan stood hunched and slightly apart, elbows on the counter, a glass of stout hovering just below his dimpled chin. He raised the glass slightly, flashed a little sneering grin and emptied the dark contents down his throat. He refilled from the bottle, tilting the glass at an angle, allowing the dark liquid to trickle gently along the side.

"So, who's going to win the big race, then, Frankie?" asked Stephen.

Frankie sneered again and JJ wondered if he'd ever had an uncynical moment in his life.

"Obviously, it's Punch's race to lose."

"He's the favourite with the bookies, all right," said Stephen.

"Last year's winner, just coming off a great win and only carrying eleven-stone-ten? Who's going to beat him?" Frankie planted his glass emphatically on the counter.

JJ handed Stephen a fresh bottle of beer.

"Thanks, a mhac. No dead certs when there's jumps involved, though."

JJ passed Frankie a fresh bottle of stout.

"Sláinte mhaith, Sooey. He's by far the best jumper in the field."

"I don't know, I fancy Ussher's horse, Ballyneety," said Stephen.

"Ballyneety?" scoffed Frankie, laughing for the first time since JJ had met him.

Stephen smiled, enjoying the banter. "What about you, JJ? Know anything about the horses?"

"Well, not a lot but—"

"There's no horses in Sooey, only mules!" said Frankie.

Stephen thumped him playfully then addressed JJ earnestly. "But what, lad? I hope you're not hiding anything from us?"

"No. It's just, I don't think you should put any money on Ballyneety."

"Well, that's very insightful, Sooey," said Frankie, laughing.

"Or Punch, either."

"Well, that about sums up your knowledge of racing."

"He's not going to win," JJ announced.

"What?"

The two were astonished by JJ's wild claim.

"He can't win."

"Right, enough of this raiméis. I'm off to put on a bet."

Frankie raised his glass to his mouth.

"No, wait a minute. I think this lad knows more than he's letting on."

"What?"

They were standing over JJ now, close enough for him to feel the warmth of the alcohol on their breath and Stephen was insisting that he spit it out, tell them what he knew.

"After all, we're a team now, JJ, isn't that right?"

JJ gulped. "Well, I can't say too much."

"Oh for fuck's sake!" Frankie gulped a large mouthful of stout.

"Go on, JJ. You're among friends, friends who have been very good to you."

"Well, I was doing a bit of work for Mr Ussher."

Frankie's ears pricked instantly. "The trainer of Ballyneety?"

"I was just helping a friend."

"What friend?"

"I can't say. But he told me that Ballyneety, well, he won't be at his best for the race."

"What?"

"He's been held up? Or nobbled, maybe? Is that the word? He's been got to?"

Then JJ nodded discreetly to Frankie. "Punch too."

"The fucking favourite?" said Frankie.

"This is incredible, JJ," said Stephen. "If it's true, it could be worth a nice few quid."

"To anyone who's in the know," added Frankie with a wink.

"So, go on then, JJ, finish the story. Who got to them? Who's going to win?"

"Well, I don't know."

"Oh come on, Sooey, spit it out!" Frankie's tone was threatening now, as he leaned closer.

Stephen put a restraining hand on Frankie's arm. "We're all here for the same reason, to make some money. And this information could help us all to make a lot more. Come on, JJ, this won't go any further."

"Well." JJ looked to his left and right and leaned closer so that the three were in a tight huddle. "My friend says it was to clear the way for Civil War to win."

"Civil War?" said Stephen.

"King's horse. He's a Sligo man, isn't he?" said Frankie.

"I think so."

"You think so?"

"I don't know him."

"You sure about that, Sooey? You're not working in cahoots with him or anything?"

"In cahoots? No." JJ was mystified.

"So what do you think, Frankie?" asked Stephen.

"Well, he won it two years ago but I would have thought he was past it by now."

"His owner is riding him and he'll know how to guide him around safely," said JJ, parroting Ollie.

"Is that what your friend says, JJ?" asked Stephen.

JJ nodded.

"And if the two main contenders have been nobbled?"

"A good price, Frankie?"

"Yeah. Probably get him at six- or seven-to-one."

"Hmmm, I think that could be the icing on our financial cake, boys." Stephen was smiling widely as he drained his glass and began to pour the bottle JJ had bought him.

Frankie Ronan agreed, and emptied his glass. JJ sipped his whiskey, not sure if he'd done the right thing.

"You going to have a flutter yourself, Sooey?" teased Frankie.

"Well, I might have a shilling on. Just for the fun."

"No, no, no, JJ," insisted Stephen. "You're never going to get rich like that."

"That's all I can afford, Stephen. Saving my fare to London."

"You have ten bob coming for your day's work with me covey. At six- or seven-to-one, you could be going home with close to £4 in your pocket.

"But if he doesn't win?" asked JJ.

"But he is going to win!" Frankie's gaze was sharp. "That's what you said, isn't it?"

The question was loaded and the pressure was back on JJ again.

"Yes."

"Right," said Stephen emphatically, digging his hand into his trouser pocket. "Here's what you're going to do."

He gave JJ two pound notes – the ten shillings he'd already earned, a further ten bob advance on his earnings from stings yet to come and another pound on loan.

"You can repay me out of your winnings!" Stephen said.

He told JJ to put it all on Civil War in the big race. One, it would prove that he wasn't lying, and two, it would earn him at least £12, more than he could expect to earn in weeks of busking and more than enough to get him to London.

Even if JJ had been able to stutter a "no," he knew Stephen would not have accepted it. The potential cash bonanza was also tempting. JJ nodded tersely and took the money. McNamara then gave the astonished youth a five-pound note of his own to place on the horse.

"Holy God, Stephen! Are you sure you want to risk so much, on a horse race?"

"But there's no risk, JJ, according to your information." Stephen winked.

JJ gulped.

"I'll put on my own bet," Frankie declared, grinning smugly, and he left.

Stephen sent JJ off to the bookie's and arranged to meet up again just before the start of the big race at his new pitch, on the far side of the whiskey tent.

Luckily there were a number of enterprising bookmakers in the centre section of the track. JJ didn't fancy showing his face back in the main enclosure again. As he passed between the back of the whiskey tent and one of the fortune teller's caravans, an arm stretched out and grabbed him around the neck. Before he knew it, he was in a stranglehold against the back of the gypsy caravan. He couldn't see his assailant's face but his voice was unmistakable.

"Right, Sooooey, I'm not as trusting as my business partner, so you're going to take me to this 'friend' of yours. I'd like to hear for myself that what you told us is true."

"It is!"

"I want to hear it from the horse's mouth."

JJ almost blurted that horses couldn't talk, just to lighten things a bit, but he thought better of it. Frankie had shown himself to be a man bereft of any humour.

"I can't do that!"

"Why not? Coz you're going to disappear, do a runner with our hard-earned cash in your pocket?"

"No. I wouldn't do that! I promised my friend." JJ was also extremely reluctant to return to that side of the track.

"Well, if he's a true friend, he'll understand."

Frankie released his grip and shoved JJ ahead of him.

Ollie was furious and refused at first to confirm anything JJ had said. But sensing that JJ was genuinely scared and recognising that Frankie Ronan was not a man to be trifled with, he grudgingly repeated all he had told JJ.

Satisfied, Frankie instructed JJ to accompany him to the bookie's. Just before they left, Ollie grabbed JJ by the sleeve and snarled that he needn't bother showing his face again, that he was no longer a friend of his. JJ was about to ask for the money he was owed for his morning's work but Ollie had already turned his back and returned to preparing Ballyneety for the big race.

As they stood at the bookie's stand, in clear view, JJ shuffled, glanced left and right and jumped every time he saw anything resembling a uniform, cowering sheepishly until the threat, perceived or otherwise, had passed. There were queues at all of the stands and they were situated so close to each other that it was difficult not to get jostled and bumped. As he waited four back in his queue, Frankie one place ahead of him, someone bumped forcibly against him and grabbed his arm.

"Hey!" JJ glared angrily at the uncouth stranger.

"Aisy! Calm. I know who you are."

"What?" Then JJ recognised the blocky young fella from earlier.

"I'm Liamy. I met you the other evening. When we sprang the captain," he explained in a whisper.

"The captain?"

"From the Hole in the Wall? You wouldn't come with us that time."

"Oh, yes." JJ smiled but his attention was drawn back to the bookie's stall as the queue moved closer to the board. The chalk scrawl displayed Civil War at odds of six-to-one.

"I saw you grappling with those Fusiliers."

"Yes. Thanks for your help. But I wasn't with them. I have nothing to do with the likes of them."

"I know," said Liamy, squeezing JJ's arm tighter. "Nor should you, a mhac. You should be with us."

"But I don't want to be with anyone," pleaded a confused JJ, as the queue moved forward again.

"We're against everything those braggarts stand for."

"Right."

"We've a chance to teach them and their likes a lesson, for once and for all. There's going to be some big stuff, dramatic stuff kicking off today, and if I were you, I'd want to be a part of it, right from the start."

"Dramatic? Is it acting you're talking about?"

"No acting, a chara. The real thing."

"The real thing?"

Frankie was placing his bet.

Liamy glanced furtively about.

"It was called off yesterday but we got word this morning that it's going ahead today."

"Today?"

"We're rounding up as many fellas as we can," he added, then looked JJ straight in the eye. "So, are you with us?"

"Sorry, Liamy. I'm only a singer, an actor. I'd be no use to ye at all."

"We treat all men equally."

"Right, Sooey, place your bets." Frankie had placed his and was now glowering at this stranger.

"Right." JJ slinked past Frankie's glare and stepped up to the bookie.

"If you change your mind, we'll be leaving shortly after the National." Liamy gave JJ the thumbs up and disappeared into the crowd.

"Who was he?"

"I don't know. Nobody. I think he thought I was someone else."

Frankie seemed satisfied enough with the vague explanation, and waited while JJ put first his own two pounds and then Stephen's fiver on Civil War to win at 6/1.

Bets placed, Frankie placated and safely back among the hoi polloi again, JJ sat for a few minutes to compose himself. He was overtaken by a wave of nostalgia. As he gazed wistfully over and beyond the city of tents, caravans, wagons, cars and all the hustle-bustle, he felt homesick. It was not that he missed the life he had at home, certainly not. It was not that he didn't still want the dream he was chasing; nothing would sway him from that. It was simply that an incredible amount had happened to him in a short space of time. His life had been utterly transformed, without any time to take it all in.

When he had been back in Ballysumaghan and things got on top of him, or he was missing his mother, he had a favourite spot that became his bolt hole. You had to trek across some fields for over half an hour, through a hazel wood then across the Castle Dargan estate. It used to be owned by the Ormsby family. "They're fucking planters," his father used to say. "Came over from England three hundred years ago and stole our land, the bastards!" It had all been sold off now, to rich merchants from Sligo town. You still had to be careful going through though. If they thought you were a poacher, they'd shoot you on sight! After that you had to go through a small wood, past Lough Dargan and then there was a stiff climb up by Lough Ballygawley onto Union Rock, "Where that bastard Joshua Cooper raised the Union Jack on the 1 January 1801!" This his father would shout every time they passed the spot on their way into Sligo, shaking his fist at the rock. Jaysus, you'd swear he'd been there and seen it for himself.

Once on the top of the rock, it was an easy walk across to the highest peak, Sliabh Dá Éan. Here there was a haphazard arrangement of rocks, the remnants of an ancient passage grave, it was said, where they buried the Cailleach Beara, whoever she was, after she had lost her magical powers and drowned in the bottomless Lough Dhá Ghéanna on the western side of the peak.

The story told by the local seanachaí was that the lake was named after Mad Sweeny, a king cursed by an angry priest to wander, naked, hungry and nervous as a bird throughout Ireland. When the bird-like madman got to this part of Sligo he got into a fight with some other local hag and, during the struggle, they changed into geese and dragged each other into the lake, never to be seen again. JJ loved the story but he could never figure out how they were able to recover the Cailleach Beara's body for burial if it was a bottomless lake. Anyway, when he sat on the top of Sliabh Dá Éan, this place of hags and madmen, he could be confident that he wouldn't be bothered by anyone and, more importantly, he had the most amazing view, out over west Sligo and right down to the sea. On a clear day he could see north to the phallic crag of Ben Bulben and south-west to the breast-like Knocknaree, final resting place of Queen Maebh, and the Atlantic Ocean beyond. Some days he could even see Croagh Patrick, seventy miles south, in County Mayo. A lad could lose himself for hours in a place like that, and JJ often did.

"JJ McHale! There you are."

JJ almost jumped out of his skin with the fright and now he was intensely aware of the crowds and the activity around him again.

"Peggy?" God she looked magnificent against the light, a latter-day Queen Maebh.

"Where have you been?"

He wanted to grab her by the waist, kiss her deeply on those full moist lips and sweep her behind the nearest tent or caravan and make passionate, unbridled love to her until they both collapsed, exhausted, into a soothing sleep.

"I was looking everywhere for ya," she said, nuzzling him.

"Working. Sorry. God, you look good." He kissed her, not passionately but lightly, with a tender intensity.

She was taken aback for an instant. She held his gaze for a moment. "Huh. You're such a plawmawser, Mr JJ McHale."

"Am I?" He looked away, down at his shoes.

"What?"

"Nothing."

He was equally surprised by his sudden display of sensitivity.

"Look, I have to go to work again, so I'll see you later, after the big race?"

"What work?"

"I'll tell you everything later."

"Where?"

"The whiskey tent."

Before she could say anything more, he had kissed her quickly on the side of the mouth and scurried off.

JJ needed to be by himself for a while. He needed to sing. To ground himself before becoming McNamara's callow shill again. He sang without thinking. He sang without considering what the audience might want to hear. He sang not bothering about what would reflect the mood of the day and the event or what might persuade people to part with their hard-earned coppers.

> I am a bold rake and this nation I've travelled all round
> In search of a fair one her equal was never yet found,
> She was neat in each limb and her skin far whiter than snow –
> And if I don't gain her quite crazy to Bedlam I'll go!

There was only a trickle of coins for there was plenty of competition. He didn't care.

They may talk of Flying Childers and the speed of Harkaway,
Till the fancy it be wilder, as you list to what they say,
But for real bone and beauty, tho' you travel near and far,
The fairest mare you find belongs to Pat of Mullingar!

The pitch-bending, hurgle-gurgle of a hurdy-gurdy wafted from fifty feet away.

. . . For to gain the great prizes and bear them awa'
Never counting on Ireland and Master McGrath!

Less than fifty yards away, JJ could hear then see two of the buskers from the previous Saturday playing up a storm. The fiddle player with the pheasant feather in his battered top hat and the fawn coat pinned full of old replica war medals and his companion with the bodhrán, white beard and red trousers. He was going to have to be at his very best to rise above their raucous harmonics.

"Ri-too-ra-loora-lah, Ri-too-ra-loorah-laddy/ Ri-too-ra-loora-lah, Ri-too-ra-loorah-laddy-oooh!" Pipes and fiddle squealed out a lively jig, "Molly's Favourite", while the hurdy-gurdy barrelled out a barely recognisable music-hall favourite, "Nellie Dean".

JJ switched to a popular ballad. "As I was going over the far fame'd Kerry mountain/ I met with Captain Farrell and his money he was counting!"

Pipes and fiddle swung into a giddy reel, "Saddle the Pony", and the hurdy-gurdy segued into "It's a Long Way to Tipperary". JJ needed to up his game to compete, so he responded with a rousing version of "Lanigan's Ball".

"She stepped out, I stepped in again/ I stepped out and she stepped in again/ She stepped out and I stepped in again learning to dance for Lanigan's ball."

Pipes and fiddle were on to a poignant version of "The Wind That Shakes the Barley" that scratched against the hurdy-gurdy warbling "Pack Up Your Troubles".

Then JJ reprised one of his favourites. "Ooooohhhh, if I was a blackbird, I'd whistle and sing/ And I'd follow the ship that my true love sails in!"

Then, almost spent and inspired by his earlier recitation, resurrected from his school days, he launched into another narrative poem as he wandered about the central enclosure, trying to find a less discordant pitch. "A bunch of the boys were whooping it up in the Malamute saloon;/ The kid that handles the music-box was hitting a jag-time tune;/ Back of the bar, in a solo game, sat Dangerous Dan McGrew."

People paused. A small audience formed. This was something that resonated with all, a story known to every school child, young and old.

"And watching his luck was his light-o'-love, the lady that's known as Lou."

The copper coins trickled intermittently but JJ remained undeterred, not concerned with profit. He was on a roll. "When out of the night, which was fifty below, and into the din and the glare,/ There stumbled a miner fresh from the creeks, dog-dirty, and loaded for bear."

Having a ball, he was.

"The rag-time kid was having a drink; there was no one else on the stool,/ So the stranger stumbles across the room, and flops down there like a fool."

In his element.

"In a buckskin shirt that was glazed with dirt he sat, and I saw him sway;/ Then he clutched the keys with his talon hands – my God! but that man could play."

At one with the world yet standing out from his surroundings, like a diamond in a barrel of walnuts.

"Then on a sudden the music changed, so soft that you scarce could hear;/ But you felt that your life had been looted clean of all that it once held dear;"

And then he saw her again. The girl who had scorned his "Anima Christi" in the church the previous morning. "And the stranger turned, and his eyes they burned in a most peculiar way;/ In a buckskin shirt that was glazed with dirt he sat, and I saw him sway;"

Today, in the sunlight, she was even more captivating. There was no unflattering hat shrouding her dark ringlets, bound in a loose ponytail, like his mother often used to make, by twisting the hair through itself. Her eyes were sharp and keen, her skin pale, almost translucent.

"Ohhh, soft!" JJ shouted inappropriately. "What light through yonder window breaks?" Another half-remembered gem from school.

Not a total waste of time after all.

She glanced, perhaps distracted by the sound, but JJ couldn't tell if she heard the words. Maybe she remembered him from the morning before.

"It is the east, and Juliet is the sun!" he continued undaunted, buoyed and encouraged by the growing audience. "Arise, fair sun and kill the envious moon," he was declaiming now, the attention-seeking actor using the permission the words gave him to ham it up.

She had to divert, to get past this irksome distraction and keep up with her companion, a tall, thin man with a long face and prominent nose. He reminded JJ of a horse.

"Who is already sick and pale with grief," he continued without missing a beat, as he scuttled through his audience to get ahead of her again. Many spectators were sufficiently intrigued to stay with him, their ranks swollen by others who stopped out of curiosity.

"That thou her maid art far more fair than she." He played this final line directly to her and, with an expansive gesture, shared it with his audience. There was a spontaneous cheer. She stopped. She had little option. This odd, ranting lunatic was standing right in front of her now. She was surrounded, hemmed in by a mob of unwelcome, un-asked-for observers.

JJ was in full flow. "Be not her maid, since she is envious/ Her vestal livery is but sick and green/ And none but fools do wear it; cast it off!" He emphasised this final line with another expansive gesture and again invited the audience into his world. The girl gave him a quizzical look, bemused, caught off guard. For an instant, JJ thought he could see right into those dark, mystical eyes, into her soul or her heart – he was never quite sure of the difference. Whichever he was seeing into, though, it was not at rest but conflicted. A strange sadness overwhelmed him in that moment. It took a little of the wind out of his sails and all of the artifice out of his performance.

"It is my lady; O! It is my love."

She blinked. Her quizzical look turned to disbelief, scorn even. As JJ delivered his next line with gusto, snapping back into the energy of the performance, she tried to step around and past him as before. But he anticipated her move and back-pedalled to keep ahead of her, maintaining eye contact.

"It is my lady; O! It is my love," he reiterated, playing to the audience again, willing them to endorse his declaration, then dropping dramatically onto one knee and taking her right hand in his, "O! That she knew she were."

The crowd cheered loudly. The girl glared in horror, clearly embarrassed by the spotlight he was shining on her.

"Miss McNally!" called her companion. He had barged through the spectators and was standing between them, his hand outstretched, "Molly!" His face was stern, disapproving. Molly looked up, as if waking from a strange, unearthly spell, a geasa. She snapped away her hand and strode past JJ, almost knocking him to the ground. Her companion gripped her elbow and led her quickly away.

"She says nothing, yet she speaks volumes: what of that?" JJ misquoted, rising and gesturing rhetorically to the audience. They cheered and applauded and hurled coppers at him with seeming abandon. He remained oblivious for a moment, watching this intriguing, elusive woman disappear into the crowd, his smile broadening and lighting up his face.

"Molly." He savoured the word, rolling it around in his mouth, the soft, bilabial *m* opening out to the rolling vowel, then into the sensual alveolar double *l*. A coin struck him in the face, rudely waking him from his delightful reverie. Whoo! What had just happened?

That must be what real acting feels like, JJ thought. He had gone into a kind of trance, become someone else, almost literally. Now that was what he wanted to do, what he wanted to be. He thanked his dwindling audience then stooped to pick up his bounty, quietly reciting an extract from another speech in that same play that surged up from somewhere deep within the well of memory. "And in this state she gallops night by night/ Through lover's brains, and then they dream of love."

He jingled the fistful of coins he had gathered then dropped them into his jacket pocket, still smiling broadly. Things were looking up again. His luck was turning. He fingered the bookmaker's tickets in his other pocket. He was more than ready now to be the best shill in Ireland.

"Molly, my Irish Molly, my sweet Macushla dear/ I'm fairly off my trolley, my Irish Molly, when you are near."

13

The Big Race

———✦———

STEPHEN MCNAMARA WAS NOT PLEASED when JJ eventually reappeared only ten minutes before the start of the big race. He sprang instantly into action, slipping easily into character and not at all put off by Stephen's seething glare. So good was the banter between them, so foolish and naive did JJ present, in contrast to Stephen's smug confidence, that people were fighting each other to stake money against the arrogant magician and feed off the young rustic's good luck. Less than five minutes into the big race, though, the crowd dispersed and swarmed against the railings that bordered the racetrack or piled onto the array of vehicles that had parked up in the central enclosure, snatching every accessible viewing point.

"You were late!" barked McNamara as he gathered up his accoutrements.

"What matter, Stephie?"

McNamara glowered at the young lad's sudden familiarity.

"That was a great session! We cleaned up!"

"We were lucky."

"Not luck, Stephie. Pure skill, boy, pure skill. We made a killing!"

"There was more money to be made. We needed to make hay before the sun went behind the clouds!" said Stephen, indicating the crowds now gripped by the race.

Even the most uninterested day tripper was transformed the moment the starter raised his flag. Everyone bet on the National, some thinking they knew more than the bookmakers and tipsters; some going on the scores of tips that hummed along the grapevine in the hours leading up to the race; some picking a horse's name that held some significance for them, or owner's colours they liked; some simply sticking a pin in the race card.

"And my name is Stephen, all right?"

JJ was suitably chastened. "All right, Stephen," he said, surveying the scene as the eleven horses pounded around the track, cheered on by the huge crowd of spectators. "Sorry. You're right. I understand."

Inside though, JJ was still feeling like the tallest, luckiest, happiest man in Fairyhouse. He had never felt so self-assured and confident before and he was determined to feel like this again and again and again. Not only was he more certain than ever where his destiny lay, but he felt he knew now exactly how to go about reaching it.

"Not a bother. We'll settle up after the race," Stephen replied with a wink.

By the time JJ had wrestled and elbowed his way through the crowd to find a decent spot at the railings, the horses were just galloping past to begin their second and final circuit in the three-mile race. The thunderous pounding of hooves was exhilarating. The horses gasped and snorted for breath as each one strained to give his all. JJ had memorised the names and numbers from the bookmakers' boards and could tell that the field was being led by Turkish Maiden, who was well clear and going at a ferocious pace. He could just make out numbers 3 and 4, Punch and Civil War, in the main bunch, the jockeys in orange with grey arm bands and scarlet with a green sash respectively. Then he spotted Ballyneety's number 8 towards the back of the field, in a group of three, jockey in black with yellow sleeves. These were a few lengths off the pace, and Ballyneety looked well below par, already almost spent. The red-capped jockey struck him with his crop several times, hard.

Whether from fear, desperation or pride, the animal dug deep and made another tremendous surge as they thundered past. Then JJ lost sight of the field as it moved behind the crowd and around the first sweeping bend.

When they came into view again, Ballyneety had somehow managed to make contact with the main group and was nestling against the inner rail in joint seventh, just behind the sky blue and crimson hoop of All Sorts. The battle was beginning to ratchet up as they approached the next fence and the gap to the leader had closed. They were still going at a fierce clip and he could see Punch struggling to stay on the pace, as Ollie had predicted, while Civil War was moving up from sixth to fifth. The pace-maker, Turkish Maiden, hit the solid birch obstacle hard. The brown mare's knees buckled and her head dipped, but the jockey managed to keep her on her feet and himself on her back, through a combination of strength and amazing dexterity. His feat was acknowledged by a chorus of cheers;

"Good man Lynn!"

"Willie Lynn. Great jockey."

"The man's a miracle worker."

"His brother Jack is on All Sorts."

By then, the majestic Ruddygore had sailed over, followed closely by Punch and a tiring Earn Thought alongside All Sorts, with Sultan and Ballyneety neck and neck a length farther back. Ballyneety stumbled on landing, however, and lost a bit of ground.

"What the fuck is wrong with that horse?" cried a desperate punter.

JJ bit his lip.

The excitement was intense, the sense of expectation palpable, and the volume rose exponentially, as each punter cheered on his or her chosen steed and swore at every mistake made. JJ soaked up the atmosphere.

Then a flash of green on the other side of the track caught his eye. Was that Sergeant O'Connor he'd seen? He followed the imposing figure for a moment until it stopped, turned and seemed to stare straight at JJ. Now he could see for sure that it was the irrepressible policeman, straining, it seemed, to confirm his sighting maybe. JJ ducked behind a couple of punters, confident that he had avoided detection on this occasion. He shimmied, rose on tiptoes and glanced to and fro, as he attempted to follow the fortunes of his horse and track O'Connor's movements. He lost sight of the sergeant in the crowd a few times but he was aware that the policeman was heading in the direction of the winning post. That was that then. He knew the man had an interest in betting, so presumably he was searching out the best vantage point from which to watch his horse cross the line. JJ sighed with relief and turned his attention to the race again.

Just as JJ located the field, the distinctive red cap of Ballyneety disappeared from view as the horse went crashing out of the race. The horse's tired body had ploughed through the next fence and collapsed under the astonished jockey, causing horse and rider to tumble several times before coming to a stop in two separate heaps of flesh and bone, over twenty yards beyond the obstacle. Once the rest of the field had jumped clear of them, the jockey got gingerly to his feet, but the horse remained still. JJ was concerned for Ballyneety and distraught for Ollie. After what seemed like an eternity, the gelding raised his head and thrashed about desperately, in an attempt to get back up, and eventually made it onto his feet, helped by the jockey and a course attendant, but he looked distressed and was limping badly. JJ spotted Ollie sprinting along the rail. His heart went out to his friend.

Then his attention turned to a commotion down by the winning post and he spotted Sergeant O'Connor again. Apparently oblivious to the events unfolding on the track, he was remonstrating with two course attendants who were refusing to permit him to cross the track. O'Connor's head jutted forward like a bull's, as if he might just charge through regardless, but the attendants seemed equally intent on blocking his progress. Indeed, he would be taking his life in his hands were he to attempt to cross the track right now, as close to ten tons of horse flesh would soon be thundering past that very spot at a rate of knots, and would mow down anything in its path. Again, JJ felt secure, and who was to say it was him the sergeant was after in any case? He kept one eye on the policeman, nonetheless, and the other on the race.

Within seconds, a combination of hierarchy of needs, the law and brute force prevailed, though, and JJ watched the sergeant burst past the two men and through the unlocked gate and cause great hilarity among the surrounding spectators as he waddled and stumbled across the freshly rutted turf. About a furlong beyond this cartoonish scene, the thoroughbreds loomed into view again, as the field approached the final bend.

JJ was gripped again, shouting, clenching his fists and jumping, too busy to give the sergeant his full attention. With only three fences left to jump, the battle for position was at its most intense. An exhausted

Turkish Maiden was just about holding on to the lead. Remarkably, Punch had edged into second, ahead of a valiant Ruddygore, with Civil War well placed on their heels. Earn Thought continued to struggle in joint fifth, alongside a spritely All Sorts, ridden by Willie Lynn's brother. So, apart from Punch's surprisingly strong run, the race was going exactly as Ollie had forecast. JJ was confident that Civil War seemed full of running and, nestled against the inner rail, was perfectly positioned to make his move. As they approached the fence, the only change was that All Sorts had moved into fifth on his own, ahead of a fast-fading Earn Thought, who had given his all. One of the back-markers cantered off to the side towards the exit to the stables, his day's work done too.

"Come on Civil War! Come on, yourself. Good lad!" roared JJ.

He was distracted again by the sight of Sergeant O'Connor, remonstrating now with the course officials on JJ's side of the track. Given the proximity of the field of thoroughbreds, they were unlikely to show much resistance. The sergeant seemed to glance in JJ's direction once or twice, but surely he couldn't pick him out in this crowd? JJ slid behind a couple of cheering punters, just to be sure, and continued to concentrate on the race, peering above shoulders and between arms as required.

The lead horses were in a bunch now, so how they jumped the next fence would be critical. Urged on by their riders and the cheering spectators, they all sailed over, bar All Sorts that is. Put off by a sudden, cynical move off the rails by Civil War, he hit the fence hard and his legs buckled. The jockey, Jack Lynn, slid down the horse's neck and was hanging on by his fingertips. His brother Willie, coming up behind on stable mate Turkish Maiden, responded instinctively. He pulled alongside, stretched out his left arm and gave his brother the leverage he needed to get back into the saddle. An audible, spontaneous "Ooooh!" echoed through the crowd, as Jack Lynn steadied himself again and drove his mount forward with a couple of sharp swipes of his crop. Both brothers had lost valuable ground and it looked like their race might be over. Civil War had made his move off the rail and was on level terms with Punch, who was giving his all on his inner, and a weakening Ruddygore on his outer.

JJ, all thoughts of Sergeant O'Connor banished from his mind, was leaping, screaming and beating the air with his fists, as the horses approached the final fence and his bet, his wonderful, destiny-fulfilling wager was within seconds of coming good. Then every muscle in his body tensed as Civil War mistimed his final leap and ploughed through the obstacle. The jockey seemed to have anticipated this and was able to stay solid in the saddle, but the jump had winded the horse and cost him ground. Ruddygore and Punch remained as they were, while All Sorts, Jack Lynn having piloted him brilliantly over the last, came alongside and slotted neatly into the gap left by Civil War. So they galloped down the home straight, all well and truly off the bridle, under pressure from their riders and straining for the finish line. The valiant young Ruddygore was losing ground with every stride and Punch, although out on his feet, was pushing for all he was worth. But All Sorts was easing ahead and looking relatively comfortable, while Civil War was driving with all his strength to stay with him.

JJ, apoplectic with joy, anxiety, excitement and fear, was shouting himself hoarse as he watched his horse battle it out with the less fancied All Sorts and a valiant Punch somehow managing to stay close.

"Come on, Civil War! Come on, boy! Come on!"

The finish line just wasn't coming quickly enough, though, and All Sorts seemed to be cruising. But JJ refused to accept that.

"Come on, Civil War! You have it! You have it, boy!"

With less than a hundred yards to go, Civil War was being squeezed out, stuck between the rails and a fresher-looking All Sorts.

"Come on, boy, come on! COME ON!"

Then, as if the tension in an elastic band had suddenly been released, All Sorts, with beautiful, long, fluid strides, sprinted clear of the others to win comfortably, by several lengths. Punch, who had run an amazing race, given what Ollie had said of him, held on to second place, ahead of a resurgent Turkish Maiden, who battled it out with Civil War for third and fourth.

The horses galloped past JJ's vantage point in a flash of sky blue, orange, dark blue and scarlet, before slowing to a stop further down the track. Being fifty yards or more from the post, JJ didn't have the best view of the finish, but it was clear from the deflation of those who had been cheering Civil War and the elation of those who were still cheering All Sorts that the latter had indeed won the day. JJ collapsed onto the railing, exhausted and disappointed. The enormity of what had happened slowly sank in. He hadn't simply not won the fortune he had expected to but had lost virtually everything he had earned over the past two days, plus he now owed Stephen McNamara one whole pound! Worse still, he had also caused Stephen and Frankie Ronan, to lose a considerable portion of their own earnings. Not that he should have to accept the entire blame for that. He had tried to keep the information from them. They had forced it out of him and out of Ollie. He doubted they would see it like that, though.

Then he thought he caught a glimpse of Sergeant O'Connor being swung around in a sort of victory headlock, in the midst of a wild scrummage of jubilant punters, celebrating with uncouth abandon. Yet another reason to judge discretion the better part of valour and flight the only practical option. He tried to bury his bitter disappointment and gather his thoughts as he pushed and shrugged his way through the crowd, not entirely sure where he was going to go or how.

Acting purely on instinct and thanking his lucky stars that Stephen and Frankie were nowhere to be seen, JJ slipped furtively between two canopied stalls. He scurried towards the far side of the track, away from the grand stands, the entrance and all the danger that awaited him there. He passed behind the whiskey tent, forgetting that he had arranged to meet Peggy there, then around an empty horse-drawn wagon. He was checking back over his shoulder when he almost ran straight into Stephen McNamara.

"Jesus! You frightened the life out of me, Stephen."

"Did I?"

"That was some magic trick, appearing out of nowhere like that," JJ said, and he managed a giddy laugh.

McNamara didn't laugh. "Where you going, JJ?"

"Ehm. Nowhere. Just. I was just . . . going to take a piss."

"Off you go, then. Don't let me stop you." And he leaned against the wagon waiting, mar dhea, for JJ to relieve himself against the wheel.

"Ach, no. Sure I'm grand now."

"Are you? Well I'm not fucking grand, JJ. In fact I'm as far away from fucking grand as it's possible to be right now, JJ!"

"Right." He wished he wouldn't keep repeating his name like that.

McNamara took a step closer. "What the fuck happened, JJ? Civil

War? A dead cert? Couldn't be beaten?"

"It's not my fault, Stephen."

"Then whose fucking fault is it?"

"That's what I was told."

"I've lost a hell of a lot of money because of you and your fucking information!"

"I know. I know. I lost too, Stephen."

Tiny bubbles of white spittle were foaming at the corners of McNamara's mouth and he was pointing a sharp finger in JJ's face. "Fuck you and what you lost. What are you proposing to do about my fucking money?"

"What can I do?"

"Pay me back, you fucking óinseach!"

"But I have nothing, Stephen!"

"Me too, Sooooey."

JJ turned sharply. Frankie had crept right up behind him.

"This is all I have in the world, Frankie," he pleaded, taking out a fistful of busking coppers from his jacket pocket.

"You stupid fucking bogger!" said Frankie. He swung his tightly clenched fist but JJ anticipated and dodged the blow. The hammer of a fist swung over JJ's head and smashed instead into McNamara's jaw. The magician roared and fell back against the wagon. Frankie winced too with the pain of the mistimed blow and stumbled off balance. JJ stuffed the loose change back in his pocket, ducked under and around Frankie, pushed him onto McNamara before racing around the wagon and back in the direction of the whiskey tent. Just as he rounded the corner of the tent, the bould Sergeant O'Connor emerged from a fruitless search within, to find himself face to face with none other than his elusive fugitive.

"Well! You little fucker. You'll not get away this time." O'Connor took a stride forward.

JJ took a stride back and turned to flee, but a fuming Frankie was fast approaching from that direction, Magic McNamara staggering behind, holding his jaw.

"Shit! All right, Sergeant, you've got me," he said, holding his wrists out in front of him.

"You're damn right, I have." He stepped forward, his arm outstretched to grab JJ by the collar, his midriff unprotected.

"Sorry about this."

The sergeant flashed a quizzical look as JJ swung his right boot and caught the policeman full in the groin. O'Connor doubled over, groaning in pain, grasped his privates and slumped to his knees. JJ leapfrogged the policeman, just as the other two arrived at the whiskey tent. Frankie was athletic enough to leap over the slumped obstacle but McNamara ran headlong into it. JJ was as quick a runner as Frankie, and younger, so he was able to maintain his lead but, recalling how his horse had been undone in the race, he wasn't taking anything for granted. He wove a haphazard route through the crowd but failed to shake off Frankie. Then an opportunity presented itself in the form of a large, slightly denser group around a bookmaker's stand up ahead. He roared at the top of his voice to draw attention to himself.

"Woohoo! Come on, All Sorts!"

The crowd turned to look.

"I'm a rich man because of you!" he bragged.

The crowd cheered spontaneously and JJ threw his fistful of coins in the air. As the coins descended, men, women and children swarmed, anticipating a windfall. They jostled and pushed, scraped and gouged to get at the scattered lucre. Frankie couldn't adjust quickly enough to avoid running right into the midst of the mayhem, which created enough of a diversion for JJ to get away. He continued to sprint towards the track and his less-preferred exit route, but it was his only option at this stage. He bounded over the inner railing like a race horse, stumbled across the rutted track and vaulted the outer railing before eventually coming to a stop, in relative safety, down the side of the wooden grand stand. Panting, he slumped and rested his hands on his knees, gulping to get his breath back. This day was not progressing at all as it was supposed to.

"There you are!"

What? Who was after him now? Had he not made good his escape, even for long enough to draw breath? He glanced up to see Peggy marching towards him, hands on hips.

"I'm beginning to think you're trying to avoid me, JJ McHale!"

"Peggy! No!"

"Where were you?"

"I was . . . at the whiskey tent," he said, suddenly remembering their arrangement. "I tried to find you beyond to tell you. We decided to move over here to the posh side. Too much competition the other side. Made good money too. You should've done the same."

"Maybe I should have. I certainly wouldn't have been any worse off."

"What's wrong, a leanna?" He looked away, hunched his shoulders and sighed.

Peggy took his face in her hands and looked him straight in the eye. "Nothing."

He couldn't hold her gaze. He was anxious that his pursuers might still locate him.

She pulled his face around so that he was forced to look at her again. "Don't treat me like a child, JJ."

"I'm not—"

"I think you're brilliant. You're great to be with. Jesus, it's not like I've kept it a secret. I thought you felt the same." She stopped abruptly, turning her statement into a question. One he had to answer. "Well?"

"I do. At least I did."

"And now?"

God! Why was he finding this so difficult? Just say yes, I do feel the same. Lie. That's what he'd always done and it had always worked. It's what they want to hear, isn't it? Not the truth. They don't want that. They want the right answer, cloaked in the appearance of truth. That would keep her happy for another while, until the next gap in their understanding appeared, a little wider next time, and thus it would continue until the gap became a chasm and the inexorable parting would happen naturally. Then her place would be taken by the next sweet-voiced, soft-complexioned, doe-eyed beauty that would inevitably present herself. That had been the pattern, the way it had been for as long as JJ could remember being physically and sexually attracted to women. But something was different this time. He didn't know what, but he was acutely aware that something had changed in him. It was probably all the stress the day had brought: the mishaps, mischances and miscalculations. His world was in a tailspin. It was like his blood had been infected by some strange malady and was flaring, galloping through his veins like a herd of febrile thoroughbreds. He needed to be alone for a while, get his breath back, clear his head, organise his thoughts and decide what to do next.

"You don't need to lie to me, JJ McHale. I'm not some silly, country girleen, you know."

"I know."

"And so you should. I love being with you and I'd love it to continue for a while but I didn't come up here looking for a man. I'm going to Dublin city, to take up a good job in the post office and make a bloody good life for myself, give myself a future I couldn't even dream of if I stayed below in the bogs of Leitrim!"

"Jesus, Peggy, you're amazing."

"And you're going to go off to England or America or wherever."

"Yes, I am. Yes!"

"So don't lie to me, lad."

"I'm not. It's just . . . I don't know what's going on. A lot has happened today."

He held her firmly by the shoulders, looked her straight in the eye.

" You're a fabulous girl but . . . I've drawn a bit of trouble down on myself."

"What trouble?"

"Well, a couple of things have got a bit out of hand, grown some horns. It's a long story, but I need to sort it all out. Then I'll come to you and we'll talk and I'll be able to tell you how I really feel. But not right now."

"All right, JJ, all right. Good luck to you, boy." She kissed him briefly, earnestly, on the lips. "If I see you again, great. If I don't, then so be it." Her smile was thin and wistful.

"Right, you fucking bogger, let's have this out once and for all!" Mickser and his four comrades stood full-square about thirty feet away. Mickser's bony fists were clenched, his eyes dark.

"Shit!"

Peggy turned to look at the tight group of Fusiliers then smiled broadly. "Ah will you look who it is. Mickser, isn't it?"

"Stay out of this, you!"

She walked up to Mickser, undaunted, providing a pretty and seductive line of defence for her erstwhile lover. "Stay out? Sure isn't it me that this is all over?" she asked rhetorically, caressing Mickser's arm, bringing her face close to his.

"Not anymore, a grá!"

"Come on, Mickser, you know it's me you want." She was kissing his cheek now, searching out his mouth.

"Get off!" He pushed her away but she clung on resolutely.

"Peggy!"

"Fucking whore!"

JJ seethed.

"Come on, Mickser, let's go somewhere quieter, show me what you're really made of."

She was tugging at Mickser's sleeve now. He was shaking her off, violently.

"Fuck off!"

He covered her face with his hand and pushed hard. She stumbled. JJ caught her before she fell. Mickser stepped forward. His comrades held back for now.

"Go, JJ! Run!" Peggy pleaded, a thin line of blood trickling from her nose.

"Come on, bogger, are you going to hide behind a girl's skirts?"

"Don't be an eejit, JJ. Get out of here while you can!"

Instead, JJ stepped forward and squared up to Mickser. "Look," he said evenly, "I have nothing against you. You started all this by being rude and insulting to this fabulous girl who's worth ten of you!"

He had barely got the final word out of his mouth when a deep roar caused both men to look to JJ's left.

"Stop! Now!" It was O'Connor. "In the name of the law!"

JJ looked back at Mickser but too late to see the right hook that smacked into his jaw. The blow sent him reeling backwards against the wall of the grand stand. He was stunned. His head was spinning. Through foggy eyes he watched the scene before him play out like some weird dream. Peggy leapt on top of Mickser, cursing and swearing like a drunken shawlie, scratching his face and gouging his eyes. Mickser was crying out, thrashing and flailing to get her off him, still intent on finishing the job he had started on JJ. His comrades, too, more cognisant of the police presence than Mickser, were trying to get the Amazon of a woman off their comrade's back. Then Sergeant O'Connor strode forward, imposing himself on the situation.

"Right! That's enough! I'll take care of this now! Stop, cease and desist!"

The tussle continued unabated, however, fuelled by Peggy's rabidness and Mickser's determination. Then there was an instant when JJ's head was sufficiently clear and his pursuers sufficiently distracted for him to slip away again. O'Connor realised this just as JJ did and grabbed him by the collar with his free hand.

"You stay right where you are! Now, the rest of ye desist!"

Mickser's friends tried to reason with him. JJ tried to encourage Peggy to stop. Mickser railed. Peggy squealed. O'Connor stretched and grabbed her by the shoulder with his free hand and attempted to wrench her off the soldier's back. Then the strange, incongruous tinkle of a couple of bicycle bells sneaked in through the noise of the melee followed by a sharp whistle and a shout that drew JJ's attention.

"Hey, young fella, are you with us now?"

Two men were hurtling towards them on bicycles, the young Fenian, Liamy, who had approached him earlier in the betting queue and a second man, older and thinner. JJ was gobsmacked. He turned towards the cyclists just as Peggy snarled loudly and bit into Mickser's ear. Mickser's pained response spun the tight group of Fusiliers, Peggy and policeman through ninety degrees, throwing everyone off balance so that the sergeant was forced to release his grip on JJ's collar and use his hands to stop him crashing against the side of the grand stand. By then the two bikes were alongside and had slowed enough for JJ to jump onto the cross bar.

"Come on, hop up!" shouted the thin, wiry man on the second bike.

JJ ducked under the sergeant's arm, kicked Mickser in the arse and hopped onto the bike, shouting, "Thanks, Peggy!"

"Go on, JJ!" she roared, having released her grip on Mickser's ear. Mickser's reflex caused the group to spin again, tumble against the sergeant and collapse in a heap on the ground.

JJ whooped loudly as his pilot lost his balance for an instant. The bike wobbled precariously, scattering a group of revelling punters and almost crashing against a stall near the exit.

The driveway from the racecourse to the main road, although stony, was flat, allowing them to build up a head of steam, before swinging right onto the roadway, with its smoother macadam surface. Thankfully the first half mile or so was downhill so they were able to pick up some speed before the first stiff hill. Liamy, on the lead bike, in his grey overcoat and black flat cap, was a butty sort of a fella, blocky, with big farmer's arms. He smiled and spoke to JJ like they were fast friends, and somehow JJ had a strong feeling that they would be. The battered old black bike that he himself was riding side-saddle pillion, reminded JJ of Bartley Comer's old boneshaker that had been his first means of escape. It was being pushed and steered by Micheál, an older man, maybe late thirties, beginning to lose his hair at the front. He was certainly a fit man, able to keep up with Liamy without it seeming to take any more out of him.

Liamy did the talking, quickly, breathlessly, the wind taking half his words, so that JJ was not much the wiser after his explanation of who they were, what they were about and where they were headed.

"Anyway, you're with us now, whether you like it or not."

His new fast friend seemed adamant, despite JJ's pleas to be left off in Ratoath or at the nearest train station. From what he could glean, that wasn't the plan. There was a plan, though, one that involved trains and railway tracks and comrades and the "commandant". This final title Liamy announced with added gravitas. As they pushed up the hill, JJ's pilot reminded him that after his run-in with Sergeant O'Connor, every RIC man in Meath would be on the lookout for him.

"If they don't get you, those army lads will."

Once they reached the top of the hill, they were able to freewheel down the other side and continue at an impressive pace for the next mile or so, into the village of Ratoath. The deserted streets looked bleak now that the throng had moved to the racecourse. Out the other side, they headed in an easterly direction. Due to the determined progress of the bikes, Micheál's pincer-like grip and the fact that his options were severely limited, JJ had little choice but to cling on tightly and enjoy the ride.

14

Skirmish

———•———

MICHEÁL WAS WARY AND WATCHFUL as they cranked steadily along the mostly flat, tree-lined roads. Liamy was relaxed and chatty, despite the efforts of the wind to silence him. He explained that Cathal O'Cofaigh, JJ's "cellmate" in the Hole in the Wall, was his captain but their commandant was a Kerryman, a schoolteacher and a bit of a poet. JJ tried to discover what he was commandant of but Liamy was vague. JJ wasn't sure if Liamy had misheard him or was just being guarded. It was clear, though, that they were ready and willing to follow this commandant wherever he led. JJ again tried to convey to whichever man would listen that he had no intention of following anyone or anything other than his dreams.

"Dreams?" echoed Liamy, laughing heartily and throwing his head back so that he almost swerved into the ditch. "You're beginning to sound like himself now!"

"Who?"

"The commandant! A great man for the dreams he is too."

This final remark drew an amused snigger from the otherwise pensive Micheál.

After another fifteen or twenty minutes, they had covered a further three miles and were approaching Rath Cross, according to Liamy's running commentary. The road they were on crossed the main road north out of Ashbourne to Slane and they slowed for the first time. Finally JJ would have an opportunity to jump ship, or bike, slip away and leave these two desperadoes to be led into whatever lunacy the commandant had in mind, while he set about finding his way into Dublin.

"Hauld up here a bit, a mhac," growled Micheál, and Liamy immediately swung his bike to the left, pulled on the brake and hopped off, all in one smooth movement that belied his unathletic physique. Micheál slowed cautiously, applying a pumping action to the brakes and dragging his foot along the ground. JJ was unable to judge their centre of gravity or his own equilibrium, so when they eventually did come to a stop and Micheál supported their weight on his straining left leg, JJ failed to counterbalance his pilot and fell backwards into Micheál's arms. The sudden, unexpected weight caused Micheál to stumble backwards himself and it took all his wiry strength to prevent the bike, himself and his passenger bumbling into the ditch in a heap. JJ's instincts kicked in, too, prompted by several colourful swear words from Micheál, and he managed to jump clear in time.

"Fucking óinseach," Micheál said.

"So this is it, then, Liamy?" JJ chimed, as he composed himself.

"It certainly is, my friend."

"The parting of the ways," JJ announced, smiling and extending a hand. "Well, it was nice knowing you."

"A bit early for that yet, young fella."

"Oh?"

"We're only stopping here to meet the others."

"The others?"

"Daoine ag teacht," shouted Micheál in a strange kind of stage whisper.

"That's probably the lads," Liamy called back, walking into the middle of the road to get a better view to the north.

"Bí cúramach, ya feckin' eejit!" Micheál said, using his odd stage whisper again as he crouched down against the corner of the wall and pulled out a bloody revolver. JJ was beginning to wonder what the hell he had stumbled into. Men going around on bicycles with guns in their trouser belts?

"Take it easy, Micheál," Liamy said, still standing in the middle of the road and straining to see who or what was approaching.

JJ was alongside him now and also peering into the dullish light from the north. It was clear from the dust that it was a vehicle of some sort, apparently horse-drawn; there was certainly no engine to be heard.

JJ turned to look in the opposite direction, into the sun. By his reckoning that was roughly the direction in which lay Dublin. So it was reasonable to assume that the approaching vehicle was heading that way and could take him closer to his desired destination, if not right into the city itself. That would be a real stroke of luck. When he turned back, the approaching vehicle was close enough for JJ to distinguish its outline and confirm that it was definitely horse-drawn.

"It's them, Micheál. Has to be," Liamy announced.

"Is the motorcar not with them?"

"What motorcar?"

"Dr Hayes's. I can't hear it."

"Maybe he's not with them?"

"Well it'd be very surprising if he wasn't, Liamy. And anyway, the commandant is definitely with them and I don't hear his motorcycle either." Micheál sounded anxious and was still crouching for cover in the corner of the ditch on the western approach to the crossroads.

JJ peered to get a better view and saw now that the men approaching were in uniform, a dark uniform, that same dark green he had been fleeing from all weekend. "Are your boys in uniform, Liamy?" he asked.

"Maybe one or two. Most of us just wear our own clothes."

"Those lads are definitely in uniform."

"Are you sure?" Liamy was squinting. "Hmm, well, the commandant and Dr Hayes will be in uniform," he mumbled.

JJ sensed Liamy's confidence wavering.

Micheál shouted urgently, "Get off the fucking road, you pair of amadáns, it's the fucking RIC!" No stage whisper this time.

"What?"

That would not be good for JJ.

"No. Whisht!"

Liamy's hearing compensated for his poor vision. JJ could only hear the faint pounding of horse's hooves and the rattle of the steel-bound wheels of the horse-drawn sidecar, close enough now to remove any doubt that it contained five rifle-toting RIC officers, flanked by a further four on bicycles.

"I hear an engine!" shouted Liamy. "A motor car engine!"

JJ turned to look south again and could see now what Liamy had heard. A cloud of dust betrayed the approach of a well-tuned motor car.

"It's Dr Hayes and the commandant!" said Liamy. Delighted, he began to run in the direction of Ashbourne and the approaching reinforcements.

JJ followed instinctively, moving towards possible salvation and away from probable arrest and incarceration.

"For fuck's sake, take cover!" The panic in Micheál's voice as he roared at his two callow accomplices shocked the youths into reassessing the situation.

Time seemed to slow almost to a standstill. Liamy turned to see the police cavalcade bearing down on them. The faster-moving Volunteer cavalcade was closer, too, and they could see now that it comprised Dr Hayes's burgundy Oxford bullnose two-seater, the commandant on his tan-coloured New Hudson motorcycle, with several cyclists following at a distance.

Several shots rang out, like thunderous whip cracks. JJ couldn't tell who had fired them – the policemen, the Volunteers, Micheál or all of the above.

"Take cover!" shouted Liamy, propelling JJ with a shove to the back of his shoulder, which only served to knock him off balance as he strained to ascertain the closest point of safety. Liamy galloped and sprang headlong into the ditch, his frame again belying his ability to cover the ground as sprightly as a whippet. JJ's normally nimble legs seemed to fill with liquid as he stumbled, tripped and tumbled awkwardly into the same ditch, practically landing on top of Liamy and twisting his ankle in the process. There was silence for an instant. Time froze.

Then all hell broke loose.

JJ had never seen or heard anything like it before, never mind been smack bang in the middle of it. Shots rang out from north, south and west. There was shouting and panicked cries. Engines roared, wheels skidded on the stony road surface and brakes squealed as men and machines were forced to do things they had never had to do before.

JJ managed to get his head just above the top of the ditch to witness the RIC horse rearing wildly, terrified by the whistle, crack and ping of bullets all around him. The driver, alone now in the sidecar, struggled to keep control of the animal. JJ could make out another three constables shouldering their rifles and taking unreliable cover behind the shifting vehicle. It took him a moment longer to notice the fourth policeman lying motionless on the road beside the wheeling sidecar. The driver, clearly deciding it was best to cut his losses, jumped clear then tumbled and collapsed in a heap on the side of the road. Moments later, though, he shook himself back to life and took cover behind a roadside water pump, revolver in hand.

The four RIC cyclists had continued in the direction of the rebel motor car. When they got as close to the Oxford bullnose as they dared, they spun their bikes off the road, two to either side, and sprang athletically into the ditch. By then their fellow constables were ranged around the unsteady sidecar and the terrified horse, firing at the three occupants of the motor car, who were using the vehicle, stalled at an acute angle across the centre of the road, as a shield. The commandant had driven past the car, towards and past the RIC sidecar, steering his motorcycle with his left hand and firing his revolver with his right. About thirty yards beyond the policemen, he swung the motorcycle around and rode back again in a similar fashion. This all proved too much for the police horse, which bolted down the only real escape route open to him, the fourth road in the junction. This left the RIC constables exposed and forced them to dash for cover wherever they could. A second was wounded in the leg before he could make it to the relative safety of the ditch. The bolting horse also created a diversion that allowed the Volunteer cyclists to dismount and take up strategic positions in the ditches on both sides of the road and at the western corner of the crossroads, where Micheál still held his original position.

In the midst of this mayhem, a shocked and terrified JJ was cowering in the ditch, without a gun, without a cause, without any preparation whatsoever for what was unfolding. What of the men around him? They seemed practised, as if this was not the first time they had fired a shot at a fellow human being, the first time they had been shot at themselves. But this was no army, these were clearly not professional soldiers. They were Liamy and his friends, farmers, labourers, shopkeepers. Surely they too were trembling, living on their nerves. JJ couldn't tell but he was certainly more frightened than he had ever been in his life. He also sensed that there was an inexplicable, infectious exhilaration that went with being in a theatre of battle, fearful that his life could end but excited by his very survival.

It was also painful when several Volunteers came hurtling into the ditch on top of them. One landed on JJ's injured ankle, causing him to roar. Another smacked against the back of his head, driving him face first into the dirt and filling his open mouth with clay and acrid blood from a split lip. Almost instantly he was surrounded by blasts of gunfire at his ear. A bullet whistled so close to his neck that he was sure he must have been hit. He screamed again and put his hand to his neck to stanch the flow of blood, only to find the merest of scratches. A pistol was shoved into his hand and a fierce voice with a country accent barked an aggressive command.

"Stop fucking screaming and start fucking shooting!"

Oh dear Lord, how exquisite and at once awful to discover that the owner of the gruff voice and feral attitude was none other than Molly. His Irish Molly. His Juliet. Here she was again, straddling him in the confines of this shallow roadside ditch, her open raincoat revealing a military-style uniform beneath, her wonderful ringlets scrunched and trapped beneath a misshapen fedora. She turned away and began firing. This was no meek Juliet. This was a terrier, a tigress, firing her weapon as if possessed and roaring at JJ to do the same.

"Are you wanting to be killed?" she roared. "Fire!"

He attempted to explain quickly that his presence there was accidental, not intentional. He tried to justify his deep-seated pacifism, to query what the hell was going on anyway. But this was no place for debate. There was no time for discussion. This Molly made crystal clear when she turned her back on her antagonists for a moment to reload the magazine of her rifle.

"If you don't stop whinging and start fucking shooting, either they'll kill you or I will!"

Left with no option, JJ raised his newly acquired pistol shakily above the brim of the ditch, keeping his head well down, and fired a shot as instructed, but harmlessly into the air. The recoil hurt his wrist. He massaged it quickly before firing again, this time nestling his hand on the grassy verge to support it. He couldn't even see what he was firing at, didn't want to see. He didn't know much about guns but felt sure he would need to be much closer to his adversaries to do them any serious injury with a pistol. Just to be sure though, he continued to fire upwards, in no direction in particular and at no particular target.

"There you are, a chara." Liamy rolled alongside him. "Good to see you're all right."

"Jesus, Liamy, what the hell is going on?"

"Don't know in fuck. This wasn't part of the plan. But we'll need to drive them back, so we can get out of here and regroup."

"Regroup? I thought you were going to get me to Dublin."

"You don't want to be in Dublin now, a mhac."

"Yes I do!" JJ glared open-mouthed at his new "comrade". He didn't understand, and before Liamy could explain, a bullet whistled past their heads and thumped into the grassy ditch behind them. "Jesus Christ! Jesus fucking Christ, Liamy!"

Something inside JJ snapped. He stood up, his head and abdomen above the ditch, and fired four or five shots in quick succession, snarling as he did. "This is not my fight. This is not my fight!" Then his pistol clicked. Empty.

Liamy and Molly dragged him back down into the safety of the ditch.

"Get down, you fool," Molly snarled with a curl of her lip.

"It's mad, isn't it? Have you ever felt this alive before?" said Liamy.

"Are you not scared?"

"I'm shitting myself!"

"Then why? You don't have to be here. We don't!"

"But we are, a chara. So it's kill or be killed, isn't it? Simple as that, JJ."

Liamy put his rifle butt to his shoulder, raised his head above the ditch and fired a single round, then he was back down again.

"Fucking Mausers," he growled, as he loaded another cartridge into the exposed chamber. "Useless."

"No it's not, Liamy. It's not that simple at all!" JJ shouted.

Liamy raised his eyebrows and grimaced, then swung his rifle to his shoulder to fire another shot. He was up and down like a yo-yo, choosing his targets carefully, trying to make every precious shot count.

JJ had noticed the slight petulant whine in his own voice. He had sounded like a child lost in the dark. His hands were shaking. The noise was deafening now. If he believed anything his priests and teachers had told him, he would have prayed, prayed hard to their God to be rescued from this horrific nightmare and delivered safely into the city so that he could get back on track again, reset his compass, set a new course if he had to. He looked up again just as Molly looked down at him, a hardness in her gaze, her face drawn and strained. Her eyes, though, the deep green gulf of them, mirrored his own sense of loss, fear and confusion. For a brief instant, he thought he read pity there. Not the patronising pity of someone who feels superior but the genuine empathy of a fellow traveller. But in a flicker, as if he had stumbled on a private, intimate scene, the curtain was drawn and all became hard and cruel again.

"For God's sake, man, this is no place for snivelling boys!" she growled as she dropped a handful of bullets at his feet. Then she turned away again to face the firing line, her efficient killing machine clasped in her delicate hands.

JJ was enraged. Her callousness disgusted him. But he was embarrassed too. He was behaving like a little boy. But why should he be ashamed? This was a perfectly natural reaction to death and needless killing. He wiped his sleeve across his face, picked up the bullets Molly had dropped for him and reloaded the revolver. It occurred to him to just drop the gun and walk away, maybe hold his arms aloft in surrender, face his punishment as a common criminal. He was not here by choice. But that was ridiculous. He knew it. He was unlikely to get more than a few steps without being struck by a hail of bullets from one side or the other. He could just lay down the gun and sit there, though, in this impromptu trench and wait for the horror to pass and his fate to reveal itself. That would cause him some embarrassment, yes, if the Volunteers managed to repel the attack, even an odd sense of guilt for letting down his newfound "comrades", who had rescued him from certain arrest and become, well, his friends. But that was something he had experienced before and certainly something he had the self-confidence now to deal with. It might also mean spending some time in jail if the RIC came out on top. That would be difficult but not impossible, and maybe, before a judge, he could explain how he had been mistakenly arrested to begin with. But there was something else happening in his body that he couldn't explain. He felt a deep, strong desire or need to please Molly, a compulsion to win her approval. He couldn't understand why. Yes, he was used to doing things to make women happy. But that was just the fleeting kind of happiness that would endear him for long enough to achieve his own gratification. So without thinking any further, he allowed instinct to take over. He drew in a deep breath, cocked his pistol and turned to face the firing line.

Another bullet whizzed past his face and hit something close to him with a dull, soft thud like a fist thumping a pillow. He heard the pained cry just before he turned to see Liamy fall backwards into the ditch, his arms splayed, his rifle spinning through the air. There was a wide-eyed, startled look on the young Volunteer's face. Jesus! Was he dead?

"Oh, Christ fucking Jeeesus!" Liamy said through tightly clenched teeth.

"Are you all right?" was the best JJ could manage. He slid down by his friend's side.

"Does it look like I fucking am?"

JJ was flapping like a startled goose.

"Oh Christ! That is fucking sore. Jeeesus!" Liamy closed his eyes tightly for a moment.

"Where did they get you?"

"Shoulder, I think." He turned his head towards his left arm.

JJ lifted the flap of his friend's coat and was nauseated by the sight of the thick, burgundy liquid that was oozing from a small hole just above where people put their hand when they're indicating their heart. The lad's shirt was already soaked and his jacket was reddening quickly too.

"Jesus, Liamy, Jesus!"

"Do something, JJ. Do something!"

Now it was Liamy who was like a lost child. JJ snapped into action.

"Yeah, yeah, of course. Jesus!"

JJ pressed his hand on the seeping hole and started calling for help, shouting that his friend had been shot and that he needed help. Now! Liamy told him to calm down, that no one could come while they were still pinned down. He suggested a hanky or something to stop the bleeding. JJ hadn't the heart to tell him that a hanky would be useless, so fierce was the flow.

"Here." Molly threw JJ her woollen scarf, hardly taking her eyes from the combat. JJ gathered the scarf into a ball and pressed it tightly against the wound.

Liamy grabbed JJ's wrist and stared into his eyes. "I'm not dying, JJ, am I? I don't want to die, a mhac." He was almost whimpering.

JJ felt sorry for him but was relieved that he wasn't the only one who was struggling to hold back the tears. "Shut up, you óinseach," he said. "You haven't a notion of . . ." He couldn't bring himself to say the word. "It's only an auld scratch. You'll be fine."

Liamy smiled thinly. JJ noticed a thin film of perspiration on his white face. Liamy winced and groaned through gritted teeth.

"Please!" JJ shouted. "We need a doctor. Is there a doctor, for fuck's sake?"

Liamy tightened his grip on JJ's wrist. He groaned again. His breathing was shallow, rasping. JJ winced at the pain in his own wrist and this time he did pray, silently, an old prayer in Irish that his mother used to say.

"They're pulling back! They're pulling back!"

The words were being shouted, whispered, passed along the line, and as the information filtered through, the firing abated.

The exposed police squad was outnumbered and the route to the nearby barracks a couple of hundred yards to the south was cut off. They had been given a faint glimmer of hope when three armed policemen had appeared at the wall of the barracks, drawn out by the sound of gunfire. These had opened fire on the Volunteers from the rear. It was in this unexpected exchange that Liamy had been wounded. But once the Volunteers turned some of their fire onto the barracks wall, the commandant doing another drive by on his motor cycle, the policemen quickly retreated to the safety of the barracks. With this hope extinguished, the RIC squad out on the road decided that retreat was the more sensible option. They used the ditches and hedgerows as cover and left their two dead colleagues to the mercy of the rebel bandits.

As soon as the police squad had withdrawn, the commandant barked an order to regroup, before firing up his motorcycle and heading east along the Garristown Road. The Volunteers emerged from cover with swift, efficient caution. This kind of thing they had clearly rehearsed over weeks, perhaps months, of drilling and training. They moved out onto the road and stealthily along its verges, guns loaded and trained on any potential points of ambush. Several walked backwards, forming a rearguard. The men to the fore checked the RIC fatalities and divested them of their weapons and ammunition, while the others remounted their bicycles. JJ had continued to call for help until a doctor finally made his way over to them. The long face, the prominent nose. JJ recognised him instantly as the man who'd stolen Molly away from him at the races. He didn't seem to recognise JJ.

"Where are you hit, Liam?"

"Left shoulder, Dr Hayes."

Dr Hayes was quite flippant about Liamy's wound, which was disconcerting at first but ultimately strangely reassuring. If he wasn't worried, then neither should they be.

"Thanks, JJ. But Jesus it hurts."

"Hold still," barked the doctor. "We don't have time to linger here. I'll patch you up for now and do a more permanent job when we get back to base camp."

Happy that the doctor had the situation in hand, JJ hobbled back onto the road, his ankle quite swollen now. He limped over to the doctor's car and rested against it to survey the scene. Most of the Volunteers, Molly among them, had slung their rifles over their shoulders, remounted their bicycles and were ready to head off. One of the dead policemen lay in full view on the road where the sidecar had initially come to a stop. He was supine, arms and legs outstretched, like a child might lie to feign death in some game. But he was feigning nothing. A pool of dark, thick liquid, more like oil than blood, had congealed around and under his torso. It looked like he'd been shot directly through the heart. How vulnerable and vital an organ it was. JJ was overwhelmed for a moment by a powerful sense of the finality of death. He had seen death before of course, had personal experience of it, not least his mother's untimely passing. But he had never seen it happen before, to a human being, and in such a violent fashion. Now all he could think of was the mother or wife or children who were waiting for their son, husband or father to return, unaware that they would never see him alive again, never speak to him, touch him, caress him, kiss him or feel his warm, reassuring embrace. JJ limped a bit closer, drawn like a moth to a flame, seduced and enchanted by the enormity of it all.

When he got halfway, he stopped again on seeing the second dead policeman off to the side but closer to him. He had obviously fallen forward in the same direction he had been running when he was shot.

His face had hit the ground before he'd had time to get his hands down to break his fall, and the ditch had halted his forward momentum too abruptly for the rest of his body that was following behind. The result was grotesque, absurd and almost comical. His face was turned towards JJ, his eyes gaping wide, his tongue lolling like a panting dog. His torso had concertinaed up around his neck like a massive, posthumous shrug of the shoulders; his knees were doubled up, his arse raised in the air. Before he could stop himself, JJ was wishing for a more dignified pose in his own dying moment. He quickly cast that and all thoughts of death from his mind with a shake and an involuntary shudder.

There was urgent activity around him again. Micheál was shouting the order to pull out in two separate groups and make for Garristown to pick up supplies, then continue on to Rogerstown. Dr Hayes had patched up Liamy and helped him to his car. Liamy was waving at JJ now and grinning ridiculously. The doctor had given him "something for the pain". As JJ rejoined his friend, the bicycle convoy pulled out. He noticed the doctor stoop over the first of the RIC corpses. He wondered why. Clearly they were beyond any medical attention. Dr Hayes dropped to one knee, closed the man's eyes and made a rudimentary sign of the cross. His lips moved quickly and silently for a moment.

"Are you crazy, man?" Micheál shouted from the rear of the departing convoy. "Leave the fuckers be and get to hell out of here. His own can take care of all that."

"His own?" the doctor replied. "Can you not see? This man is Patrick Gormley from Navan. The boxer. So who might his own be, Micheál?"

Micheál shook his head dismissively, cranked his bike and set off in pursuit of the disappearing convoy. Dr Hayes moved quickly to the second corpse and repeated his dignified little ritual before returning to the car.

"Right, sonny, what are we going to do with you, then?"

It took JJ a second to realise that the doctor was speaking to him. The convoy was out of sight, Liamy was still grinning widely from the passenger seat of the doctor's car and an eerie silence had descended on the crossroads. Dr Hayes asked JJ to cycle Liamy's bike the twenty miles or so to Rogerstown. JJ assured him he couldn't even cycle it two miles with his ankle the way it was. There was no going anywhere, really, for him now. The doctor examined the injury, hemmed a little sceptically and assured JJ that a good soak in the cold seawater would see it right as rain again. At least the doctor had transport that would get him out of this place to the sea and a chance to draw breath, reassess things. JJ was also anxious to ensure that his new friend Liamy was going to be all right. The doctor hooked the bike onto the back of his car and squeezed JJ into the two-seater, with Liamy in the middle between the two of them. JJ grinned stupidly and talked gibberish for most of the hour it took them to drive to the base camp at Rogerstown, near Rush and the sea.

15

Tarry With Me in Green Woods

———*———

JJ HADN'T NOTICED THE DAY become duller, but now, as he waded in the cold saltwater that lapped against the beach at Rush, about fifteen miles north of Dublin, the sky was a mass of clouds and the grey light made even the golden sand look a bit worn and weary. Following the doctor's advice, he had taken off his shoes and holed socks, rolled up his trouser legs and was bathing his injured ankle in the chilly brine to reduce the swelling. It seemed to be working. Certainly the pain was not as intense. He had left Liamy with Dr Hayes, who had been delighted to inform his patient that the bullet had gone clean through. No surgical intervention would be required, which, he added gravely, was good news given their rudimentary supplies and mendicant living conditions. JJ had never heard some of those words before but got the gist of the doc's meaning from his earnest demeanour. Dr Hayes also admitted that there was probably significant ligament and muscle damage and the bullet may even have chipped a bone on its way through. So poor Liamy would be in pain for a few days and his movement restricted. He was unlikely to be of much use in battle, but he was determined nonetheless.

"As long as I have a hand fit to fire a pistol, I'll be there on the front line!"

The doctor praised his courage and commitment but recommended food and rest before making any rash decisions, adding that Liamy had lost a lot of blood. JJ too had wanted to endorse the doc's words and tell Liamy that he was insane to even contemplate taking any part in whatever fighting lay ahead. But he felt guilty for not being able to do more for him, so kept his counsel.

Now, alone in the water, JJ could reflect on the events of the past twenty-four hours. His luck had changed from bad to good to bad and back again so many times that he didn't know if he was coming or going. On the positive side, there was no going back. So he had to accept where fate had thrust him and keep heading in the direction he was still convinced his dreams and ambitions lay. As long as he was progressing and didn't allow himself to become disheartened, he would be fine. That strange, lonesome, homesick feeling was back again, though. If only he had someone to talk to, someone to offload his frustrations onto, that would help. Not that he'd ever had anyone like that back home in Sligo, not since his mother died at any rate. A large wave splashed up above his knees and soaked his trousers.

"God damn and blast you, you little fecker!"

The words were out of his mouth and blown away by the fresh sea breeze before he realised it was a phrase of his father's, especially when JJ had made a hames of some task or other. He even thought he had sounded like his father just then, railing at the sea that responded with another even livelier wave, which sent him scuttling ashore. No, God damn it, he would never turn into that man. Never!

When he looked up, his eye was drawn to the island lolling about two or three miles offshore. It looked sort of like a man, although the head was not well defined. He was floating on his back, his eyes closed, JJ imagined, and arms outstretched, allowing all his worries and cares to drift skyward, to be swallowed by the dark, tumbling clouds. He turned to face south, hoping for a view of the elusive city; not quite the city of gold but an important step on his way to El Dorado. All he could distinguish was a headland about six or eight miles away, where the shoreline curved out into the sea again, obscuring any land that lay beyond. Nothing about this adventure of his was proving easy or free from obstacles. He turned to his lolling-man island again and, with arms outstretched, raised his face to the darkening clouds, closed his eyes and unleashed a long, deep sigh. After a brief pause, eyes still shut, a tune floated onto his lips. He hummed it quietly at first, unsure which from his vast repertoire it was. Several bars in, the words began to dance about in his head and soon made their way onto his lips and out into the fresh, salty air.

It was on a summer's morning, all in the month of May
Down by the banks of Claudy, I carelessly did stray,
I overheard a maiden in sorrow to complain,
All for her absent lover that ploughed the raging main!

JJ kicked wildly through the sea water as he trumpeted the final line of verse one.

I stepped up unto her and gave her a surprise.
I own she did not know me, I being in disguise.
Hmm, hmm, hmm, hmmm [the words escaped him]
How far do you mean to wander this dark and weary night?

By the time he reached the jaunty chorus, his spirits had lifted and he was kicking the waves again, half skipping, half dancing and finally singing out at the top of his voice to the vast sea and the empty beach.

But do not trust your Johnny, for he's a false young man,
But do not trust your Johnny, for he'll not meet you here,
But tarry with me in green woods, no danger need you fear.

"That ankle doesn't seem to be giving you too much bother now."

JJ turned, startled by the voice. The next words of the song fell limply from his mouth until none emerged at all from the gaping hole between his nose and chin.

Molly was smiling broadly.

"What?" he grunted.

She was laughing now, at his sudden awkward shyness. He was stung that she would mock him like that but all sense of injury dissolved as he watched her laughter perform a miracle before his eyes. Her face broadened and opened, her eyes sparkled, her shoulders shook, her hair swung loosely about her head now that she carried the battered fedora in her hand.

"Oh, yes, the sea water."

"I see." She made a face that implied a sudden understanding that caused him to think she was ribbing him. She began to remove her own boots.

"Dr Hayes's advice."

"Ah, a very clever man."

She rolled up the trousers of her uniform, exposing her alabaster calves, and joined him in the water. He felt a tingle at the notion that the same water was lapping playfully against both his legs and hers.

"Yes," he said finally, and they paddled in silence.

Where had she come from? How had he not seen or heard her approach so that he could have been prepared, fit to match her quick, sharp wit? He looked about the beach to discover that it was no longer the deserted idyll it had been when he arrived. There were fifteen to twenty men, standing in groups of three or four. Some stood silently on the beach gazing out to sea; several lay on the sand imitating JJ's lolling-man island. Two men sat on the rocks. Many of them were smoking. The few who spoke did so in hushed, almost reverential tones. JJ sensed a solemnity about the silence, broken only by the swashing and shkittling waves and several squealing gulls. The beach had become a sort of open-air church.

He turned back to Molly who was watching the gentle but relentless waves wash against her legs. She looked up. Their eyes met as if for the first time. There was silence for a moment.

"So, where did you wash up from?"

"Me? Ehm . . ." He looked out at the sea and the island, as if she had meant the question literally. "I'm from Sligo."

"You're a long way from home, so."

"I was at the races."

"I know."

Silence.

"Well, it's a story and a half," he joked, trying to make light of it, "but things didn't quite work out as intended, then Liamy and Micheál just happened to be in the right place at the right time." He smiled, shrugged and nodded with a gesture that said, "So here I am now."

"And that's how you ended up in the wrong place at the wrong time."

"Yes," he said sheepishly. "Sorry."

He wasn't really sorry, though. It wasn't his fault he had ended up in the middle of a bloody skirmish. It wasn't his fault he wasn't a trained combatant. In fact, he wanted to tell her boldly, he had no interest whatsoever in battle of any sort and had only one cause – his own. He did feel guilty for adding to her difficulties and probably putting her life at risk.

"That kind of carry on is just not acceptable in the line of fire."

"I know, but—"

"I mean we were all bloody scared!"

"Were we? You didn't look frightened."

"I was terrified. Good God! It was the first time I'd ever . . . I mean Jesus Christ." Her shoulders hunched and she seemed to sigh, or maybe it was a sob.

"Are you all right?" He moved instinctively to put a hand on her shoulder.

She snapped bolt upright again and stepped back. "I'm fine!" The sudden backward step threw her off balance. She stumbled.

JJ continued his initial movement and managed to grab her by the hand to prevent her falling. She grabbed his other hand to restore her balance. Her hands were cold as ice but not unwelcoming. They stood for an instant, their hands still clasped. It was only seconds but she didn't let go. This would normally be the moment when it would happen. He would tilt his head a little to one side and gaze warmly into her eyes, clasp her hands a little more tightly. She would take a half step closer, tilt her head slightly in the opposite direction and slowly close her eyes as she brought her lips closer to his. They would kiss, gently at first but then more deeply, longingly, wrapped in each other's reassuring embrace. So he took the initiative, stepped closer, clasped her hands more tightly in his and slowly closed his eyes as he brought his lips –

Boom!

They both jumped with fright and looked to the west and the source of the blast. She snapped her hands back. The explosion had caused everyone on the beach to react. Those not standing leapt to their feet, instantly on guard, already battle-hardened. Was it a surprise attack, or was another Volunteer unit in action nearby?

"Jesus Christ! What the hell was that?" A thick plume of smoke rose from the railway viaduct further up the estuary, the main rail link between Dublin and Belfast.

Molly quickly regained her composure, now that it was clear what had happened. "We've blown up the railway. Stop reinforcements coming in from Belfast." She sat down on the sand, hurriedly putting on her socks and boots.

"Reinforcements? What the hell is going on here, Molly?"

She stopped still at the sound of her name.

It took JJ a couple of seconds to realise he had said it aloud, right in front of her.

"How do you know my name?"

"The racecourse. When we met. The doctor called you by name."

She thought for a second, seemed to recall the moment, then returned to her socks and boots.

"Sorry. I'm JJ, by the way." He held out his hand but realised immediately what a stupid, ill-timed gesture that was and withdrew it.

"There's a war on, JJ, in case you haven't noticed." She said his name with extra emphasis, like his teachers used to when he had misbehaved or asked a stupid question in class.

"I know that," he snapped defensively, "but that's in Europe. Is it coming here now?"

"No, you idiot. This is our war, an Irish war. Our strike for freedom!"

With that, she jumped to her feet and marched up the beach to where they had all thrown their bikes when they arrived. JJ was angry, embarrassed and confused.

The beach had emptied and a cavalcade of cyclists was forming on the road back to the farmhouse, their billet for the night.

"Well it's not my bloody war!" he shouted after her.

16

The Two Commandants

———•———

THE TEMPORARY BASE CAMP WAS situated in the grounds of an old two-storey farmhouse, set in a tiny valley less than a mile from the mouth of the estuary. The house was constructed of rough-cut stone, plastered front and back but with the stone on the gable ends exposed. The farmer still lived there with his wife and several young children. He was not an activist but was sympathetic to the cause, believing that his family might have a better, more prosperous, more Irish future were they governed by their own. His children played or performed chores in and around the farmyard. They were on their Easter holidays from nearby Corduff National School, the same school he'd gone to himself.

The Volunteers were billeted in shakedowns of straw in the outhouses. The walls were plastered with daub, sufficient to keep out serious draughts and comfortable enough for the animals. There were three of these, arranged in the courtyard and on either side of the main house. Any livestock had been let out to grass by this stage of the year, so the buildings were empty, apart from a clutch of hens and several temperamental geese. Nonetheless, with upwards of sixty men and four women to be catered for, conditions were cramped, although relatively warm and dry. The owner insisted that the leaders eat at his table and sleep under his roof. So Commandant Ashe, Adjutant Dr Hayes and Battalion Quartermaster Frank Lawless accepted graciously. There was also a corrugated-iron hay barn to the rear of the main house, but since it sat atop eight stout wooden posts, the lack of walls left it exposed to the elements. Not many of the men were happy to bed down there, especially when the rain came and the wind off the sea picked up.

And didn't the rain come! By the time JJ made it back, it had been drizzling steadily for about fifteen minutes, not heavily but enough to soak his hair and darken the top half of his coat. Although there was still light left in the day, the rest of the brigade, or whatever term they used for this motley crew of farmers, shopkeepers and labourers, had started to settle for the night. Some had taken up sentry duty in the area around the farmyard; others ate and got some sleep so that they could take over in several hours. So it would continue, at four-hourly intervals, until morning. Some food was being prepared in the house, pots of potatoes and loaves of bread, while other rations, brought by the men themselves or provided by Frank Lawless, were cooked over two large open fires in the centre of the courtyard. JJ could only imagine just how busy the same Frank Lawless had been that day and in the previous days and weeks. As BQM, he had responsibility for all provisions and ordinance. If you needed a gun or explosives, you went to Frank; if you wanted a uniform, you went to Frank; if you got fed and watered as you sat in a rural farmyard in north county Dublin after a long and traumatic day, your gratitude should be to Frank.

When JJ enquired how Liamy was, he was told that he had been brought into the farmhouse to be treated and cared for during the night. JJ made his way up to the house and within minutes was sitting on an upright wooden chair beside his friend. Liamy was sitting up in a bed made by stuffing a huge sack with straw and placing the makeshift mattress on the stone floor. He was sipping a bowl of broth, which had come from a large black pot simmering on the hearth. Once he had established that Dr Hayes had cleaned his friend's wounds thoroughly and dressed them properly, JJ was full of questions about what was going on, about how Liamy had ended up befriending him at the racecourse and, wittingly or otherwise, leading him into the middle of something that he knew nothing about and cared nothing for.

Liamy seemed a little offended by the aggressive questioning but understood JJ's confusion and frustration. He began by explaining that everyone in the farmyard that evening, plus an additional sixty or so men in the area, had been ordered to attend major manoeuvres on Easter Sunday. But at virtually the last minute, that order had been revoked by the leadership in Dublin, whoever they were. This had left Commandant Ashe, Hayes, Lawless and many others confused. So Lawless had been dispatched to Dublin on Sunday evening, on Ashe's Hudson, to query the countermanded orders and seek some clarification. He had arrived back to Ashe's residence sometime after dark with clear orders to go out the next day, Easter Monday. They immediately got the word out to their men as best they could.

"That's why myself and Micheál were in Fairyhouse. A gang of our lads, once they heard the manoeuvres were cancelled, decided they'd go racing."

Liamy and Micheál and some others, including the doctor and Molly, had been tasked with rounding them up, along with anyone else who was willing to throw their lot in with him. They were to send or bring them to a prearranged rendezvous point at Rath Cross, where they would receive further orders.

"That's what we were doing when that blasted RIC squad came along and sparked off the skirmish." Liamy glanced at his wounded shoulder with a look of disgusted disappointment.

JJ also learned that the explosion that shattered his tender moment with Molly on the beach was down to the ubiquitous Frank Lawless. He had driven to the railway bridge over the causeway, with sixty pounds of dynamite lashed to the carrier of Ashe's motorcycle, and an armed escort of four men on bicycles. He refused to let anyone else risk it, as the gelignite had started to ooze from some of the dynamite. This made it unstable and liable to ignite spontaneously. Apparently that was why the explosion had been less effective than intended.

All of this was news to JJ. According to Liamy, the plan had been to blow up the bridge, cutting off the rail link between Belfast and Dublin, which would be advantageous in a long-running campaign. JJ didn't really grasp what he meant by that last bit. At any rate, the dynamite failed to blow a hole in the bridge; instead it merely lifted and bent a short section of the track. This would cause only temporary disruption.

"So who is this Commandant Ashe fella when he's at home?" JJ asked.

"Kerryman originally. Principal in Corduff. Good footballer. Great leader."

"Is there anything he can't do?"

"Probably not."

They both laughed.

Then JJ looked out the window at the busy farmyard. He was feeling pessimistic about what he had landed himself in the middle of but was glad that his friend was in good spirits and seemed to be receiving excellent medical attention.

Outside, the rain was heavier now, as darkness seeped in. Since JJ didn't really know where he was, the prospect of some food and a warm, dry place to sleep was very attractive. He bade Liamy good night, pulled his collar up around his neck and went back out into the courtyard. As he walked from the farmhouse, he looked around with a mixture of bewilderment and amusement. How had he ended up in a farmhouse in the middle of God knows where, among a band of armed strangers, apparently intent on striking some sort of blow for freedom on behalf of his country, against the oppressive English? He had never really thought of his country in those terms, terms that made it sound like it could be owned by anyone, let alone by him and his fellow Irishmen. He had always seen the country simply as the place where he lived and the place he wanted to escape from. Nor had he ever seen the English as oppressors. In fact he had had little or no dealings with the English or their agents in his day-to-day life; well, until he met the redoubtable Sergeant O'Connor that is. And he had always had his own personal oppressors: his father, school, a preordained life path. No one had ever offered to fight for his freedom. Indeed, he had for long seen England as a place to escape to, a place of opportunity and a gateway to his ultimate golden cow, America.

JJ stood for a moment, taking in the scene. The men sat around in groups, eating, smoking, chatting, having already all but adapted to their new surroundings, their new roles, as if they had been somehow born to this life. There were between twenty and thirty in the yard. About twenty wore the same or similar uniform – a grey-green serge tunic with matching two-buttoned knickers, puttees of light Irish serge and a haversack, with a bandolier hung across their chests like a sash. Others had just slung the haversack and bandolier over their everyday clothes, either caught unprepared by the second change in orders or because they hadn't yet acquired a uniform. Liamy had told him that all equipment had to be bought and paid for by the men themselves.

THE BALLAD OF JJ MCHALE

As he stood surveying the courtyard, his eye was drawn to the tall figure of a man standing in the doorway of one of the outhouses. It was his shirt that caught JJ's eye, a wide-sleeved, flouncy white shirt that flapped enthusiastically in the wind. It was the man Liamy had called "the commandant", the same man he had seen with Molly in the church on Easter Sunday. JJ had to admit he cut a dashing figure in the chiaroscuro light of the doorway. Still in his motorcycle gear of black leather boots over black leather trousers held up by a pair of braces, he was a fine specimen of manhood. Leaning against the door jamb, a china teacup in his hand, he gave the impression of nonchalance but his gaze was alert, his demeanour courageous, and he held his head like the high-principled man he clearly was. With skin darkened by the sun, a full head of thick, wavy curls and the carefully manicured moustache, he looked like a high-ranking English officer or a film star, like bloody Douglas Fairbanks or someone. He must have women swooning and falling at his feet too.

"Dia dhuit, a mháistir Ághas," cried the farmer's children as they passed him.

"Dia dhaoibh, a leanaí," he answered, smiling and ruffling the hair of the oldest boy. As the children ran to the house, Ashe drained his cup and went into the shed.

"Sit down, a mhac. You're blocking the sun."

JJ looked at the hefty young man who had spoken and then at the mist drifting down from the darkening sky. He was nonplussed.

"Come and join us, before your feet take root," said another man in the same group. They were sitting on their haversacks in a loose circle around a couple of plates of bread and a small pot of cold spuds, coats slung over their shoulders against the drizzle. JJ realised that he had been staring at the commandant for longer than was appropriate and so was glad to accept the invitation.

"It's been a tough day for everyone, boy," said the second man as JJ sat on a rock behind him.

"A rale baptism of fire," said the first, bursting into a laugh that came all the way from his ample belly and offering JJ his large hand to shake. "Bennie McAllister," he added warmly. "Great to have you with us."

"Ehm . . ."

"I'm Christy Nugent," said the second man as he too shook JJ's hand.

"What'll we call you?"

"Ehm, JJ. I'm JJ McHale."

"McHale?" says McAllister. "That's not a local name."

"No. I'm from Ballysumaghan. Near Sooey. Sligo."

"Jaysus, that's an awful long way to come for a scrap."

"Yeah, you see, the thing is—"

"These are the lads you'll be fighting alongside. My two brothers, John and Mick, Willie Norton, Peter Wilson, Bartley Weston, Nick Teeling, Peadar Blanchfield and that's your captain, Eddie Rooney, over with Commandant Ashe."

"My captain?" JJ asked, his eyes followed the man's stumpy finger to the outhouse, where the commandant, Ashe, was in conference with several of his junior officers.

"Have some food," said one of the men he'd just been introduced to but whose name JJ couldn't recall. He was a smiling, fresh-faced young fella, not much older than himself.

"Thanks."

JJ hunkered and dug his hand absentmindedly into the pot of spuds, distracted by the sight of Molly, hatless now, her hair blown askew by the sea breeze and made to glisten by the light rain. She walked across the courtyard and directly up to Commandant Ashe. She approached him with an openness and familiarity that indicated friendship rather than subordination. His smile was welcoming to say the least. They didn't embrace or anything, but from the moment Molly entered his line of vision, Ashe's demeanour changed. It was like a planetary shift: he who had been the sun, orbited by others held in thrall by his gravitational allure, became a smouldering Mercury to her dazzling sun. Once before him, she adopted a formal, military pose, including a cursory salute that drew a twinkling smile from the commandant. He half-saluted in return and addressed her in what sounded like a mock-authoritative tone, before dismissing his cohorts with a nod. Once alone, he took her hand in his, but she quickly withdrew it, and he seemed to acknowledge her embarrassment.

As JJ munched on cold spuds and sipped hot tea from a tin mug belonging to Peter Wilson, he stole glances at the charismatic couple.

They stood as close as possible without actually embracing and chatted for a long ten minutes, relaxed and completely at ease. His companions, too, chatted, ate and smoked away, oblivious to the churning in JJ's innards. Ashe had feelings for Molly that appeared to be reciprocated. Clearly, they were a couple, lovers, and probably had been for some time. That was it and that was that. So why couldn't he just leave it be? She was a beautiful young woman with high ideals; he was a dashing, well-educated young man with prospects. Why should they not be attracted to one another? The wonder was that JJ was so fixated, found himself choked and immobilised by envy at the very thought of this other man even touching Molly, let alone being intimate with her. Ashe offered his hand a second time and seemed to invite her to join him in the more comfortable farmhouse. Mercifully, she declined politely and seemed to indicate that her proper place was with her comrades. Ashe nodded. They both smiled and gazed wistfully into each other's eyes for what seemed like an eternity before going their separate ways for the time being.

"She's not bad? The commandant's mott?" growled McAllister. "Not my type at all though."

"What? Oh." It took JJ a moment to tune back in and grasp McAllister's meaning.

"I like them with a bit of mate on them, something to grab hault of," the big man continued, drawing an outline of an imaginary woman with his outstretched hands.

"Isn't that right, byes?" he bawled, and the rest of the company, led by his brothers, guffawed in response.

The rain had eased to a drizzle when JJ decided he should sort out a place to lay his head for the night, having accepted that his current situation was effectively irreversible until at least the next day. He had just stood and was stretching his tired limbs when the doctor's burgundy Morris Oxford two-seater noisily rounded the bend off the main Lusk to Rush road. It swung into the courtyard, scattering hens, geese and loose pebbles and putting everyone in the yard instantly on guard.

The doctor was not alone in the car. Beside him in the passenger seat was another Volunteer in an officer's uniform. His tunic was almost three-quarter length, of grey-green serge with a high stiff collar and Cossack-like cap. A leather holster, sheathing a pistol, was suspended by two long leather straps from his Sam Browne belt so that it sat quite low on his hip.

"That's a Savage semi-automatic," Liamy would later tell him. "American. Deadly yoke."

The uniform was completed by a pair of matching bow-legged jodhpurs, black leather puttees and boots.

Commandant Ashe looked up from where he still stood, just inside the door of the outhouse. He'd been studying a map, which he had spread out on an upturned barrel, and was making scrupulous notes in what looked like a school jotter. The car had barely drawn to a stop when the officer leapt out and strode purposefully across the yard to Ashe. His bearing was impressive, accentuated by the fine cut of his uniform and the confidence and authority of his walk. He was hyper-alert, casting glances left and right as he crossed the yard. There was an odd look about him, though. His long pointed nose gave him the look of a hawk or an eagle.

When he reached Ashe, the two men shook hands firmly, warmly, and exchanged greetings in Irish. Within seconds Ashe had gathered up his map and the two had disappeared into the farmhouse. Once he had parked the car and retrieved his medical satchel from behind his seat, Dr Hayes followed them.

Commandant Mulcahy was introduced to the men that night at twenty-one hundred hours, as Captain Rooney had put it. JJ had to get Peter Wilson to explain that it was military-speak for nine o'clock. Anyway, at nine sharp, around fifty Volunteers, not including those on sentry duty, sat around a large fire in the centre of the courtyard. The rain had let up briefly. Announced by Ashe as joint Commanding Officer, Mulcahy delivered a speech that was half morale boosting and half tactical. He stood with his weight thrown forward onto the balls of his feet, his arms spread wide and his shoulders slightly hunched, like a bird about to swoop onto his unsuspecting prey. At times he reminded JJ of the local football manager giving his brother's team a rousing talk before an important grudge match against local rivals, Geevagh. At other times he sounded like a teacher explaining a complicated mathematical problem to a class of top students who knew exactly what he was talking about, unlike JJ who only understood snippets of the jargon that peppered the speech. He did pick up enough to know that these men were determined to complete what they had started and at virtually any cost, including their lives. They were clear that there was an enemy, who that enemy was and how they intended to defeat him. This Mulcahy fella sounded like he really knew what he was talking about and, while Ashe cut a dashing, courageous figure that men would follow into the very jaws of death, Mulcahy was a man who knew how to stir men's ire, heat their blood and call them to duties they might otherwise shirk. His knowledge and grasp of military tactics was strangely reassuring. JJ got drawn in too and could even conceive of obeying this man's orders himself, cycling into battle, an Enfield slung over his shoulder, images of the new republic flashing through his mind, were he at all inclined in that direction.

"Right, men, so this is the plan of campaign."

A hush fell over the assembly and all eyes and ears were on the commanding triumvirate. All except JJ's that is; his eyes were busily surveying the faces of his peers, perched like young fledglings awaiting the life-sustaining morsels being delivered by their industrious parents. Naturally his eyes soon found and rested happily upon Molly. The speech gradually faded into the background, until it became little more than an accompaniment to the music of the breeze in the trees, a poor second fiddle. Although her gaze was fixed on Ashe, her attention given to Mulcahy, her enraptured state gave her an aura that was almost beatific. JJ could easily have taken that beautiful image and spun it into an imaginary icon of mythic proportions, given her the qualities of a Greek or Roman goddess and written her into the script of a tragic love story, worthy of Mary Pickford or Lillian Gish. But the lack of sophistication in her demeanour, the honesty in her face, unobscured by make-up, and the unflattering paramilitary garb prevented such frivolous romantic idealisation. He was beginning to feel drawn to her in a much deeper way. He kept searching for an image, a phrase from a song, something that would help him to label this attraction, give it a name, a category that might help him to better understand it, so he could deal with it and get on with his life. All he could come up with was a moth and a flame.

Mulcahy declared that they would be doing things differently from how they had planned and practised.

"Simply seizing strategic enemy strongholds and defending them to the death is not practicable or sensible out here," he declared. "Instead, we're going to have to box clever, stay one step ahead of the enemy, keep on the move. Otherwise we'll be like sitting ducks in a fairground."

Many of the men grunted and nodded in agreement and there was visible relief that he was talking sense and grabbing the bull by the horns. Most were from a farming background and respected this kind of decisive, pragmatic action.

Mulcahy explained that their small battalion would be more efficient split into four columns of ten to fifteen men, each under the command of a captain. The four remaining senior officers – himself, Commandant Ashe, Adjutant Hayes and BQM Frank Lawless – would constitute the command staff. Each day, one company would be detailed with protecting the integrity of the base camp as well as foraging for and procuring food supplies for the entire battalion, while the other three would conduct strategic raids. For increased security, the raiding companies would move in a prearranged formation: the leading company as an advance scouting party, the endmost as a rearguard, while the commander and his staff would travel with the main body in between. The companies would alternate daily. Two raids were planned for the following day. The details of these raids would be withheld until the morning briefing to ensure secrecy. He then handed over to BQM Lawless to delineate the four companies.

JJ had had enough by this point and thought this an opportunity to skulk off to his temporary lodgings for the night.

"You! Stop!" Mulcahy bellowed at the top of this voice, so loud and sudden that JJ was startled and turned to see who had drawn such anger upon themselves.

"Where the hell are you going, man?" It was Mulcahy again, still bellowing and glaring directly at JJ, unless there was someone else behind him. He looked to see but there was no red-cheeked Volunteer cringing in a corner. So he shrugged and started on his way again, failing to grasp the gravity of his case.

"Good God!" he heard behind him.

"Stop that man, now!"

Two men jumped to their feet and stood directly in JJ's path. One of them was Cathal Ó'Cofaigh, looking as disgusted as Mulcahy sounded angry. The man who wasn't Cathal was mugging to JJ to look at Mulcahy quickly and contritely. JJ turned fully and only then realised that the entire command staff was glaring at him.

"You haven't been dismissed yet, man!" bellowed Mulcahy.

"Oh, I see now." JJ was smiling inanely at the silly misunderstanding. "See, I'm not with ye," he explained with a shrug.

"What?" This was the loudest bellow yet. "Not with us? What are you, then? A spy? Are you an infiltrator? Have we got a quisling among us?"

The men looked about uncomfortably, embarrassed that they might have missed a spy in their midst.

"No, sir. No, no. I'm no spy, sir." JJ's use of the word *sir*, whether out of habit – his father liked to be addressed so – or nervousness, seemed to ingratiate him with the officer, just a little.

"Then what are you, lad? Not a coward, I hope? A deserter?"

JJ felt a rush of heat to his cheeks. He had certainly shown himself to be cowardly in the face of death that day. Certainly he lacked the courage to risk life and limb that the other men had demonstrated. Is that really what courage is? As for deserting, well if that meant to depart and leave these men to fight for their cause without his questionable assistance, then that's exactly what he was planning to do.

"No, sir," he said eventually. "At least I hope not. I only mean that this is not my fight, sir."

"Not your fight?"

Shit, he'd obviously touched a nerve that would set Mulcahy off on another rant.

"This is everyone's fight, damn it to hell! If you are of this country and value freedom and equality before the law, then this *is* your fight! If the blood coursing through your veins is Irish blood, then this is *your* fight. You are either with us or against us, man, and if you're not against us, then this IS YOUR FIGHT!"

It took JJ only a few seconds to realise that this did not offer him a way out. Nothing for it then other than blunt honesty.

"No, sir."

Mulcahy's visage darkened to match the night sky.

"I mean yes, sir."

Mulcahy looked to Ashe who was the picture of disapproval but appeared to have no explanation to offer.

"I mean, sir, I was on my way to Dublin and, well, it's a long story but Micheál and Liamy rescued me from, well, from a situation and the next thing I knew I was in the middle of a skirmish with someone else's gun in my hand and bullets whizzing past my head, left, right and centre."

"Is this true? Where is Micheál?" Mulcahy scanned the silent assembly.

"Here, sir." Micheál raised his arm sheepishly. "Liam Kenny recruited him, sir. I had no idea he was not committed to our cause."

At this point, Dr Hayes stretched across and whispered in Mulcahy's ear. This seemed to ameliorate his mood slightly.

"Right! Dr Hayes has vouched for you for now, sonny. So sit down, for God's sake! When we have finished here come to our quarters so that we can interview you further. If there is anyone else here who had any dealings with this man they too should report to us later."

With that, Mulcahy instructed Lawless to assign the men to their various companies once Commandant Ashe had said a few words. Ashe's speech was shorter, less detailed, more measured and tempered.

"Thanks, Dick. Delighted to have you on board."

There was spontaneous but dignified applause.

"I've known this man a long time and, take it from me boys, you could not have a better man at the helm. Follow any order he gives, as if it came from Pádraig Pearse himself."

He glanced at Mulcahy, nodded, smiled, then turned to face his men again.

"Difficult times lie ahead of us, boys. Your courage, energy and commitment will be tested to the hilt. And I know the bloody confusion at the weekend hasn't helped. That's why we're half the number we should be."

The men muttered and moaned in agreement.

"Now, we're all volunteers here, so, if anyone is having any doubts after today's action, well, there's still time to 'buail an bothar'. If you're not fully commited to what's ahead, you're free to leave, without fear of mockery or recrimination."

Mulcahy looked a bit askance at this, but JJ perked up. Surely that provided him with a way out. Finally, Ashe launched into spontaneous song, to remind his men of their purpose and put some fire into their bellies.

> Last night I had a happy dream, tho' restless where I be.
> I thought again brave Irishmen, had set old Ireland free,
> And how I got excited when the cannons loud did roar
> It's grá mo chroí, I'd like to see Old Ireland free once more.
> It's true we had brave Irishmen, as everyone must own,
> The Liberator, O'Connell, true, Lord Edward and Wolfe Tone.
> And also Robert Emmet, who till death did not give o'er,
> It's grá mo chroí I'd like to see Old Ireland free once more.
> Allen, Larkin and O'Brien died their country to set free,
> And see to-day brave Irishmen are struggling hard for thee.
> Both day and night they'll always fight, until death they'll
>   ne'er give o'er,
> It's grá mo chroí I'd like to see Old Ireland free once more . . .
> Oh grá mo chroí I long to see Old Ireland free once more!

By God, the man could sing. He had the small audience of fifty or so tough men and four ladies in his thrall. The final line of each verse was sung in rousing chorus, full of passion and determination, and by the song's end, many were close to tears. These men were deadly serious about what they wanted to achieve – true zealots. JJ respected them for that. They too had a dream to which they were committed and he must show the same resolve in the pursuit of his. If he did, if he followed their example, he could achieve anything. Ashe was utterly inspiring, but JJ was jealous as hell of this man who was so capable, so talented and seemed to have such an effect on Molly. It left him in little doubt that Ashe had her heart and that any designs and desires he harboured were best scattered to the breeze like so much dust.

The interview was held in a small room off the kitchen of the farmhouse, a sort of parlour. The wallpaper was striped, smoke-aged, and a large threadbare rug covered most of the dark wooden floor. The furniture was sparse. A long, floral, straw-filled couch ran the length of the wall, under the only window. On the mantle of the open fireplace opposite was an eclectic display of family photos, a happy family – mother, father, four children – all smiling, the sort of family anyone would wish for. Right above the mantle there was a dark, foreboding painting of a grim-faced Jesus on the cross, who seemed to be glaring directly at JJ, no matter where he stood in the room. The only light came from a hissing oil lamp on a small round incidental table close to the dresser.

There was only the incidental table, so the commanding triumvirate sat to attention on three upright wooden chairs. JJ slouched and paced the tiny space.

"You want to be an actor?" Mulcahy looked as if he was chewing on a slice of lemon.

"I am an actor. Sir."

"Well, sure, lots of us do a bit of play acting, in the evenings, the weekends," Ashe said and laughed lightly.

"No, I want to do it for real. Like Chaplin."

"Who's Chaplin?" Mulcahy asked.

"Charlie Chaplin, sir."

"In the pictures," said Ashe, smiling. "The Tramp."

"In America," JJ added. At last. Someone understood him.

"America?" Mulcahy seemed to have bitten on his imaginary slice of lemon.

"Yes. Well, first I need to get to London. That's where he started."

"Who?"

"Charlie Chaplin. So, that's why I'm trying to get to Dublin."

Mulcahy pursed his lips and appeared to move the slice of lemon from one side of his mouth to the other.

"An actor would be a good man to send as a spy," he said finally, glancing at Ashe.

"Surely would, Dick."

JJ stopped pacing. Squared up to the two Commandants. Saw his father's face in theirs.

"Look, I have no interest in spying on you lot or on anyone else for that matter. I don't know where ye've all been living but no-one I know is goin' around shoutin' about fighting the bloody English and all that. We're too busy living our lives!"

There followed a stony silence. Mulcahy's face contorted. JJ sensed he was gearing up for another ear-splitting tirade.

There was a knock on the door.

"Enter!" called Ashe.

A pale, impish Liamy staggered in, leaning on Molly's shoulder.

"He wanted to say something in favour of the Sligo man," she said apologetically.

"You should be resting, young man!" The doctor was on his feet and helping Liamy to a chair.

"I tried telling him," said Molly.

She caught JJ's eye briefly and seemed to blush. Then she looked to Ashe, but didn't hold his gaze, doubtless feeling a bit of a nuisance.

"I'm the one recruited this man, in Fairyhouse," said Liamy. "He's a good man and certainly no traitor. He was thrown right into the middle of a skirmish without the slightest warning and performed heroically. I'm tellin' ye," – Liamy became teary – "this man saved my life today."

Mulcahy raised his eyebrows to their limit.

"Is this true?" Ashe was addressing Molly. "You were there, Miss McNally."

"Well, yes, I was there."

"And did this man perform heroically?" Mulcahy asked, without a trace of sarcasm, fair play to him.

"Well, it was a chaotic situation. I gave him my revolver and, well, yes, he did use it, eventually."

"And did he truly save this man's life, Adjutant Hayes?"

"There was a lot of blood loss. Had he not stanched the flow, it's difficult to say how much longer Liam might have survived."

"Well," said Mulcahy, "these are neither the actions of a coward nor a traitor. You will remain with us for tonight, Mr McHale, and you will be free to make your own decision in the morning. But bear in mind that this cause needs as many able-bodied, committed young men as possible."

JJ glanced at Ashe. He wasn't smiling.

The interview was concluded and the rain was falling again, sheeting in off the sea, propelled by a strong wind. JJ helped Molly to bring Liamy back to his sickbed, before returning to their billets, JJ still limping a little. It was only then that he realised, with more than a little delight, that because they were both assigned to C Company, they were effectively sharing a billet, albeit separated by a wooden milking stall and in the company of ten other Volunteers. The wet weather, the exertions of the day and the prospect of an early start to an even more eventful day had impelled everyone to bed down early. Most were already asleep when JJ and Molly got back. There was another moment of mild embarrassment as JJ stood before her, just inside the door of the outhouse.

"Well," he said lightly, "that was some day and no mistake."

She looked at him as she might an enemy intruder or some ne'er-do-well who was about to assault her. "'Twas," she said, either thrown slightly by his sudden directness or unsure how to respond to such an inane comment. She dropped her head and stepped past him. "Good night, then."

JJ smiled as she shuffled to the far end of the billet, but inside he was wailing. He had never come across anyone who had affected him so. He seemed reduced to an incompetent, babbling child around her and like a glass suddenly drained of its contents whenever she left his side. This was pure daft and it had to stop right now, right there and then. Grab the bull by the horns. What would Mulcahy do?

JJ shuffled through the billet to where Molly had made her rough bed, stepping on someone's toes in the darkness.

"For fuck's sake!"

"Sorry."

When he got to Molly, she turned and gasped, clearly startled, as she clutched her coat around her as if she feared what this daft young man might do next.

He needed to sort this and quickly. "Sorry," he said. "It's just, well, I'm sure you've noticed and I'm sorry if you have and if it's made you feel uncomfortable, but, really I mean, this has never happened before but, well, these feelings, the feelings I have, the way I feel, I mean, I know that you and the commandant are, well, probably are, an item. I mean it's obvious to all, and so I shouldn't even presume, but, well, I can't help the way I feel but I can see that it is making you uncomfortable."

Her eyes were wide, her mouth agape, like someone had shown her into a room she never knew existed, in a house she had lived in her whole life.

"And, well, you have your cause, you and the commandant and I have mine, so . . ."

He extended his hand so suddenly and firmly that she jumped back with the fright and shrieked enough to rouse one or two of the men nearby.

"It was lovely to meet you, Molly, but we must part. The very best of luck to you."

One of the men lifted his head above his great coat, which he had wrapped around him as a blanket. "What the hell is going on?"

"Nothing. Everything is fine now, thanks," JJ said, smiling, convinced he had done a good thing, the right thing.

She was glaring at his hand in disbelief.

"Well?" he asked.

He raised his proferred hand higher, repeating his offer.

"You all right, Miss McNally?" the half-asleep Volunteer said.

"Ehm, yes, thanks." She shook JJ's hand, holding only his fingers.

The ripple that shuddered through his body was ridiculous in its intensity, for such a simple gesture, so he put it down to the cold and damp of the outhouse.

"Goodbye, then." He smiled again as she took her hand away and his heart sank lower than it had for a long time. He shook his head and snorted lightly at how silly this all was, really, and then withdrew quietly to his own little corner.

17

The Girl I Left Behind Me

——•——

It's a spectacular summer day in Ballysumaghan. The sun is high and the azure sky mottled with puffy cumuli. JJ and his mother are in the bog, lying stretched out on the flat of their backs on the soft, warm summer heather, laughing at the constantly changing shapes of the clouds as they drift by. But then the scene is overshadowed by a more ominous bank of darker clouds. These take on the shapes of hideous monsters and slouch across the sky, dimming everything as they go. JJ and his mother try to run, to escape, but he finds himself alone and in a fantastical valley surrounded by many-headed beasts with deadly claws and monstrous shark-like teeth. He calls out to his mother, runs aimlessly around, desperately trying to find her. He loses his footing and slides down a steep slope, then falls headlong from a precipitous crag, still pursued by the clawing, rapacious monsters. Next he plunges without warning into a deep whirlpool, where he is churned, swilled and whipped against jagged rocks by an angry tide, as an array of overgrown fish, with poisonous tendrils, razor-like teeth and armoured scales tear at his flesh, leaving him bloodied and covered in welts and gashes. With a huge, energy-sapping effort, JJ manages to leap clear and falls supine onto the soft and constantly shifting sand of a barren desert. The sand and sweat sting his wounds until the pain becomes intolerable and choking thirst drives him on. Mistaking the shimmering, rippled sand for refreshing water, he falls to his knees and gulps whole handfuls. When he realises his mistake and tries to call for help, for something to slake his thirst, to salve his wounds, he is choked, unable to utter more than distorted, guttural whimpers.

JJ awoke during this final sequence to find himself on all fours on the straw-covered floor of the outhouse. His mouth was stuffed with golden stalks, his shirt ripped open and sweat poured down his face, neck and back. He was still trying to beat off the hideous, deformed monsters who were trying to drag him down into their netherworld. Finally his arms were grabbed roughly and pinned tightly behind so that he could do nothing to defend himself. Once he surrendered to his captors, his vision began to clear and the forms took on a more human shape. Distinct facial features emerged to replace the hideous visages that had haunted his fitful sleep; calm, reassuring voices replaced the beastly howls and bellows. He finally realised that he had been dreaming and was surrounded not by ogres or demons but by two or three of his new comrades. Once he relaxed, his arms were released and the air peppered with several incoherent expletives, as the men returned to sleep. Two soft hands still clasped his cheeks, one stroking him soothingly, the other gently removing the straw from around his mouth. A hushed voice uttered reassuring platitudes. His eyes adjusted to confirm that it was Molly.

He rubbed the back of his head.

"One of the men threw a boot at you."

"Oh."

He stared at her, could barely speak. He was embarrassed by his behaviour but delighted it had caused her to be so concerned, to show such tenderness. "Thank you," he finally muttered.

"I would have done the same for anyone else."

"And, again, I'm sorry. You must regret ever clapping eyes on me."

She didn't answer but she didn't look away either. She did take her hands away from his face, though.

"What was disturbing you?"

"I'm not sure. A nightmare. I was fleeing something horrible, something that was trying to destroy me, then I was trying to retrieve something I'd lost I think. I don't know. Hmph." He shrugged, blushing slightly. "Foolish."

"No."

They looked at each other again for an instant.

"Sometimes I feel the same," Molly admitted.

He left a pause for her to continue or not, as she pleased.

"I sometimes feel like I've left behind all that I knew and am careening into a future that I know nothing of and with nothing to measure it against."

"Yes," he said, almost breathlessly.

"These are difficult times, changing times. I feel we will all wake up from this dream we are living and we, everything, will have changed beyond recognition."

She looked a little confused, unsure of herself. He hadn't seen this vulnerability in her up to now.

"They can't force you to stay."

"I am here of my own free will and because I believe what we desire is worth fighting for."

"Sorry."

"That's all right. JJ?"

He nodded.

She smiled. God, she had a beautiful smile.

"I believe that sometimes it falls to a particular generation to be the ones who change things or spark a change that is necessary, has been necessary for some time, no matter what the cost. I believe we are that generation, JJ, and that the cost is likely to be high."

"So you believe in destiny?" he asked, excited.

"Yes, I suppose I do."

He held her gaze for one moment longer. The air was hushed, broken only by the regular breathing and occasional snores of their sleeping comrades. He leaned forward gently, anxious not to startle her, angled his head a little and pressed his lips to hers. She didn't resist. She angled her head a little too, pressed her lips softly onto his. He brought his hand along her upper arm and to her cheek, but as soon as he stroked her cool skin, she drew her head back slightly but remained close enough for him to still feel the warmth of her breath. She looked puzzled but not angry or upset.

JJ thought about kissing her again but had an inkling she might not allow it, that it might even destroy whatever it was that was hovering between them. The door of the outhouse creaked open, allowing in just enough light to illuminate their intimacy. The noise of the rain seemed suddenly invasive; the cold air made them shiver. They looked over to see Ashe standing in the doorway. He was nonplussed to say the least, shocked to his core, quite probably, but definitely surprised to find his girlfriend with this stranger from Sligo, in a position that was open to misinterpretation.

"Tomás!" She stood and stepped towards the door.

JJ knew he should have left it to her to explain but his nervousness and genuine fright got the better of him and he began stuttering half-explanations that sounded more like invented excuses than clarifications and utterly undermined Molly's attempt at a reasonable, truthful account.

"I was—"

"We were just—"

"He had a nightmare—"

"I was crazy, bawling, screaming. She was—"

"We had to restrain him—"

"Believe me, I was like a lunatic. The others, it wasn't just her. Molly . . ."

She was standing before Ashe, who remained silent. JJ was still on his knees, too anxious to stop explaining for long enough to stand up, and blissfully ignorant of the ridiculousness of his pose.

"He's all right now, just going back to sleep."

"Sleep. Yes. I need to. We all need to. End of nightmares. Gone. Finished!"

"Is something wrong, love?" she asked Ashe.

The suddenness of the word and the tenderness of the fricative consonant stung JJ sharply. She was staring up at the tall Kerryman with all the concern of a long-time lover.

Ashe gave JJ one last withering, incredulous look before turning his attention to Molly, irritated at the unexpected lack of privacy. "I just wanted to let you know. An order has come from Dublin. We've taken the GPO." He allowed a brief, judicious pause for them to share the excitement and import of the news.

JJ remembered that the GPO was where Peggy was due to start work the next day.

"But Connolly wants us to send half our men in tomorrow as reinforcements."

"Oh?" was all Molly said.

"I may take command of that squad."

"I think you're needed more out here," she said, "but . . . if you think that's best."

"I don't know what's best. I think our role out here is crucial." He gently removed a flake of straw from the corner of her mouth with his index finger.

She blushed, touched her mouth. "What does Commandant Mulcahy think?"

"Hmph. He thinks we should ignore the order. Continue as planned."

"I see."

He waited an instant to allow her to expand. She didn't.

"Anyway, we'll be making a decision first thing in the morning. I just wanted your thoughts in advance."

"Well, you know what I think, Tomás."

He nodded, smiled thinly then kissed her full on the lips. JJ thought she held the kiss for longer than Ashe had intended it to last, certainly too long for JJ's liking.

"Oíche mhaith, mo ghrá gheall."

Molly smiled coyly and returned to her bed at the far end of the shed.

"Oíche mhaith, a mhac," he said to JJ. "Tá súil agam go gcodlóidh tú níos suaimhní ó seo?" He closed the door tightly.

"'Night!" JJ shouted, mostly for Molly's benefit.

The closing door and JJ's shout roused a couple of the men again.

"For fuck's sake!"

"Shshshshsh!"

"Go to sleep, you fucking leibide!"

JJ sank slowly back onto his makeshift bed of straw.

Next morning JJ awoke before his body was ready to. The camp was a flurry of activity. Everyone moved quickly and deftly as bags were packed, weapons primed, ammunition belts checked. Breakfast was eaten in the open air, the men standing or sitting in an almost sombre silence. JJ, still limping a little, moved on the fringes of the group but could not but be affected by the mood. These men and women were facing into the most dangerous day of their lives. Yes, they had faced death the previous day, but that had come upon them unexpectedly. Today, with the news from the city that the rising or rebellion or whatever they were calling it had escalated beyond the point of no return, the prospect of death was very real. Today, too, they rode out with graphic, first-hand knowledge of what gunshots, bullet wounds and instant, violent death were like.

Naturally Molly was caught up in this milieu as well but she seemed to be going out of her way to avoid JJ. Peter Wilson tried to engage him in conversation as they shared some salty ham and hard-boiled eggs. He asked excitedly what JJ thought their first mission might be, where their first target would lie. Would the enemy be expecting them or could they take them by surprise?

"That'd be great, JJ, wouldn't it, to catch the feckers off guard?"

JJ was polite but unable to respond with the same enthusiasm or even hazard a wild guess as to what lay ahead. Wilson on the other hand was full of opinion, bursting with speculation and so fuelled by adrenalin that he seemed almost exhilarated. What would he be like in the heat of battle, should it come to that?

Would it truly come to that? Could this really be a fully fledged rebellion that had been gestating for months, even years, without him and half the country having the slightest inkling? He refused to believe it. This was just another detour. He'd most likely stumbled upon little more than a small band of fervent, zealous Fenians, one of several radical cadres that had decided to take matters into their own hands. There were one or two in Sligo, he knew, in every county maybe. But with limited armaments and a serious lack of military strength, their tilt at the might of the British forces in Ireland would be akin to waving a small stick at a raging dragon. They might be a minor thorn in the side of the authorities for a couple of days, before being surrounded, infiltrated, overwhelmed and crushed by superior numbers, greater fire power and better organisation. This event would doubtless put JJ's dreams on hold for that time, but as long as he kept moving forward and remained focused on his own destiny he would eventually find himself in the right place at the right time.

But he was confused too, wracked with doubt and no longer so sure of his bearings. These rebels, on the other hand, were men of certainty, sure-footed and decisive, qualities that had been alien to JJ until he made his own impulsive break, less than a week earlier. But, in those short few days, had he not become like them? Should he not follow their example and continue on his own journey with renewed vigour, rather than follow them recklessly and blindly into battle? Why was he even stopping to think about that? He owed them nothing, well, apart from his rescuers, Liam and Micheál, but that debt could be repaid later and without having to risk life and limb. Yet he felt an illogical, inexplicable guilt for deserting them. Their paths had crossed by accident and he had nothing in common with them, so why did he care what became of them? In any case, anything that might befall them, they would have brought upon themselves with their crazy notions and overblown cause.

He spotted Molly again, watched her cross the courtyard with measured, purposeful steps. She was deep in thought as she slung her rifle over her shoulder and adjusted her ammunition belt. She looked up at the lowering sky and grimaced. She approached Captain Rooney, saluted and discussed some matter of import for a moment or two. Then they both smiled warmly, saluted again, and she returned to her bicycle to prepare it for action. Departure time was imminent. JJ went into the farmhouse to see Liamy.

His young pal was sitting up at the kitchen table with a mug of tea in his hand and a grin on his face that would brighten the dullest winter evening. He was enjoying the warmth and comfort of the farmhouse and was in great spirits as he joked with the farmer's wife.

"Oh now, say nothing." And he leaned in conspiratorially. "You know why a farm is the hardest place to keep a secret?"

"No, why?" she asked, already smiling in anticipation.

"Because the potatoes have eyes and the corn has ears!" he whispered before exploding in raucous laughter.

She chortled, as much at Liamy as at the joke, flicking him across the shoulder with her dish cloth as she went.

"You're a comical young fella, so you are." She left them to chat about whatever it was young lads chatted about in these turbulent times, and went about her own mundane chores.

JJ questioned Liamy about what was going on. It seemed the hundred or so men in the battalion had indeed been preparing for well over a year. Only a little over half of their total number had turned out, because of the confusion over the orders. Liamy had been involved with Redmond's Volunteers, as he called them, for several years but had left after the start of the war. As he recalled, things had begun to step up not long after that and he was recruited into the Fingal Volunteers by Battalion Quartermaster Frank Lawless. There was a desperate fear of betrayal, he admitted, so things were always kept hush hush until the last minute. They had known that there were plans to strike against the British while they were preoccupied with the war in Europe but there had been no hint of when, or what exactly that strike would entail. It looked now like it was in fact much bigger than he or any of his friends had envisaged. JJ told him his own brothers had been out messing around with the Volunteers a few times but confessed that most people around Sooey had very little meas on them.

"Sure it's the same around here. It's hard to get people up off their arses. They're happy to make do with things the way they are."

"Ha, you're one to talk," JJ said.

"By Jesus, make no mistake, boy, I'll be back out there again tomorrow, you wait and see." Liamy raised his injured arm with his good hand in a gesture of defiance.

JJ smiled at his friend's courage and determination. "I have no doubt you will be, Liamy."

"Hopefully I'll see you there too, JJ. We could do with you." Liamy extended his good hand.

JJ didn't answer but he took his friend's hand and shook it firmly, with genuine affection.

Mulcahy was perched on the front step of the farmhouse, looming over his force of men and four women. His troops stood in pairs in their respective companies, headed by their captains. JJ limped past Mulcahy and Ashe, suitably cowed, and scuttled to the back of C Company. He was happy then that he could relax for a few minutes, gather his thoughts, until he noticed that he was standing right behind Molly. Ashe's eyes burned through him for a moment but there was nothing to be done at this stage, and she kept her gaze locked firmly on the commanding officers. Mulcahy explained the new orders to the battalion, the same orders Ashe had revealed to Molly the previous night. He declared the GPO as the headquarters of the new Irish Republic and told them the leaders had requested thirty to forty men from the battalion as reinforcements but insisted that it would be imprudent to shed so many. He said they would instead be sending between twelve and fifteen men, several from each company, to be nominated by their captains. This would leave behind four companies, with around twelve Volunteers in each.

JJ smiled. This was his opportunity to get out, make an exit without losing face. The gods had smiled on him again just when things seemed at their bleakest. Mulcahy outlined the plan for the day. The battalion would proceed to Swords to raid the RIC barracks there and capture its quite considerable arsenal. They would then raid the barracks in Donabate, before setting up camp at a new location, to be disclosed later . The officers withdrew and the battalion disbanded, each company circling its captain. In the spontaneous choreography, JJ and Molly came face to face, almost bumping into each other. He held her gaze for an instant but she quickly averted hers and manoeuvred her way around and past him to the opposite side of the emerging circle of C Company. That only made matters worse. Although they were no longer in close proximity, they were directly opposite each other, with the captain between them, so could not avoid making eye contact.

The suddenness of the encounter threw poor JJ into another whirl of confusion. The guilt he had felt before with Liamy was nothing compared to this kaleidoscope of emotion. He was so drawn to her, so wanted to remain in her constellation, so wanted to simply watch her, watch her face crinkle slightly and her lips purse as she became thoughtful, watch her stride across the courtyard, watch her long coat swirl as she leapt onto her bike, her back straightening as she pushed the pedals into action.

Molly was not chosen to be part of the detachment being sent to Dublin; JJ was, as was his new friend Peter Wilson. Fantastic and not surprising. He should have been delighted, jumping for joy. If he hadn't been chosen he would have volunteered, insisted on being sent. But when he heard Eddie Rooney call out his name – in fact he just pointed and said "you" – he had an instant sinking feeling, a tightening of his scrotum, a fluttering in the pit of his stomach. It reminded him of that moment, all those years ago, when he had kissed his mother's icy cheek and finally realised she was dead. Molly was smiling and busy again, delighted to be staying where the action was and, presumably, where her heart was too. When he caught her eye, her smile died for an instant. JJ had an incontrollable impulse to go straight up to her and tell her again what he was feeling. There was a sudden look of terror in her eyes as if she sensed his impulse. But before he had time to act, Molly was gone and Ashe was standing behind him, addressing him quietly but firmly.

"This is your chance now, boy, to get to Dublin."

"Oh, yes."

"Take it. No, grab it," – he clasped JJ's shoulders tightly – "with both hands, boy. Grab it with both hands and don't let go!"

"Right." JJ grimaced slightly, his shoulders paining him.

"And if you have any sense you'll stay there. There's nothing for you here. Do you get my drift, boy?"

"Drift? Right, yes." JJ's head was spinning and his shoulder hurt. "I'll go to Dublin, but I'll not stay there!" he said, more boldly than he had intended. He wished Ashe would let go of his bloody shoulders.

"What?" Ashe tightened his grip.

"Ow!" JJ winced and wriggled free, glared defiantly at the commandant. "I'm going way beyond Dublin, sir. Way beyond. Dublin is only the start for me!"

"Right. America?" Ashe smirked. "Good, good." He nodded. "The further the better," he concluded, smiling thinly, and left JJ standing alone in the middle of the courtyard, a somewhat forlorn figure amid the purposeful milieu.

JJ's bicycle, once Liamy's bicycle, was leaning like a corner boy against the gable of the farthest shed from the farmhouse. As he picked it up, he felt a presence at his shoulder. Not Ashe again, surely?

"How's the ankle?" Molly asked gently.

He turned abruptly, surprised. She was alone. He peered over her shoulder to confirm there was no sign of her officious boyfriend.

"Should be all right for cycling." He smiled, wriggling his foot stupidly, like a kid in the playground. "Yeah, it's fine. Thanks."

She glanced quickly over her shoulder, stepped closer and furtively removed a revolver from her coat pocket. "Take this."

He looked at the weapon for a moment, stunned, before raising his hands. "No, thanks."

"Look, you eejit, you're heading into a war zone. You're going to need this." She thrust it at his chest.

"Is that so?"

"Yes! Do you really have no idea what's going on?"

"No, actually, I don't." He was angry now, angry at her, at Ashe, at this whole bloody mess, and mostly at himself for feeling the way he did about her. "What do you care anyway?"

She had no answer. She sighed impatiently, glanced over her shoulder and pushed the gun at him again. "Look, it's nothing special. You're nothing special. I just don't want you getting yourself killed for the lack of a gun, that's all. I'd do the same for anyone."

He took the revolver, grudgingly, but grabbed her hand before she could withdraw it.

"Come with me. With us. Go to Rooney, tell him you think you'd be more useful in the city, say you want to be in the thick of things, you're sick of being on the fringes. I don't know, whatever it takes."

She remained wide-eyed throughout this outburst, desperately trying to retrieve her hand until finally she interrupted him. "Stop! Stoppit! Stop this nonsense now!" She snatched her hand back, rubbing her wrist where his grip had reddened it. "I'm staying here, where I belong. Now go. And don't come back!"

She spat the final three words and stormed off. JJ looked at the dark, cold steel in his hand and shoved it into the inside pocket of his jacket, where its weight seemed to quadruple, dragging the jacket out of shape.

18

The Rocky Road to Dublin

———✦———

AN HOUR OUT FROM ROGERSTOWN, the cyclecade was wending its way cautiously along Spittal Hill in Swords. They had got to that point without incident by keeping to the quiet, leafy lanes that dissected the north Dublin landscape. If they had been lovers escorting their sweethearts and not insurgents heading into battle, these laneways would have been romantic, bucolic idylls. Under the circumstances, the lush, verdant vegetation provided excellent cover. They had meandered first along Rogerstown Lane then turned briefly onto Turvey Avenue, before skirting Newbridge Demesne, the vast Donabate estate of the Cobbe family, with a reputation locally as beneficent landlords. Then via Cobbe's Lane and a series of rutted tracks, well known to the local lads. They had continued on wider but still quiet roads, through Lissenhall, Ballymadrough and Seafield, before finally turning onto Spittal Hill. There were fifteen men in total, led by Captain Dick Coleman, and they had travelled with one man riding point, about a hundred yards ahead of the main group, and another two riding rearguard a hundred yards behind. The remainder of the company was split into two groups of six, cycling two abreast at twenty-yard intervals, with Coleman riding solo in between, equidistant from both sections. This formation, the captain had explained, was to avoid detection and allow time and space to react to surprise encounters or ambush.

Probably unsurprisingly, JJ was riding rearguard, alongside Peter Wilson. This suited him perfectly. Since the roads and laneways had been quiet thus far, he had enjoyed the little jaunt, forgetting for a time the seriousness of what he was caught up in and taking in the scenery. The terrain was flatter and richer than that of his home place but with many of the features common to land that is close to the sea, especially the fresh salty air. At one twisty section of road around Seafield, when the requisite distances put all the advance cyclists out of sight, he briefly considered taking a detour. If he allowed Peter to get ahead of him, he could dodge down a side lane, separate from the group and make his own way into the city. Common sense, for a change, overruled impulse and he decided to remain with people who knew where they were going rather than risk getting lost and ending up God knows where. He also thought it would be mean to put Peter in a difficult position.

There was noticeably more activity along Spittal Hill as they progressed into the more populous parts of Swords. Mostly it was people going about their daily business, but with edginess in their movements, anxiety in their faces, alarm in their reactions as the cyclecade came trundling out of nowhere, around their corner of town. At the bottom of Spittal Hill there was a left turn onto the bridge, where the estuary narrowed to become the Broadmeadow River. As JJ and Peter rounded this bend, the tail of the company came into view again, much closer than either had expected it to be. Maybe they had quickened up without realising it and drawn too close. But then JJ noticed that they too had closed ranks, become bunched as first two, then three, five and seven cyclists came into view up ahead. Next they heard the unmistakable cracking sounds of gunfire. They saw the men ahead swing their bicycles into either side of the road, leap off and spring onto and behind the walled ditches.

Peter quickened, instinctively; JJ slowed instinctively. The men ahead had shouldered their rifles and were returning fire. JJ couldn't see their target but assumed it was the police and that they had been ready, on alert, expecting trouble of some sort in the wake of the previous day's skirmish in Ashbourne. Adrenalin gushed through his veins, his head throbbed, his heart thumped as he freewheeled southwards along the top cross of a T-junction on an inevitable course towards the conflict. Peter, fifty yards ahead, was already ducking and weaving to avoid the rifle fire that cracked all around them, bullets pinging and whistling through the air.

"Roadblock, JJ!" roared Peter. "RIC! Take cover!"

JJ slowed further, scanning his surroundings for cover. Peter leapt from his bicycle, which wobbled riderless for a ridiculous moment or two before crashing to the ground as its erstwhile rider threw himself against a wall, slinging his rifle off his shoulder. JJ was still a little way back from the centre of the conflagration and about to do something similar, when he was overwhelmed by a sudden sensation – the opposite to a sense of loyalty. He gritted his teeth in defiance, squeezed the back brakes as tightly as he could and turned the handlebars. The back wheel skidded on the loose tinder and in an instant he was facing in the direction he'd just come from. The manoeuvre slowed him almost to a stop, so it took him several seconds to build up momentum again and his calves began to burn. Several bullets pinged off the walls to his left, another couple off the surface of the road to his right, one split the rear mudguard, and a ricochet disconnected one side of the carrier from the frame. JJ wasn't sure if the shots had been fired by the so-called enemy or the Volunteers, but he didn't look back to check. Instead he lifted his arse out of the saddle, put his head down and pedalled for all he was worth back along the road to the T-junction. Here he hung a spectacular right turn, nearly parting company with the bicycle, and careened eastwards, down a deserted Estuary Road, like a bullet shot from a Lee–Enfield.

He continued down Estuary Road, along the waterfront, without pause, without even lifting his head. His efforts had the same energy and vigour that had taken him clear of Bartley Comer's gun, his father's repression and all in Ballysumaghan that reminded him of his dead mother, the previous Wednesday. After close on two miles, at a place with walls yellowed from years of bleaching raw linen, he had no option but to follow the road around a tight, sweeping right-hand bend. Just up ahead a large brewery wagon had broken an axle and shed its load. The driver was unyoking the horse but flagged JJ down when he saw him approaching. JJ tugged on the back brakes again and skidded to his left onto a narrower road, through a large hamlet built around a cotton mill. There were forty or fifty houses, half with slate roofs, half with traditional thatch. The streets were as busy as those around Swords had been and his sudden appearance and urgent haste drew a few quizzical glances. A further half mile on, he slowed at another T-junction. A road sign indicated Malahide to his left and Dublin city to his right. Only then did he dare look back. He was alone. He hadn't been followed. Delighted and relieved, he turned right and followed the main road through Kinsealy, Balgriffin and Coolock, until, after about forty minutes of cycling, breathless and sweating, his calves tight, JJ had no option but to slow and take a breather.

It was only when he slowed that he noticed his back wheel was catching. On investigation he found that the split mudguard was the cause. He trundled to a stop beside a row of cottages that looked relatively new. It was only when he had dismounted that he discovered how badly damaged the rear of the bike was. He was astonished he'd been able to keep going at all, so tight was the back wheel. His ankle was also paining him again and he was sweating profusely. He pulled in alongside the cottages, laid the bike against the pillar of one of them and sat on its low brick wall. He took off his right boot and holed sock to massage his ankle and foot. There was a pub on the other side of the road, a single-storey building, not much bigger than one of the cottages. The name Kyle's was hand-painted in blue on a sign above the door. He thought he heard someone singing inside but it was too indistinct to be sure. A milestone twenty yards south told him he was only three miles from the city centre. He smiled and breathed deeply.

Although he was so close to the heart of the metropolis, this place had the feel and pace of a rural village. There were more people stirring and more traffic on the road than he would have seen in a week sitting on a wall in the middle of Sooey, though.

"All right, mister?"

JJ wheeled around to see two thin, scruffy boys of around thirteen or fourteen, both sporting fresh, tight haircuts. The one who had spoken was smiling broadly, the other had his head inclined slightly downwards and was squinting up as though he were used to looking from behind a long fringe, giving him a shifty appearance.

"Do you need some help?"

As the smiler tried to engage JJ in conversation, the other lad sidled around to his blind side.

"Ehm, no, thanks. I'm grand."

He glanced around at the shifty young fella but the smiler was already sitting beside JJ on the wall, uncomfortably close.

"Where are you comin' from?"

JJ was beginning to feel like the man he had seen pickpocketed in Ratoath. The shifty one lifted up his bike. JJ grasped it firmly. The young lad scowled.

"Just lookin'."

"I hope you're not thinkin' of headin' into the city," the smiler said.

JJ kept a firm grip on the bike. Shifty turned to look down the road as if unperturbed and uninterested.

"I am. Why?"

"Jaysus, all sorts of quare things goin' on in there by all accounts."

"What kind of things?"

"Some mad lads with guns took over the post office, I heard. Police and soldiers everywhere now."

"So it is true."

"That's what we heard anyway, isn't it, Heno?"

"I heard the Germans had invaded," said Heno flatly, looking down the road as if checking to see if the German flag had been hoisted already.

Smiler had also managed to get closer to JJ so that he felt like he was being caught in a pincer movement that would lead to an attempt to purloin whatever meagre possessions he had, so he decided to come clean and save the youngsters their blushes, and him the unnecessary irritation.

"Lookit, lads, I don't have anything, bar a couple of coppers, so ye're wasting yeer time with me."

"What are ya talkin' about?" said Smiler, not smiling now, his face wide with umbrage.

Heno turned around, his interest piqued again.

"I didn't come down in the last shower, lads."

"We were only trying to be friendly, mister."

"You looked lost," Heno added emphatically, almost squaring up to JJ now.

"I'm grand, thanks," JJ said, bending to put his sock back on, keeping his hip pressed against the bike.

As he stretched to get his boot, Smiler mirrored his movements and got his hand to it before JJ.

"Hey!"

JJ lunged at Smiler and Heno grabbed the handle bars with both hands.

"Just trying to help," Smiler said, the boot in his hand as he took a step back.

"Give me my boot!" JJ stood, taking his weight off the bicycle enough to allow Heno to yank it free. "Hey!" JJ shouted and grabbed the dislocated carrier just before it was out of reach.

"Do you not want yer boot, mister?" Smiler dangled the boot in front of JJ's face.

JJ tried to grab it with one hand while still holding the bike with the other.

Heno yanked again, knocking JJ off balance.

"Aw come on, lads, for fuck's sake!"

"Come on what? Do ya want the boot or the bike?"

"Givvus the fuckin' bike," snarled Heno.

"No!" JJ snapped. All the stress, anxiety, rejection and impediments of the past days bubbled to the surface and exploded in the face of these two cheeky, impertinent, irksome whippersnappers. Who the hell did they think they were and what the hell did they take him for? Some stupid, wet behind the ears, country fella who couldn't tell his arse from his neighbour's elbow? Well fuck them.

"Keep the fucking boot, ya eejit!"

He yanked the bike fiercely back from Heno, who clung on for all he was worth but almost toppled forward in the attempt.

"Take your hands off my bike, ya phucaide, or I'll knock your big leibide of a head off your fucking shoulders!"

Heno's eyes widened and he looked to Smiler for direction. Smiler jumped onto JJ's back, grabbing a fistful of his hair and whacking him with his own boot.

"Go on, Heno. We need that bike!"

"I'm tryin', for fuck's sake! He's a madman!"

JJ was beating Smiler off with one hand while pulling the bike for all he was worth with the other. He was fighting a losing battle, though, and was wondering what the passers-by made of what was happening. He was astonished that no one had intervened.

"Hey! You two!" a male voice called from the other side of the road. "Are youse on the run, yez bloody gurriers!" he shouted as he crossed over to them. Next he was pulling Smiler off JJ's back.

"I've got this one now, sonny!"

Smiler was beating the stranger with JJ's boot while continuing to tug on JJ's hair.

"These bloody bowsies are on the run from the industrial school above. Thieves and gougers, the whole bloody shower of them!"

JJ's grip on the bike was loosening. Heno gave one final yank and JJ lost his balance. He and Smiler fell backwards together, on top of the stranger, pulling JJ away from the bike long enough for Heno to snatch it.

By the time JJ had regained his balance, Heno was pedalling for all he was worth towards the city, followed by Smiler on foot, waving JJ's right boot above his head like a trophy.

"We just needed the fucking bike, mister, to get away from this shithole!"

JJ made an attempt to give chase. He needed that bike to get out of this shithole too. But between the lack of a boot and his sore ankle he quickly realised it was fruitless. Damn it!

Smiler hopped onto the crossbar of the bike and the two fugitives made good their escape.

"Bastards!" JJ roared in their wake.

"Sorry about that, my friend."

JJ might have kept possession of his bike and his boot, had this helpful stranger not shown up when he did. Now he had neither.

"Not to worry. Thanks."

"No problem. Anyway, they won't get too far if they're thinkin' of headin' into the city. There's bloody mayhem in there by all accounts."

"Really?"

"Yeah. A bunch of lads from around here marched in yesterday. Shinners. Mad in the head if you ask me. Anyway, better shoot the crow. You'll be all right?"

JJ looked at his stockinged foot as if it was a complex algebraic equation. "Yeah, I suppose. I'll have to be."

"Good luck, then."

"I could do with a bit of that, all right."

The pub was dark and smoky. There were ten or eleven people inside, as far as JJ could make out, and all except one were men. The singer he had heard faintly from outside was a tall, hefty woman wearing a faded brown coat. She sat in the far corner with a half-finished glass of Guinness in front of her. She looked mysterious, even a little sad as she stared into her drink. When she lifted her head, though, she smiled at him and her whole face lit up. She saluted him with her glass, then drank. JJ hadn't the price of a drink, so he just tipped his hat and wondered why he had come in here at all. Maybe he'd been drawn by the possibility of music, curious to confirm if he had in fact heard someone singing. He also hoped someone there might have been able to provide an old pair of boots. The clientele took the opportunity to look him up and down, muttering quietly to each other, regarding him with undisguised suspicion. No one offered a pair of boots. He certainly didn't feel welcome and was sure the proprietor would ask him to leave once he returned from whatever task had taken him into the living quarters, especially when he discovered JJ hadn't the price of a drink. Still, he had nothing to lose, and at least the old woman seemed happy to see him.

"Hey!" she called, waving her left arm vaguely in the direction of the bar, without looking. "Hey!" she bellowed. "Barman! Barman! Give this man a drink. Barman!"

"Shut up," barked one of the other drinkers. "He's in the back."

"What?"

JJ wondered if perhaps she was deaf.

"He's in the back!" a second man shouted.

"He can't hear you."

"Ah, for fuck's sake! What kind of a fucking pub is this anyway?"

"Shut up, Biddy, or you'll be out on your ear," said a third man in a dark suit. He was standing on his own, apart from the other customers. He spoke with authority, loudly but without shouting.

"Ara fuck off, Marcus. Stingy auld bollox."

JJ felt even more self-conscious now that he was the cause of this discord without even opening his mouth. He made a move to go.

"Stay where you are, young man," said the auld one, pointing with an arthritic finger. "He'll be back in a minute and we'll have a drink together."

JJ sat down and smiled at the curious stranger. He noticed that there was a banjo on the bench beside her; its strap was the belt off her coat.

"Do you sing?" she asked as she picked it up and adjusted it into the playing position without waiting for a response.

"Well, yes I—"

Too late. She was already picking out a staccato melody on the strings by way of an intro. She began to sing in a low, husky but unquestionably feminine voice.

> On the banks of the Roses, my love and I sat down,
> And I took out my fiddle to play my love a tune.
> In the middle of the tune, oh she sighed and she said,
> Oro Johnny, lovely Johnny, would you leave me?

She was tuneful and melodious but the song was a little doleful and the theme seemed to drag her down so that she almost disappeared into herself, her volume lowering with every line, her head sinking, her voice weakening. Even the twinkling strings of the banjo failed to lighten the mood. The men continued to talk among themselves. She hummed the first two bars of the next verse, then threw her head in the air, laughing dryly.

"Ara will you listen to the daft auld bird, draggin' the whole place down with her lamenting. We need something brighter," she said. And without missing a beat, the tempo of her picking increased and the strings of the banjo seemed to skitter and giggle as she sang.

> There was three farmers in the north, as they were passing by,
> They swore an oath, a mighty oath that barley corn should die,
> One of them said drown him and the other said hang him
>   high,
> For whoever will stick to barley grain, a begging he will die.
> With me fal-la-la-the-dee, toor-a-lay, a begging he will die.

During the final line of the verse she nodded at JJ to join in. He didn't need a second invitation. "They put poor barley in a sack of a cold and rainy day/ And brought him off to culm fields and buried him in the clay."

Her voice was loud, rasping, bursting with energy and passion, almost like a foghorn in the cramped pub.

JJ sang along exuberantly. "Frost and snow began to melt and the dew began to fall/ When barley grain put up his head and soon surprised them all." He was feeling their mutual exclusion and sense of rejection. It was a song of defiance, a proclamation for the downtrodden and abused, all those gifted with the voice of individuality who have had their spirit crushed and buried by oppression, a declaration that the seed will rise again in spring. By the time they reached the end of the song, both were on their feet, JJ half skipping, half dancing as he sang, Biddy kicking her heavy, swollen feet as best she could, as she continued to pluck and sing. She put every fibre of her being into that final verse, every decibel of her voice.

"The barley grain is a comical grain, it makes men sigh and moan/ For when they take a glass or two they forgot their wife and home."

She was singing it at the other drinkers now, striding among them, her words prodding like firethorns. She nudged a couple of them with her hefty shoulder, almost knocking them off their perches. JJ followed, his hand on her shoulder, echoing her passion and matching her volume.

"The drunkard is a dirty man, he used me worse than all/ He drank me up in his dirty maw and tumbled against the wall!"

She so enjoyed these final two lines that she reprised them, turning to JJ, elongating the last note until she had no breath left in her lungs and sustaining the final chord on the banjo by playing it in triple time.

This was around the time the proprietor entered from the living quarters, red-faced and fuming. His regulars liked a quiet drink at this time on a Tuesday, especially with all the rumours flying about the place from the evening before. He was shouting but the singers couldn't hear him. The final exertions so exhausted Biddy that her face was nearly purple. She stumbled, then lunged forward, spreading her arms wide. JJ grabbed her but couldn't adjust quickly enough to take her weight, increased by her sudden momentum. The banjo went clanging to the ground and the unlikely, ungainly couple went crashing into two of the drinkers seated on stools at the counter, sending them, the stools and their half-full pint glasses flying, finally ending in a disorganised heap of limbs, stool legs and broken glass on the flagged floor.

"In the love and honour of Jaysus! What the hell are ye tryin' to do to me?"

They heard the proprietor this time, at least JJ did.

"I told you not to be goin' on with any of yer auld messin', Biddy, or you'd be out on yer ear!"

"Owww on yer eee-arrrr!" said Biddy, mimicking the drawl of his accent and laughing.

JJ was laughing, too, and trying to pick himself and Biddy up off the floor. He was enjoying the discomfort and righteous indignation of the uptight poker-up-the-arse drinkers who hadn't even had the courtesy to bid him good day when he came in. Some of them reminded him of his father and that made him laugh even more, that and Biddy's infectious giggle.

"Get out, ya crazy auld bitch!"

"Crayzeee auld bitch!" she mimicked.

"Get out! And take yer mangy auld lap dog with you! Go on!"

They were hoisted onto their feet by the landlord and a couple of his mewling customers and marched out the door, before Biddy had time to do another mocking impersonation of the demented owner.

Once outside in the cold, bright light of day, JJ was suddenly aware of just how drunk Biddy was. She was giggling uncontrollably and unable to stay on her feet without the support of a wall, or JJ's shoulder. She clutched the banjo in her left hand and JJ noticed that one of the strings had snapped. He asked her where she lived, if she knew anyone nearby who could take her in, if she had any family. But her answers were incoherent or nonsensical. The best he could ascertain was that she lived in the city somewhere. What the hell had he taken on himself now? He asked a few passers-by if they knew her. None answered; a couple even made a point of stepping off the footpath as they passed, peering down their noses at the drunken couple. He couldn't just leave her there on her own, in this state. So he had no option but to strap the banjo around her back and start walking her, like a wounded combatant, towards the city. Hopefully the walk would sober her up and she might become more cogent.

After fifteen minutes of walking, staggering and stumbling, JJ's limp exaggerated by his lack of a right boot, they reached the Bradshaw Estate in Clontarf. The perimeter was delineated by a cut-stone wall with a line of huge oak, sycamore and beech trees behind, through which could be seen the carefully maintained lawns of Clontarf Golf Club.

The fairways cut swathes like runways through the longer, rougher wild grass. The fairway closest to them led to the beautifully manicured twelfth green. The whole picture seemed utterly incongruous to JJ after the undignified scene on the streets of Artane and in the pub, not to mention the rudimentary conditions and discomfort of the past twenty-four hours. The bucolic picture, framed by staunch walls and veiled behind stiff, decades-old trees, represented the wealth and privilege of a world that was inaccessible and alien to the likes of JJ and Biddy and most if not all of the people he had met over the past week, certainly all of the people he had grown up with.

As JJ stood staring in through the trees, Biddy dropped her banjo on the ground and slid down the wall, until she was sitting, her head slumped forward. She was standing when JJ had left her propped against the wall, mumbling angrily about "fuckers!" and "bastards!" and "the whole fuckin' lot of them!", making no sense but releasing a lot of frustration. It was the third time she had ended up on her arse since being thrown out of the pub. She was trying to sing now, too, but what emerged was mostly just lilting or mumming. What few words escaped were too muffled to decipher. The melody shifted disconcertingly so that JJ couldn't work out what song she was trying to sing. As he turned to pick her up again and resume their trek into the city, his eye was caught by something metallic glinting in the shrubbery behind the wall, among and between the trees. On closer inspection, he saw spokes and the outline of a wheel, a bicycle wheel. There was a man's bicycle half-concealed in the shrubbery, thrown there, discarded in a hurry. Was it useable? Was it in fact his own?

Seconds later JJ was the other side of the wall, tearing at the shrubbery between him and the bike with his bare hands, crushing it down with his booted foot. The extra weight on his injured foot caused several darts of pain. JJ eventually pulled the bike free and howled as a thorn pierced his stockinged foot. As he hopped on his booted foot, struggling to extract the thorn, he also spotted his missing boot in the shrubbery. He happily reshod his right foot and finally confirmed that the bike was in fact his, or as much his as it had ever been. He was delighted to have found it again, then crestfallen to discover that the back tyre was flat, pierced by the split mudguard. He was pleased, nonetheless, that the little gurriers hadn't got far on their misdeed.

While he was tossing the useless bike back into the shrubbery, he noticed an army infantry support truck come to a stop on the road with a squeal of brakes. Several young British troops leapt from it and approached Biddy.

"Roight, you! Up! Now!"

JJ watched from the cover of the shrubbery, unsure whether or not to intervene. "Get up, you silly old cow!" a second trooper sneered.

"Maybe she's injured," said the third.

They might take her off his hands, bring her home to wherever she lived.

"Bollox!" swore the second man, a corporal. He kicked her a couple of times.

"Fuck off!" Biddy mumbled from the depths of her stupor.

"She's fucking pissed!" said the first trooper, laughing. "Oi, wake up, Granmaw," he said as he hunkered down, shaking her vigorously and slapping her face a couple of times.

JJ suppressed an impulse to leap to her defence.

"Fuck off!" Biddy slapped back ineffectively. "Mnhucking bastarrrrs!"

"Whoa! Got a bit of a tongue on 'er, ain't she?"

Biddy grabbed the squaddie's face with a claw-like right hand.

"Ow, you fucking bitch!"

The second soldier struck Biddy's right arm with his rifle butt. She squealed in pain and released her grip on his colleague, who put one hand to his wound and struck her on the face with his other fist.

"Fucking bitch!"

"Leave 'er. Let's get going!" ordered the corporal.

The injured squaddie grabbed Biddy by the hair, pulled her roughly away from the wall and kicked her again. As he raised his rifle above his head to strike her, JJ could restrain himself no longer. He thrashed through the shrubbery and leapt over the wall.

"Hey, leave her. She's with me."

The effect was like hurling a large rock into a pond. Biddy was pushed to the ground face first as all three soldiers sprang back, the corporal drawing and cocking his pistol, the other two raising their rifles to their shoulders. Two more jumped out of the vehicle. They were all shouting over each other, not hearing anything JJ was saying.

"What the fuck?"

"Look out!"

"Who are you?"

"Get down!"

"No!"

"Put your hands on your head! Hands on your head!"

"Back against the wall, you fucker!"

"No but—"

"Against the fucking wall!"

"Are there any others?"

Three soldiers were waving their rifles around while two more had theirs focused on JJ's chest. JJ spread his arms as he pleaded to be listened to.

"No, she's—"

"Hands on your head! On your fucking head!"

"Please, let me just . . ." He stooped to pick Biddy up but before he could budge her, he was grabbed roughly by the back of his jacket and hurled against the wall.

"Check behind the wall!" barked the corporal.

"Cover us!" roared one squaddie as he and another hopped the wall in a well-rehearsed move, their rifles trained as they scoured the environs for enemy operatives.

JJ, slightly winded, was supporting himself on the wall, the muzzle of a rifle lodged between his shoulder blades.

"Please, she's with me," he said breathlessly.

"Shut up!"

"Anything there?" bawled the corporal.

"No sign of hostiles."

"She's . . . she's my mother. Just let me pick her up."

"She's drunk! Not much of a son, are you?"

"No, she's . . . she's not well . . . Consumption."

"Who are you? What are you doing here?" barked the trooper, pressing the muzzle deeper into JJ's back.

"Ehm . . . Liam. I'm Liam Kenny. We were on our way home."

"And where is home?" asked the corporal more calmly, taking control of the situation.

"In the city," was the best JJ could come up with.

Before the young corporal could insist on something more precise, he was interrupted by one of his men, searching the undergrowth.

"There's a bicycle here, Corporal. Looks like it's just been ditched. Been shot up too!"

"Roight matey, arms out, spread your legs."

"What?"

The muzzle dug deeper still so that JJ had to spread his arms and grab the wall to prevent his face being smashed. The squaddie kicked JJ's legs apart with his big hob-nailed boots.

"Where are you coming from?" asked the corporal.

"What?"

"Where?" shouted the corporal as JJ got the butt of the rifle full in the back.

"Argh! Artane. Artane I think it's called."

"You think?"

"It is. Yes. There's a man there. A healer. He treats her, my mother."

"A fucking witch doctor, eh?"

"No, but, well she, we don't have money for doctors."

"Fucking peasants and witches, the lot of yez. Search them," he ordered.

Shit. This was really spiralling out of control. Less than two minutes ago, his biggest problem was how to get this larger-than-life, drunken old woman to safety. Now, he was surrounded by five jumpy English soldiers who had their guns trained on him. And they were about to search him and find that shagging pistol in his breast pocket, the one he hadn't even wanted in the first place, wouldn't have accepted only it was Molly who had presented it to him. Fuck! How could he get out of this? The pistol was sure to send these hair-trigger squaddies into a tail spin. Would they even give him a chance to explain it away as self-protection against any crazy, treacherous rebels he might encounter? That might ingratiate him to the squaddies, give the impression that they were all on the same side.

It was around this point that Biddy began to regain some awareness. She shuddered expansively and hauled herself onto her knees. She squatted for a moment, dazed, taking in the scene, sobering a little and beginning to recognise the seriousness of the situation. The squaddie who'd had his rifle lodged in JJ's back had put it aside to search him. As he placed his hands on JJ's shoulders to begin frisking him, JJ plunged his hand into his own breast pocket. At the same time, Biddy lumbered to her feet and began flailing her hands above her head, bellowing like a fog horn. JJ whipped out the pistol. Biddy charged the soldiers. JJ wheeled around and smacked his unsuspecting captor in the face with the pistol butt.

Screaming like a dervish, Biddy punched, grabbed and scratched the two squaddies closest to her. As the two young men struggled to restrain her, JJ grabbed his stunned captor around the neck, held the pistol to his head and cocked the hammer. The two squaddies wrestling Biddy, distracted by JJ's actions, released their grip on her. Seizing the opportunity, Biddy kicked the one nearest her in the groin and snatched his rifle, but lost her balance and staggered backwards against the wall. This distracted JJ but before the squaddies could react, the impact of striking the wall caused Biddy to pull the trigger of the rifle. The shot sounded like an explosion, amplified by the leafy canopy. Although the barrel was pointed harmlessly at the ground, the bullet ricocheted into the thigh of the squaddie she'd snatched it from.

"Oh, Jaysus, what have I fuckin' done?" Biddy cried.

One of the squaddies rushed at her but she instinctively swung the rifle upwards, so that it was aimed directly at his chest. He stopped in his tracks.

"Now that I know how this thing works, you'd better be careful, sham!"

The rifle shot had instantly focused everyone's attention again and now it was JJ's turn to bark out the orders. He pushed the pistol against the temple of his captor become captive.

"Right! Put your weapons down or I will shoot this man." Christ, he thought, could they not hear the tremor in his voice? Could they not see his hand shaking? He pushed the gun even harder into the man's temple to stop the shake, causing the terrified young squaddie to whimper pitifully.

There was silence for an instant before it was shattered by the scream of the soldier who had been shot in the leg. The shock had silenced him momentarily, but now that blood was spurting from his wound the full horror hit home. The bullet had severed an artery. The man's plaintive cries and the sight of the blood made JJ nauseous but he fought off the urge to puke, or worse still, pass out. So he had one soldier held at gun point, another was bleeding to death on the roadside, a third was in a stand-off with Biddy and the final squaddie and his corporal had a rifle and a pistol trained on JJ.

"So, what now, Oirish?" asked the corporal.

"Good question," said JJ, genuinely nonplussed. He noticed the corporal gulp.

"Neither of you will get out of this alive."

"Maybe we won't, but neither will this man, or your chap on the ground, and I don't fancy your mate's chances against my mother, either."

The corporal gulped again and glanced at the hefty balladeer, one eye closed, her rifle hovering less than a foot from the soldier's heart. The man on the ground roared again, pleading for help. JJ saw beads of sweat glistening on the corporal's forehead. He wasn't much older than JJ.

Emboldened, JJ said, "That's a high price to pay for some peasant and his drunken mother."

The corporal ordered Smith to take care of the man on the ground. The young soldier drew cautiously back from Biddy's rifle and slowly removed his belt to make a tourniquet for his mate.

Biddy swung her rifle onto the corporal and smiled.

"Now!" shouted JJ, hoarse, a quiver still audible in his voice. "You need to get that boy to a hospital quickly, Corporal, or he'll bleed to death."

The corporal licked his lips, blinked three or four times in quick succession.

JJ was immersed in his role now, confident that he had the upper hand. He breathed deeply and fixed the corporal with a steely gaze. "I'm going to keep this man as a hostage. You two throw your weapons over the wall and get everyone back into the truck. Save that man's life, while you still can."

JJ could see the wheels turning in the corporal's head. It was a surreal situation. The whole incident had taken less than three minutes to reach this extraordinary climax. Surely he would realise the loss of three good men, including himself, was a ridiculous price to pay for one lone wolf rebel and his witch of a mother.

A moment later the corporal said, "Smith, Roberts, get Jackson into the truck!"

His two subordinates looked dubious for an instant, a little taken aback by the order, but delighted to be able to save their friend's life and their own too. Roberts hurled his and Jackson's rifles over the wall and then moved swiftly and skilfully to get Jackson into the back of the truck. The corporal, his pistol still trained on JJ's head, checked with the hostage that he was all right. The man confirmed with a nod of the head. The corporal promised JJ that he would personally find him and kill him if he harmed Manley. JJ flinched; one of his knees buckled slightly. He decided that any response would only weaken his position. The corporal returned his defiant gaze, then flung his pistol over the wall and left with his tail firmly between his legs.

19

Shooters, Looters, the Tramp and the Queen

———•———

ABOUT AN HOUR LATER THE slightly burlesque duo reached Fairview. They had cut through the practically deserted golf club and out onto the Howth Road on the opposite side. While crossing the course, they had encountered four middle-aged golfers who either had no idea what was afoot in the city, or they knew but treated it with utter contempt and disdain. While JJ had tucked his pistol into the waist of his trousers, Biddy kept her rifle barrel resting between Manley's shoulder blades as they marched the forlorn squaddie ahead of them, with no idea what they were going to do with him. The four intrepid golfers didn't exhibit the slightest hint of trepidation. So JJ ordered them to take responsibility for the young soldier – he was enjoying his new authoritative role – and to ensure that he was returned unharmed to his own barracks or any barracks. The golfers didn't flinch, remained phlegmatic.

"Indeed," said the oldest, moustachioed gent.

And so the pair marched on, Biddy keeping her rifle trained on the four ball turned five until they were out of sight on the far side of the hill leading from the ninth green. She then slung the rifle over her shoulder like a cavalier infantry-woman or an extra in an amateurish Gilbert and Sullivan production.

In Fairview they needed to rest. Biddy had become quite sober and was feeling the effects of the drink, as well as the trek. The area between the village and the sea was little more than mud flats, with part of it used as a dump for some of the city's rubbish. The Dublin–Belfast railway line ran along the far side, but once you crossed that you were at the sea. Drawn by the salt air and the prospect of the soothing ebb and flow of the tide, the pair made their way to the water's edge. Biddy bathed and massaged her calloused feet while JJ sat on a rock, his injured foot dangling in the brine, and allowed the repetitive rhythm of the sea to lull him into a meditative torpor.

"Did I hear you tellin' them soldiers I was your mother?" Biddy asked eventually.

"Hmm?" JJ tuned in, slowly. He shrugged. "It's all I could think of."

"What was she like?"

"Who?"

"Your mother."

"Oh. I don't really remember. She died when I was very young."

"Sorry to hear that. She was beautiful, no doubt?"

"Yes. Very beautiful."

"Well, that's maybe a good side of death then."

"What?"

"Well, if you die young and beautiful, that's how you'll be remembered."

"I'd rather have had her around."

"Of course you would. But what if she'd aged badly? Like me? Ended up a fat, drunken auld wan?"

"You're not. And anyway, that's not all there is to beauty."

"Ha! You're a fucking plawmawser and no mistake. I'd say the girleens love that."

JJ smirked, looked wistfully across at the hump she called Bray Head on the opposite shore.

"You know what I mean. She'll always be young and beautiful in your memory, whereas I'll always be fat, loud and troublesome."

"Sounds to me like that's the way you like to be seen."

She released a loud legato laugh, her natural contralto rumbling above the sounds of the sea, the gulls providing a harmonising soprano.

JJ threw his head back and joined in the rasping chorus.

"I'm hungry now but I'm back on home ground, so come on, let's go."

As they trudged barefoot through the silt and back to the main street, she told him that she lived in Summerhill, only fifteen or twenty minutes away. She assured him there'd be a welcome for them there and some grub too.

"We might even sing a few auld songs, a mhacín." She smiled and strummed the auld banjo before slinging it over her shoulder again.

When they reached the street, their feet were caked in sandy mud. JJ advised Biddy to keep her rifle out of sight behind the low wall that bordered the mud flats. She sat on the same wall and JJ brushed the silt and dried mud off her feet. She laughed when his touch tickled but thanked him as she put back on her stockings and shoes. As he brushed the dirt from his own feet a man came scurrying along from the direction of Fairview Strand, to their north. He ducked down and glanced over his shoulder to his right as he crossed from Hayes Conyngham pharmacy on the corner opposite. JJ noticed now that the windows of the pharmacy had been shot out, the front door boarded up, although the shop was still open for business. The man approached JJ and placed an arm on his shoulder, huddling close. He spoke in a slightly hushed tone, repeatedly glancing over his shoulder and back down towards the river, the Tolka he called it.

"I wouldn't dilly dally around here if I was youse, my friends."

"We were just about to go up to Summerhill," said Biddy.

"Oh Jaysus! Sure it's as bad up there!"

"Well that's my home and it's where I'm goin."

"Well, stay well clear of Annesley Bridge Road," the man warned, pointing at the road between the pharmacy and the bridge.

He told them a fierce battle had raged most of the previous day and into the night around the bridge and up and down that stretch of road. The rebels had been transporting guns from nearby Croydon Park to the city when they were surprised by a British force marching in from the British Musketry School, out on Bull Island to the east. The band of young, ill-trained, trigger-happy soldiers were also en route to the city centre when they happened upon the rebels. Many civilians got caught in the crossfire as the battle raged on the streets for several hours. The rebels then took cover in the houses along the street and on roofs, while the British took up strategic positions on the opposite side, on Wharf Road and around the port. A sniper battle continued for another twelve hours, with anyone who moved becoming a target.

"Several residents were shot dead, mistaken for rebels by the British or for soldiers by the rebels. Murdered because they had twitched a curtain, their curiosity getting the better of them, or tried to drag a wounded man to safety. One man just walked past a window that a sniper had in his sights."

He showed them where one man, presumed to be a rebel, still dangled from a chimney stack where he'd been shot as he tried to steeplejack his way up to a prime sniping position. They looked down past the pharmacy to a factory complex he called the manure works and sure enough, JJ could see a tiny, insect-like figure dangling from one of two chimney stacks.

The safety rope had been attached to the steeplejack's waist so the tiny figure swayed slightly in the wind, his arms and legs splayed pitifully. There was something sad, forlorn and slightly pathetic about the tiny, lifeless figure suspended in death above the angry streets.

"Why doesn't someone take the poor fucker down?" Biddy asked the stranger.

"Anyone insane enough to climb up that yoke would surely meet the same fate!" He concluded that things had quietened down since morning, with only occasional volleys. He still didn't feel safe, though, with shooting and looting and all sorts of mad exploits. He'd heard some of the looters in the city had even been shot dead for the sake of the few measly bits and pieces they'd managed to grab.

"The city is gone mad! Mad!" he declared finally before scurrying off with urgent caution, along Fairview Main Street and into Merville Avenue.

Biddy suggested they should head up Fairview Strand, where the gentleman had come from, take a left at Gilbey's Wine Merchants into Ballybough Road and on up to Summerhill. The names of the streets meant nothing to JJ but he was sure Biddy knew her way around this part of the city and at least she remembered now where she lived. JJ wanted to leave the rifle behind, worried that it would make them a target. He even thought about ditching his own pistol. But Biddy was adamant that they hold on to both weapons.

"We don't know much about what's happening, a mhac. We might end up having to defend ourselves, against both sides!"

The thought sickened JJ to his core but he was in unknown territory now.

Biddy concealed the rifle beneath her long coat. It made walking more difficult but discovery less likely. "At the very least, I'll get a nice few bob for this above in the Hill!"

When they reached Summerhill there was quite the commotion, just past the junction with Buckingham Street. JJ had become used to landing in the middle of commotions by now but there was a real sense of carnival to this one. He couldn't believe the sight that was materialising as they approached. It was like they'd walked onto the set of a Keystone film. A bawdy, colourful group of about ten boys, men and women were returning from an expedition into the city and were singing, dancing and skipping their way down the middle of the road. The women were dressed like the tenement dwellers they were but also wearing elaborate lace, silk and flower-adorned hats as fine as any he had seen in Fairyhouse. The men too sported incongruous hats and coats that belied their impoverished state. They also carried armfuls of similar couture or small items of furniture and ornaments. One woman had filled her scarf with silver trinkets and gathered it at the corners to form an improvised swag bag. Several of the barefoot children in ragged hand-me-downs carried handfuls of expensive-looking chocolates. One girl dug her hand into the centre of a huge, creamy gateau and scooped out helpings to share with her companions. Then, in the midst of it all, emerging from the back like a spectre in a dream, strutting penguin-like down the middle of the road, was Charlie Chaplin himself.

"Good Jesus," said JJ, "it's Charlie bloody Chaplin."

"What are you talkin' about, a mhac?" said Biddy.

"Look!" JJ's finger was shaking with excitement as he pointed at the apparition less than a hundred feet away.

"It's a mirage. The hunger can cause that."

How could this be? JJ could see him, see his hero as clear as day, as clear as he could see the rest of the crowd. He was wearing the tilted black bowler hat, the ill-fitting tailcoat and sporting his iconic black moustache. He swirled the cane by his side, waddled with his feet pointed outwards, the same way JJ had seen him do in all the photos and the one film of his he'd been lucky enough to see.

"It's him, it has to be."

"Why the hell would he be bothered coming to a place like this at all, not to mention when it's crawling with crazy rebels and jittery soldiers who might blow his head off as quick as look at him?"

The man was close enough now to distinguish his features more clearly. The suit was ill-fitting but not loose around the midriff, because this "Charlie" had a round little belly that Chaplin didn't. He also bantered with the others in a broad Dublin accent and, on closer inspection, his suit was brand new, unlike the threadbare cast-offs that Chaplin's tramp wore. Finally, as he was only yards away now, JJ could see that the trademark black moustache was just a streak of mud or coal, applied by a finger to complete the illusion. The chirpy impersonator elaborately tipped his bowler and greeted them with his poor version of a middle-class Dublin drawl.

"Good afternoon to yiz and isn't it a pleasant one for an auld stroll."

JJ was crestfallen. Biddy thought the whole scene hilarious. It turned out the smash and grabbers had stolen the clothes, furniture, ornaments and confection from the expensive department stores in the nearby city centre. "Everyone is doing it!" they said. "The whole bleedin' city is on the rampage!" Apparently the shenanigans in the GPO had spread further through the streets, so there were no police, only army, and they were too busy dealing with the rebels to be bothered with a few looters. They'd heard rumours, though, that some looters had been shot by the rebels.

"But we had no bother," one of the younger girls chimed, "and sure wasn't it worth the risk anyway."

The group cheered as she raised her booty for all to see. It was a great opportunity for the poor of the city to taste some of the pleasures and luxuries usually denied them. "Sure wasn't it great auld gas!"

"And isn't yer man done up like Charlie Chaplin a right scream altogether."

JJ enjoyed the funny side of it too but he was beginning to feel like he was living in a dream world, where everything was topsy-turvy and it was getting hard for a man to know whether he was coming or going. Biddy on the other hand, ever the pragmatist, had already bartered the rifle in return for a couple of healthy portions of the more nourishing food that had been purloined earlier in the day: Shaw's quality ham with cold spuds, olives, anchovies, tinned mock turtle soup and caviar from a jar. JJ found the fish roe far too salty and bitter for his liking. The main course was washed down with an exquisite Château Lafite followed by a dessert of almonds and luxury chocolates. The feast had been acquired from Findlater's on Sackville Street, the city's finest grocer and wine merchant, JJ was told. After this lavish buffet, he and Biddy tuned the banjo and led the group in a rousing sing-song.

The spirit of fun and opportunistic good fortune remained but a sombre note was struck when several of Biddy's friends recounted dramatic tales of street battles fought between rebels and soldiers, with many innocent bystanders getting killed in the crossfire. Several had close friends who had been wounded or suffered injuries from falls, as they fled the fighting. One man had just learned that his cousin had been shot dead by a sniper. It was unclear whether it was an accident, a case of mistaken identity or simply a trigger-happy renegade who placed little value on life. Several others claimed they had heard that a young boy of only thirteen from the Summerhill area had been shot dead. So the atmosphere was a curious mix of frivolity, larceny and mourning.

By nightfall, the feasting and storytelling had developed into a rowdy, all-out street party. A huge fire had been lit using wooden boxes, old furniture and abandoned carts. A good deal of spirits had been consumed, and as the evening drew in, more musical instruments were produced, tunes played, dances improvised and songs sung. Biddy was welcomed home like a returned emigrant. They loved her, her spirit, her wisdom and her music, and they treated her like a queen.

"You're the Queeeean of Summerhill, Biddy!" they cheered.

As her companion and rescuer, her de facto son, JJ, was afforded an equally warm welcome. Within an hour he was at the centre of the festivities, if they could be called such under the circumstances, wielding a half-empty bottle of whiskey and singing a rousing rendition of "Lanigan's Ball" to the encouraging cheers of the assembled residents. They also had a couple of cases of the finest looted whiskey to oil the wheels of conviviality.

If JJ hadn't got so drunk on the whiskey, the hysteria and the singing, he would have been appalled at the slovenliness of the accommodation Biddy and her extended family called home. A small farmer's cottage in the West of Ireland, devoid of a woman's touch, was not the neatest, cleanest or most pleasant place to grow up, but JJ had never experienced anything as acrid and stifling as the stench of bodies, rotten food, urine and faeces that assaulted his nostrils when he staggered into Biddy's tenement. He retched but assumed it was the copious volumes of whiskey he had consumed that was the cause of his nausea and not the rancid atmosphere. If he wasn't seeing double, he would have counted fifteen other occupants, between adults, adolescents and children. Each mooched about until they found a space just about large enough to accommodate his or her own form. Twisting, turning or spreading oneself wide were not options. As JJ stood in wonder in the corner, watching this dance, the now-empty whiskey bottle still clutched in his hand, the images began to blur, a loud buzzing permeated his skull, his breathing became laboured, until finally he slid down the wall and crumpled in a heap, his chin nestled on his chest, and began to snore quietly. As he slept, the room continued to glow orange and red from the myriad fires that blazed in the centre of the besieged city on the other side of the window.

20

The Lancer's Horse

———✦———

AWARENESS SEEPED INTO JJ'S BRAIN through the slit of his half-open eye. The room was dark but for one sharp shaft of light coming through a hole in the tattered old curtain. JJ followed the streak of light. If it had been a sniper's bullet, it would have pierced Biddy through the heart as she lay snoring loudly on a brand-new mattress that had come from Arnott's department store on Henry Street. He blinked his second eye open and watched the dust particles bounce and glide in the shaft of sunlight, entranced by their mesmeric dance. He winced slightly then, as a sharp pain began at the base of his skull and sliced slowly through his head and into his left eye socket.

A moment later the whole building seemed to shake and everyone was suddenly awake, the younger ones screaming in terror as several ferocious bangs rang out across the centre of the city. Each explosion was preceded by a kind of dull thud some distance away.

"Jaysus. What the hell was that?" JJ asked his roommates.

"Sounds like it's coming from the river."

"I heard there was an English gunboat down at the port."

Everyone stared at the window, mouths agape, as another fierce blast rang out, followed by a dazzling flash of orange light. This rebellion, this war or whatever it was, was ratcheting up and would have to be taken seriously by everyone, whether they liked it or not.

JJ's roomates jumped to their feet, ready to flee if necessary. Some crawled boldly to the two tall windows to see what was happening to their city. The women were screaming, convinced the shells were exploding right outside the building. The children cried, whined, grabbed and clung to their mothers' dresses, their fear transformed to panic by their mothers' hysteria. The men became instant, urban guerrillas, creeping stealthily about the room, pulling the women down, ordering the children to lie flat, while those who had crept to the windows edged back the curtains to get a better view. JJ caught sight of the next explosion, only about half a mile south. First there was the huge bang and the window panes rattled; next the bright flash from the combustion of the peroxides; then the ball of smoke that puffed into the air, blocking out the sun for an eerie moment.

"That's the post office," declared one of the men.

"Jaysus, they're fucked now for sure."

JJ slumped down, his back to the window, as the banging ceased, replaced by the intermittent crackling of rifles and the insistent rattle of machine guns. It was only then that he became fully aware of the filth of the room. Washing hung from improvised clotheslines, one in the doorway that led to a smaller sleeping area, another attached to the ceiling. There was an open cabinet built into the wall in a corner of the room, full of dirty pots and pans, tin mugs and plates. More utensils hung from a chipped mantel that sat above what had once been an open fireplace, blocked now by an ancient, battered stove. JJ imagined the house when it had been inhabited by its original owners, now doubtless living in a comfortable mansion in the suburbs; a fire maintained by a paid servant heating the room; family portraits, expensive ornaments and a clock decorating the mantel. Perhaps even the very clock that stood in its centre now, stopped at ten minutes to ten. Only a wedding photograph and a picture of the Sacred Heart decorated the wall now, a meagre nod to domesticity. Underneath, a worn, stained washboard and a portable urinal, full of piss and shit from the night, undermined any effort to create a civilised environment.

JJ saw that most of the occupants had slept in their clothes on the bare floor or on old sacks, with barely enough room to lie down. Biddy had her new mattress and there were two tattered mattresses in the other much smaller room; one for Biddy's son and daughter-in-law, the other shared by five of the younger children. The other adults – cousins, uncles, aunts – had slept wherever they could find space, anaesthetised by the alcohol. The awful stench stung JJ's nostrils. He belched. The whiskey reflux combined with the overpowering smell was too much for him. He leapt to his feet and ran out into the corridor in search of the front door, but unfamiliar with the building's layout, he didn't find it in time. He spewed up against the wall of the corridor and again all over the floor. It was mostly liquid so the area covered was wide. The smell, as nauseating as that of the room, soon blended with the general odour of the place and was scarcely noticed by the residents, accustomed as they were to squalor.

In contrast, the air outside was fresh, almost sweet. JJ inhaled huge mouthfuls, dragging it deep into his lungs then blowing it out quickly so that he could refill them instantly. His head was thumping by now, his throat dry and raw. His stomach ached and groaned, upset by the stale alcohol and stifling room. It was empty too and in need of sustenance. The sun was shining brilliantly in a virtually clear blue sky. The morning was alive with birdsong. If it weren't for the cracking of rifle fire, he might have thought he was in the most idyllic city in the whole of the British Empire. The street burst into life as throngs of people came streaming out of the row of tenements. JJ looked with utter disbelief at the sheer volume of human life that spilled from the dilapidated buildings. Obviously every room was at least as cramped as his own had been. The mood again was light, excited. The residents were anxious to get closer to the centre of things again, to get a ringside seat, as if they were attending a boxing tournament.

Biddy stopped to encourage JJ to join them. "This'll be better than any of those movie pictures you were going on about last night!"

He had indeed gone on at length about his love of films and had probably even divulged his ambitions to the uninterested revellers. So Biddy's comment was delivered with a sprinkle of whimsy. But she also meant that this was as real as you could get, so it would be foolish not to get as good a view as possible.

"Come on, JJ."

He smiled, waited for a second, the crowd continuing to stream excitedly past. Then he followed, even breaking into a jog.

The main body moved en masse westwards along Summerhill and swung left onto Gardiner Street, heading for Talbot Street. This would get them as close to the post office as was possible, which most agreed was the centre of things. The rebels had made a speech from there on the Monday, before occupying the building. As the mob flowed swiftly along the streets like human lava, rifle shots rang out above and around them. Some sounded so close that many crouched as they ran and others even threw themselves face first onto the ground, terrified that they would be killed. One man thought he had been shot when something stung his ankle. He roared with pain and toppled to the ground, rolling around and clutching his wounded leg.

"I'm shot," he cried. "Ah Jaysus Christ! They shot me. The bastards!"

The people around him dived for cover in doorways, behind steps, huddling together like terrified children. Several men hauled the wounded man in off the road and attended to him in the doorway of a tailor's shop. It turned out that he had only been hit by a stone, propelled by the boot of one of the procession. Once word of what had actually occurred spread there was much slagging of the poor man who had genuinely believed his demise was imminent. People who moments earlier had lain on the ground terrified that they too were about to die, laughed and joked as they skipped along, eager to get even closer to the action, oblivious of the irony. JJ couldn't quite understand this impulse, but was nonetheless curious enough to follow the herd.

The mob halted abruptly at the top of Talbot Street, at the junction with Marlborough Street, when they saw a stout barricade halfway up North Earl Street. It was constructed of carts turned on their side, beer barrels, sandbags, benches, mattresses, a butcher's table and an expensive-looking couch with two matching armchairs, apparently commandeered from the nearby Clery's department store. There were forty or fifty British soldiers hunkered behind the barricade, their rifles directed through strategic gaps in the structure and trained on the General Post Office less than fifty yards away on the far side of Sackville Street.

JJ spotted two large flags on poles atop the roof of the post office. One, a green flag with a yellow harp, was the Irish flag; the other, a green, white and orange tricolour which he had never seen before, fluttered behind a statue of a lady holding a spear in one hand and a harp in the other. Someone said the rebels were calling it the flag of the "new republic".

There was no antagonism towards the British soldiers from the mob, nor did the soldiers seem hostile towards the crowd. This was partly due to the fact that the soldiers were somewhat preoccupied, but also the good-natured quality of the banter. JJ was taken aback by the informality and lack of urgency, which made the whole scene almost comical. While all around them the rifles cracked and bullets ricocheted, the ordinary people of Dublin spoke to these British soldiers as if it were half time in an important football match and they had got access to the dressing room of the home team.

"Have yiz not finished them off yet?"

"I hear they only have hurleys in there with them."

"And pikes!"

"Should youse not be out in France fighting a real war?"

"Sure let them fire away, lads. That shower inside in the post office will run out of either bullets or nerve before too long!"

The crowd laughed loudest at this last comment, but as if the rebels had heard, a shower of rifle fire rained down onto the barricade from the roof of the post office. Even the bravest, most seasoned combatant kept his head down during that fusillade.

The crowd went from raucous laughter to terrified screaming in an instant and fled back down Marlborough Street like a herd of stampeding steers. As he too fled, JJ glimpsed one of the soldiers at the barricade fall, without even a whimper, shot through the eye. Several minutes later the mob wheeled left through Findlater Place and flooded onto Sackville Street beside the Parnell Monument. Twice their number was already assembled there ahead of them. The street was packed with people. Old and young, rich and poor mingled democratically, discussing the events, the rumours, the likely outcomes, and viewing the fire fight a hundred yards down Sackville Street as if it was a film playing in the Rotunda Room behind them.

JJ remained alert, much more concerned about the serious, life-threatening danger that surrounded him than his companions appeared to be. He saw a dead horse not far from them, lying on the ground in a pool of congealed blood. It had a saddle and livery that indicated it was an English cavalry horse. JJ could see what he thought were two bullet wounds, one on the horse's shoulder, the other on his face, but the blood had flowed mainly from his throat, which had been slit from ear to ear. It was a pitiable sight. Although JJ had seen two RIC men killed by gunshot, a dead rebel dangling from a chimney stack in Fairview and another young soldier slain by a sniper's bullet just moments ago, the sight of this innocent, lumbering, aristocrat of an animal lying lifeless on the street, its mouth frozen in a comical toothy grin, caused a great sadness to wash over him. His knees buckled slightly; he felt nauseous again. He sat on the edge of the footpath, breathed deeply a few times and sobbed. He was astonished at his reaction. Biddy put a hand on his shoulder and asked if he was all right.

"Grand, thanks," he lied. "The whiskey."

There was a lull in the firing then, which provided an opportunity to listen to some of the banter from the other spectators.

"So what do you make of all this then?" asked a well-dressed man with a middle-class accent.

"Amazing thing," answered a second man, in a broad city accent. "They'll be beaten of course."

"I hope so. Damn bloody nuisance, this whole blasted affair!"

"Sure they haven't the numbers. The military will overrun them."

"I daresay you're right."

"Let's hope they can hold out for a few days more, though. Otherwise Dublin'll be a laughin' stock. 'Couldn't even organise a proper rebellion!' they'll be saying."

JJ thought that a curious attitude but was too distracted to get involved. He was watching three boys between ten and twelve years of age. They had slunk out from the crowd and advanced down the street, using doorways, lamp posts and abandoned vehicles as cover. They eventually made their way to the dead horse. What the hell were they at? The firing was likely to commence again at any moment, if some sniper didn't already have them in his sights. Then JJ spotted the purpose of their little sortie. On the ground, about four or five feet from the dead horse, lay a shiny steel sabre with a leather handle and coloured lanyard – too great a prize for these boys to ignore.

A woman in a shawl, obviously the mother of one of the boys, pushed her way to the front of the crowd and started shouting at them to come back.

"What the hell do yiz think ye're at? Do yiz want to get yeerselves shot, yiz feckin' eejits!"

JJ couldn't hear what the tallest boy shouted in response but he waved a dismissive hand and they proceeded on their mission.

"Get back here now or so help me I'll kill yiz!"

The spectators laughed at the unintentional irony, but JJ shared the woman's anxiety as the boys made their final dash from cover. They raced across the wide-open street towards the dead animal just as the firing started again. Rifle bullets pinged off the ground around the boys' feet. The firing was coming from rooftops, so it was impossible to be sure who was doing the shooting, but JJ thought it was coming from the rebel side of the street. Why would they do this? Why would anyone fire at young boys simply up to a bit of devilment? Maybe their intention was to scare the boys, deter them from danger by deliberately missing the target? Or maybe they were just poor shots. At any rate, two of the boys did turn back, suitably chastened, but the tallest lad continued, determined to obtain the object of his desire. And obtain it he did, but not without difficulty.

When he reached the dead horse, he skidded to the ground, using the animal's body to protect him. As he did so, two bullets pierced the stiffened skin of the animal, unnervingly close to the boy. He had just five feet of open ground to cover to get to the sabre, its cold steel glinting in the mid-morning sun. The direct firing had stopped, although the sporadic gun battles farther down the street and around the river continued unabated. Cleverly, the boy tried to stretch out to retrieve the sabre, keeping his body low and flat and using the horse's corpse as a shield.

"Ah, Jaysus, he's going to get killed. They're going to kill my boy!" his mother howled.

He couldn't quite reach, so he scurried out from behind the cover of the animal on his hands and knees and snatched the sword, just as a bullet pinged off the road only inches from his head. It was a miracle he hadn't been hit. A huge cheer rang out as he raised the sword above his head in triumph. He turned, bounded over the huge corpse and sprinted for cover.

Two more shots cracked like vicious whips. The first struck a wooden shop door; the second hit a lamp post with a loud, metallic ring and entered the boy's body just above his hip bone. His body arched back, his knees buckled and he fell to the ground, tumbing several times before being halted by the edge of the footpath.

During all of this he held on to the sword. With a somewhat

anguished smile, he raised it a foot above his head. Some of the audience cheered stupidly. The boy's arm collapsed onto the path and his eyes closed tightly. His mother was keening like a banshee, certain that her son was dead.

"We have to help him," JJ heard himself say.

"Are ye mad? Ye can't go out there!"

"You'll be shot too!"

"Come on, son," Biddy said, grabbing him by the shoulder. "They won't get the both of us."

Before he had time to weigh up the odds, he and Biddy were darting out of the crowd and weaving their way along the street, using doorways and lamp posts for cover, just as the boys had done. A couple of shots rang out but it wasn't clear if they were directed at the daring duo. JJ got to the injured boy first. He lifted him and saw he was bleeding badly from his side. He was moaning and mumbling but JJ couldn't make out what he was saying. He put his own head under the boy's arm and began to drag his limp body off the street. Biddy arrived then and took his second arm. With the boy's weight supported, they were able to move swiftly back towards the relative safety of the crowd and the monument. Several more rifle shots rang out, a couple pinging close by. Biddy tripped, stumbling slightly, but managed to stay on her feet, and seconds later they had made it back to safety. The lad's mother began to fuss over him, half crying, half berating him. A doctor came forward from the crowd and used his jacket and a scarf to stanch the flow of blood and press-ganged several men into carrying the boy into the Rotunda Hospital across the street. It was a lying-in hospital, but it was a hospital and that was all that mattered on a day like this.

JJ turned to thank Biddy for her help to find her lying against the base of the monument, sweating, her breathing laboured and her hand pressed against her ribs.

"What's wrong with you?"

"Don't know. I've a desperate pain in me chest."

JJ had a closer look and discovered that she was bleeding.

"Damn it!"

"What?"

"They've shot you. Come on." He had already put her arm around his neck and begun to lift her.

"Ah Jaysus, I'm fucked so, a mhac."

"You're not! As long as I'm here, you're going to be fine."

He roared at people to clear a path. Another man helped him by taking her other arm on his shoulder. She was quite a weight. Just as well the Rotunda was so close.

There was chaos inside the hospital. JJ was ordered to take Biddy straight through to a ward. As if he knew where the wards were. He hobbled on regardless, nurses, sisters and orderlies hurrying left and right. A red-faced nurse, crossing the long corridor, seemed to appreciate his predicament, and took Biddy under her free arm.

"Thanks," said JJ. "She's been shot."

"You know it's babies we deliver here, not bullets?" She smiled, as she directed them down a perpendicular corridor. How could she joke at a time like this?

"I didn't know where else to go."

"You're grand. We're really short-staffed though. A lot of the girls couldn't get in, so most of us have been on duty for almost twenty-four hours."

She brought them into a ward with eight or ten beds and they put Biddy between the wounded boy and a woman who, the nurse said, was in the early stages of labour. The doctor from the street was still there, rolling up his sleeves, glad to be able to help out in the straitened conditions. JJ asked him to take a look at Biddy's chest wound. He was busy with the wounded boy but he ordered a triage nurse to check her out.

After a brief examination, the nurse was able to tell JJ that the bullet seemed to have hit a rib. The rib had probably cracked but had also diverted the bullet straight out through her back, just under her shoulder blade. The nurse was confident that the rib had prevented the bullet puncturing her lung and saved Biddy from much more serious injury. JJ was still concerned at her laboured breathing but the nurse assured him it was due to the pain from the cracked rib. She cleaned and dressed the wound and told JJ he could take her home in about half an hour, once the doctor had examined her. Biddy insisted she was fine with that, so JJ returned to the street and the crowd still swarming around the Parnell Monument.

He found himself in the company of a man from the country who was in conversation with a labouring man from the city. The crackling of rifle fire was almost drowned out now by heavy shelling at the southern end of Sackville Street. The shells, fired from the gunboat on the Liffey, pounded a number of tall buildings at the farthest corner of Sackville Street beside Carlisle Bridge. These buildings had also been occupied by rebels. The well-dressed countryman had come to Dublin for a holiday over the Easter weekend and had not been able to return home. They watched intently as a couple of shells burst through two windows in one of the Carlisle Bridge buildings and exploded. A third shell hit the red-brick building on the opposite corner, sending a cloud of red dust pluming skywards and splintered bricks hurtling to the ground.

"I hate to see the like of that being done to other Irishmen," said the rural gent.

The Dubliner explained to him that the gunboat had bombarded Liberty Hall early that morning but that Connolly's Labour men, the Citizen Army men, he called them, had got out well beforehand and were now in the post office along with the rest.

"I know those men," he said, "and the men I know wouldn't be afraid of anything."

"What chance have they got, do you think?" asked the country gent, sensing that this man knew something.

"Not a hope in hell," he replied without hesitation. "They never said they had, and never thought they would."

"Why do it, so?" asked the bemused country gent.

"To wake up the country, I'd say," said the labouring man.

"Hmm. So do you think they'll hold out for long?"

"Hard to say."

The country gent pointed towards the houses that were being bombarded as another two shells smashed into the walls. "That'll root them out quick enough."

"No doubt it will, but what then?"

"Well, I won't be waiting around for the answer to that one. I'm off to find a way to get back down home. My people will be wondering if I'm dead or alive."

As JJ continued to loiter uneasily among the crowd of onlookers outside the Rotunda Room, he was struck again by the unsettling unreality of it all. Biddy and the young boy could both have been killed, and for what? A shiny British cavalry sabre? And then there was the dead horse. He was tempted to find a way back out like the country gent. Not to return home, though, certainly not that, but to draw back from the incomprehensible fiasco and wait for the dust to settle, literally. But he had to wait for Biddy now and where would he go anyway? It was clear from the ruinous state of the main thoroughfare that there was no hope of getting any farther forward, never mind getting out of the country. And as for the prospect of any theatre work or busking, well that was right off the agenda until the curtain had fallen on this real-life drama and the mess had been cleaned up.

And who could tell how long that would take?

"Look at yiz, yiz bowsies! Yiz are only a shower of fuckin' tossers, standin' around pullin' yeer bleedin' wires!"

The voice was female but harsh, guttural and hoarse. JJ craned to see if he could identify the source. It was the first time he witnessed the middle-class spectators actively separate themselves from a member of the eclectic audience. They parted like the Red Sea as she staggered through, cursing them in language more obscene than anything JJ had ever heard, even from the coarsest farmer at a fair. They turned their noses up, some even producing kerchiefs to protect against the smell, mar dhea.

"Disgusting!"

"Vile!"

"A walking disease!"

The girl was no older than twenty, in a brown shawl and floral apron. Her face was pretty, with a youthful softness. JJ wasn't sure if she'd made a bee line for him as a kindred spirit, in age if not class, or if she had just been funnelled towards him by the motion of the other spectators. Either way, she was standing before him, a barely perceptible grin playing on the corner of her full mouth. He could see now that her eyes, too, were soft like a kitten's. She startled him by turning on the crowd again, staring directly at the men, and letting fly with another vitriolic salvo.

"Yiz should be fuckin' ashamed of yeerselves! Call yerselves fuckin' men? Men? Have yiz any fuckin' pricks at all between yizzer jaysusin legs? If yiz have, then march out onto the street there and prove yizzer not scared of yizzer shites and face them fuckin' bullets like real men!"

She turned her attention back on a gaping JJ just as abruptly.

"What the fuck are you gawkin' at, ya fuckin' culchie?"

"Ehm . . ."

"Never mind," she said. "Have you a fag?"

"Sorry, no."

"Jaysus! I'm dyin' for a smoke. Maybe one of this shower of bollixes has one?" And she was gone again, pushing through the crowd, delivering another colourful tirade as she went.

Less than a minute later she had returned with two cigarettes and a single match. "Here," she said, proffering one of them with a look that did not brook a refusal.

"Thanks," JJ answered, taking the cigarette without hesitation.

As she leaned in to light it, he could smell the strange mix of alcohol, body odour and the faintest hint of rosewater.

"You're a good-lookin' young fella." She squinted, her right eye half closing as a puff of cigarette smoke hit it.

JJ was taken aback, but he wasn't at all convinced it was meant as a compliment. "Thanks."

"Why the fuck aren't you down there fightin' with those boys, then?"

If he were to answer that honestly he might antagonise her further.

"I have two brothers in there," she said. "It's madness." She sucked hard on her cigarette and turned to look him in the eye. "They haven't a fucking hope, have they?" Her exhaled smoke created a veil around her anguished face.

JJ couldn't answer and he didn't think she expected him to.

"It's fuckin' brave, though. Fair play to them, poor fuckers." Tears welled as she gave him one final glance before disappearing into the crowd like a sylph.

JJ pulled sharply on his cigarette, clasping it firmly between his thumb and middle finger, his index finger hovering, barely touching the flaxen paper. The tail of ash fell from the end and fluttered to the ground. He squinted against the sun, now high in the sky to the south of Sackville Street, hovering somewhere over the Dublin–Wicklow foothills. Rifles continued to crackle repeatedly. The rattle of machine guns added to the cacophony, along with the irregular, ear-splitting crescendo of heavy shells. It was only then he noticed the arched canopy of a cinema about fifty yards away on the right-hand side of Sackville Street, just short of the huge pillar with the tiny admiral on top. He could just about make out the name, The Pillar Picture House. The bill for the film currently playing was partly ripped, but there was no mistaking the life-sized image emblazoned on the massive poster. It was Charlie Chaplin, starring in a thirty-minute, sea-faring adventure, *Shanghaied*. JJ wished that someone would shanghai him there and then and take him out of this crazy situation.

As he continued to suck on the cigarette, he imagined Charlie the tramp wandering into the disreputable part of town, the red-light district down by the docks, probably a little drunk, and getting clubbed and hauled on board ship. Then he would come to, far out to sea, and wonder how he had got into this peculiar pickle. Several comic capers would ensue as he did his best to try to escape. There would be a woman too, of course. A pretty maiden, unhappy, stuck with a man who no longer loved her and waiting to meet the man of her dreams – Mabel Normand, Clara Bow, Edna Purviance or maybe Florence La Badie. Yes, she and Charlie would begin at loggerheads, unable to get on, she suppressing her true feelings, he compromising her position by paying her too much attention. But they would soon realise that they had to work together to escape their oppressors.

JJ jumped as a huge blast lit up the inside of the post office, scattering bricks, stone and spewing clouds of smoke and dust into the air and onto the street. Jesus! How could anyone in there have survived that? He threw the half-finished cigarette onto the ground, not bothering to stub it, and went back to the hospital to collect Biddy.

When JJ and Biddy re-emerged the situation had transformed utterly. The firing had intensified and the crowd was scattering in fear and panic. The rebels had got up onto the roof of the Rotunda itself and into a three-storey house on the corner opposite. They were firing down from the roof of the hospital and the windows of the house. The proximity of the fighting and the constant rattle of bullets overhead had finally spread alarm through the crowd, who feared for their own lives now for the first time. As JJ and Biddy scampered along the street, past the Rotunda Room, keeping their heads down and staying close to the walls, alarm turned to terror. The British had set up a couple of machine-gun positions at either end of Great Britain Street to deal with this new rebel threat; or maybe the rebels were responding to them, it was difficult to tell. As JJ and Biddy attempted to cross Sackville Street to return to Summerhill, a tremendous fusillade was unleashed. The crowd screamed and scattered further, some taking cover where they could, others deciding to make a run for it. A woman of around thirty was hit several times and crashed lifelessly to the ground. From the way her shawl was wrapped around her shoulder and across her chest, it looked to JJ like she was carrying a babe in arms. His impulse was to stop and help but Biddy grabbed his arm and dragged him back past the hospital and up the opposite side of Rutland Square.

This didn't feel any safer though, as the whole street was swept by stray bullets. There was a full scale fire fight underway and they were caught right in the middle of it. When they reached the turn at the top of the square, a deafening volley of shots rang out and they could see that Granby Place was swarming with soldiers. The rebels were mostly on the rooftops or at the high windows of the buildings that lined the square and were firing down on the soldiers in the streets. The British troops were equally hair-triggered and unsure of who was enemy and who was not.

Biddy quickly took the initiative again and guided JJ across the north end of the square, still crouching low. But, at the junction with Frederick Street, they were met by another deafening racket. The British had set up a machine-gun position outside a laundry on the corner of Dorset Street and were spraying the top of the square with bullets. Biddy and JJ were forced to double back and turn north up Granby Row. After the Black Church, they turned onto Mountjoy Street. From there she led him onwards, down onto Eccles Street and past the front of the Mater Hospital, also doing its best in extremis to look after the sick and injured being brought to them from all sides and by all means; some carried, others limping on the shoulder of a friend or loved one. One unconscious man, bleeding heavily from an abdominal wound, was wheeled in on a street-trader's hand cart. Eventually they re-emerged onto Drumcondra Road and paused for rest. Biddy was still having difficulty with her breathing and clearly in pain.

They stopped at a house with a low cut-stone wall and railings. Biddy sat on the steps of the house and winced, clutching her side, panting. There was a short document tied to the railings with string. It was a military proclamation.

What was it about this city and proclamations?

"Are you all right?" Biddy asked him.

"Hmm? Yes. What about you?

"Oh, I'm grand, sure. Nothin' a good slug of porter or a dram of uisce beatha wouldn't cure." She smiled.

JJ stared blankly at the document.

"You look troubled."

"Oh. Really? So this is some hooley I've landed myself in the middle of, is it?"

"Well that was a deft little jig you did when the machine gun started up."

He scowled. She laughed. "Ha,ha,ha. With a boom, boom in the sorting room/ And the bang, bangs out on Sackville Street," she sang, improvising a melody, skipping a rudimentary aon, dó, trí. "Between the jigs and betwixt the reels/ There will be wigs upon the Green."

"Jesus, Biddy!"

"Ah sure you'd have to laugh." And she did, then winced and held her ribs.

"You're unbelievable, you know that!"

"Look, we're still standin', aren't we? And if we stay out of the limelight from now on, we'll be fine."

"Hmm." He dug his hands deeper into his pockets, hunched his shoulders.

"I've a feeling it's not just that though."

"Look, Biddy, I don't like being shot at, right! I don't like seeing people killed right in front of my eyes either, or people almost dying in my arms. I didn't come here for all this. I came here to be free, to follow my dreams. But this is some fucking nightmare! So I'm sorry if I'm not inclined to laugh or sing or whatever it is you think I should be doing right now!"

"Jaysus, you're well able to talk once you get goin', aren't you?"

JJ turned away. He was sorry for losing his temper and for taking it out on her. It wasn't her fault, after all. But he wasn't sorry for getting it off his chest. He really was angry and frustrated. He felt impotent, like his future was in the lap of the gods, whoever the hell they were.

"See, it's good to say it out, let off some steam."

"Sorry. I didn't mean to—"

"Yer grand. Sure isn't that what I'm here for."

He smiled thinly. "Hmph. Come on, let's get you home."

She didn't stir.

"And what about you? Where are you going to go now?"

He was surprised by the question. He had thought about it, yes, but hadn't come to any conclusions. "Don't know."

"You're welcome to stay with us. Until this is all over at least."

"And when will that be?" He was cross again.

"I can't see it lasting more than a few days. It's the British Army for feck's sake!"

"Hmmm." He turned so that he was facing north-east, his gaze wistful.

"Where would you like to be right now?"

"Right now? On a boat to England! Or at least working to earn the fare."

"Really?"

"Yes!"

"Right, then. Just lie low with us for a few days and when this is all over, you can take up where you left off. Come on." She hauled herself to her feet and started to walk, but after only a few feet she stopped. "See!" She returned to his side. "Tell me. Pretend I'm your mother." She smiled and sat again.

"I don't know." He smiled too. "I met this woman . . ."

"Ha! I might have known it."

"No, it's not like that."

"Right."

"She's in love with someone else. They're both . . . they're rebels. Fighting. Up around Ashbourne. I suppose they'll get married. If they don't die together first. For the 'cause'!" He raised his fist sarcastically.

"So why is she on your mind, then?"

"I don't bloody know! Sure, I liked her, wished she was with me and not him. But I've liked girls my whole life, so . . ."

"This one is different, though?"

"No. But . . . why can't I forget her, Biddy? I keep seeing her. Hearing her voice. Jesus! Wondering if she's alive or dead."

"Ach, that's just because you can't have her. You men are all the same."

"It's not that. Ugh, I don't know."

"Well, there's probably only one way you'll ever know." She looked at him as if the conclusion was obvious. He looked back at her as if she had just asked him to solve a quadratic equation.

"You need to go back to her."

"What? But she's in love with someone else."

"Well, she was. But then she hadn't met you yet. And judging from your reaction, you must have felt something from her."

"Sort of. But maybe that was just my imagination."

"Did anything happen?"

"Well, she did kiss me."

"What?"

"Sort of."

What does that mean?"

"I was injured. Had a nightmare. She felt sorry for me."

"Sounds like a very nice girl."

"But when I asked her to come with me and if she cared about me, she pushed me away."

"Well, son, if you're going to be put off that easily, I don't hold out much hope for your dreams and wild ambitions!" She got up again as if to walk off.

"When I want something, I do whatever it takes to get it. You don't know the shit I had to go through just to get this far."

That stopped her. She faced him with slits of eyes, like a sniper fixing a target in her sights.

"Then go back there and show her how you really feel."

She turned and marched off down Lower Dorset Street towards the canal bridge, not a bother on her. Finally, he threw his hands in the air and followed her.

JJ was as used to death by now as anyone would ever want to be. Losing his mother at such a young age, it shadowed his life, even if he wasn't always aware of it. But he had always thought of death as a furtive thing, a shadowy pooka that crept in when no one was looking, when your back was turned, a silent, insidious burglar of life. But over these past few days he had witnessed it leap out into the open, take centre stage, like some masked highwayman, a Zorro or a Dick Turpin with whom you might go marauding up and down the roads of Meath and through the streets of Dublin, wreaking havoc with gay abandon. And what sort of people were these city folk, who almost welcomed the fervid excitement it brought riding on its coat-tails? Where was the morbidity, the dread, the apocalyptic fear that should accompany its every visitation? Dublin seemed to be laughing at the brutal battering it was taking, making no complaint, nor crying any dirge for the dead. Maybe this was just the outward show though; the brave face that must be presented to the world; the wit that was their only weapon against the constant suffering, inequality, squalor and now indiscriminate, wasteful death.

As they approached the North Circular Road, a squad of Dublin Fusiliers was crossing the canal bridge up ahead, marching towards the city centre. Biddy told JJ she would take a right turn and skip back towards Summerhill. When she asked what he planned to do, he said he would try to get up to Meath, as she had advised. He thought if he could commandeer a bicycle and get back to Swords, he could retrace his steps from there. He might make it back before nightfall or at least first thing next morning.

"Well, all's fair in love and war. Isn't that what they say?"

She took his hand firmly and shook it. "Yer a grand young fella. I'm glad I met ya."

He put his arms tightly around her neck and gave her a big hug.

"Ah Jaysus, go easy would ya."

"Thanks, Biddy."

"For nothing! Now go on. Off with you. And try to get yerself somethin' to eat."

"Cripes, yeah. I'd forgotten I had a belly."

"Jaysus, I could eat the hind leg of the lamb of God!"

JJ laughed, glanced at the approaching Fusiliers and waved Biddy off. She skipped towards the corner, but before she could get around it, four or five rifle shots rang out in quick succession. They ducked instinctively as the bullets pinged off the wall beside them. One left a near perfect circle in the window of the corner house.

Biddy screamed. "For fuck's sake!"

"Jesus Christ!" JJ roared as two more bullets pinged off the footpath. "Stop! For fuck's sake! Stop, would ye!" he shouted, raising his hands.

"Stay where you are!" shouted an English voice.

"Don't move," added a Dubliner, "or we'll shoot yiz!"

"Run, Biddy, run!" shouted JJ.

She could barely get beyond a trot but set off as quickly as she could and disappeared, hand clutching her side, into a laneway. Several more shots rang out and whined past JJ's head, smacking against the walls behind him.

"Stop! Leave her! She's my mother. She's just going home." He waved his hands about in a pathetic gesture of pleading and submission. By now the Fusiliers had reached him and the instructions being roared at him were only a beat ahead of the violence that insured his compliance.

"Get down! Down! Down!"

JJ was grabbed by the arm. A hob-nailed boot kicked the back of his knees. They buckled and a rifle butt, levelled between his shoulder blades, sent him crashing onto the path.

"Filthy fucking rebel."

Several pairs of boots clattered by his head and continued onto the North Circular Road in pursuit of Biddy.

"Are you one of them, Paddy?"

A boot pressed on his back and his arms were wrenched violently behind him. "Where were you coming from?"

"Where you going?"

Now JJ was being frisked. He remembered the revolver. Shit! That damn and blasted fucking revolver! Why hadn't he got rid of it?

"Home!"

"With your mother?"

"No. I mean I don't live with her. I live in . . . Fairview." He was delighted he had managed to recall the name of the area.

"Fairview. Croydon Park! That's where half of these fuckers are based, Sarge!"

"No. I have nothing to do with this!" JJ said through gritted teeth.

"Gun, Sergeant!"

He hardly felt the squaddie rip the revolver from his inside pocket and could just about see him hold it aloft between finger and thumb like a foul-smelling article, his face curled up in disdain.

"You fucking bastard!"

A steel-capped, hob-nailed boot smashed into his jaw. As the buzzing in his head began to fade and inky blackness cloaked his eyes, JJ thought he heard the clatter of boots and someone shout, "She got away, Sergeant."

21

Churched

———◆———

WHEN JJ CAME TO, THE place, the room, was shadowy and sliced through by shafts of brightly coloured lights. Blue. Red. Yellow. The air was flecked with hundreds of floating dust particles and there was an almost pleasing musky odour. He lifted his chin slowly off his chest. He sensed a mustiness in the air, too, and a tomb-like cold chilled his bones. He began to make out shapes. Chairs? No. Benches. Long benches. Rows of them. Gaps in between. Leading to a large, elevated table. No. An altar. It was a church. He could make out the stained-glass windows now, candelabras, the tabernacle. It was only when he tried to stand that he realised he was tied to a chair. Not very well tied, he thought, as he jiggled his wrists, but tight enough to restrain him. His chin was sore but his head was clearing. He remembered the nervous, excitable squaddies and Biddy's attempted escape. He checked about but there was no sign of her. He hoped that meant she had lost her pursuers in the warren of streets that she knew so well. Like someone who has just returned an animal to the wild, his emotions were mixed. Naturally he was delighted she was safe but he was sad she was gone and that he might never see her again.

As he surveyed his surroundings, he could distinguish bodies, a lot of bodies, in uniforms, sprawled out on the tiled floor around the baptistery. Were they dead? Or maybe wounded? There was no sign of any medics. No nurses. No medicinal odours. He heard a loud snore then another. They were asleep, exhausted presumably, after several days of fighting with little or no rest. There were others stretched out on the tiles of the chancel. But why in a church? Commandeered as a billet and doubling as a temporary lock-up? He was beginning to understand that there was a strange spontaneity to this conflict, things were happening off the cuff, being dealt with on the hoof. Claiming that he was not a rebel and attempting to explain how he came to have a revolver stuffed down the back of his trousers would be pointless. But he would at least have to attempt to reason with his captors if he was to have any hope of getting out of this in one piece.

When he looked to his right, he saw a British sentry guarding a door. There was another posted at the door on the opposite wall, standing beneath the seventh station of the cross, a gaudy painting of Jesus on his knees, having fallen under the weight of his burden and being scourged by a cat-o'-nine-tails. There were piles of haversacks, belts, boots and rifles heaped on the front pews and around the altar. He noticed another figure in a chair at the far end of the church, to the right of the altar, and could see that he too was tied and sitting with his back to JJ. His head was lowered but it was unclear whether he was injured or just asleep. JJ's mouth was dry; his stomach grumbled loudly. He hadn't eaten in almost twenty-four hours. He couldn't tell what time of day it might be – the light was diffused by the stained glass – but he felt sure it was no later than early evening. Just then, the sentry to his right noticed him stirring and whistled to his companion at the other door, who cocked his head, glanced at JJ and made his way wearily to the baptistery.

Minutes later the sentry was with JJ, his rifle slung over his shoulder, a large billycan in his hand. He ladled tepid water into JJ's gaping mouth. The water dribbled then overflowed. JJ coughed, sending water spluttering from his mouth and nose.

"For fuck's sake!"

The accent was Irish. Not Dublin but not from JJ's part of the country either.

"Sorry, too fast," JJ muttered.

The soldier tutted but adjusted his pouring rate so that JJ was able to drink without choking. The water tasted of old tin and was too warm to be refreshing but it quenched his thirst and he felt better.

"Thanks."

The soldier shrugged, threw the ladle into the billycan and began to walk away.

"Where are you from?" JJ called after him.

The sentry stopped, half turned, leaned his head to one side and glared at JJ as if he'd just called him an offensive name or insulted his progeny.

"Shut your fucking mouth and speak when you're spoken to."

He returned the can to the baptistery and resumed his post with the same lack of enthusiasm as he'd shown JJ.

The time dragged by. Probably close to four hours passed. The snoring continued intermittently. The sentries remained at their posts, leaning against the cold granite walls to keep from drifting into sleep. JJ thought he nodded off once or twice, but the gnawing pain in his stomach kept sleep at arm's length. He passed the time by skipping through his vast repertoire of songs, singing quietly, and all the time wriggling and picking at his ligatures, which were definitely loosening. It gave him something to be doing, sure.

> Attend you gallant Irishmen and listen for a while
> I'll sing to you the praises of the sons of Erin's Isle
> It's of those gallant heroes who voluntarily ran
> To release two Irish shamrocks from an English prison van
> On the eighteenth of September, it was a dreadful year
> When sorrow and excitement ran throughout all Lancashire
> At a gathering of the Irish boys they volunteered each man
> To release those Irish prisoners out of the prison van.

When the silence and tedium was eventually broken, it was shattered. The only warning of what was to come was the faint crunch of boots on the cinders of the churchyard outside, muffled by the thickness of the walls and the heavy oak doors. The doors to JJ's right were flung open as if they had been kicked and they slammed against the granite walls, almost crushing the dozing sentry. A British officer strode in, at the head of a company of around fifty troops, barking orders and immediately taking centre stage in front of the altar. JJ found it difficult to discern the detail of the orders but they were clear from the tone and volume nonetheless. The sleeping men were to wake, rearm and return to duty while the men who had just returned could grab themselves a couple of hours' sleep. There were some meagre, cold rations, fresh water, oh, and they had captured another vile rebel prisoner. The captive was knocked to the floor, just for good measure, before being hauled to a third corner of the church and also bound to a chair. The men who had been asleep did not rouse like normal sleepers might, sitting up, stretching stiffened limbs, yawning and rubbing sleep from half-open eyes. These men were instantly on their feet, alert, eyes blinking wide open. They pulled on combat jackets and rearmed with the efficiency, if not the lightness of foot, of a well-choreographed dance troupe, and within five minutes they had gobbled, gulped, assembled, roll-called and re-entered the fray through the still-open church doors, which were then shut firmly in their wake. It was like the church had been swept by a mini typhoon.

The newly arrived troops chatted quietly as they threw off dusty jackets and boots and the air was thick with the smell of cordite. They didn't eat, which JJ thought might improve his chances of getting a morsel, but they did drink thirstily, before bedding down as best they could. A few smoked before allowing much-needed sleep to overtake them.

JJ's ligatures were now loose enough for him to move his hands around and find the knot. It was pulled tight but he had plenty of time to work on it. He began to pick and tug and he noted that the sentries hadn't been changed, presumably on longer shifts given the reduced demands of their posting. No doubt they'd rather have been out in the thick of the action, preferring the intensity of danger to the boredom of sentry duty. JJ couldn't make out much of the new prisoner. He guessed he was in his thirties and seemed quiet, even a little shy and sensitive. His skin was pale, hair black, with a slight quiff to the left. He was probably also quieted by fear of the fate that awaited him. JJ didn't want to think about that. Rebels could expect a long period of imprisonment and some serious punishment, he imagined. But JJ wasn't a rebel, hadn't broken any laws. Could he convince his captors of that?

He called his sentry, the man who had attended to him previously. Needless to say, he was unimpressed at being summoned like some sort of waiter. So JJ had to beg for food for himself and his fellow prisoners. The guard reluctantly relented and fetched a lump of stale bread, a couple of ladles of water and a slice of spam each for JJ and his two colleagues. He served the other two first, to make a point. As JJ chewed the hard, dry bread, he chatted to the soldier.

"You're Irish, yes?"

"What the fuck do you mean by that?"

"Nothing. Just. I don't understand all this, what's going on, like."

"All what?"

"Well, Irishmen in English uniforms fighting Irishmen in Irish uniforms or no uniforms at all, fighting Englishmen?"

"Irish, English, French, German! What the fuck does it all mean?"

JJ was astonished at the response. He shrugged, stupidly, inanely.

"I've come home from France where I was knee deep in mud and blood and vomit and shit, where thousands, fucking thousands of Irishmen, Englishmen, Frenchmen, Germans and whoever the fuck else stupid enough to be there, are being killed, slaughtered and butchered and for fucking what? For fucking who? So fuckers like you can come out and fight for freedom? Whose fucking freedom? Not mine, that's for sure!"

JJ was startled. "I'm not fighting anyone," was all he could say.

The sentry dropped the can noisily on the tiled floor. Water splashed over the rim. He brought his face close to JJ's, his finger to JJ's right eye and snarled, "Listen to me, you smart alec fucker. You lot are the fucking traitors here. What sort of men fight you when your back is turned? Stab you in the back like fucking cowards?"

"They're not my lot!"

"You're all the fucking same." He dismissed JJ with a flick of his hand and stooped to pick up the billycan of water.

"No, I'm no more like them, the rebels, than you are," JJ said. "I'm not fighting and I don't understand all this killing either."

The soldier stood and seemed to be listening now. He didn't walk off at least.

"Look, it's a long story so I won't bore you with the detail, but I'm just a lad from Sligo who . . . All I wanted was to be an actor and I came to Dublin on my way to London, not to get mixed up in some mad fight for what? Freedom? I don't know about you, but I was quite free thank you very much until all this started. So, like you say, whose freedom are they fighting for anyway?"

"Quite a speech. Must be the actor in you."

"I'm not acting now."

The sentry swung his rifle off his shoulder, laid it against the nearest pew and sat wearily on the edge, with a sort of resigned sigh.

"Was it really bad over there?" JJ asked gently.

"Believe me," said the young soldier, "it was as near to hell as I ever want to get."

JJ allowed the statement to hang in the air.

"The filth. The fear. The stench. Sometimes it's the stench that gets to you the most. That mix of shit and rotting flesh. It gets right inside you, right into the pit of your stomach, into your soul maybe."

"Jesus, how can you bear it?"

"Can't. Just have to. The only way out is a bullet. If you lose your nerve, an enemy bullet will get you. If you try to run, one of your own will."

"Any hope it will end soon?"

"I was on my way back for another six months. So no. Not anytime soon. And here I am now, having to shoot my own countrymen. That's just as nonfuckingsensical!"

JJ allowed the long silence that followed to settle, pausing the work on his knots.

"Why did you join up?"

His sentry gave him a sceptical sideways look. "I'm Balance, Richard. From Coolattin, Wicklow. I don't know about where you're from but around our place, anyone old enough to join up did. Some even lied about their age so they could. It was the natural thing to do, the right thing to do."

"I'm JJ McHale, from Ballysumaghan near Sooey, in Sligo. Lads up our way were too busy trying to survive to be bothered going off to a war in France, or to any war."

"Well, weren't they the wise men?"

Richard Balance told JJ about trenches packed with wounded men, the crippled, the maimed, all screaming in pain, crying for their mothers. The ones who were closer to death sat in a dazed heap, a stare fixed on some dim point in the distance or the tiny flickering portal to an unfathomable future existence. He spoke of friends, their arms ripped off at the shoulder by a shell blast, or their faces half torn away, leaving a naked jaw bone and a row of yellowing teeth. He spoke of the yellow gas that visited an awful, insidious death upon those without a mask or with one that was defective, leaky. But the hand-to-hand combat was the worst, he said, the death at close quarters. It happened whenever a resourceful group broke through the line and piled into a trench. Bayonets, mallets, axes, anything that was to hand, served as weapons as men tore and scratched at faces, eyes and throats. The moment when your blow or thrust had struck home was instantly recognisable in the expression on your opponent's face, in the final fierce flame in his eyes. Then the flame fading as life seeped from the body at the end of your blade. The stinking breath on your face becoming shallow, blood sometimes gurgling in the throat, as the body slid lifelessly to the ground at your feet.

As the young soldier spoke, the images he created seemed to play out again on an invisible screen behind his irises. The more detail he described, the more he seemed to fade from the room, almost disappearing into the depths of his recollection. JJ listened intently to the young English soldier from Wickow and was moved by his poignant recollections of the horrors he had lived through. But he was even more intent on his ligatures and on loosening that knot.

The soldier went silent. JJ stopped.

The sentry hauled a deep, heavy breath into his lungs and dragged himself back into the reality of the church. He sighed and glanced across at his colleague, who was regarding him with suspicion, glaring like a displeased schoolteacher at one of his star pupils uncharacteristically out of his place without permission. He stood as he turned back to JJ. "More water?" he asked. He seemed unsure of where they had left off or for how long he had been talking. He held out a full ladle.

"Thanks."

But before JJ could get his lips to the ladle the relative quiet was broken again by a banging and clambering on the door to his right. Richard Balance's attention was drawn away as his companion jumped to attention, armed his rifle and bellowed, "Who goes there?"

"Let me in! Let me in now!" came the piercing voice of a woman.

The sentries exchanged quizzical looks.

"You have my son! Under false arrest! Let me in I say, now!"

Richard glanced at JJ, who shook his head. He dropped the ladle back into the billycan as his fellow sentry opened the large wooden door. He had barely opened it wide enough to allow entry when a veritable whirlwind of women barged fearlessly in, crowing, wailing and demanding.

"Where is he? Jack? Jack? Yiz bastards took him and him doin' nothing! Nothing at all! Wouldn't hurt a fly, God love him."

All this while being restrained by the sentry who was, in turn, being mauled by the woman's three confederates.

Richard was just about to grab his rifle and rush to the aid of his companion when JJ pulled his hands free of his loosened binds, pushed Richard off balance, not even thinking of the irony, grabbed the barrel of the rifle and swung it like a hurley, catching the sentry on his left temple with the butt.

"He couldn't even get rid of a few rats outa our place when I needed him to," roared the woman who headed the gang of backstreet harridans, "not mind get rid of ye lot out of the country. Let go and let him go now. He's a writer not a fighter!"

By now, Richard was lying dazed on the floor of the church and JJ was running towards the unguarded door. Several of the sleeping soldiers were roused enough by the commotion to raise their heads but none spotted JJ until it was too late. The second sentry did see him and, realising what was happening, abandoned the crazy woman and grabbed his rifle. JJ had already hauled open the other door and was galloping like a colt across the yard towards a side gate that would take him he knew not where but away from his captors, and that was enough to be going on with. The second sentry dashed out the door in pursuit of the escapee and managed to get a shot off but only as JJ disappeared through the gate and out of sight.

"Focking baastehd!" he heard the soldier shout in a cockney accent as he fired a second shot that thwacked harmlessly into the shrubbery beyond the gate. JJ knew the sentry could not desert his post to give chase, so he was safe.

JJ had no idea where he was as he galloped and stumbled down a muddy laneway and out onto a narrow street. Lines of washing were strung between the houses. He could smell the sea but couldn't see it. The sun was quite low in the sky, beginning to sink behind the buildings; it was later than he expected. Now that he was out in the open, the intermittent artillery fire was louder and felt closer. The crackle of rifle fire had become the accompaniment to his life at this point. All he could do for now was keep running until he could get his bearings, or ask directions, or at least get far enough away from the church to stop and figure out where he was and how to get out of this godforsaken city. He rounded a corner at the bottom of the street and swung into a wider street. The rifle fire became even louder, closer, more intense. A sustained volley rang out from the far end of the street, knocking chips out of the road and the buildings on either side.

He stopped, ducked and saw that there was a barricade halfway up the street, with a group of Volunteers crouched on the near side of it, holding off a handful of soldiers. He could tell they were rebels because only two were in uniform. The volley had come from the other side of the barricade. JJ scurried into a doorway, hoping he hadn't been spotted. As he crouched with Richard Balance's rifle clutched between his knees, shots ringing out in all directions and artillery fire pounding out from somewhere not far to the south, he stared at the row of buildings opposite and sighed deeply. Why, at the first sign of violence, that day back at Rath Cross, had he not just stayed put, allowed the violence to pass him by, sat it out and bided his time until, like an April storm, it had blown over, drained itself dry. Then he could have continued on his way unimpeded. But it hadn't been that simple, had it? What he'd thought at the time was nothing more than an isolated incident in a remote hamlet in Meath had escalated in tiny increments, almost imperceptibly, each step dragging JJ deeper and deeper in until he was trapped, lost in a maze of conflicting motives and loyalties.

At least over in France, where the real war was happening, and notwithstanding the horror Richard had described, the fight was against a single enemy. But here, now, in this war, it was bizarre. Everyone spoke the same language, most were born and lived in the same country, and all seemed to have more in common than in difference. He felt bad for having knocked Richard senseless with the butt of his own rifle. He had nothing against the lad after all, liked him, even, from what he had got to know of him during their brief chat.

Just then a tall man with a mop of red hair and a strong jaw came around the corner and strode right up the centre of the street.

"There yiz are, yiz fuckers."

He was dead set on the barricade ahead and seemed oblivious to the occasional bullet that hit the road or one of the buildings near him.

He stopped about fifty feet past JJ, ten feet short of the barricade, and stood with his hands on his hips.

"I want my cart back! Hey, d'yiz hear me?"

"Get down, ya eejit. You'll be shot," shouted a young Volunteer, before turning back to fire a shot through a slit in the barricade.

"I need that cart to make a livin', for fuck's sake!"

There was no response from the contingent manning the barricade.

"It's all I have!"

A bullet whizzed through the air along a line halfway between the carter and JJ. The man jerked his head, the first sign that he was at least aware that danger lurked. It didn't divert him from his goal, though. He strode right up to the barricade and in between several gobsmacked Volunteers. With bullets ricocheting on every side, he grabbed the butts of the arms of his cart which were pointed skywards.

"What the hell are you doin'?"

"Are you mad?"

"Leave that be! Leave it be!"

He was not for turning. With a massive heave and by applying all his strength, he hauled the arms of his upended cart downwards until the cart was righted.

"Jesus Christ!"

"Get the fuck away, you mad bastard!" cried one of the older men.

As the carter began to pull his precious cart away from the barricade, leaving a gaping hole in its wake, he was pursued by one of the men in uniform, the company commander, JJ guessed. He pointed his revolver directly at the carter and spoke in as even a tone as he could muster. "Why don't you leave that cart where it is now and go back home, a chara?"

The carter glared back him.

"Why don't you go and stick that fuckin' gun of yours up your hole and leave us all be!" He continued to pull his cart away from the barricade. The uniformed commander ducked as several bullets pinged and whined but then raised his pistol again.

"Halt! Now!"

He didn't.

"I order you in the name of the Irish Republic to halt!"

"You and your fucking republic can go and fuck off!" shouted the carter, as he turned his cart and started to push it home. Presumably he had no idea that he was putting his very life at risk.

"Final warning!" He fired a warning shot in the air. "Halt or I'll shoot!"

Several shots from English rifles ricocheted off the road, more thudded into the barricade. JJ cowered. The uniformed Volunteer flinched. The carter shouted some obscenity back at him. The man in uniform raised his pistol again and pulled the trigger. The back of the carter's head seemed to explode, spraying blood and bone. His legs turned to rubber. He collapsed and slumped forward onto his cart.

"Jesus Christ!" shouted JJ. "Jesus Christ!"

He jumped to his feet and without even thinking ran to the wounded carter. The dead carter he discovered when he got there and lifted the man in his arms, saw the blank, wide-eyed stare, felt the warm blood stream down over his hands, soak into his shirt. He felt his bowels loosen, had to struggle to preserve his dignity.

The Volunteer commander coldly ordered his men to replace the cart in the barricade. They did so automatically and efficiently, oblivious to the fact that JJ was holding a dead, innocent Irishman in his arms. He sank to his knees under the man's weight, too shocked to say anything.

"Shit!" cried one of the men at the barricade.

"Reinforcements!"

"How many?" asked the commander as he threw himself against the barricade.

"Too fucking many."

The firing intensified almost immediately as volley after volley rang out from the enhanced British line and JJ lay flat on the ground beside the dead carter. The fifteen or so Volunteers responded as best they could, clearly husbanding their ammunition.

Before JJ knew it, the uniformed commander was back at his side, hunched on one knee, waving his gun around and barking orders. His face was gaunt, grey and weary. The peak of his hat shadowed his eyes so that they looked like two black holes in his head. There were darkened blotches and spots of blood splattered on his tunic.

"Leave him!" he roared. "You have a rifle. Get in there!" He waved his pistol in the direction of the besieged Volunteers.

"No," shouted JJ, standing and throwing the rifle to the ground.

"Take the damn thing. I'm not joining in your little fucking war."

"Get in there now!" the officer snarled through clenched teeth and dug his pistol into JJ's chest.

Several bullets ricocheted only feet away, causing them both to drop as close to the ground as possible.

"No! You have no authority over me!" JJ's voice, hands and legs trembled.

"This is the only fucking authority around here." He pulled back the hammer of his pistol with his thumb and rammed it against JJ's forehead. "Now get in there or I'll fucking shoot you too!"

JJ might have called his bluff but for the dead man at his feet. He bent slowly, picked up Richard Balance's rifle and shuffled, stooped, ahead of the officer to join the other men at the barricade.

Once in position, the hopelessness of the situation was abundantly clear. With nothing to their advantage other than this makeshift barricade, they faced a force of more than fifty British soldiers, by JJ's reckoning. The soldiers had been split into three companies. One company was stretched in two lines across the street about thirty yards away; one on their bellies, the other hunkered on one knee behind. These kept the barricade under a constant hail of bullets, while the other two companies advanced along either side of the street, using doorways, steps and abandoned items of looted furniture for cover. These were the primary targets of the men behind the barricade but accuracy became increasingly difficult under the intensity of the volleys raining down from the far end of the street.

"Concentrate on the targets closest to you, lads. We need to make every shot count," ordered the commander. "And you too!" he roared into JJ's ear.

JJ scowled. He would fire the rifle but he would not pick a target. He slid the rifle through a slit in the barricade, closed one eye as if eyeing a human target, and fired three or four shots over the heads of the British riflemen, while shrinking under the thuck and thump of bullets that lodged in his section of the barricade. God damn it! This was lunacy. He was going to die here; he knew it. Just then he felt a pressure, a great hulking weight against his left shoulder. He tried shrugging it off but it was too heavy and was knocking him over. When he turned to curse whoever it was, he jumped with fright as he found himself virtually nose to nose with the commander. His head was hatless, his eyes wide open, an intense blue, now that JJ could see them in the light. His teeth were clenched and his lips parted in an expression of intense rage. But as the massive weight of the man continued to press down on him, JJ realised the expression was fixed; the man was not breathing. It was only then that he spotted the quickly widening ruby red patch around a small hole in the left breast pocket of the man's tunic. He jerked back and threw the man to the ground, partly from shock, partly disgust, and sat there for what seemed like an eternity, frozen, unable to act, as the battle raged around him.

Eventually one of the Volunteers noticed the body.

"Jesus Christ! He's gone."

An older man, also in uniform, glanced over his shoulder.

"Mahony's been hit, lads. Looks like he's dead," he said almost casually, and resumed firing on the ever encroaching enemy force. The man reminded JJ of someone. An actor he'd seen in a show once, back in Sooey, perhaps?

"Fucking hell!"

Waves of fear and doubt rippled through the small band of rebels. Whatever courage or adrenalin had sustained them under Mahony's uncompromising leadership had evaporated. The inevitability of their fate seemed to finally have dawned. JJ watched the dogged fighting men become young, terrified boys again and decided this might be a good time to make a run for it.

As if he too had sensed this change, the older man turned away from the battle, and as he replaced the magazine in his rifle, he addressed the men with a calm that JJ found extraordinary under the circumstances. He had definitely seen this man in action before.

"The game is up here, lads. We should have pulled back earlier. You've all fought well, bravely. Go! Now! There's many more days fighting to come, so go on. Go!" He turned and continued firing at the swarming enemy. One or two of the youngest needed no second prompt. They scampered, heads down, back along the street, staying close to the buildings on either side. JJ did the same, relieved and incredulous that he was still alive and escaping again. Always escaping. How long could this continue? Two other men remained at the barricade, making three nameless heroes to keep the advancing soldiers at bay long enough for the others to get away with their lives.

The light of day was fading, now that the sun had dipped below the roofs of the houses. There was no way that JJ was going to get out of the city before dark. He still had no idea where he was and had no friends among this band of rebels. Even if he had, they dispersed like shotgun pellets once they reached the end of the street. At the first abandoned house he came upon, JJ found a way in through the flimsy hoarding and retreated as far to the rear of the house as he could, where he settled down by a glassless window for a long, lonely night of fitful sleep. He never for a moment considered that the only reason a house would be abandoned in this part of the city was because it was in imminent danger of collapse.

As darkness descended, he thought about the dead carter. Was he still lying in the street, beside his cart, the instrument of his livelihood that had become the cause of his death? He imagined his distraught wife and children, so cruelly robbed of a breadwinner and a soulmate. He wondered too if the three heroes at the barricade had paid the ultimate price or survived, surrendered perhaps? And was the man who had effectively saved his life really someone from JJ's past? An archangel, if you believed in that sort of thing, sent to protect him. Tears streamed down his cold cheeks as outside the sky again glowed red and orange from the fires blazing throughout the centre of the city.

22

Lead Thou Me On

————•————

PALE, COOL DAYLIGHT STREAMED IN through the glassless window as JJ's eyes popped open. Sleep had obviously overtaken him, eventually. There was an astonishing, eerie silence. The building creaked and groaned, like an old man stretching after an uncomfortable sleep. A lump of plaster and a cloud of dust fell from the ceiling. There was no sunshine, the sky shielded by a thick dawn fog.

The street outside was deserted and visibility was reduced to about twenty or thirty yards. This was good because it provided cover but bad because JJ wouldn't spot any danger until it was on top of him. So he kept his ears trained as he shuffled along, tired, hungry, thirsty and alone. He was also effectively lost and there was no sun to guide him. He forced his brain to reconstruct the previous evening, the direction he had entered the house from. That was south. He and Biddy had been heading more or less east when he'd been captured, towards a place she'd called Drumcondra and the road to Swords. Once there he could easily find his way back to Rogerstown. So if he followed this street north, then at some point he would be able to turn right and head in a more easterly direction again.

Once he found the river, the Tolka, he would be better able to figure out which road would take him back to where he'd left Molly. When he reached the first junction, he had to strain to read the street signs, which told him that he was on the corner of Seville Place, Amiens Street and North Strand Road. The junction was dominated by a large cast iron structure with five lanterns at the top. Next he heard, then saw, water spouting from a lion's head on the base. It was the sweetest water he'd ever tasted. Refreshed, he turned right and continued over a railway bridge until he heard the crackle of sporadic gunfire up ahead. He decided to turn left up the next street, Charleville Avenue, which soon brought him to another junction. There was no street sign visible but he smiled broadly nonetheless. He recognised the streetscape. He was back in Summerhill. If he turned left he would be able to find Biddy and her family in Buckingham Street but if he turned right, he was certain that would take him back the way they had come on Tuesday afternoon, back down Ballybough Road and past Gilbey's Wine Merchants on the corner of Fairview Strand.

At Gilbey's everything was quiet and still, but the windows of the shop had been smashed to pieces and the walls were peppered by a pebble-dash of bullet holes. The firing he'd heard earlier must have been coming from the area around the bridge at Fairview. So, instead of continuing back down Fairview Strand, he turned left and walked along Richmond Road, past the Dublin Whiskey Distillery and parallel to the river. Fifteen minutes later, he reached Drumcondra Road. This was where he needed to turn right again, head for Swords, away from the river and the city. But he was tired and weak from hunger. He needed to rest. He sat on a window, close to the bridge that crossed the Tolka.

The sun was beginning to burn off the fog so the mist had developed a translucency that, together with the eerie silence and the absence of other human beings, gave the streetscape a slightly ethereal quality. First, he heard the crunch of wooden wheels on macadam accompanied by an odd, inhuman keening that was part crying, part babbling, with a hint of singing. Slowly then, like a ghost materialising before his eyes, a figure appeared out of the mist. It was a man, pushing a wooden handcart, not dissimilar to the one the unfortunate carter had given his life for the previous evening. The man was moving laboriously and mumbling, muttering, rocking to and fro. The mumbling and muttering was underscored by a constant mewling keen that cut JJ to the quick, making him shudder. Then the man broke into a line or two of a song that JJ didn't know: "Lead, kindly light, amid th'encircling gloom/ Lead thou me on."

As the stranger crossed the bridge and drew closer to where JJ was sitting transfixed, he wheeled to his left and up a road parallel to the river and away from JJ, who could see now that there was a small, four-foot box on the cart. A coffin. And he was better able to decipher some of what the man was muttering.

"My daughter . . . They killed her . . . My little girl . . . gone . . . gone from me now."

Then the grief-stricken father sang quietly again as he was swallowed by the mist. "Th' night is dark an' I am far from home/ Lead thou me on."

JJ got to his feet and was about to start walking again when the intensity of the sunlight at his back increased and cut through the mist before him, like a torch in the dark. As the feathery wisps of mist hovering above the water dissipated he could just make out a shape. The shape was dark, solid and mechanical. It looked like it could be a bicycle. Was this possible? Even if he did believe in a providential God, he hadn't even prayed to him. He walked over to the stone bridge, entranced. Sure enough, there was a heavy black delivery boy's bicycle, complete with large basket on the front, lying at the foot of the parapet. It looked like it had been dropped there, abandoned in a hurry, the rider in urgent need to be somewhere other than on a bicycle, delivering messages. JJ was sure there was an interesting tale attached but that would be for another day. Right now he had far more pressing business. He checked the basket. There was a loaf of stale bread that any regular customer would have returned but which was like a banquet to JJ. The milk in the basket was far too sour to drink, the raw pork chops with kidneys utterly inedible. So he threw the milk and meat at the side of the road and set off, crunching the hard bread.

The bike was heavy and the route mainly uphill until just before Swords, so it took every ounce of his energy to keep the thing moving. After less than an hour, though, he reached the outskirts of the village, where he encountered a woman in her front garden, feeding her chickens and collecting the morning's eggs. She was suspicious at first of this lone young cyclist, coming from the city that everyone knew was under siege. The delivery bike was incongruous to say the least, and JJ must have looked somewhat battle weary. But he soon disarmed her with his charm and a brief summary of his eventful couple of days. She wilted and offered him some hot, wholesome food and refreshing spring water. She also had tales for him. The barracks in Swords had been raided the day before by a band of rebels on bicycles who'd come over from Lusk or Rush, she wasn't sure. They'd also cut down the telegraph lines and it was said they'd captured a load of weapons. She'd heard they went on to do the same in Donabate and Garristown. That had to be Ashe, Mulcahy and the battalion.

"So where are they now?" he asked.

"Well, how should I know? I have no truck with the likes of them blaggards! Will you have another cup of tea?"

"No, thanks. That was great. Best be on my way again."

She folded her arms, tilted her head to one side and glared with a combination of scepticism and disappointment. "I thought you said you weren't one of them."

"I'm not."

"Hmm."

"My friend is. I need to talk to her, before it's too late."

"If it's not already," the woman said and began to clear away the crockery and cutlery, as noisily as possible.

Reinvigorated by the food, rejuvenated by the water and revitalised by news of Molly and her gang, JJ was back on his bike and pedalling vigorously north-west out of Swords. Following the woman's directions, he turned right at Lispopple Cross and headed north until he reached Garristown, just over an hour later. He wasn't too surprised not to have encountered any military since leaving the city, but he had expected more of a police presence. When he got to Garristown, he learned that the barracks there had been evacuated and disarmed the previous day in anticipation of a raid from the Fingal Volunteers, as Mulcahy and Ashe's gang had come to be known. The police were running scared, and while anyone he met was utterly opposed to what these upstarts were at, there was a respect for their efficiency, an admiration for their consistency. So effective were they that nobody knew where they had camped the previous night or where they were likely to strike next. The best guess on the latter was based on the fact that the police were reinforcing the barracks in Ashbourne, making it the most obvious target. As to the former, they could be camped in Rogerstown, where he'd left them, or Ratoath, where he'd joined them, or anywhere in between. It would be like trying to find the proverbial needle in a haystack. He could simply hole up close to Ashbourne and wait for the expected raid, but then it would be too late to talk properly to Molly. Too late to persuade her that she was fighting a lost cause. Too late to save her life given that the police were forewarned and would be forearmed.

So it was with a heavy heart and without conviction that he trudged out of Garristown and towards Ashbourne. The sun was high in the sky by now. He estimated it was about ten o'clock; the clock on the mantel in Swords had read half past eight as he was leaving. The fog had burned off some time ago and there was heat in the sun. The countryside was flat but beautiful green farmland. If it weren't for the current situation, it would surely have been busy with farmers and labourers, husbanding crops or harvesting fresh vegetables for the city markets. It was, however, strangely quiet. The city had effectively been cut off since Tuesday, so people, naturally reluctant to venture out, were doubtless only making necessary trips. The reputation of the Fingal Volunteers and the constant risk of being caught in a skirmish or crossfire from an ambush must also have been a deterrent. So the only sound, as he trundled towards Ashbourne on that sunny Thursday morning, was the whir of the wheels, the click-click of the pedals, the birdsong and the occasional lowing of a cow or bleating of a sheep or goat.

But then something else leaked into the soundscape. It was faint, barely audible at first and difficult to distinguish. But it was getting closer, louder and clearer. It reminded JJ of the sound a sling shot makes when it's swung around in the air. He slowed, looked for places on the side of the road that he could retreat into if necessary. He was jumpy, he knew, overly alert to potential danger. The events of the past few days had ensured that. It was probably nothing but it was such an unusual sound that he couldn't ignore it. There was a little gateway up ahead, set back from the road, with plenty of foliage on either side.

He stopped, hopped off the bike and took cover beyond the gate. The noise continued to grow louder, got closer, quicker, and within minutes had rounded the corner and was whizzing past his little bolthole. A cavalcade of bicycles, ridden by men in great coats, with rifles slung over their shoulders. It was them. They whizzed by too quickly for him to identify anyone but he had seen one woman, who wasn't Molly. He counted fifteen or sixteen cyclists. The sound faded but was replaced by the swinging sling-shot sound again, coming from the same direction. The first group had been the advance section. The next group would contain Mulcahy and Ashe. Probably best not to reveal himself to them just yet. But there should then be a rearguard. If he inserted himself between these two groups, he could follow the mid-section to their next location, without being discovered by the rearguard. He hoped with all his heart that they were not already on their way to raid the barracks in Ashbourne. Either way, this would be his only opportunity to speak to Molly. He had to go for it.

Less than five minutes after the first section had passed, the mid-section went by. He was wrong about Mulcahy and Ashe, though. There was no sign of them. No sight or sound of the New Hudson. But he thought he spotted Frank Lawless, so maybe he was the senior officer for the purpose of this excursion. That could mean that they weren't on their way into action. Surely the joint commandants would be there if that was the plan? This was a glimmer of hope.

As the sound of the cavalcade faded, JJ hopped back onto his Clydesdale of a machine and cycled after, as hard as he could. At first he was unable to get within sight of the cyclists ahead of him but after a sharp left turn at the ruin of an old windmill, there was a straight stretch that allowed him to see the rear of the leading group disappear around a bend several hundred yards ahead. After about another mile of bends and twists, there was another straight stretch. He expected he would again see the tail of the group ahead but he couldn't. He was surprised to have dropped that far behind in such a short distance. He slowed. Without the wind whistling in his ears he could hear the rear guard not far behind him. Nothing for it. He would just have to bite the bullet and confront whatever awaited him.

He hopped off his bike and waited at the side of the road. The rear guard appeared around the corner less than a hundred yards back then disappeared again, to his right, as if they'd just been swallowed by a fairy rath. Intrigued, JJ remounted and cycled back to the spot, where he discovered a secluded entrance to a tiny boreen. The boreen led to a disused farmhouse with two roofless outhouses and a rusting, crumbling hay barn. The entire Battalion was busying itself setting up camp just as they had in Rogerstown several days previously, when he had been one of their number.

As he cautiously advanced, his view of the camp was obscured for a time by a low hill that rose between the entrance and the old farmyard. His eyeline shifted abruptly downwards as his bike hit an immovable object and he shot out over the handlebars and crashed in a heap onto the grassy boreen, breaking his fall with his hands. He was disoriented, so the first things he was able to discern clearly were the barrels of a pair of rifles that were almost touching his face. He flinched and pulled back. He could now make out two familiar faces. The boorish Bennie McAllister and his mate Christy Nugent.

"Well, Christy, would you look at what the fucking cat dragged in."

The interrogation this time took place out in the open. Ashe and Mulcahy sat behind a makeshift table made from old planks, one end resting on an empty barrel, the other on the handlebars of a rusted ploughshare.

"So you must have been in the post office, then?" Ashe asked, while Mulcahy eyed JJ sceptically.

JJ looked from one to the other before answering, "Well, no." No point in bluffing.

"But that's where Dick Coleman was headed. Where is he?" asked Mulcahy gruffly.

"Ehm . . . well, we got separated."

"What?" Ashe asked.

Mulcahy scoffed.

"There was an ambush." The best lies contained a grain of truth. "On the way into Swords. We had to split up. I did make it as far as Sackville Street in the end, but the post office was surrounded by British troops. There's a gun boat bombarding them from the Liffey."

"So what did you do? Did you even fire a shot?" Ashe asked.

"I did, yes. I spent a day as a prisoner, in a church."

"But you managed to escape?" said Mulcahy, apparently impressed. Ashe looked doubtful again.

"Yes. Then there was a gun battle."

"Where?"

Ashe was being a hard-nosed bastard, not looking at all happy to see him back. "Don't know. Near Fairview, I think."

That seemed to ring a bell with both and fit their view of what JJ should have been up to. He had to keep this story going, though, if he was to have any chance of speaking to Molly.

"But they brought in reinforcements. There were over fifty of them. Only fifteen, sixteen of us. We were going to be overrun. The commander got shot. Killed. Second in command ordered us to run, save ourselves for the next battle."

"So why are you back here?" demanded Ashe.

"Ehm . . . Dublin is cut off. It looks like it's going to fall, any day now."

"No!" Mulcahy leapt to his feet, slammed a fist on the makeshift table. "That's treasonous talk!"

"But it's not just me. Everyone is saying it."

"Then they are traitors too. I will not hear that sort of talk in this camp. Do you understand?" Mulcahy was leaning close to JJ, looking deep into his eyes. This wasn't about truth any more or even who was right and who was wrong. For Mulcahy and Ashe and their men, who had remained so loyal, this was about seeing something through to its logical conclusion, as they saw it. Failure would not even be considered.

"If I had stayed where I was, I would have been recaptured or killed. I thought I might be more use out here, if you'll still have me?" This was probably the most barefaced lie JJ had told in his life.

"Someone get this man a rifle," Mulcahy roared, then to JJ, stabbing him in the chest with his index finger, "Be back here at eighteen hundred hours for a battalion briefing."

Mulcahy gathered up his papers and left. This was good news for JJ. No briefing till six o'clock. It was only around midday now, so plenty of time to find and talk to Molly. But where the hell was she? Why hadn't he spotted her?

A large, firm hand slapped down on JJ's shoulder.

"Good to have you back, a mhac!" chanted Ashe.

JJ looked up sheepishly at the taller man. Surely he didn't mean that.

"It's good to be back . . ." – he wasn't sure how he should address him – ". . . sir. Good to get out of the city."

The Kerryman wrapped his arm around JJ's shoulder and led him, as if they were best buddies, across the deserted old farmyard.

"You must tell me more of how things are in the city. Any information will be useful to us in planning our strategy for the coming weeks."

Weeks?

"It doesn't sound like anyone wants to hear what I have to say."

"Mulcahy? Don't mind that. He's just concerned about morale. We had to let five or six lads go home this morning." Ashe's face betrayed his disappointment.

"How come?"

Ashe released his grip on JJ, guiding him instead with a hand on his back, leaning close, dropping his voice, as if revealing a secret "Two were just too old. Not up to it physically. The others hadn't the heart to go on. Thought we should have had reinforcements by now. Said they'd heard rumours that Dublin was ours. You know the way lads are." His flicker of a smile implied Ashe knew something JJ didn't but should have.

"I wasn't making that up, about the city. It's only a matter of time until it falls."

"Mmm, I heard you." He ruminated for a moment.

Why the hell was he being so friendly? Did he sense the real reason JJ had returned and was he just keeping him close?

"Well, all the more reason for us to hold firm and gain as much ground as possible. This may well turn out to be a rebellion that swells from the outside inwards rather than what had been expected."

"Right, yes."

As Ashe smiled broadly down at him, JJ felt like a small boy facing the school bully.

"Go to the barn now like a good lad and get yourself kitted out. See you at six." Ashe winked and was gone.

JJ stood for a few minutes in the centre of the farmyard milieu. Everyone was busy, industrious. Each man seemed to know what to do, exactly what was expected of him. In the three days since he'd left them, they had become a well-drilled, closely knit unit. JJ realised that he was now part of this too. He had effectively volunteered himself, and it was no longer Ashe and Mulcahy he would have to convince he was genuine, but the men, these men, who had befriended him, taken him in and would do so again, but only if they were sure he was there for the same reason as them, was committed to the same cause. But he wasn't. He was only there for Molly and, while he might be willing to put his life in danger for her, even die for her, he would not, could not, kill for her.

"Jaysus McHale! The dead arose and appeared to many!"

JJ jumped, smiled and then laughed as Liamy strode right up to him, typically uninhibited, threw his good arm around him and pulled him in for a huge bear hug.

"What fucking rock did you crawl out from under?"

"Liamy, it's great to see you, you bowsie, ya!"

"Oh? You picked up a bit of the auld Dubelin lingo," he said in a mock city accent.

"Jaysus, I've had some few days, Liamy. If you only knew the half of it."

"It's been pretty hectic around here, too, but all goin' very well. Come on, let's make a sup of tea and we can catch up."

He threw his good arm around JJ's shoulder and directed him to the rickety barn.

JJ had rehearsed his reunion with Molly many times over the past couple of days. He was an actor, he needed to know his lines, find his character, especially when it was a new situation, something he had never done or experienced before. His favourite version had her bent over her bicycle, repairing the chain, her long coat flapping in the breeze, the sun low in the sky behind her. As if she had sensed him coming, she would turn her head, then straighten, the sun glinting in his eyes, making her an unreadable silhouette. He would be unsure for a moment if it was a smile or a grimace that played on her lips. But on stepping up to her, his eyes no longer blinded by the sun, he would see that she was smiling. There would be surprise in her eyes, too, and delight, like when someone you haven't seen for a long time turns up unexpectedly.

"You need a hand, Miss McNally?" he would ask playfully.

"I'm grand, thanks," she would reply but without returning to her task.

He would hunker down and fix the recalcitrant chain back onto its cogs. He would stand again, waving his oily hands with a Chaplinesque grin. She would do likewise before throwing her arms around him and hugging him warmly. While in her embrace, he would whisper, "I missed you." She would pull back gently, straighten her coat and re-establish some decorum, a show of face, but he would know that he had her, that her heart was his and not Ashe's.

It was nice to imagine that's how it would be, but he was far too world-weary by now to believe that it could go so smoothly. No. It would be awkward and too public. Too many eyes and ears for them to exchange private words, say what they really felt. Even a revealing glance would be difficult. She would have to appear stern and disinterested. He would be unsure at first if that was how she really felt. He would feel he had wasted his time returning. Feel ridiculous for even hoping she felt the same way about him. But then there would be a barely perceptible flick of the eyes and she would leave the company. He would follow her discreetly, after a moment or two, once he was sure that no one else had noticed her private signal. But when he emerged into the dusky light, she would be nowhere to be seen. Intuition or some sixth sense would lead him in the right direction, until her delicate hand would reach out from a doorway or from behind a wall and whisk him into a dark, secret corner. They would not embrace immediately because she would still be annoyed at his prior effrontery and angry that he had left her. He would argue that he only left because she had rejected him. She would tell him again that she had thought she was in love with Ashe and had never expected to feel love for anyone else, until JJ had come along. He would ask her to say exactly what she meant. She would admit that she knew now she loved JJ and couldn't live without him. They would embrace. Then kiss. And from that moment onwards both their lives would be changed for ever. They would have to be sensitive to Ashe's feelings, naturally, careful about when and how to reveal their love, and there could be no public displays of affection yet. He would simply be content to be in her company, knowing that he had her heart.

"What the hell are you doing back here?"

Molly stood before him like that statue he'd seen atop the GPO, a rifle in place of a spear in one hand, the other stretched outwards in a question. He was sitting on a loose rock, his back to a low drystone wall, drinking tea and chatting with Liamy when she descended, the sun behind her and indeed blinding him. Her long coat was flapping in the breeze but it was clearly not a smile that played on her lips. She was, indeed, looking at him as you would at someone you hadn't seen for a long time who had turned up unexpectedly, but her tone left no doubt that his return did not fill her with delight. JJ was gobsmacked, all his rehearsal in vain. She glared at Liamy, and before JJ could respond, Liamy awkwardly excused himself, tossing the dregs of his tea onto the grass as he left.

"I told you to stay away. You're not wanted here. You don't fit in!"

"I've never really fitted in anywhere, Molly," he said, standing up. "It's good to see you too."

"You see, you see!" she chanted.

He didn't.

"It's like it's all just a game to you. This is real, JJ."

She remembered his name. He was delighted, but then that could be a bad thing too.

"Real life!"

"I know. And you're right to be angry. But a lot has happened in the past few days, Molly."

She shifted uneasily when he said her name. Tutted impatiently.

"I'm not the person I was," he said.

"Well, that's great. I'm happy for you. But why the hell does that mean you have to come back here, upsetting things?"

"How am I upsetting things?"

"Ugh! Good God! You are the dimmest person I have ever met. You really are."

"I came back to see you, Molly."

She shut her eyes, gritted her teeth. "Would you please stop saying my name."

"I need to talk to you, Molly."

"Right, look, it doesn't matter. You're back. I don't understand why. I don't want to know why. It's got nothing to do with me."

"It has everything to do with you, Molly!"

She raised a warning finger. "Just . . . just keep to yourself, follow orders and stay away from me, then everything will be fine, or at least as fine as it can be, considering what's ahead of us all." She turned to leave.

"But that's exactly what I need to talk to you about."

She didn't stop, her coat flapped wildly as she stomped off.

"Molly!"

He must have shouted that a little too loudly. Several heads turned from what they were doing for an instant, then quickly returned to their tasks.

"JJ?" Liamy stuck his head out from the shadows of the barn. "Come on, let's get you kitted out."

23

The Rovers Return

———∗———

THE BRIEFING WAS DELIVERED FROM the same makeshift table where JJ's interview had been held. The use of pencil-drawn, line maps on scraps of paper belied the preparation and attention to detail that had gone into the plan for the raid on the Ashbourne police barracks. Several copies of the map were passed around as Mulcahy outlined what would happen. The raid would begin at 9.30 a.m. As usual, one company of ten to twelve men would remain to guard the camp and procure food and provisions. An advance party of ten men, led by a Captain Charlie Weston, would travel by bicycle to Rath Cross.

They would abandon their bikes at the crossroads and proceed on foot, under cover of the roadside ditches, to the front of the barracks. Once they had secured safe positions, with good cover, they would call on the police within to surrender. It was expected that the men in the barracks would not have the stomach for a fight. Mulcahy was confident the reputation the Ashbourne Battalion had garnered would put the fear of God into the isolated RIC, as had been the case in Garristown the previous day.

The remainder of the battalion, about twenty-five men, would proceed to Rath Cross, fifteen minutes behind the advance party. This would allow time for a last-minute change of plan should the advance raiding party run into any difficulties. There were strong rumours that reinforcements were being deployed to Ashbourne from barracks in Meath and as far away as north Kildare in order "to put a halt to our gallop", as Mulcahy put it. If this were the case and there was not an instant surrender, they would proceed to the more important target at Batterstown, to blow up the Midland Great Western Railway bridge, cutting off the crucial rail link between Athlone and Dublin.

On a nod from Mulcahy, Weston explained that two points on the far side of the Rath crossroads were good sniper positions with excellent cover, one behind an old fallen tree, the other behind the ruin of a stone shed. These positions would be occupied by Christy Nugent and Billy Rooney, brother of Captain Eddie Rooney. Weston handed back to Mulcahy, who urged the men to get a good night's sleep and be prepared for any and every eventuality the next day.

"Like the best football or hurling teams, lads, we have a plan going into the game, but everyone will have to be able to adapt as the conditions change, because they always do."

But this was no game.

Mulcahy gathered up his bits and scraps of paper and returned to the farmhouse, deep in conversation with Ashe. There was no song this time.

JJ hadn't been allocated to a particular company, so he presumed he would remain with C Company under Captain Eddie Rooney. At least that would allow him to stay close to Molly, protect her if necessary. On the other hand, with a bit of luck they might be selected to stay behind at base camp, and he would have some time with her there, away from Ashe, to convince her of the folly of continuing with this failing enterprise. Liamy confirmed that JJ was still in C Company but, apart from Weston's crew, no one would be told where they were going until the morning.

"Mulcahy is a fierce careful man, JJ."

"Not careful enough."

"What are you saying?"

"You have to believe me, Liamy. Things are disastrous in Dublin. The rebels are outnumbered and pinned down. There's heavy guns pounding them day and night. The city is an inferno."

"You're a powerful man to spin a yarn, a chara."

"I'm not exaggerating. Why would I?"

"So what do you think we should do? Give up?"

"Yes, while you still can. I don't know . . . live to fight another day, if there ever is another day."

"But we've won every scrap so far. We've taken every barracks in the area. Cut off communications. Captured explosives, guns, ammunition. We're on top here, JJ. Why should we quit?"

"I don't know. Maybe if the whole country was like you boys . . ."

"How do we know it isn't, JJ? Maybe the whole country is out, and it's only a matter of days till the Brits realise they're the ones fighting a losing battle and give us what we're looking for."

"And what's that, Liamy?"

"Jaysus, lad! Freedom! Freedom to govern ourselves, to shape a future for ourselves, to be ourselves and not be answerable to a foreign king or kaiser."

Liamy was not for turning and JJ couldn't blame him. This was his place; these his people, his friends. They were on a path that seemed to be leading exactly where they wanted it to, so why should they quit? Maybe, if something like this had happened around Sooey and JJ had found himself part of it, he would react in exactly the same way. He understood that people sometimes get caught up in events and get carried along by a prevailing mood, a collective excitement, a kind of fever. JJ hadn't been infected, but could he cure Molly?

There was a small copse of sycamore, ash and chestnut at the back of the disused farmhouse, just coming into foliage. JJ leaned against the trunk of a gnarled chestnut tree and ran his eye over the sorry stone structure. It was showing all the signs of long neglect: half the chimney had collapsed, the roof was holed, the glass was gone from several windows, smashed in several others. An outhouse attached to the main house was roofless and the gable wall was crumbling. He wondered who had lived here. Why had they left? Where had they gone? To the local workhouse? Or a new life in America, if they hadn't died on some coffin ship? He'd seen similar abandoned homesteads back in Sligo, empty since famine had ravaged the country only sixty-odd years ago.

He wandered a little deeper into the copse, soothed by the birdsong and the light breeze that ruffled the upper branches of the trees. For a moment or two, the events of the past few days and the dilemmas of the coming days drifted away and his shoulders became light again. He looked up at the clouds dotting the cobalt sky. He had to squint against the brightness until the sun slipped in behind a large cloud. There was a rustling, something or someone approaching at pace. He turned. It was Molly, returning from a bracing walk. She stood with her hands on her hips, frowning.

"What the hell are you doing here?" she asked, but he didn't sense anger. Frustration? No. She was irritated. Yes, he was an irritant. But that wasn't necessarily a bad thing. The sun could be an irritant until you got used to it or found a little shade.

"Why did you really come back? Get too hot for you in the city?"

"No," he replied, trying to be enigmatic.

"Did you even make it to the post office?"

"No, but I got close enough to be glad I hadn't."

"Hmph!" She moved around him.

He skipped after her, got ahead of her again and stood in her path so she had to stop.

"Good God, you're like a flipping shadow! No, like a piece of dirt that I can't shake off my shoe!" She leaned closer to deliver this insult, quietly and with venom.

God, she was spirited! He could get the faint smell of rosewater, mixed with the sweet salty odour of perspiration. He smiled.

"I came back for you." He stared deep into her dark-green eyes.

"You're an idiot, you really are. A proper óinseach!"

She tried to step around him again but he stopped her with a hand on her shoulder.

"Maybe I am. What of it? Lunacy seems to be the order of the day these times."

"What?" She slapped his hand away.

"All this. What ye're at. It's lunacy. Ye haven't a hope. A few hundred against thousands. Give it up, Molly, before it's too late."

She started to walk away.

"Get away while you still can," he shouted after her.

She was gone. He could have given chase but there was no point. She didn't want to hear what he had to say. She was blind to anything that questioned what she was doing. She was committed, indoctrinated into a cause that was not really her own but that she had made her own. Maybe he had got this all wrong. Maybe she really did love this Ashe fella. And why not? He was handsome, dashing, romantic probably. He was a poet, for God's sake, and a man of action, willing to risk life and limb for this cause. What a combination! He was like some knight of old. But that was just infatuation, wasn't it? The sort of thing JJ had felt for many women and girls in the short few years since he discovered the delights of the female. What he felt for Molly was deeper. That didn't mean she would feel the same for him, though. So maybe he was an óinseach. His father had used that word often enough to describe him.

He stood there in the clearing between copse and dilapidated house. Maybe it was time to give up this foolhardy pursuit of a woman who probably despised him and who had given her heart, or at least her fidelity, to another man.

"Time to cut your losses, JJ lad, and get back onto your own track again," he said to himself. He looked around him. He could easily slip away through the copse, hike across the fields to Garristown, without anyone noticing. No one would even miss him, truth be told, apart from Liamy. No doubt the beautiful Molly would feel her shoe lighter, relieved of its unpleasant attachment. He turned to do just that, but there was no energy or drive in his steps. He got only five or six yards before stopping, his feet rooted to the ground.

There was a great communal meal prepared for that evening. The foraging had gone well, and the local people seemed more supportive of their rebels than the city folk had been of theirs. That was one of the benefits of living in a rural community: everyone knew everyone else. So even if they didn't agree with your politics, even if they didn't want to get personally involved in your activities, when push came to shove, you were one of their own – PJ's son, Katie's nephew, or niece, Mary-Ellen's grandchild. There was spring lamb roasted on a spit, a vegetable broth and fresh-baked soda bread. There was even a bottle of poteen passed around, and some bottles of stout. The men were careful not to overdo the alcohol, though; they would need clear heads in the morning. They imbibed sufficient to relax tense bodies, release repressed spirits but no more. Several sang their party pieces and one young lad recited an epic poem about Fionn and na Fianna that he remembered from school. Tomás Ashe took centre stage for the performance of the night, singing the poignant, the beautiful "Róisín Dubh".

Is fada an réim a lig mé léi ó inné go dtí inniu,
trasna sléibhte go ndeachas léi faoi sheólta ar muir;
Is an éirne chaith mé léim í cé gur mór é a sruth;
'S bhí ceól téad ar gach taobh díom a bhíonn mo Róisín Dubh.

Molly looked lost in the undulating melody of the old Irish air. It was like her heart rose and fell with every glissando and mordent, fluttered with every trill, skipped a beat with every turn and did a somersault in her chest with every acciaccatura. JJ felt upstaged, outmanoeuvred and well and truly defeated. He hung his head in acceptance of the older man's superior talent, knowledge and worldliness. If he hadn't been feeling sorry for himself, he might have spotted Molly glance over at him as the singer began the third verse.

Mhairbh tú mé, a bhrídeach, is nárbh fhearrde dhuit,
Is go bhfuil m'anam istigh i ngean ort 's ní inné ná inniu;
D'fhág tú lag an bhfann mé i ngné is i gcruth,
Ná feall orm is mé i ngean ort, a Róisín Dubh.

He might have noticed the wistful fog that misted her eyes, the confusion that furrowed her brow as the words cut through to her heart, to her very soul, as Tomás Ashe had. JJ did catch her eye briefly when he raised his head again, just as the singer finished the song to rapturous applause and loud cheering. But by then, Molly too was clapping as enthusiastically as the rest. He should have left earlier, when he had the chance.

He was about to take his leave of the informal group gathered around the embers of the cooking fire when Liamy shouted for him to perform.

"Come on, JJ. You're the actor, do a turn for us, go on!"

"Ah Jaysus, no, Liamy. It's too late."

"Too late?" Liamy raised his eyebrows for added effect.

"Go on, McHale, show us what you can do!" chanted a few others.

"I mean, I'm tired."

"Ara fuck tired, go on!" Liamy insisted.

Ashe remained where he was, standing astride the gang like an ancient chieftain. Like Conchubair holding court over the Red Branch

Knights, a crooked grin on his face as he enjoyed watching his rival squirm. Yes. He remembered the story from school. He was Diarmuid and she was Gráinne, except Molly would never contemplate running away with him. Try as he might, he had failed to put her under his spell. Well, if he was going to be a laughing stock, he might as well play the jester outright.

"Right so, right so, right so," he chimed in a nasal Dublin accent. He rose to his feet, his shoulders slightly hunched, stretched his fingers and splayed his hands, as he visualised the scenario he was about to unfold. A ripple of laughter, mostly mocking, poppled around the assembled group.

Slowly JJ began to weave slightly as he embodied the drunken waiter-narrator of the popular Percy French parody.

"Good evening, ladies and gentlemen, and to the rest of ye too."

There was a tiny ripple of a titter.

"I'm James Murphy Esquoire, or Jamsey to his friends, and I live and work in Dubelin Towen, where I had the honour and appropriation of being invited to wait on the Queen of England herself, Queen Victorious, at the Viceregal Lodge in the same Dubelin Towen on the occasion of Her Highness' visit to this Emerald Isle, accompanied by a gang of her lownesses. I can assure you fine people that I waited longer for her than I waited on her, but in any case, this is the gisht of the speech she delivered to the assembled lords, ladies and arse-lickers, after guzzling her dinner with great gusto, never farting once and only belching twice."

There was hearty laughter, as the audience began to warm to this bawdy, ribald character. JJ straightened, as much as such a drunken waiter might, twisted his face into a contorted version of the late queen's chubby, aquiline features, waved an effete left hand in occasional gestures of pompous superiority and put on James Murphy's finest British-Dubelin accent.

> "Me loving subjects," sez she,
> "Here's me best respects," sez she,
> "And I'm proud this day," sez she,
> "Of the illigant way," sez she,
> "Ye gave me the hand," sez she . . .

He mimicked pinching her arse, then instantly mimed her reaction to being pinched, which drew great laughter from the audience of Volunteers.

> "When I came to land," sez she,
> "And that Maud Gonne," sez she,
> "Dhressin' in black," sez she,
> "To welcome me back," sez she,
> "And all that gammon," sez she,
> "About me bringin' famine," sez she,
> "Now Maud'll write," sez she,
> "That I brought blight," sez she,
> "Or altered the saysons," sez she,
> "For some private raysons," says she . . .

Whenever JJ felt he was losing his audience, he would throw in a few physical jokes, slur, confuse or mispronounce his words, using the waiter's drunkenness to excellent effect. They particularly enjoyed his malapropisms. In the light of current events, he was going to skip the section about the Irish regiments who had fought in the British Army during the Second Boer War, but then thought better of it. In for a penny . . .

> "So drink to the min," sez she,
> "That have gone in to win," sez she,
> "In the gap of danger," sez she,
> "There's a Connaught Ranger," sez she,
> "And somewhere near," sez she,
> "There's a Fusilier," sez she,
> "An' the Inniskillings not far," sez she,
> "From the heart o' the war," sez she . . .

There was such booing and heckling during this section that he had to raise his voice above the racket for the final salvo.

> "But what they can't draw," sez she,

"Is the lion's claw," sez she,
"And before our flag's furled," sez she,
"We'll own the wurruld," sez she,
"We'll own the wurruld!"

Silence greeted the final lines, and JJ was sure he'd finally alienated his audience beyond recovery, when up piped Bennie McAllister, beating the air with his fist, the drop of poteen gone straight to his head.

"Well, ye won't own this part of the fuckin' wurruld, so ye won't! God save Ireland!"

This drew a huge, passionate cheer from the crowd.

"God save Ireland!"

And Bennie had saved JJ's bacon.

"Good man, Bennie," added JJ, remaining in character, lest they confuse the sentiments of the Queen's faux speech with his own. "Now, I might finish with a little ditty from Dubelin Towen."

Come single belle and beau, unto me pay attention,
Don't ever fall in love, 'tis the divil's own invention.
For once I fell in love, with a maiden so bewitching.
Miss Henrietta Bell, down in Captain Kelly's kitchen.

JJ noticed Ashe bristle, and Liamy gave him the crossest look ever. What harm? He'd enjoyed it. It was the chorus next and everyone joined in, oblivious to the subtext.

With me toora loora laa, me toora loora laddie
Me toora loora laddie aand me toora loora laddie.

After several more verses and choruses, JJ left his audience amused and entertained, with their spirits lifted. These men didn't have stones for hearts, not even Ashe. Especially not Ashe. Their blood coursed as hot and fervid through their veins as did his. He was pleased with his choices, fitting antidotes to the gravity and sadness of Ashe's song.

*

As dusk turned to night, JJ was back at the copse behind the farmhouse, finishing a cigarette he'd got from one of the lads. He took solace from the calming if somewhat haunting stillness of the spot.

"Your little . . . show earlier was . . . very funny."

JJ turned with a smile and a flourish of the hands. "JJ the jester, that's me." He stubbed out his cigarette on the tree trunk.

"You're good at what you do."

"I'm not sure your boyfriend would agree."

She flinched and dropped her chin. "Sorry?"

"Mister Ashe? I don't think he was amused."

"Oh. Well, it's hard for him to laugh these days."

"I know, I didn't mean . . ." This conversation was not going to go anywhere.

"He's a talented man."

"He is. In another place, in another time . . ."

They sat in silence for a moment.

JJ decided to press her, gently. "I'm sorry if I offended you earlier."

"You didn't," she said, without looking at him.

"You seemed a little upset."

"Look, JJ, you have your dreams that you're committed to, don't you?"

He shrugged.

"Well I have my dreams, too. We have our dreams. So it's right we should pursue them with all our energy."

"Yes, of course you should."

"Well then?"

"But I've had to accept setbacks and obstacles along the way. I've had to change course, swerve down unfamiliar roads. I'm not saying you should give up your dreams. I have no right to tell anyone to do that. I'm just asking you to take a step back, for now, to regroup and figure out a new route, because the one you're on right now can only lead to failure. And then what?"

She seemed, for the first time, to actually consider what he had said. "Maybe sometimes you have to sacrifice your own selfish dreams so that others, maybe later, obtain the freedom you crave and that you know in your heart you're entitled to but have been denied. I don't know. I just know that things in this country cannot continue as they are and I believe they will not. But someone has to take a stand."

She had been looking away from him, at the ground, then into the distance, perhaps at some vague, filmy, unformed image of a future. She turned and looked him straight in the eye. "That's why I must see this through to the end. Whatever that end might be."

If JJ had been in any doubt about what he felt for her before, he was absolutely certain now.

"Anyway, why does it matter so much to you?" she asked.

"Because I love you, Molly."

She looked horrified, but then, maybe because he hadn't followed the declaration with an attempt to kiss her or maybe because of its simplicity, its directness, her expression softened.

"I should go," she said, but without moving or taking her eyes off him.

"This may be the last chance I get to tell you."

"Right."

Her beauty had a strangely tragic quality in the fading light. There was a sudden cacophony of birdsong as an avian shawl descended on the copse for the night. Slightly startled, she turned her head towards the racket. JJ stepped closer. She faced him again. A piece of hair had come loose and dropped over her eye. He pushed it back. He kissed her gently on the lips. They parted slightly for an instant. He hoped she was feeling what he was. He kissed her again, a long, deep, passionate kiss. She slipped easily into the warmth of his embrace. They stumbled slightly, back against a towering chestnut tree. He pushed himself against her, caressing her arms, her shoulders, her breasts. Then she stopped, pulled back, stared in astonishment at him. He had been acting on instinct, surrendering to desire; now he was inert, unsure what to do next. She frowned, then embraced him again and held him in a long, tight embrace. When she pulled away again, she held him at arm's length, by his shoulders, and looked him in the eye.

"Ugh! JJ McHale, what are you doing to me?"

"Don't go, Molly."

She dropped her eyes, shook her head slightly and left. He took a step after her but knew there was no point in following.

24

The Battle of Ashbourne

———✦———

NEXT MORNING, THE CAMP BEGAN to come to life around 7 a.m. JJ had slept fitfully, so was glad it was time to get up. Breakfast was basic – tea, bread, some meat left over from the previous evening. Volunteers were busy oiling, cleaning and preparing weapons and equipment for the day's action. They were quieter than usual, their conversation sparse, intermittent and practical – what was to be done, where and when. The irrepressible Bennie McAllister couldn't resist an occasional joke or smart comment. He above anybody seemed to relish what was ahead of them. JJ prepared as he had slept – half-heartedly, in fits and starts.

Liamy noticed. "You know JJ, if you haven't got the stomach for this, then don't go."

"What do you mean?"

"A bunch of lads went home yesterday morning. This is no place to be if your heart isn't in it."

JJ didn't answer immediately.

Liamy lit a cigarette, handed it to his friend. "No one will think you're a coward."

"I don't give a shite what people think of me, Liamy." JJ dragged deeply on the cigarette as his friend lit another for himself.

"If it's Molly?"

JJ glared at him.

"I mean, are you really willing to do this for a woman, JJ? Especially one who's in love with someone else."

"You don't know that."

"Ah Jaysus, JJ, are you blind?"

This was another conversation that was going nowhere.

"Look, Liamy, thanks for being concerned. But it's grand. I'm grand. I'm ready for this." He was lying, but he fastened his knapsack with vigour and noisily checked the chamber of the rifle he'd been given, smiling broadly at Liamy.

"Come on, then. Let's give these fuckers what for, huh?"

Liamy smiled thinly. JJ slung his rifle over his shoulder and marched over to the assembly area, his cigarette dangling from the corner of his mouth.

Liamy stubbed his own cigarette on the ground.

"You're some actor, JJ McHale."

Mulcahy began his address to the assembled battalion with a quote that JJ didn't recognise: "Brave Irishmen, our cause is common. Like you we hold as indefeasible the right of all nations to liberty. God save Ireland!"

He needed to say little more. His men were acutely aware of the dangers facing them, the need to be vigilant, sharp and determined. He nominated B Company as base company for the day – which meant Molly would be involved in the raid – then handed over to Weston to call out his advance unit. He called the names quickly, without fuss, and as they were called, each man marched to his bike and stood by, ready to leave. The last three names to be called were Kenny, Duke and McHale. JJ didn't even hear at first, or heard but didn't register that McHale was him, his name. It was the look on Liamy's face that alerted him, then his jaw dropped. He looked at Weston for confirmation, but the captain had already moved off. He looked to Molly, who was nonplussed, busying herself with her kit. He looked at Ashe who glanced at Molly then returned a flat, emotionless stare.

"McHale, move your arse!" roared Bennie McAllister.

As JJ joined Weston's advance party of ten, Ashe led the battalion in a rousing rendition of their unofficial anthem.

> Never till the latest day shall the memory pass away
> Of the gallant lives thus given for our land

But on the cause must go, amidst joy and weal and woe
Till we make our Isle a nation free and grand.

God save Ireland, said the heroes
God save Ireland, said they all
Whether on the scaffold high
Or the battlefield we die
Oh, what matter when for Erin dear we fall.

JJ cycled back down the rutted boreen at the tail of the advance party with the song still ringing in his ears. His mouth was dry, his stomach hollow and beads of cool sweat formed on his brow.

Rath Cross was about two miles from the farmhouse, so it only took around ten minutes. A few hundred yards before the crossroads and on a bend in the road, a barrier was being constructed by an RIC Sergeant and a local constable, using several barrels and some large planks. Their rifles lay against the ditch and they were felling a telegraph pole to reinforce the barrier when the Volunteer company arrived.

Weston gestured to his men to halt. As they slowed, JJ's heart began to thump like a sledgehammer against the wall of his chest. Weston and two others hopped quickly and stealthily off their bikes, without stopping completely, swung their rifles off their shoulders and confronted the two policemen. It was only then that JJ recognised his old adversary, Sergeant O'Connor.

"Are you lads the Fingal lot?" the sergeant asked, unclipping his holster before any of the rebels had a chance to speak.

"I hope you're not thinking of resisting?" Weston said, levelling his rifle at the sergeant's chest. Two more rifles were pointed at the constable, who instantly raised his arms above his head.

"Jesus, no, I don't get paid enough for that."

Sergeant O'Connor gave the constable a withering look but had to accept that they were outnumbered. One of the Volunteers relieved him of his revolver while another picked up their rifles. A flicker of recognition flashed across his face when O'Connor spotted JJ.

"Are there many others? In the barracks?" asked Weston.

There were rumours circulating that a British naval brigade had landed in Dundalk to confront the Fingal insurgents.

"Just the usual crew," the constable revealed helpfully.

Sergeant O'Connor scowled again. They were handcuffed with their own cuffs.

"Any chance of a smoke, lads?"

The constable was given a cigarette and Weston asked for a volunteer to escort the pair back to base camp. No one offered, all eager to be involved in the action rather than relegated to the role of nursemaid.

JJ's hand shot up. "I'll go, Captain."

He noticed O'Connor give him a quizzical look.

"You have to stay with us, McHale," said Weston.

Ned Stafford cursed when he was selected instead.

"Do I know you?" the sergeant asked JJ as he came alongside.

"No."

O'Connor gave a twisted, sceptical look.

"The voice. That cocky gimp. Yes. The races! You're that sleeveen of a pickpocket that gave me the runaround!"

The gang of Volunteers stopped what they were doing.

"I'm no fucking thief!" shouted JJ and he levelled his gun at O'Connor's chest. His hands shook, his face reddened and waves of indignation swept through his body.

"Is that the sort of ye, then," taunted the sergeant, "a bunch of thieves and murderers?"

"Shut your stupid mouth," roared JJ and he pressed the gun into the policeman's chest.

O'Connor sneered defiantly.

"You're a fucking idiot! I never robbed anyone in my life!"

JJ forced the sergeant back with the rifle. He lost his balance, found himself trapped against a gate, JJ's rifle digging into his chest.

There was an instant when JJ thought he would pull the trigger.

"JJ, don't!" shouted Liamy.

Charlie Weston stepped between them and gently pushed JJ's gun down and away from the pompous policeman.

"Take them away, Ned."

Weston's Company, now down to nine men, continued on to the crossroads. There they abandoned their bikes in the ditches as planned and he led them across the road and down to the barracks in single file, crouching and using the hedgerows, banks and drainage ditches for cover.

JJ was still in shock at the extremity of his reaction to the sergeant's accusation. His hatred and indignation had lit a fire in his brain that burned fiercely. He really had wanted to teach the arrogant bastard a fucking lesson! JJ breathed deeply and tried to clear the fuzz of the experience from his head.

Within a couple of minutes, the company had taken up firing positions behind a high bank set back from the road and directly across from the entrance to the barracks. Nugent and Rooney took up their sniper positions behind a fallen tree and an old shed. The barracks was quiet, confirming what the constable had said. Weston sent two men down either side of the barracks, leaving himself, Bennie McAllister and JJ to cover the front. Weston called for the barracks to surrender, in the name of the Irish Republic, claiming they had the place surrounded and there was no point resisting. JJ gripped his rifle with sweaty hands and licked his dry lips, as Weston stood on top of the bank and called out a second time for the building to surrender. This time there was a response. Several shots rang out from the steel-shuttered windows and ricocheted close to Weston. He dived for cover and ordered a volley to be fired at the barracks in response.

JJ thought this a good opportunity to demonstrate a willingness to fight. He fired liberally at the walls of the building, confident that he would cause no injury. Weston and McAllister seemed surprised at his apparent exuberance, but suitably impressed. Their volley was immediately answered with another from within, and so it continued.

Ten minutes later the second company arrived at the crossroads, with Ashe at its head on his New Hudson motorcycle. They were followed another ten minutes later by the third company under Captain Lawless, with Mulcahy and Dr Hayes in the two-seater Morris Oxford. Both companies took cover behind and in the ditches at the sides of the crossroads. Mulcahy and Ashe would have expected that the barracks would have surrendered by now and the battallion would have been on its way to Batterstown. There seemed little they could do for now, though, but lie low and watch from their position at the crossroads. There were no windows or doors at the rear or sides of the barracks, so no chance of outflanking the garrison. Nor was there any way the garrison could escape or mount a counter attack. It was a stalemate that the Volunteers would inevitably win, even JJ could see that, but time was not on their side and there was still the possibility of reinforcements arriving and outflanking them.

Then JJ spotted Ashe waving his arm to beckon one of his men, then watched Peadar Blanchfield, a slightly gormless-looking young fella with prominent front teeth and a shock of red curls, make his way up the line. Blanchfield and Ashe seemed to exchange a few brief words and the lad produced something from his coat pocket that JJ couldn't identify. Ashe nodded and they took off like a pair of rabbits, chasing along ditches and down the far side of the road like athletes.

It took them less than a minute to make it down to Weston's group across from the barracks. Charlie Weston was clearly delighted to see Ashe. Greetings were implied, not expressed, though. Ashe didn't seem to notice JJ.

"No stir from inside, Charlie?"

"Not a gíog. Apart from the odd volley. What do you think?"

Ashe smirked, winked, then gave Blanchfield the nod. The lad dug his hand into his coat pocket and whipped out a sort of canister. He primed the homemade device and hurled it at the front door of the barracks. JJ jumped when it exploded with a huge, ear-splitting bang and produced a hell of a lot of smoke.

"Woohoo!" trumpeted McAllister. "That should flush the fuckers out!"

But it seemed to have inflicted little or no damage.

"I was hoping it might give us a way in," said Ashe. "Go again, Peadar, see if we can't blow in that shaggin' door!"

Blanchfield drew a second canister from the other pocket of his great coat and repeated his actions, landing the device even closer to the door this time but with a similar result. The device was all flash and no force, it seemed. But the besieged garrison weren't to know that. They had been pinned down for over half an hour, with no apparent prospect of relief or escape, so morale must have been low. Maybe these explosions were the final straw for the beleaguered policemen then, because they ceased firing, and minutes later a white dish cloth fluttered from one of the upstairs windows. Ashe had obtained the desired surrender. Weston clapped him on the back.

"Well done, sir."

"Well done, Peadar," said Ashe, giving Blanchfield the thumbs up.

Next he jumped onto the top of the bank, whistled shrilly and waved his arms wide to indicate to Mulcahy and the others back at the crossroads that they had been successful. JJ was in awe of the tall man again.

Weston commanded those inside the barracks to come out with their hands raised. This was great. Much easier than JJ had expected, and he had managed to appear involved without any risk to life or limb. The other men began to gather themselves and rise onto the top of the bank, rifles still trained on the front of the building. The four men at the sides of the barracks moved around to the front garden to accept the imminent surrender.

Just as the door swung open and the first dark-green uniform emerged from the shadows, hands raised, a hail of bullets spit off the road and pinged off walls, sending stone chips and dust flying. Everyone crouched and scrambled for cover. The policeman in the doorway ducked back inside and slammed it shut again. The firing was coming from beyond the crossroads, a couple of hundred yards back up the road.

"Shit!" spat Weston as he and Ashe dived for cover behind the bank again.

"What the hell is that?" barked Ashe, practically into JJ's ear.

"Reinforcements!" roared McAllister. "Bastard rumours must have been true."

JJ lifted his head cautiously and peered back up beyond the crossroads, where he could see that around eight to ten motor cars had pulled up at the side of the main road and more were screeching to a halt further behind. Nugent and Rooney had been first to register their arrival and were already sniping at the new arrivals. Then the two companies at the crossroads, having switched their attention away from the barracks and onto the halted motorcade, also opened fire on the RIC reinforcements.

"This is going to make a right bags of things now," Ashe said to Weston, both men looking worried for the first time since JJ had known them.

JJ watched a stream of uniformed RIC men flow from the parked cars and take cover behind the vehicles, under the vehicles and on both sides of the road. There were cars lined up as far back as he could see.

"Jesus Christ," he whispered.

Ashe looked across at the barracks door, closed tight again. "I suppose those buggers will hardly stir out now."

"Unlikely."

JJ felt cold sweat trickle down his back. He clasped his rifle tighter to stop his hands shaking. Judging by the numbers of police at the crossroads, the Fingal Volunteers didn't stand a snowball's chance in hell. Ashe directed two of the men in the garden of the barracks to stay put and keep it covered. He ordered Weston, McAllister and JJ to follow him back up to the crossroads and left Blanchfield in situ to cover the barracks. JJ couldn't believe it. Ashe was taking them right back into the line of fire. His comrades were already leaping the bank, scampering across the road, over the ditch and into the field on the opposite side. Ashe pushed JJ ahead of him along the same route. All of this was done under a stream of enemy fire, although their efficacy and accuracy were reduced by the sniper fire of Nugent and Rooney. When Ashe and JJ reached the crossroads, they took up positions behind the ditch alongside the rest of the battalion. From there they had a much clearer view and could count as many as thirty large motor cars stretching back up the main road towards Slane. The leading cars were only a short distance from the cross and well within range. JJ had his back against the ditch. He swallowed hard and licked his dry lips. Mulcahy roared at him to open fire.

"For fuck's sake, man!"

JJ could see that they had better cover than the RIC, who were skulking behind and under the parked cars. The road also sloped upwards and away from the Volunteers, so they could see clearly under the cars, making easy targets of those sheltering there. But he also estimated that the Volunteers were outnumbered at least two to one. JJ turned reluctantly to face the swarms of RIC and had an instant, barely controllable urge to surrender, throw his rifle down, raise his hands above his head and step out from behind the ditch. He realised how stupid that would be, though. If the police didn't get him, Mulcahy, Ashe or one of the two snipers would. He tried to catch Molly's eye. Maybe she was feeling the same, like a lamb to the slaughter. But no, she was focused only on her targets. Even Liamy was totally absorbed, despite his injured arm. JJ took aim again and began firing liberally at the wheels of parked cars, at walls, trees, anything inanimate he could find. He prayed that he would not miss one of his targets and do harm to another human being, then prayed that his prayers would be listened to after such a long lapse.

He was astonished at the accuracy of his comrades. The policemen were panicked, unsure where the enemy was or how many Volunteers they were up against. They were firing erratically, in all directions. The Volunteers on the other hand were able to concentrate on the policemen who were under the cars or exposed on the roadside. There was no firing coming from the RIC barracks to their rear, presumably because they feared hitting their own men. Although it was only the second time the men of the Fingal Battalion had come under persistent fire, they remained calm, responded like veterans and quickly inflicted significant casualties on the police force, without sustaining any themselves. They had them well and truly pinned down. But how long could they hold out? JJ turned to take his hands off the hot metal of his gun for a few moments. Liamy offered him a canister of water to cool it.

"Thanks," muttered JJ wryly, in no hurry to cool the gun and return to combat. Surely Mulcahy could see that the odds against them were insurmountable? Why hadn't he ordered an organised retreat while they still had the upper hand? Would he not now consider laying low until more definite information could be transmitted from the city.

"How many do you reckon, Charlie?" asked Mulcahy, as he hugged the roadside ditch beside Captain Weston.

"Over a hundred, I'd say, sir."

"Damn! Pity it's not a thousand!" said the commandant with a half grin that made him look a bit demonic.

"Don't worry, lads!" shouted Mulcahy above the racket of the gunfire. "We'll soon deal with these fellas."

JJ admired his confidence but questioned his sanity.

"Just keep them pinned above the crossroads, Charlie. If they get down below it we're fecked."

"Will do, sir. We have Nugent and Rooney sniping from the far side as well."

"Good," said Mulcahy. "Maybe we could get a couple more lads across there?" He clapped Ashe on the back to indicate the question was rhetorical. "You might take that on, Tomás?" and then he was gone, like a spectre.

Or maybe you could just get a couple of lads killed trying to get to the other side of the road, JJ was thinking.

"Keep that going here, Charlie. Right, lads." Ashe looked thoughtfully at each member of the company, halting for a second longer at JJ. "Bennie, take Kenny and McHale across to that corner opposite," he ordered McAllister, pointing at the corner of the crossroads diagonally opposite. He assured them there was good cover there, provided by a high wall with a deep water course behind it.

"Good cover if you manage to get there alive!" JJ said.

"What's that, McHale?"

"Ehm . . ." Shit, he hadn't meant to say it aloud. Well, sheep or a lamb now. "I just think it's madness, that's all."

"Your job isn't to think, McHale, it's to follow orders. Now go!" shouted Ashe.

"Come on, McHale, don't be such a fuckin' weasel!" said McAllister, hitting him on the shoulder and standing.

"We'll never make it across!"

A bullet whistled right past McAllister's head, causing him to hunker down behind the ditch again.

"Easy, JJ," said Liamy.

"We'll be mown down!"

"Are you afraid, McHale? Is that it?" said Ashe.

"Yes!"

"JJ!" Liamy grabbed his friend by the arm.

"You're a bloody coward McHale!" sneered Ashe.

JJ snapped his arm back from Liamy's grasp. "I probably am, but you know, dying is one thing, dying needlessly is another."

"Are you saying I'd knowingly send a man to his death?"

JJ didn't respond.

"I would never, never ask another man to do something I wouldn't do myself!"

With that, Ashe grabbed JJ by the shoulder of his jacket and hauled him to his feet. Jesus, he was strong. McAllister and Liamy immediately stepped in behind, so that JJ became the meat in a reckless sandwich.

"Cover us, Charlie!"

"Will do, Tom!"

Weston and his men fired several carefully aimed volleys at the besieged police, while Ashe, JJ, Liamy and McAllister scampered across the open road, ducking and weaving to dodge the bullets that pinged, skipped and whistled about them. They were only feet from relative safety when JJ felt his ankle sting, the same one he'd injured before, and a bolt of sharp pain shot up through his body.

"Argh! Jesus. I'm hit. I'm shot, lads!" he cried out as he toppled and hit the grassy verge like a sack of coal dumped off the back of a moving truck. Half his face was lodged in a patch of mud, his mouth full of grass, and then it was like he was floating. The two horses of men that were Ashe and McAllister had grabbed him under the arms and hauled him through a gate at the corner of the field, while Liamy fired several covering shots at the police. Seconds later they were all safe behind the cover of a high fence.

"Where?" asked McAllister.

"Leg," groaned JJ.

Bennie McAllister quickly checked JJ's leg, while Ashe and Liamy fired on the RIC.

"It's your ankle. You just twisted it, you óinseach! Now come on," said McAllister, dragging JJ up by the lapels like a disobedient child, "be a fucking man, would you!"

JJ took his place sheepishly beside the others, finding a spot at the corner of the high fence that provided maximum cover, while still giving him a good view of the enemy. The enemy! Jesus, what did that even mean? He had no enemies here. Even Ashe was merely a rival.

"McHale! For fuck's sake, man!" roared McAllister.

"Mulcahy and the other lads are depending on us," said Ashe calmly, trying to motivate rather than bully.

JJ grudgingly resumed firing, again choosing inanimate targets and praying for accuracy.

The deployment of these extra rifles to the west side of the crossroads meant the RIC were under fire from three sides now and prevented from moving forward. The policemen hugged the ground for dear life, while their leaders reassessed their options against an enemy they couldn't see or quantify. Their firing had become sporadic as a result and even more ineffective. They had reached a stalemate and an eerie silence settled heavily on the scene. JJ noticed several bodies lying motionless on the road near the abandoned cars. He had to presume these men were either dead or so badly wounded they were incapable of moving. Several others hauled themselves to relative safety, groaning and clutching bloody wounds.

"What's the plan now, sir?" McAllister asked.

"Sit tight."

"I'd say we could take them," said McAllister. "One good push."

"No. Too many of them." Ashe looked at his pocket watch.

Maybe JJ wasn't the only one who thought retreat might be the more sensible option.

"Commandant Mulcahy is gone back to get Lawless and his company. Better chance of outflanking them then."

JJ began to wonder what had become of Molly. Was she thinking about him or about Ashe? Or just trying to stay alive like everyone else?

After a hiatus of about fifteen minutes, JJ and the others became aware of firing on the northern flank of the RIC column, beyond the line of parked cars. Within a minute, policemen were chasing down the road towards them, attempting to flee the assault from their rear. This made them easy targets, as the Volunteers on both sides of the crossroads opened fire. Several fell, rolled and tumbled until their lifeless bodies lay slumped or stretched on the road, or half in and out of the ditches to the side. Others fell similarly but were able to drag or shuffle their wounded bodies to relative safety in the same ditches, where still others had managed to dive for cover. The RIC squad was in a collective state of panic and confusion.

"Good man, Dick!" Ashe said with a knowing smile.

"He's some fucking man for one fucking man, what?" said McAllister as he shot down another policeman as if he were shooting a pigeon in the woods.

JJ couldn't bear to look and was unable to move a muscle. He was scared, sickened and trapped. Just like the police. The net result of their reaction to Mulcahy's attack was that the police ended up packed into a tight group, huddled together in an open spot on the road, with only six to eight cars to provide cover, handing the initiative to the Volunteers. Victors need good luck, as well as good strategy.

During the lull that followed this latest frenzy, JJ could see Charlie Weston move his group across the Garristown Road opposite and into a field closer to the RIC position, behind a labourer's cottage. With Mulcahy and his men in an equally strong position behind the RIC, the pincer was tightening. On noticing this, Ashe decided he should move to the other side of the watercourse, to get a more advantageous position on the west flank and link up with Mulcahy.

"This is it, boys. I think we have them. They're just stalling for time now."

"Just say the word, sir," said McAllister.

"Come on, McHale."

He grabbed JJ and dragged him with him, leaving Liamy, McAllister and Rooney to cover any attempt by the RIC to break down the road towards the barracks.

As they moved stealthily up along the roadside ditches and hedges, JJ caught glimpses of the death and devastation the Volunteers had inflicted on the relatively defenceless policemen. He also noticed that two of the bodies lying on the road were not wearing uniforms. Civilians? Why were they there? Both lay as if they had been running from the cars when they were killed. One had bled profusely from the head, the other from the stomach and the back of his leg. Ashe whistled for JJ to follow. He was moving ahead twenty yards at a time, then whistling for JJ to follow.

As Ashe made his next move forward, leaving JJ to cover his back, a noise from the other side of the hedge drew JJ's attention. It sounded like something was thwacking off the foliage, keeping pace with his steps, until he reached a small gap in the hedge. JJ stopped and turned instinctively, then jumped back when the head and abdomen of a police constable burst through the hedge. It reminded JJ of one of those jack-in-the-box toys. He froze, bemused, terrified. The policeman paused, wide-eyed, a sitting duck, only yards away from an armed rebel, and yet, miraculously, still alive. In an instant he was through the hedge and charging at JJ with his pistol trained on his forehead, screeching like a madman. It was the screeching that alerted Ashe and triggered JJ's reflexes. It all happened in less than two seconds. With no time to think, JJ's finger tightened on the trigger, just a flicker quicker than the policeman's did on his. JJ hadn't even time to take aim properly, but his rifle happened to be pointing at the man's chest. The bullet caused the charging policeman to pitch forward violently, his hands flailing, the shot from his pistol whistling ominously but harmlessly past JJ's left ear. The man crashed on top of JJ, headbutting him on the bridge of the nose and trapping him beneath his dead weight. JJ began shouting or screaming or crying – he wasn't sure what sounds were coming out of him.

Before he knew it, Ashe was alongside, swearing at JJ to shut the fuck up as he hauled the dead policeman off him. As the body rolled away from JJ, he saw the man's eyes, wide open but not yet lifeless. The policeman's chest was soaked red, his body twitching and his breathing a strangled, choking gurgle. Two more rifle shots rang out. Ashe had shot and wounded another policeman who had come to investigate, driving him back onto the roadside.

"Quick!" Ashe shouted. "Come on!"

He gave JJ a hand up and they scampered further up along the hedgerow. JJ's ankle ached, his hands shook and a thin line of blood trickled down from the bridge of his nose. Less than a minute later, they were lying behind a hedge again, above the RIC and in the company of several of Mulcahy's group who had crossed to this side of the road. Through the teary haze that was blurring his vision, JJ saw that Molly was part of this section. She was pleased to see Ashe, who made a beeline for her. He placed a reassuring hand on her shoulder.

"Tá tú sábhailte."

"Agus tusa." She touched his hand for an instant.

"We have them now." He smiled. "I need to talk to Dick."

"Tabhair aire," she said as he moved away, scurried up along the hedge and across the road.

No room for kissing in the trenches. JJ lay on his back in the ditch and stared upwards. The clouds began to spin, and he felt his stomach heave. He rolled onto his side and vomited. Rolling onto his back again, he closed his eyes tightly, glad of a moment's respite, trying to come to terms with what had just happened. What had he done? He had killed a man, for fuck's sake.

His eyes burned under the lids.

"That looks nasty."

When JJ opened his eyes, Molly was crouching over him. She touched his nose tenderly.

"It's just a bit of a bloody nose!" he said testily and pushed her hand away.

"Sorry."

She backed off slightly.

He grabbed her wrist. "Molly, I just shot a man. Shot him dead. He was as close as you are now, Molly." JJ was close to tears.

"If you hadn't, he would have shot you, JJ, and it wouldn't have cost him a thought."

"You think not?"

There was a pause. No gunfire. No birdsong. Had even the air stopped moving?

"Where is he?"

"Tomás? Gone across to Mulcahy. They need to figure out a way out of this mess."

"I'm glad you agree. "

"More of a mess for the police," she said. "I don't know why they don't just surrender."

"Give up, you mean? Hmm, some commanding officer too proud to accept defeat and a crowd of sheep too daft or scared to save themselves. Sound familiar?"

Molly ignored the question. "I need to move back up the line. Mind yourself." She touched his hand tenderly before she moved back to her own position, thirty yards or so away.

JJ was staring at the sky again. He knew if he closed his eyes he would see the dead policeman's face, that terrified, accusatory stare.

Movement just above where Molly was positioned caused her and her comrades to spin around and open fire on a perceived threat from behind.

"Jesus, they're on top of us!"

"How the hell did they manage that?"

A volley was returned, causing them to dive flat onto the ground. Then a few shouts and calls to "ease off" clarified the confusion. Two Volunteer patrols had been firing on each other. No one had been killed or hurt but valuable ammunition had been wasted. Ashe reappeared, imploring people to keep their wits about them.

Down the road, a small rabble of about a dozen policemen, who had been pinned down by Weston and his section for over an hour now, threw down their weapons and emerged from the ditches with their hands in the air. Weston marched the prisoners up the Garristown Road.

An angry English voice thundered from the midst of the group of policemen closest to JJ's position: "What the devil are you cowardly blighters up to? Hell fire and damnation to you! There will be no surrender, do you hear? None!" And he began firing at the group of prisoners, at his own men.

The frightened prisoners stumbled and dashed into the safety of the ditches.

"The commanding officer," a stage whisper from the ditch confirmed.

"Looks like an inspector," said another Volunteer as he took aim and fired a shot that struck the roof of the car the officer was using for cover, missing him by only inches. The inspector spun around and returned fire, before taking cover again.

"Right, lads, it's time to make our move," Ashe shouted.

If JJ hoped he meant move out, he was to be disappointed. The order had come down the line from Mulcahy to close in on the encircled enemy and press home their advantage before the RIC commanding officer realised the rebels had only half the men he had. As the Volunteers crouched behind the roadside ditch, awaiting the signal to attack, each man lost in his own thoughts, his own prayers, the inspector sprang from cover again and leapt onto the roadside bank just above JJ's position. With his pistol directed skywards, he roared at his men: "Attack! Attack!"

The instant Mulcahy saw the inspector move, he roared, "Hullalloo!", the signal for the Volunteers to attack. The inspector, realising that the enemy was launching a pre-emptive strike from three sides, spun a full 360 degrees, firing indiscriminately in every direction. All hell broke loose. The Volunteers moved forward. Still under better cover than the police, they were able to pick their shots, while the panicked, surrounded policemen were facing too many points of attack with no distinct targets. The seemingly crazed inspector remained on top of the bank, exposed to fire from all sides but miraculously avoiding the hail of bullets that passed him as he continued circling and firing. JJ moved up along the line to where Molly was positioned; his only purpose in this chaos was to protect her. He had no need to fake it in the confusion, so instead he fired close to anyone who looked about to shoot in their direction, forcing them to duck for cover.

Crennigan, a blocky young Volunteer next to JJ, managed to get the inspector in his sights.

"I have him now, begod."

But before he could squeeze the trigger, the inspector spun again and fired his revolver, shooting the young Volunteer in the face, killing him instantly. JJ felt something warm and moist splash onto his cheek and saw Crennigan's body collapse backwards, the side of his face shattered beyond recognition. JJ's stomach heaved again and he began to fire erratically, in a frenzy, at anything that moved.

"JJ, are you all right?" Molly called.

His gun jammed. He had no idea how to release it, just tapped and banged at the weapon to no effect.

"What's wrong?" Molly asked.

"It's jammed."

"Damn! Stay down!"

He didn't need to be told twice.

The inspector stopped spinning. His stare was demonic. His eye had caught a movement in the hedge, only feet away. JJ could see that he was glaring straight at Molly, who was firing at two policemen entrenched in the ditch on the opposite side of the road. He was transfixed, his pistol pointed directly at Molly's head. Frank Lawless must have spotted this too, as he quickly turned his rifle on the inspector. The whole thing happened in an instant, the blink of an eye. JJ threw his useless, disabled gun at the inspector, sprang to his feet, sprinted the few yards to where Molly was and leapt on top of her, just as two deafening shots rang out. The inspector staggered, wheeled around towards the source of the shot, his pistol limp in his hand. His knees buckled. He collapsed and rolled down the bank onto the road where he lay motionless, dead.

JJ was lying on top of Molly, her arms wrapped around his shoulders. Blood from a wound in the middle of his back seeped into and through his jacket. He smelt her fresh rosewater scent through the sweat and the mud and the cordite and smiled. With some considerable effort and help from a couple of comrades, Molly got JJ off her and onto his back on the grass. He saw her face now. A sad expression. A tear in her eye, he thought. Then, the last thing he saw was a procession of wispy clouds against the cobalt sky. He thought he heard his mother singing faintly in the distance.

"Go dtórródis go gcroiúil mé, trí oíche is trí lá . . ."

The sun glinted off something metallic, causing a shaft of fierce, bright light to pierce the corner of his eye, which turned everything white before fading to black.

"JJ? JJ!"

Silence.

25

Beautiful Dreamer

———◆———

A LIGHT HAZE. DUST PARTICLES and wisps of smoke floating in the beam of a huge arc lamp. It is a film studio. There are two doors. The door on the left has a large gold star on it, the door on the right has a sign saying "EXTRAS".

The door on the right opens and a handsome young man emerges, dressed in an ill-fitting servant's costume. He closes the door, stops for a moment and looks wistfully, longingly at the gold star. He lights a cigarette, and with a resigned shrug proceeds onto the set.

The set is the entrance hall of a lavish mansion, with an expansive staircase in the middle. Orchestral music emanates from above. A statuesque beauty, the heroine, is dressed for a ball. She is fanning herself and pacing nervously. The handsome young man toddles up to her and boldly introduces himself. She regards him disdainfully but nods politely. He draws on his cigarette and, with an endearing tug on his ear, releases the smoke in perfectly formed circles. The heroine laughs heartily.

An angry, obese man in his fifties, the director, storms forward, ranting, and orders the handsome young man be ejected from the set. A large man grabs him by the collar, drags him away and throws him towards a door marked "EXIT".

Alone and disgruntled, the handsome young man looks at the gold star again, and with fixed determination enters the star's dressing room.

Moments later, the door with the gold star opens. The handsome young man emerges dressed in the uniform of a nineteenth-century

Cossack, complete with sabre and sheath. The suit is much too big for him. He hoicks up the trousers. As he walks onto the set, he bumps into the side wall, causing it to wobble. The heroine starts. The director fumes. An embarrassed, gum-chewing wardrobe assistant rushes over and straightens the Cossack's hat on the handsome young man's head. He regains his composure and strides confidently onto the set. The director looks surprised to see the star actor earlier than expected. But he's here now, it seems, and ready to work, so who is he, the mere director, to argue? He orders an instant change to the shooting schedule and begins to talk his "star" – the handsome young man – through the action of the scene.

The heroine looks sceptical. This is not the actor she was expecting to play the scene with, but there is something familiar and engaging about the handsome young actor in the oversized uniform that appeals to her.

The stage is set, the extras in place, the lights fired up and the camera rolling.

"Action!" the director calls, but when he spots his "star" smiling impishly and flirting openly with the heroine, he produces his best faux-polite smile and suggests to his "star" that it might be better for the scene if he were to begin off set and make a grand, braggadocio entrance. The handsome young man watches, mesmerised, as the director demonstrates by flinging his arms aloft and wide in an effusive gesture.

"But if you have a better idea for the scene, that's OK, too," he adds sheepishly, anxious not to upset his "star" before they have even begun.

"Oh, right. Grand. No. Grand entrance. Yes. I think I can do that. Sorry."

The heroine looks quizzically at her impish co-star. "Do I detect a brogue?"

The handsome young man grins mischieviously, tips his hat and makes his way off set.

The director returns to his chair, a smug grin brightening his normally dour face, clearly confident that he can get this difficult scene in the can in no time at all.

"Action!" he cries.

The handsome young man, in the comically oversized Cossack

uniform, swings around the top corner of the hallway. He sees his beautiful heroine waiting, fanning herself. He stops dramatically as if stunned by the effect of her beauty, expands his chest like a peacock and waves his right arm wide and high in a gesture that says nothing, really, but looks terrific. The director's chair creaks. Does that mean he's seriously worried or elated, the handsome young man wonders as he hitches up his trousers and strides forward, until his hat slips down over his eyes again and he walks smack into the newel post of the sweeping staircase. The crew gasps. He clutches his stomach and pushes the hat back up onto his head. Winded and embarrassed, he laughs it off with a shrug and returns to his starting position. The crew titters. The director summons the gum-chewing wardrobe assistant and sends her to the actor's assistance.

Pushed to the pin of her collar, the young wardrobe assistant can think of nothing better than the gum in her mouth. Without revealing her secret to director or actor, she sticks the wad of gum inside the back of the tall hat then pushes it tight against the grateful actor's head. She nods to the director who calls firsts, standby and action.

The handsome young man repeats his expansive entrance but has forgotten to hoick up his trousers, which immediately slip down to his knees. The crew laughs aloud, the director's face reddens. The handsome young man grins for an instant before tripping over his trousers and crashing face first onto the floor. The crew gasps and the heroine puts her hands to her mouth but the undaunted actor hops deftly back to his feet, hauls his trousers up and, with another casual shrug, swivels on his heels and offers the crook of his arm to the heroine and links her up the wide staircase to the ballroom. The crew laughs, several clap, and the director eases back into his chair. Not what he was going for, but if the crew likes it.

Meanwhile, the real star of the film strides into the studio wearing a fur-collared cashmere coat and a broad grin. He is humming a popular music-hall ditty and his dilated whiskey eyes glisten in the sunlight that floods through the studio door he has left open behind him. He sniffs deeply. His smile becomes a smug grin and he rubs his nose with his thumb and forefinger as he strides in through the door with the gold star on it. He doesn't notice the scowl on the security guard's face as he shuts the studio door.

Moments later, the real star re-emerges from his dressing room, his mood dramatically altered.

"Where the hell is my goddamn costume?" he roars. "Someone will pay for this! Heads will roll!" He strides out of his dressing room in his underwear, roaring for a wardrobe attendant, threatening his lawyer and vowing to close down this goddamn studio.

"Quiet on set, please!" the director roars from the set.

Off set, the real star, clearly unused to being told to shut up, grabs a stagehand, and hauls him back against the wall of the studio. He clasps him around the throat and snarls into his face, his eyes wide and red, tiny flecks of white foam drying at the corners of his mouth.

"Where is my fucking costume, you cretin?"

"I don't—"

"If it isn't in my dressing room within one minute, that's sixty seconds, I swear I will have your balls served up on a plate!"

"But I . . ."

"And cut!" cries the director.

Spontaneous applause, cheers and whistles follow immediately.

The real star's head whips around, his grip on the man's throat relaxing enough to allow some air through.

"That was wonderful. Excellent. Let's go on that again. Close-ups. Begin with Miss La Badie. First positions!" he hears the director chanting.

"Are they working out there? On my film?" the real star asks the bewildered stagehand.

"I loved when you stood on her dress and it came away. Keep that in."

"Great. Will do."

"Godammit, they are!" says the real star.

"And maybe this time," he hears a young actor say, an Irish accent he's sure, "the shock could cause her to swing her arm, knock me off-balance and I could tumble back down the stairs?"

"Excellent!"

"What the hell is going on?" The real star turns back to the stagehand.

The terrified stagehand has no answer for his assailant that wouldn't put his very life at risk, and no breath to express it if he wished to. His eyes flash to his right, over the shoulder of his attacker. The real star follows the man's gaze, to see a handsome young actor take up his standby position, and wearing his stolen fucking costume!

"Hey you!" he calls, dropping the stagehand, who slides to a sitting position on the floor, and making a beeline for the young thief. "You!"

"Quiet on set!" roars the director.

The young actor turns his head just as the real star arrives. He grabs the handsome young actor by the throat and, with a demonic stare, shouts into his face.

"Why the fuck are you wearing my fucking costume?"

"Sorry?" he squeaks through his constricted airway.

"Who the fuck are you and what the hell is going on?"

"Quiet!" the director shouts, astonished by this utter disregard for film-set etiquette.

"Shut the fuck up, you ignorant cretin!" the real star shouts back.

This gives the handsome young man an opportunity to deliver a well-aimed knee to the real star's groin.

The real star folds, grabbing his privates with both hands. The handsome young man slides under his arms but before he can slip away, the real star grabs his Cossack hat with one hand, while still cradling his injured jewels with the other. The handsome young man ducks and tries to back away but the gum has stuck fast and hardened, so when the Cossack hat comes away from his head, so too does a clump of his hair. He squeals in pain and instinctively charges at the star's midriff. The hat coming free throws the real star off balance, so that their combined momentum brings them smashing through the flimsy walls of the set and out onto the floor of the mansion hallway. They tumble and roll across the floor, toppling other Cossacks, guests and two impressive looking faux-Greek columns like bowling pins, before finishing in a clumsy heap.

The director leaps out of his chair.

"For fuck's sake! You're sabotaging my fucking picture, you asshole!"

"I'm rolling on this, boss," says the cameraman with a wink.

"What? Oh, right. Good," says the director, and so it is only several minutes later, after a comical chase, involving actors and extras, up the grand staircase, back down again and eventually off set, that he finally cries, "cut!" Then he sacks the real star, who is escorted unceremoniously from the studio by two self-satisfied security guards.

The handsome young man slinks sheepishly back onto set, and is greeted by ambiguous expressions from his fellow actors and extras. The heroine, her coiffure disturbed, her petticoats exposed, glares at him, like a teacher at her favourite pupil, whom she simply cannot bring herself to admonish. Finally the director comes back on set, puts his hands on his hips, puffs his cheeks and looks around the ransacked set at his cast and crew wondering if he has enough material on film to make a picture of all that has just happened. Then the young Irishman's trousers drop down below his knees again. He looks down then back up, a look of utter dismay on his face.

"And cut!" comes a voice from behind camera.

The real director walks forward and shakes hands with the actors who played the director and the heroine, then clasps the hand of the actor who played the handsome young man.

"Well done. You're a genius."

"Thank you, Mr Chaplin, sir. It's an honour to work with you."

His fellow actors gather round to congratulate the young Irish actor, as Chaplin, the real director, walks off set and into the darkness.

Epilogue

———•———

As JJ EMERGED FROM THE darkness and blinked against the white light that flooded the room, all he was aware of was the ticking of a clock and the sound of steam pushing through the narrow spout of a kettle. As the light became a haze and the haze began to clear, his eyes picked out the vague outline of a pendulum clock hanging on a wall. He tracked the sound of the steam until his eyes settled on the battered body of the kettle, suspended from a blackened hanging arm over an open fire. The kettle seemed to breathe his name.

But then the breath took on a melody and a tone until finally he realised it was not the kettle but the delicate voice of a young woman.

JJ?

He blinked the steam and dust from his eyes, and the form of the woman began to materialise. She appeared to be sitting. He assumed he was lying down. Was that the sky or a ceiling above him?

"JJ, it's me, Molly."

It felt like he was dreaming. He blinked again, and sure enough the beautiful face of his Irish Molly was staring down at him. She smiled.

"It's good to have you back."

His head was raised up by several jackets, just enough for him to be able to sip warm broth from a spoon. As Molly patiently held the spoon to his mouth, she explained that he was in a safe house, safe for the moment, in Meath, and still alive, thank God, thanks to Dr Hayes. The bullet – JJ couldn't remember any bullet – had narrowly missed his heart and the operation to extract it was incredibly delicate. It was a bit of a miracle he was still alive. But she assured him that he had more than played his part in their hard-won victory at Rath Cross, several days before.

"So ye won, then?" JJ asked, a little confused.

"Well we won the battle but not the war, so to speak, not yet anyway."

Molly explained that later that evening they had received word that the leadership had capitulated.

"Tomás and Commandant Mulcahy would hear nothing of surrender! Couldn't see the sense of it. The entire battalion was in agreement."

But it had become clear throughout the following day that the rebels in the city had been overrun and that apart from isolated pockets here and there, the rest of the country had not come out. They were left with no alternative but to surrender too. They were determined that the fight would resume in the future, though, and wanted to prepare for that, she explained. So their final decision was that the command staff – Tomás, Mulcahy, Dr Hayes and Lawless – would surrender, but that the rest of the battalion should go on the run, take refuge in safe houses such as this one, until their day would come again.

"So what will become of them, of Tomás?"

Molly became tearful. "I don't know, JJ. No one knows."

JJ's head was spinning, throbbing, his chest was tight and he found it difficult to breathe. He could eat no more. He gently pushed the dish away with the back of his hand and turned his face towards the window.

"Are you sure?"

He glanced at her tragic face. "Thanks."

"I can't stay, JJ."

He turned to face her. Stay? Had he even expected her to? "No. Of course."

She chose her next words carefully, assembling the sentence like a jigsaw. "Unfortunately you can't be moved yet so there's a possibility you will be discovered."

"Right."

"Taken into custody."

"I understand."

"You must build up your strength. Eat, please."

"I will."

He laid his shaky hand on hers.

She rubbed it gently. "You're cold."

"Sign of a warm heart, my mother used to say."

She smiled, squeezed some warmth into his hand and kissed it tenderly.

"You saved my life. Thank you."

She smiled thinly, leaned over him and kissed him tenderly on the cheek. He could smell her body, her person, a natural odour, not masked by man-made products. It was powerful, primal. His hands reached instinctively for the softness of her face.

"You need to go, Miss McNally," growled a voice from the doorway.

"Yes, I know."

JJ tensed. His heart quickened at the sudden realisation that he was going to lose her again. He held her face in his hands, pleaded with his eyes for her to stay. Her eyes welled. Was she urging him to speak or pleading for his silence?

"Goodbye, JJ."

She gently slipped from his grasp. He searched for something to say as she stood, buttoned her coat and walked to the door, but nothing would come, not even the words of a bloody song. Then she stopped and turned.

"Will I . . . will I see you again?" he asked.

"Who knows, JJ? Who knows what lies ahead for any of us now?"

She smiled a tragic smile and was gone.

JJ slowly turned his face to the white light of the window and thought he got the faint smell of candle wax.

Acknowledgements

———•———

Writing a novel is a mammoth task and not one that can ever be achieved by one person alone. My thanks to all of you who have helped along the way with a nudge, a word of encouragement, an invaluable anecdote or a nugget of research.

A very special thanks to Eleanor, Katie and Stephen, my family, who had to endure the euphoric highs after a successful paragraph or chapter, the cyclonic lows of writer's block and the prolonged silences of self-imposed solitary confinement. Your patience, acceptance and encouragement are very much appreciated.

Crafting a novel requires an array of skills, many of which I was not even aware of before I began. Particular thanks to my editor Robert Doran for his praise of what was good, for his weeding out of what was bad or unnecessary and for making me a better writer.

Thanks to Chenile Keogh at Kazoo and Adrian White at Inkwell for their professional advice and assistance in getting the book ready for publication.

Thanks finally to the National Library of Ireland for its wealth of material, resources and silence and to the array of other researchers and authors who have written about the period in which the novel is set, especially the many eye-witnesses who recorded their personal experiences: Fingal Volunteer boards; BHS Witness Statements; irishconstabulary.com – RIC Ashbourne 1916; JR Clarke; James Stephens; Mary Morrissey; Des Keenan; Sebastian Barry; Mark Johnson; *Land and Revolution: Nationalist Politics in the West of Ireland*

1891–1921 – Fergus Campbell; *The History of Horse Racing: First Past the Post* (John Carter); *After the famine : Irish agriculture, 1850–1914* (Michael Turner); *Irish Street Ballads* (Colm O'Lochlainn); *The Street Singer* (Brendan Murray); Ballads Online; census.nationalarchives. ie; eyewitnesstohistory.com – WWI; dublintenementexperience.com; www.maggieblanck.com; theirishaesthete.com; athenrylocalhistory. blogspot.ie; History Ireland; East Wall History Group & Hugo McGuinness; eastwallforall.ie; EPPI; into.ie – Catherine Mahon; digital.ucd.ie; maps.osi.ie; irishvolunteers.org; goldenlangan.ie; wildatlanticshanty.ie; Jockeypedia; horsetalk.co.nz; Digital Repository Ireland; filmireland.net – Early Irish Cinema.

Proof

Made in the USA
Columbia, SC
22 May 2017

Please Take ME
And put a review on
Amazon

The Ballad of JJ McHale

OR
Give me to a friend
Thank You

For my dear friend Pat Mac